PARAGON

BOOK 3 - PROPHECY'S DAUGHTER

SUSAN L. ALANDAR

Apropos Press

Published by Apropos Press

Print ISBN: 979-8-9900576-4-7

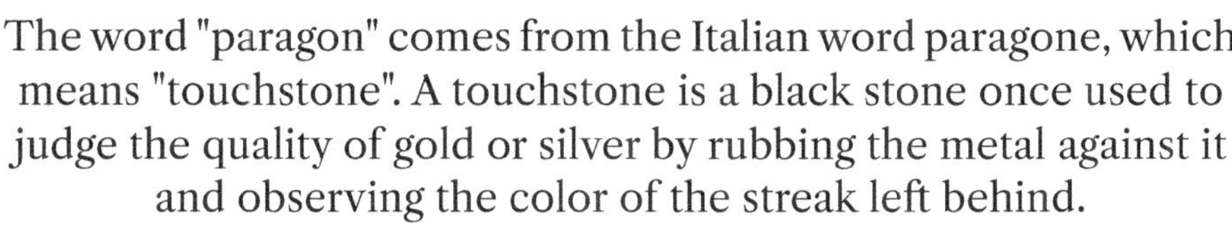

The word "paragon" comes from the Italian word paragone, which means "touchstone". A touchstone is a black stone once used to judge the quality of gold or silver by rubbing the metal against it and observing the color of the streak left behind.
The meaning today is different. It addresses an ideal. But even an ideal may be marred by what it comes against.

CONTENTS

"Life takes you to unexpected places.
Love brings you home."
—Melissa McClone

PROLOGUE

In the moments between her disappearance and reappearance on the starship *Aztlan*, Shandiin had lived a thousand years on the planet it orbited.

She'd lived a thousand years as a magic hidden goddess, as the leader of a powerful warrior race, as a friend and savior for the descendants of the colony the starship had brought from Earth.

Shandiin had, by leaving that life behind, saved them all from the insane and evil god who threatened their existence.

In doing so, she had lost everything that mattered.

The three friends who waited for her on the starship saw a brief aura of flame that took human shape, its brilliance diminishing to become the statuesque redhaired beauty who had vanished just moments before. Shandiin almost collapsed, but the man who loved her caught her in his arms. She glanced up into Zion's face, into strange emerald eyes that tore renewed grief from her throat.

They only look like his eyes, she thought. *Zion looks like Khedran. But my Khedran is gone from me, and I will never see him again.*

Nothing felt real. She vaguely heard her friend's exclamation at seeing evidence of civilization on the planet below, a planet that had been empty of any such indication just moments before Shandiin's transition. She barely perceived the computer announcing a message from the ship they had left behind in Earth's distant orbit. Her mind was incognizant as alarm and confusion reigned on the starship's bridge, until big Sarnath turned toward her, his gentle face grave with understanding that hadn't yet touched the two others.

He spoke gently. "We all heard the last words the planet spoke before Shandiin disappeared from this ship. To save the people, Shandiin had to join them, and would then be trapped there for a thousand years. It has happened, and our Shandiin has come back to us changed beyond our imagination. She needs us now."

"Is that true?" Zion's astonishment at Shandiin's disappearance and almost immediate reappearance had become horror. His grip on her tightened. "How is that possible?"

Shandiin couldn't bring herself to look into Zion's twice-familiar face. Not again, not yet. She didn't realize tears were coursing down her cheeks from the eyes she shut tight, as she sent a mental scream to the world she had left.

But Hiraeth did not answer.

PART I. A LAND MORE KIND

"Something has spoken to me in the night...and told me that I shall die, I know not where. Saying: "[Death is] to lose the earth you know for greater knowing; to lose the life you have, for greater life; to leave the friends you loved, for greater loving; to find a land more kind than home, more large than earth."
—*Thomas Wolfe*

Chapter 1

When Hiraeth didn't answer her call, Shandiin's fighting nature surged to challenge her loss, replacing grief with fury.

Zion lost his hold on her as she shoved away, turning wildly toward Sarnath, who seemed to understand what the others couldn't.

"I'm going to the stasis chambers. Diane has to die."

Egypt caught her arm before she could leave. "Why? Shandiin, what's wrong?"

Shandiin looked into the strange emerald eyes of her best friend and felt fresh grief at the sight of that familiar mutation. Those jeweled eyes had been passed on to a bloodline of amazing and beloved men, the last more beloved than she could have imagined.

It was the memory of those noble men that stilled her, and made her unable to answer. She alone knew that her daughter, Diane, was an evil predator who had used magic to violate generations of High Kings. This secret was not hers to share.

"I can't tell you why," she said after a moment. "I can only tell you that she is evil, and she has to die."

Egypt looked from her to Zion, who came to Shandiin and took her other arm, placing a gentle hand on her cheek. "Shandiin, please. Give it a moment. I think you're in shock."

She couldn't yet look into his emerald eyes, into the face that mirrored the man she'd left behind. She shrugged away from him.

He looked desperately toward Sarnath. "Can you help her?"

Big Sarnath came to her then, and when Zion stepped aside Shandiin lifted her head to face him. He immediately opened his arms, and with one look into those dark and loving eyes she finally broke.

He gathered her in. "I'm taking her to room 116," he told the others. "You handle the message from Earth. I'll take care of Shandiin."

Shandiin went with him, like a child with a father. He settled her into a big easy chair, where she curled up with her hands over her face. He left her there and opened a door directly in front of her. Then he went to make her some tea.

When he brought the steaming cup to her, she looked up at him, scraping tears away with the back of her hand. She glimpsed the door behind him, and gasped.

"That can't be real."

The door was open to a wooden porch, and beyond that a shimmering tree-lined lake. There were white-shouldered mountains in the distance, and clouds drifting in a blue sky where a hunting hawk wheeled in high, slow circles. The lake reflected it all, bright with sunlight. She could hear the chirp of birds and feel an impossible incoming breeze.

"Let it be real, Shandiin. That's why it's there." He offered her the tea.

She took the cup thoughtlessly, her eyes pinned on that three-dimensional scene from a lost world. "It's Earth, but it could be Hiraeth."

"Then maybe it is. It's what you want it to be."

"Tell me, Sarnath...what would happen, if a person went through that door?"

"They would go into stasis, and dream there until they are awakened. It's designed to be less frightening than being closed into a stasis chamber. You were never interested in stasis, so I never showed it to you before. I think you need to know, now, that it exists." He pulled another chair close, lowered into it to regard the scene with her. "Is Hiraeth so beautiful then, Shandiin?"

She kept her gaze on the scene beyond the open door, aching for the home she would never see again. "Oh, yes, it is. It's the way Earth was long ago. Pristine and full of life. And the people..."

Her voice trailed off, then, and she sipped her tea. He had sweetened it with honey. When the cup trembled, he put his big hand over hers to steady it.

"What about the people, Shandiin?"

She turned her gaze to him, regarding his plain face made beautiful by dark eyes under upswept black brows. His white hair had been left free to rain down the back of his plain linen tunic. Big Sarnath was always plain, but she knew how special he was.

"Your blood...your DNA...was included in that special bloodline, wasn't it?" When he didn't respond, she turned her gaze again to the pretend door. "Each leader born of that bloodline was extraordinary. Especially...the last one. He is truth. He is compassion. And wisdom. He has your depth of understanding. But I think he is even more than you, Sarnath. Magic took what your science created and made him even more."

"You are speaking of the bloodline we engineered to lead the people? I see. Khalen and Khandor were the first. You are telling me there was a descendant, even a thousand years later?"

"Yes. He is the seventh High King." When Sarnath tilted his head in question, she explained. "I know that sounds strange to you, but it's like the colony was thrown back in time. All their technology was taken, and the God of Order restricted any memory of science. It's a medieval realm the King rules, but it is a good one. The people are free to live as they will, within his requirement of respect for others. Their protection is his duty. With the magic gone, I wonder..." again her voice trailed away.

"You took the magic with you when you left their world," he prompted her. "When you gave up being the goddess with the aura of fire." When she turned her grey gaze to him, he smiled a little. "I glimpsed her in the moment you reappeared, before the fire faded."

Steadier, she sipped her tea again while she considered. "I think you know more than that. You always know more than you will tell. Even on the day I met you. You took my hand and seemed surprised and happy, and said 'You have seen him,' but you didn't explain who you meant."

She set the tea aside, drew in a deep breath. "It was him. You saw the seventh High King of a realm on that planet below us. I had seen him, inexplicably, on a street corner before the Earth died."

She looked up at Sarnath's unreadable face. "That can't be possible. But it's true, isn't it?"

Before he could respond his communicator signaled, and he took it from his pocket with a frown. "What is it, Egypt?"

He listened, and his eyes flashed to Shandiin's, alarmed. "Are you sure? Oh, of course you're sure. Yes, I'll tell her. We'll be there soon."

He put the communicator back in his pocket while she waited. When he hesitated, she scowled. "What? I remember a message coming in. Are we going back to Earth?"

"Yes, we are. But that's not what I have to tell you about right now." He looked at the open door, and shook his head. "You are carrying a lot of pain. I don't want to tell you what will hurt you more, Shandiin, but I must. It's about your daughter Leah."

Shandiin's vision blurred as she looked into Leah's pale face, forever still in death. She was flooded with new sorrow. This was the daughter she had loved, even honored.

"On Hiraeth she was Liethe." Shandiin spoke to the woman who was more sister than friend. Egypt stood beside her, a comforting hand on her shoulder. "She was the goddess of life and mercy, a healer." She gently stroked the cat that lay curled in her daughter's arms, who had died with his beloved mistress. "Even the cat had a purpose, there. He served as kind of a messenger for Li-ethe...and for me."

She took a deep, shuddering breath. "I don't think Leah wanted to return to the world she came from. Where she was blind, and considered disabled, and too often disregarded despite her beautiful soul. I hope Hiraeth simply allowed her spirit to remain with her. Leah deserved it."

She let her gaze slide to the closed stasis chamber next to Leah's, where Sarnath was checking the monitor. "But it should have been Diane who died. Died and gone straight to hell."

"Why, Shandiin? What happened on that world, that you want to kill your own daughter?"

Shandiin turned back to beautiful Egypt, who was even taller than her own six feet. Egypt's strange emerald eyes regarded her from a lovely dark face framed by a halo of black curls almost as wide as her shoulders. Shandiin knew she should have told her that Diane had abused the sixteen-year-old boy Egypt had considered her son. But the boy, Khalen, had become a man, and begged Shandiin not to tell his secret. So she hadn't. Diane hadn't been punished, and had gone on to commit more atrocities on Hiraeth when she had become a goddess with terrible magic power.

But Shandiin had made her promise to Khalen, and the rest of the truth belonged to Diane's victims, not to her. She could still remember the humiliation she had seen in the eyes of her cherished King. She was sure she would never see Khedran again, but it didn't matter. She was by honor bound to keep his secret.

"I'm sorry, Egypt. I can't tell you. But I'm going to unplug that chamber the first chance I get."

"I can't let you do that," Sarnath announced.

Shandiin spun to him, furious. "You don't know..."

"It doesn't matter, Shandiin, if she was a murderer or worse. She isn't the only one to be considered." He looked up, and she saw his shock and concern. "She's pregnant."

For a moment her vision shrank to a pinpoint, and Shandiin almost collapsed. "How can that be possible? Didn't you check her before she went into stasis?"

"Yes. Her pregnancy must have been too new for the tests to find." Sarnath shook his head. "I don't understand, though, how it could be visible now and not then. Both child and mother should remain unchanged, in stasis."

"It must be Khalen's," Egypt breathed. "I thought there was something going on there, before he went down to the planet."

Shandiin said nothing. Something profane had set its teeth in her throat.

For the first time in her life, she lost her will and her courage.

She sought Sarnath, and went through the door to a dream.

CHAPTER 2

Shandiin awoke in the easy chair where she had first seen the door of dreams. The door was closed, and Zion was on his knees in front of her, worry plain on his handsome face.

A King's face. She blinked, and looked away.

"What's happened?" she asked. "Why did you wake me? I want to go back to sleep."

"Shandiin, you can't. You can't just live out your life in stasis. With your power of regeneration, it could be forever, even longer than this ship would last. And you have to tell me what to do, because things have happened that involve you. We've gone back to Earth, and now we're going back to Hiraeth."

His last words were a blade in her heart, a sharp edge infected by hope and denial. She was silent while she staunched the bleeding, and that took some time.

She finally took a deep breath, then shook her head. "I don't think Hiraeth will let you in."

"We have to try. There's more than just us to think of. We're trying to save the last remnants of Earth's humanity."

She glanced around. "Where is Sarnath?"

"I know you'd rather have him than me. You made that clear ten years ago, when you first came back from Hiraeth. Why is that, Shandiin? Why can't you even look at me?"

She took another deep, steadying breath. *Ten years.* He had waited ten years to wake her, not knowing why she wouldn't look at him.

He was a true and honest man, and he deserved better than that. He deserved the truth.

So she met his worried emerald eyes, and found that she could do it without pain. Because he resembled her High King like a twin, but he wasn't him. She could never mistake him for Khedran.

She reached to touch his face gently, and he caught her hand with such gratitude it hurt her heart. "I'm sorry," she told him. "It's just that one of your special bloodline's descendants looks exactly like you. His name is Khedran, and I fell in love with him. When I left him, he was in the middle of a war. I don't even know if he survived."

He stared for a long minute. "You...loved him?" When she only nodded, he closed his eyes. "Shandiin...I am still in love with you." After a moment he opened his eyes again, and continued. "I have never stopped being in love with you. I can't let it matter, that you loved one other man in your thousand years away from me. I can and will accept that." His grip on her hand tightened, and he regarded her sadly. "What you have to accept is that he's gone. Even if he survived that war, he's gone from you. Time has taken him far, far away. In the twenty years since we left Earth, it's been a century on the ship they call the *Earthstar.* It must be even longer on Hiraeth, where a thousand years went by within minutes of my own subjective time. Relativity doesn't make sense there, perhaps because of the magic."

She closed her eyes briefly. She had already accepted what was the most probable truth. "Yes. I understand. But what is it you want from me, Zion?"

He smiled wryly. "I'm afraid what I want may no longer be in the cards. But this isn't about that. Shandiin, you need to make a decision about whether you want to return to Hiraeth with us...and it's not going to be an easy one."

She scowled. "I don't understand. Where else would I go but with you?"

"You could stay on the *Earthstar*, with the descendants of Earth's survivors, until we come back for them. It's complicated,

Shandiin, but if you want to stay on the *Aztlan*...we have to lie and say we're married."

"What?" Nothing could have stunned her more. "Zion, you're not making any sense!"

He stood up then, and ran his hands through his hair. "Believe me, I know how crazy it must sound. But that's the bottom line." He reached into his pocket, pulled out a communication device. "This is a recording of the message that came in at the same time you returned to the *Aztlan* from Hiraeth. I'm going to leave it here for you, and give you time to process everything. This cabin has a kitchen, a bed, everything you could need. I hope it won't take more than a day, but take as much time as you need. The computer is monitoring you; just signal it when you're ready to see one or all of us."

The recorded message was from Roland, the last member of the engineered family that had worked so hard to save what they could of Earth's people. When the starship *Aztlan* had departed Earth along with others from that lost world, there had been no choice but to leave him behind.

But he had reached out to his family. She listened to his message more than once.

"Hey, guys. This is Roland. I don't even know if this is getting through to you. I'm not as savvy on quantum communication as you are, but the AI computer says this should go through in real time. You've been gone fifty years now, and...shit, I don't even know if you made it to the new planet. But I'm asking for your help, so I can only hope.

"I know you felt bad about leaving me behind. I also know you had no choice because Earth was ending and you had to scram while I happened to be away. Zion, this this ship you designed for the Right Church has kept us all alive. And I can tell you helping

them save its membership was the right thing to do, even though they believed we engineered people are abominations.

"Well, the Church you knew is gone. They finally figured out that science wasn't their enemy after all, since that's what's keeping them alive in orbit above what's left of Earth. Not that they don't still hate the thought of us abominations, so I'm keeping my head down.

"They call this ship the Earthstar, *and they've replaced the Church with new leaders who have their own ideas about what's best for everybody else. They are right bastards, but if you're hearing this…well, we can't let all these people die because of them. The* Earthstar *is deteriorating. It has been for a long time, and lately I think the leaders and their also-bastard consorts have been cannibalizing parts of it to make getaway ships. It seems they think there's some place on Earth they can go, but they're wrong.*

"Most of the people here are being mind-controlled; they even put drugs in the water supplies to ensure compliance. The people are required to report anyone who doesn't comply. Women live separately from men until they are married to bear a designated number of children. But beyond all of that, the people live in terror of the Spectacle of Retribution, their version of capital punishment. Do you remember the British history about Guy Fawkes? He was sentenced to be drawn and quartered. Unbelievably, they use a modern version of that. These assholes do a living autopsy, on camera.

"Yet there are rebels even here. There are brave people living in the parts of the ship where the leaders never go. They use reverse osmosis to clear drugs from their water. They eat from what they can raise with hydroponics and what the rest throw out as garbage, and its barely enough to stay alive. It's worse than the homeless back on Earth because there's literally nowhere for them to go. Zion…and Sarnath, Egypt…you're all that's left of who we were, and I can only hope you're still out there…and I'm asking, can you help us?"

Shandiin thought about Roland, who she had known only briefly, and of his courage. She knew what it was like to wait with the desperate need to help others, when there was no hope of personal reward.

She also remembered how that life had changed her. She had become part of another world; she'd come to understand its people as she had never understood her own on earth. She had changed, and wondered how Roland might have changed as well.

Thoughtful, she used the computer to learn they were currently orbiting Earth along with the other ship called *Earthstar.*

She knew it was time to set aside her personal grief. It was necessary to look ahead instead of behind.

She let her friends know she was ready for them, and soon thereafter watched Zion, Egypt, and Sarnath come in and quietly settle into chairs around her, waiting.

"Thank you," she told them, "For your patience with me. I know it was cowardly, going into stasis so quickly after my return. I...needed the decompression." She took a deep breath. "So. I understand the people on the other ship are mind-controlled by those in power, and Roland has been secretly among them all this time? I can see why you might want to help, but not how you could."

"First," Zion put in, "I've used communication to help them repair their ship during the ten years...that's fifty years, in their time...that we've spent traveling back here."

"I'd think they'd be grateful for that."

"You'd think," Egypt responded wryly. "But using quantum entanglement for communication allows visual as well as audio, and they were horrified when they first saw Zion. There is some history that links the green eye mutation and their ancestors' fear of abominations. In their case they've accepted science, so have decided it more likely Zion and I are some kind of inhuman artificial intelligence. Zion's brilliance only confirms that belief. As far as they're concerned, the only full human on board the *Aztlan* is Sarnath, and that's who they prefer to negotiate with."

"Negotiate? What do you want from them, that you would deal with them at all?"

Sarnath leaned forward, his eyes intent on hers. "Their people, Shandiin. We want to save the people on that ship. To do so we have to get them away from this narcissistic leadership, who are the descendants of Canard, the Right Church premier. The Canards like things just the way they are, except for the danger of their deteriorating ship. They've hated having to rely on a 'witch'...as they disparagingly call Zion...to repair their own life support systems. So we told them about Hiraeth. A planet where they could live naturally, without dependence on a ship."

"Don't tell me you're going to bring the *Earthstar* to Hiraeth!"

"No. We won't take a chance on bringing technology that could destroy another planet...especially technology under the control of the sociopaths in charge of it. We won't even give them the coordinates of Hiraeth. But we will take some of their leadership with us to Hiraeth on the *Aztlan* to negotiate a possible immigration with a pre-modern civilization. I described it to them as you described it to me, Shandiin."

"I don't get it. What makes you think Hiraeth will allow this? Hiraeth's not some rock. She's alive, and she's magic. You know what she did to our first colony. And...as Zion says...the civilization I knew on Hiraeth may be distant history."

"We know all that. We know it's all balanced on a lot of unknowns. But it's the only chance we have to help the people on the *Earthstar.* Once an immigration is possible...under terms we would ensure are acceptable to us...we'd come back to take aboard the people of the *Earthstar* who want to live on a planet, and bring them to Hiraeth."

Shandiin got up to pace. "I don't like it. It's all so iffy, but even if you are somehow successful...I don't like it. There's a remote possibility Hiraeth's civilization still exists. You would be bringing in technology they would be defenseless against, and—even apart from that—a culture so different that it could destroy what exists, something I know is right and good."

"Why would you think that?" Zion demanded.

She turned on him. "Because it's happened over and over in Earth's history. Do you remember I was raised by Native Americans? They had their own civilization, one based on harmony with nature. Then came the invaders, who changed everything. The conquerors always do."

Sarnath sighed. "I understand, Shandiin. But you pointed out a lot of unknowns, and your possibility, while understandably concerning, is part of that. We can only face challenges one at a time. The people on that ship need their chance to be free, and Hiraeth is the only Earth-like planet we've been able to find. Believe me, we've looked."

She dropped back into her chair, arms crossed. "I still don't like it."

"Too late," Egypt put in. "We've already made agreements, Shandiin." She looked uncomfortable but determined. "The representatives from the Earthstar come aboard in the next 24 hours, and we're going back to Hiraeth. You have to decide whether or not to come with us."

"Well, I'm not going to go live on that ship that keeps its women separate for breeding. If I don't go with you, I'd have to go live with the rebels."

Egypt sat back. "The rebels have been integrated since Roland sent that message you listened to. He sent it fifty years ago, by their time. They are part of the general citizenry now, and some are part of the leadership's military support. Many of their soldiers are coming aboard tomorrow."

Shandiin glared. "I can't believe you agreed to that. You're bringing an army to Hiraeth?"

"They have limitations. It was part of what we had to agree to, but we've negotiated carefully about that. Trust me...this is to be a peaceful mission, not a military takeover."

Shandiin shoved her hands through her wealth of red hair. "I don't believe this." She froze suddenly, remembering, and dropped her hands to stare at Zion. "What's this shit about lying that we're married?"

He looked miserable. "Diane has already gone to live on the *Earthstar.* Her choice. She let them know there was another female aboard, and we were told firmly that unmarried females are not permitted to be near males under any circumstances. So leaving you aboard the *Aztlan* unmarried would be a deal-breaker. They've gone very backwards, Shandiin. It's like in the olden days when the navy didn't allow women aboard a ship."

Shandiin snorted. "Not that olden. Women weren't allowed to serve on a US combatant ship until 1994. Long before then they were considered bad luck and not allowed on a ship at all. Well, Egypt and I are damned bad luck when needs be." Considering, she frowned at her friend. "How come you didn't have to get married to stay aboard?"

"Not human, remember?"

Shandiin looked away, seized by a memory. Less than human, Khedran had called himself, when her opinion had been he was more than human.

But Khedran couldn't lie. Zion was willing to lie, so that she could stay on the *Aztlan.* And he loved her. She understood, now, what it was to fall in love. She'd finally taken the fall herself, and knew the joy and the pain that came with it.

She took a hard breath. "Can I talk to Zion alone, please?" she asked.

Sarnath and Egypt left wordlessly. Zion's eyes on hers were full of sorrow. "I know it's hard to lie about something like that," he began.

"Shut up. Please."

His eyebrows lifted in surprise. He waited while she regarded him thoughtfully before she went on. "When I woke up, I was in this chair, and you were on your knees in front of me. You waited for ten years to find out I loved someone else, and you accepted it. Zion, I can't make you lie for me."

He sighed and forked his fingers through his hair. "I was afraid of this. You told me a long time ago you don't believe in marriage, so why would you even pretend?"

"You misunderstand. I said I can't make you lie for me. So why don't we get married?"

He dropped his hand, shocked. "What?"

"You heard me. Will you marry me, Zion? The only thing we have to leave out of the vows is any mention of obeying. You know very well I ain't doing that. But I will honor you, and promise to be true, and to love you the best I can...just as I did before I went to Hiraeth."

"Shandiin..." He got up and came to her, sank again to his knees in front of her. "Are you sure?"

She nodded. "I can't keep running away from the truth. My life on Hiraeth is gone. It's time for me to start over. Here... with you."

Her lips curved, seeing the joy on his handsome face. "You won't regret it, Shandiin. I will honor you, vow to be true and... I will love you. Always." Then he stood, drawing her up with him to seal his promise with a kiss.

Zion wanted a traditional ceremony, to be performed by Sarnath as ship Captain. But to their surprise Sarnath frowned at the idea, and turned on Shandiin.

"What if your High King is somehow still alive?" he demanded. "Because unlike Zion, I believe it's very possible. There has to be a reason you saw him on Earth, before he was even born on Hiraeth."

Zion started to argue, but she lifted a hand to stop him. "Listen to me, both of you. Even if Khedran's still alive it doesn't matter. I left him to marry the woman who'd always been betrothed to him. I rather pushed him to her, because I didn't want him to be alone after I was gone, and he learned to love her. Do you remember making his bloodline incorruptible? He would never break a marriage vow, I'm definitely not perfect, but neither would I."

She tilted her head, considering. "Me being married to Zion isn't a problem, Sarnath. But maybe you can help me understand why I had a vision of Khedran, on Hiraeth, on the night he was born. This wasn't like the meeting on Earth; it was a true vision. He said he'd been behind me every step of my thousand years, but he couldn't be any longer. He charged me with mentoring the new King, who turned out to be himself. Then he warned me that I couldn't let him love me. I tried to comply, but I didn't understand why it was important until the very last. It turned out his love chained me to Hiraeth. I wouldn't have been able to take the gods and their magic, if he hadn't had the strength to just let me go."

Sarnath was staring at her, eyes wide. "And you didn't know this vision was the King not yet born?"

"Not at the time. Not for many years, actually. Sarnath, how can this be? How could he exist before he was even born, and know to warn me?"

Sarnath was, for once, not calm. That puzzled her. She could read alarm in his eyes even though his voice was quiet. "As for existence, souls are immortal. And time is not a boundary for...some of them. But to know the future, he had to have lived it, and purposely traveled back."

"This is making less sense all the time," Zion interjected. "Time travel isn't possible." But even with the words, his scowl became thoughtful. "Unless there's truth to the theory that spacetime isn't the foundation of the universe, but emergent from something deeper, something unknown. I never accepted that theory, but at least there's some evidence for it."

Sarnath ignored him. "Shandiin, did he say anything else?"

She slid a glance toward Zion, but answered honestly. "Yes. He warned me to guard my own heart. He told me love can be deadly dangerous, for it's the most powerful thing in the universe." She sighed. "I failed at that."

She was surprised at the look on Sarnath's face. "What's wrong?" she demanded. "You look like you've seen a ghost."

"I believe that ghost was trying to protect you." He turned to Zion. "I don't think you should marry her, Zion. It can only lead to heartbreak."

Zion's emerald eyes fired with anger. "Sarnath, I've learned to respect your theories. But this is ridiculous. A soul from outside of time warning Shandiin not to love him? It makes no sense."

"Even if it does," Shandiin added, "it doesn't apply. Khedran and I fell for each other, but we got past it. I'm not going to break Zion's heart because I love someone else, someone who agreed we had to say goodbye. I've been honest with Zion, and I always will be. I do have some ethics, Sarnath."

Sarnath regarded her grimly. "I'm very aware of that. All right, I'll call Egypt to be witness. We don't have much time, if you want this done before the Earthers board."

But they both knew he remained more than reticent.

CHAPTER 3

The ceremony was anticlimactic, a formal exchange of words on the ship's Bridge and a blessing by Sarnath as Captain of the starship. Egypt gave Shandiin a hug at the end, but worriedly whispered, "Did you marry him just to stay on the ship? Because that would be wrong, and you know it. I'd rather you both lied."

"Of course not. I do love him, Egypt."

"As much as the other guy?"

Shandiin turned away from her. "When are the Earthers getting here?"

Sarnath glanced at the monitors. "They're on their way. Shandiin, perhaps you and I should go to greet them, as the recognizable humans."

"No," she snapped. "I wasn't part of your deal and I won't pretend to like it. Zion and Egypt should go with you. The Earthers should be made to accept the fact that they're in charge right along with you. That's my dealbreaker. You know I can cause a lot of shit if they don't."

Egypt laughed. Zion grimaced, but Sarnath regarded her appreciatively. "You know, you're right. I don't want Zion or Egypt treated disrespectfully, and we haven't established the ship's officers; our negotiations never addressed that, except for the fact we would remain in command. So...I will immediately introduce Zion as the ship's Science Officer. Egypt will be my co-Captain. But Shandiin, you will need to make an appearance as Zion's wife.

This is a ten-year journey we're embarking on. You can't just hide from them."

"I don't hide." She crossed her arms stubbornly. "I'll meet them as his lowly, nagging bitch of a wife."

Egypt laughed again. "They'll probably counsel Zion that he needs to make you behave. But we have made it clear that while we would honor their customs, we are not their subjects."

"They're bringing an army," Shandiin reminded. "Egypt, how can you trust them? They could just take over the ship."

"You know me better than that. Of course I don't trust them, so they don't have the coordinates for Hiraeth. They've also been warned that if there's any attempt at a coup, the AI will recognize it and take us all immediately back to Earth's orbit. And," Egypt added with a smile, "we have a secret weapon. The soldiers they're bringing? And most of the support crew? They're Roland's."

"You're shitting me. How the hell did you pull that off?"

"We didn't. Roland did. He's been infiltrating their leadership for...overall, it's a century now, their time. And he's slowly integrated the rebels with him. The leadership has no idea they're bringing insurgents on this mission. He's also leaving a few behind to keep an eye on them, and cause enough dissension to destabilize their comfy little society. Spy work. It's always been his thing, even in books and movies." She grinned. "He is now Commander Bond."

The leader of the boarding party was Vice-Premier Ben Canard, brother of the Earthstar's elected Premier. Shandiin had learned that only members of the Canard family were eligible for election, by some descendant right no one dared to argue with. Ben had lost the big title to his brother by a narrow margin.

She didn't like him on first meeting, and the feeling was obviously mutual.

Ben Canard was not very tall, and having to look up at a woman was the first annoyance. The second was having her look down at him. "Don't speak to me," he warned. "I will not respond to a mere woman."

She shrugged. "Okay. Then I won't tell you your fly is unzipped."

Stunned speechless, he checked his pants, watched her stride away, and then turned on Sarnath. "She is insufferable! I don't want her near me again."

"I don't believe that will be a problem, Vice-Premier. May I show you to your quarters? It's been readied for you and your wife."

"My wife is not coming with me. She must watch the children, and *she*..." he paused for emphasis, "knows her place."

Sarnath lifted an upswept eyebrow. "My apologies. I was told there would be two in your quarters."

"There will, of course. My wife-consort will attend me."

Sarnath maintained his equilibrium, and started off with the Vice-Premier and his entourage. Several of the followers were meek-looking women.

Shandiin joined Egypt, who stood back to watch them go. "What hypocrites," Egypt nearly snarled. "No unmarried women, but a second 'wife' is apparently necessary to service them."

"I think history called them concubines. I guess Zion and I could have done that instead of getting married. Might even have been sexier." She grinned when Egypt slanted her a look. "I'm *kidding*, Egypt. Oh, here come the soldiers. Disciplined looking bunch. My God, is that Roland? Where are his locs? He's cut his hair tight, and looks more military than the rest of them. What a snooty command face. Are you sure he hasn't gone over to the dark side?"

"You can't expect him to break cover. He won't, even in private."

"So how can you be sure it's still just a cover? He's spent a century with them, Egypt. He could have changed. I know I did."

Egypt just shook her head while Roland signaled his soldiers to halt at parade rest. Egypt and Shandiin walked to join them, and were ignored while he addressed Zion coolly. "I presume my soldiers will be quartered away from any civilians, and have the necessary training facilities?"

"Yes, Commander Bond. Everything is as you required. I'll take you there."

"No consorts?" Shandiin asked.

There was absolutely no response to her. She and Egypt didn't exist. Roland walked off with Zion. The soldiers...all men...followed in lockstep.

"Good try," Egypt said.

"Christ. What a fucked-up bunch of people. Egypt, Roland hasn't aged a day. Is that normal for your kind?"

"We kind don't know yet what's normal. You haven't aged either, in a thousand years. Zion thinks you're possibly immortal."

"There's a scary thought. Is that park still there, Egypt?" Shandiin looked around at the curving steel hallway that had once been a parking garage. Now, she knew, ships of various sizes were garaged behind the metal doors. "This place gives me the creeps."

"That's the Aboriginal in you," Egypt laughed as she started away.

"I don't think Navajos are classified that way. Are you trying to piss me off?"

"I like it when you're pissed off. It seems more like you." Egypt led the way into an elevator, pushed a button when the doors slid closed.

"I know I'm different, Egypt. But how can you tell?"

"Falling in love over there. Getting married over here. You'll have to tell me about your adventures. But fair warning...Zion plans to write a report on all of it. He's fascinated. Will you tell him everything?"

"Yes. It might actually be good to do that, get it out."

The elevator stopped, and the door opened to green trees under a sunny sky. Shandiin lifted her face to the warmth, and smiled a little. "I remember when we brought Leah here. She couldn't see the sunlight, but she said she felt it. I know the sky and sun are a holograph, but...it's comforting."

"I'm truly sorry about Leah."

"I know Diane went to the *Earthstar*. Did anyone question her before she left?"

"Yes. All three of us. She didn't remember anything about those thousand years on Hiraeth."

"Did you believe her?"

Egypt frowned as they walked through dappled shadows under the boughs of trees that had matured over the years. "I'm not sure, and there was no way to verify. She apparently didn't even know she was pregnant. I was surprised she didn't want Zion to be her baby doctor, but instead wanted the medical facilities on the *Earthstar*. She'd always seemed obsessed with Zion. I guess she finally gave up."

Or found and lost her replacement, Shandiin thought bitterly, but didn't say.

"You still won't tell me why you wanted to kill her?" Egypt asked.

"No. I just hope I never see her again. In fact, do me a favor and don't mention her again, okay? There's stuff...I have to get past. And I won't get past that part if I talk about it, believe me."

"All right," was all Egypt said. "I can respect that."

Shandiin stopped to face her friend. "I missed you, Egypt. I made a lot of friends, on Hiraeth. But there was never anyone like you."

Egypt smiled. "Thanks for that. But I have to admit I would like to meet some of those friends. Especially the one who actually made you fall for him. He has to be something. Will you tell me about him?"

Shandiin looked away. "Give me some time. And then...yes, I very much would like to share my memories of him."

"Maybe even some juicy stuff you wouldn't share with Zion for his report?"

Shandiin looked back to see Egypt's wicked grin, and had to laugh.

She probably would. Egypt was, she realized, more sister than friend.

CHAPTER 4

Shandiin's personal version of relativity alleged that ten years on the starship was longer than a century had been on Hiraeth.

She was confined not just to a ship, but to part of a ship, because Roland had taken over half of it and required all civilians to stay out. The Vice-Premier found this perfectly reasonable, as they were separate classes. He also made it clear that the officers of the *Aztlan* were another class altogether...particularly the wife of the Science Officer. That Shandiin was included in the scheduled briefings from the *Earthstar* was a particular annoyance to VP Canard. Sarnath calmly set aside Canard's demands for her removal while Shandiin sat across the room and, apparently and manically cheerful, bared her teeth at him.

The scheduled communications with the Earthstar were in 'real time' through quantum entanglement, but not always helpful. Politics apparently abounded on that ship, and different people were their contacts, and seemed to be uncertain of their mission. Zion found this puzzling, but not troubling. His focus was on getting back to Hiraeth, and learning about Shandiin's thousand-year history, which she shared in varying degrees. Some things were, she thought, supposed to remain personal.

But even as she explained the history, she wondered if Zion could comprehend the civilizations that were born of it. The people of Hiraeth were nothing like the people they had taken to colonize that planet. Technology had been ripped away and replaced by magic. Any memory of Earth had succumbed to the gods. Reality had been forever changed as most of humanity's survivors were driven across a continent to a new land by the God of Order.

Yet, in that new land of Azlatan, the High Kings had ensured their people kept their autonomy, standing apart from dogma that would have controlled their minds. Phaelon's Laws of Order were an accepted reality, like the daily setting of their sun. Daimaine's ability to wield death and justice was fearful, but she was controlled by their trusted High King. Liethe's love and healing were welcomed with joy but not worship; she was the sun's rising, and had the same kind of impact.

Whether or not he fully understood, Zion tried his best to set forth the facts about all of Hiraeth's civilizations. His truncated report was sniffed at by the Vice-Premier. Magic gods were impossible, of course. There could be no danger from primitive people, though the possible existence of anarchistic warriors called Chaine was vaguely disturbing. More concerning was the potential of Xanthe's race of fanatics who were bent on world domination. The nomads were nothing.

What the Vice Premier found interesting was the major realm of Azlatan, where forms of wealth surely existed. He was pleased it was also a primitive society which could be easily won over with technology.

If there was a plan to use more than technology to 'win,' Canard kept it to himself. Roland, who was only seen at the required briefings, was also circumspect, and seemed in tune with his Commander in Chief. Shandiin, as was her habit, suspected the worst. He'd been too long among the enemy.

She knew the others couldn't understand the depth of her feelings for the people of Hiraeth. She held onto hope that Hiraeth wouldn't allow the *Aztlan's* passengers to disembark. She missed what had become her home, but she didn't want these strangers there. She missed Khedran...hard as she tried not to...but her aching heart hoped he had lived a long and happy life and was gone to history, so he would not have to face the changes these strangers brought. She knew those changes would be more than the introduction of electricity and everything that came after.

Perhaps Azlatan's civilization had grown to have technology on its own. Zion told her he believed that was a real possibility, but he didn't mention it to the VP.

Egypt's first interest was about the bloodline of the High Kings, but she quickly added fascination about the Chaine and their philosophy. "Reason and honor," she summarized over a shared workout in their well-equipped gym. "Understandable, since you created it."

"I only started it," Shandiin responded. "Then I watched it grow with each generation. At the end it was all their own."

"And you taught it to your High King."

"I found it helpful to the role he would have to play when I left. It's not that the Chaine aren't merciful, but they use mercy with reason, and can be very hard when their standards aren't met. The Kings were all brilliant leaders, but they cared deeply for their people who also revered them, and their justice only came hard against true evil. Khedran was the only one who had to face the conflicts of civil unrest, the lack of reverence for his rule...and war."

Egypt knew that subject disturbed her friend, so she changed gears even as she put down her weights. "But he wasn't part of the culture of your Chaine. He apparently took a wife. You said the Chaine do not marry, but believe in *amhara.* What's the difference?"

"Azlatan, like Earth, has legalities surrounding marriage and its ending." Shandiin switched a weight from one hand to the other. "The Chaine do not. They believe that a bond of romantic love is no one's business but that of the people involved. If people want to share their material wealth, they make an agreement. If they want to have children, that is another contract, with the child's welfare paramount."

"I see. So contracts replace marriage? Then what is the role of *amhara*?"

"*Amhara* applies to much more than romantic love. It's basis is the belief that love cannot exist without respect, and it has two meanings. Between people, any kind of love with respect is *amhara*. In the second meaning, it is a word of requirement relating to everything, and includes a note of gratitude."

"Everything?"

Shandiin smiled. "Think about it. Shouldn't there be love, respect and gratitude for life, and all that lives, and all of nature that is part of it and necessary to it?"

Egypt frowned. "I see. But as far as people, what is *amhara* other than an open relationship? It doesn't sound like a commitment of true love." She slid a sidelong glance at her friend. "Are they like you, then? You never believed in a soulmate, never wanted to fall in love."

Shandiin stopped her workout, took a towel to her face, and sighed. "I've learned differently, Egypt. Sometimes the union between people goes very, very deep. In those cases they are generally recognized, with a great deal of awe, as *amharen*. It's actually very rare."

"I see." Egypt regarded her thoughtfully. "Was your High King *amharen* to the woman you think he married?"

Shandiin looked surprised at the question, then considered it. "He told me he respected her, and so he could care for her. And later, I know he loved her. So the foundation for *amhara* was there." She frowned. "But I don't know if they could ever have become *amharen*. If not, it's just sad. He deserved that kind of love." Shandiin looked away. "He deserved it all."

When they approached the wormhole that would take them into Hiraeth's star-system, Shandiin went to Sarnath with a mixture of hope and worry. He agreed to meet her in the park, understanding it was her comfort zone.

"When we came through that wormhole the first time," she reminded him as they walked under the trees, "everyone had visions. The first one was always very personal and affected people emotionally."

"I remember well." Sarnath strolled with his hands clasped behind his back. "You wouldn't tell me what you saw, but I knew it affected you deeply. You began your relationship with Zion right after, which I found puzzling since you and he were of opposite opinions about the source or reason for those visions."

That vision came back to her with startling clarity. *The stars are so brilliant their light ices everything, including him...shining light through his long black hair, firing the emerald of his eyes as he turns to me with love and sadness. My dark stranger.*

She'd felt a terrible emptiness as he faded away into nothing. She had never known such loss.

Until she said goodbye to him a thousand years later.

"I saw the High King, Sarnath. I saw him and...it hurt too much, when he vanished. I decided he couldn't be real, and I needed real. Zion offered that." She immediately realized how that sounded. "It wasn't like a rebound thing. I cared for Zion then, as I do now. I just didn't know at the time that love could go any deeper than that."

"But you found out later. And married Zion anyway."

She stopped walking and huffed in frustration. "All right, Sarnath. I realize Zion deserves more than I can give him. But I do love him, and why shouldn't I? He loves me, so why is it wrong for me to love him the best I can, to marry him and keep the promises I made to him?"

He also stopped. There was sadness, but no anger when he looked down at her. "I never said it was wrong. I only tried to warn of heartbreak. Love is a dangerous thing, Shandiin, but it is also necessary."

She scowled. "Have you ever loved?"

He surprised her with a sad smile. "Oh, yes. A very long time ago. Like you, I had to say goodbye."

"I'm sorry. One of the engineered? Oh my God...was she killed, along with the rest of them?"

He shook his head. "I can't talk about it, Shandiin."

She bit her lip. "All right. I can respect that. But...I've always wondered about you. You are so different from the others. Can you tell me about yourself? The others look up to you, even Zion when he disagrees with you because of his rather rigid belief system. Are you the oldest... the first one Damon Alexander engineered?"

"I was there before they came to be. As for now, I need to get back to the Bridge. We will be nearing the wormhole soon. Isn't that what you wanted to talk about?"

"Yes. If the Earthers have disturbing visions, it may well frighten them, and I am hoping you will use that to encourage them to turn back."

"No, I will not. Zion has treated the passage as inconsequential. If there are visons, he will explain it away. We are all committed to this mission, Shandiin."

She watched him walk away, sadly unsurprised at his refusal.

She was thinking instead of his response to her question. She'd heard the High Kings deflect questions because they didn't lie. Sarnath's answer had sounded like a deflection. He hadn't said he was the oldest of the engineered.

He'd said he was there before they came to be.

If he wasn't one of the engineered, she planned to someday find out just who he was.

She entered the observation room as they neared the wormhole, remembering too well the first time she'd gone through, and wondering if there would be another vision.

She'd expected the room to be full, but it wasn't. Only Zion and Egypt were there…and Roland, who sat on the other side of the room from them. He contemplated the monitor, currently showing only white light, as though he were alone.

Shandiin settled into the chair next to Zion, a bottle of water in her hand. "Is the computer running everything while we go through?" she asked.

"Yes. As it did last time."

"I just hope your AI doesn't turn into a god again."

"If we have visions, I plan to disengage the AI. Even though I disagreed with you before, I realize now that this is when Hiraeth began reading people's minds, deciding to make gods to control the colony. And the AI became the worst of all of them."

"Yes, Phaelon was the worst. When we reached orbit and the planet yanked his software mind from his hardware, he became quite unbalanced." She frowned. "Hiraeth could only touch our minds until we reached her orbit, which is some distance beyond the wormhole. Her magic is powerful, but it has a boundary."

"I came to the same conclusion."

She smiled. "I guess I can't out-think a genius. But I am curious about that wormhole, Zion. I remember you saying your engineer Dr. Alexander discovered it, but since then I've learned that it's just outside the heliosphere…which is only three times farther than the distance from the Earth to the sun. That's much nearer than the nearest star. It's so brilliant that surely it should have been discovered before he was even born."

"It's brilliant because it's magnifying the light from Hiraeth's own sun. It's like a beacon meant to lead us to that world. But it wasn't always there, Shandiin." He turned to regard her as she sipped her water. "As far as I've been able to discover, it appeared in the sky about the time you were discovered as an infant."

Startled, she spewed water. She wiped it from her face with the back of her hand while she stared at him. "What the hell? How do you figure that?"

"We have a lot of Earth's records on board this ship. I did a lot of research about you when I discovered your odd heritage...the fact that your DNA doesn't tie you to anyone else on Earth. It took a while to determine when you were found as a newborn, on that Navajo reservation. I had to backtrack from the foster system records, where you appeared at fifteen years of age...after, according to those records, having been in an orphanage for three years. You told me they took you from your Navajo family when you were twelve."

She stared at him. "So you know how old I really am."

"I've always known you're an old lady." He grinned at her. "And even older since you came back from Hiraeth. Is that why you snorted your water?"

"No. It's the freaking idea that a bright star appeared in the sky at the same time I came along. Do you know the exact date?"

"Yes. Dr. Alexander's records say the light appeared on December 21, the winter solstice."

"That's the day before they found me."

"Possibly just the night before. They found you at sunrise, which you told me is why you are named Shandiin, meaning sunshine." He lifted an eyebrow. "Were there any wise men among those who found you?"

"Knock that shit off. It's weird enough without that. There was only one person who found me. She was a medicine woman I called my grandmother. She told me a spirit had brought me there among the sheep, and her old herding dog came to guard me. She never mentioned a bright star in the sky."

"Maybe she never made the connection."

"Because there's no connection to be made. Unless you think aliens brought me through the wormhole or...shit, that isn't what you think, is it?"

He smiled and kissed her forehead. "I don't know, and I don't care. I'm just glad you're here."

Welcome back, Shandiin. You must bring the son to me.

With the whisper came bright lights, a kaleidoscope of patterns, flashing through her vision. Zion caught her bottle before she could spill the rest of her water. "Shandiin?" He gripped her shoulder anxiously. "Are you all right?"

She blinked at him. Egypt had leaned forward to watch her in concern.

"Didn't either of you see that?"

"See what?"

She glanced toward the monitor. There was a tiny black hole in the center of the white light. "We haven't even gone through yet."

"We've just entered it." Zion looked over at Egypt. "Did you see anything?"

"No. Shandiin, tell us."

"It...flashing lights. Just for an instant. Neither of you saw that?" Realizing they hadn't, she didn't tell them about the whisper.

Welcome back, Shandiin. You must bring the son to me.

She wanted to think about that. It wasn't the first time Hiraeth had told her to bring the son if she returned. She had no idea what it meant, but now it worried her.

Because it sounded like Hiraeth was expecting her.

And she didn't want to go back there, not with the Earthers.

She got up to leave, pushing back at Zion's concern with a careful lie about flashing lights being common before she got a migraine headache. She noticed Roland still sat apart, ignoring everyone.

Sarnath met her just outside the door.

"What do you know?" she demanded. "What's going to happen?"

"I have occasional memories that may not even be my own, Shandiin. But I can't foretell the future."

"I think at least part of that is a lie," she snapped, and walked away.

There was no aberration for anyone else aboard the *Aztlan* when they passed through the wormhole. The journey from there to Hiraeth was just as uneventful.

Shandiin's last hope that the planet would reject them was gone when finally Hiraeth curved beneath them, beautiful in blue and white, dappled with the colors they had known on Earth.

She stood on the Bridge with the ship's officers, watching the view from cameras that magnified the continent passing below. They passed over the march of eastern mountains, then the great central plain she knew was called the Admech.

The ship and the view slowed when there came a shadow that split the continent in two from north to south; it was cast by the great cliff that was the eastern border of the realm of Azlatan.

Atop that cliff, she saw forests and meadows, rivers and lakes, farmlands and villages. And finally, ranging far along the edge of the western sea, there was a familiar walled city of crooked streets, dominated on the south by a great black palace.

"It hasn't changed," Shandiin murmured. She could feel her own heartbeat, strong and hard in her chest while her knees were weak as water. "A thousand years passed in minutes while you waited for me, but not since I left. From here it looks the same as I last saw it." She swallowed hard. "And Penumbra still stands."

"Is that the King's castle?" Egypt asked, peering in fascination at the monitor. "I thought it was magic. I wonder why it didn't vanish along with the gods."

"Penumbra wasn't created entirely from magic. It stands on a the remnants of an ancient volcano. Daimaine used lava to build it, creating from it a natural hard obsidian." She turned to Zion, who had been very silent as they viewed the city of Cabre. She had already explained it was known as the King's City.

"It seems your explanation to the Earthers was true," she told him. "It remains a medieval civilization, unless there is more to it than the obvious."

"Yes." He didn't lift his gaze from the city that passed beneath. "And perhaps your High King is still alive after all."

"Zion..."

He shook his head. "You're going to tell me it doesn't matter. I have to believe that's true, Shandiin." He drew in a deep breath. "I'm going to think instead about Hiraeth itself. I could never understand why a planet like Earth had many similar animals, but no intelligent civilization. Now I wonder why time hasn't changed there. A thousand years passed while you were on that planet, but apparently nothing in the twenty years since you left. It doesn't make sense."

Sarnath spoke for the first time. "It's magic, not science. My guess is that it's somehow connected to Shandiin, and twenty years have passed there as well. Her time and Hiraeth's are aligned."

"That's actually kind of scary," Egypt noted.

Shandiin said nothing. She was watching Zion walk away as the view below slipped from city to sea. He hadn't once met her eyes.

PART II. THE PATH NOT TAKEN

Every journey taken always includes
the path not taken,
the detour through hell,
the crossroads of indecision
and the long way home.
–Shannon L. Alder

CHAPTER 5

N ow she was back.

Shandiin stood on the wild grassland called the Plain of Admech, beneath a night sky sparkling with the familiar constellations she had never thought to see again. Her hair of fire and gold blew around the shoulders of her denim jacket, its color muted in star and moonlight.

She remembered a thousand years of life on this planet. She remembered her people, the Chaine, those she had loved and led through centuries until the last battle to save the land of Azlatan from its prophesied destruction...a battle she had left before its conclusion.

She wondered if they endured.

With shattering clarity, she remembered the realm of Azlatan, and the dark King she had unwillingly come to love more than life.

She wondered, with an ache in her heart, if he had lived through the Prophecy War.

And if he did, she wondered if she could bear facing him knowing the dreaded change that had come with her.

Behind her, the landing party was nearly finished setting up the base camp. To her great disappointment there had been no challenge from the living planet. If she hadn't heard the whisper of greeting as they entered the wormhole, she would wonder if Hiraeth herself yet lived, since she hadn't stopped the people from landing or immediately destroyed the technology they brought with them.

Shandiin sensed her husband come near. Pasting on a fake smile for his benefit, she turned to the man who could have been a twin of her lost dark King...who was, through genetic engineering, a distant ancestor of the High Kings of Azlatan.

He stopped next to her, hands deep in the pockets of his denim jacket, his strange emerald eyes searching the star-filled sky where it met the far horizon of this sea of grass. When his gaze finally turned to hers, it was sad.

"I imagine coming back like this is hard for you, Shandiin. I know you didn't think we would be allowed to land. It appears the planet has become more welcoming since our first trip here."

She sighed. "Maybe. But it only cements the Earthers' belief that I am a liar or a crazy woman. They don't believe in magic. You wouldn't believe in it either, if you hadn't seen the evidence with your own eyes."

"Yes. I've accepted the history you explained to me, Shandiin. You're the one without faith. You don't trust my decision to give other people the possibility of a future on a new world. You know I never felt right leaving all those people behind, to live forever on a ship."

When she turned away he tried again to convince her. "I still don't understand why you are so mistrustful of those survivors, Shandiin. Yes, I made concessions with their leaders, but so have they. Their Premier agreed that you and I would go first to make the case for a second colonization of this planet. We'll leave tomorrow after the briefing...on foot, as you demanded, instead of using a method of transport that might terrify or antagonize the people here."

She shook her head. "You don't understand why I don't trust even those people back on the *Earthstar*, who have lived like prisoners under control of these assholes? Zion, they've been brainwashed ever since Earth died, and understand nothing about nature. They will believe they have the right to do whatever they want with it."

"I would think losing Earth has changed that attitude."

"If anything, it's made it worse. They rely on technology to live. Like those before them, they will treat nature as a resource instead of realizing they are part of it." She sighed again at his scowl. "I still wish you hadn't let them know there was another planet like Earth." She gazed into his strange eyes that reflected neon green in the moonlight, wishing she could make him understand. "Hiraeth trusted me, Zion. She didn't have to let me go and take the gods that were controlling the people. She trusted me!"

"You make the planet sound like a person. How could it even have a gender?"

Shandiin huffed. "She is a living and intelligent being. To me that's a person. And she spoke to me with the voice of my grand-mother."

He shook his head. "No wonder you're so sentimental. You came back in such a state..."

"I know you thought I was just hysterical."

"You wanted to disconnect life support...to kill your own daugh-ter!"

"Diane was a goddess here, and became evil. She is evil, Zion."

"When she came out of stasis she didn't even remember being on Hiraeth, unlike you. She was in the stasis chamber the whole time you were gone, as was your daughter Leah."

"It should have been Diane who died." Shandiin's unhappy gaze shifted toward the far horizon where she had once seen a cottage silhouetted by the rising moon, and met the goddess known as Liethe. The goddess who had also been her other daughter, Leah.

"Shandiin..." he shook his head. "I'm sorry for your loss. Leah was a wonderful person. But I couldn't allow Diane to be punished for a dream she doesn't even remember. And she's gone now, with the others back on the *Earthstar*. Science is still in charge where she is, and the laws of relativity apply. Fifty years will have passed there in the ten years we were traveling back to Hiraeth.

They can't begin the immigration until we have approval from this world's inhabitants. Only then will I give them the coordinates to get here. It's very likely Diane won't even be alive when their immigration becomes possible."

When Shandiin didn't respond, he frowned in frustration. "I know you remember whatever evil she committed in your thousand years. But to her, it was all a forgotten dream when she woke. You and Sarnath convinced me that astral projection is somehow real, but she had no memory of it." He regarded her stiff shoulders, her averted head, and sighed. "You remember it all, but you were not projected. You were there physically. Why did the planet take you, body and all, and not your daughters?"

"I don't know. Hiraeth would only say I was different." She turned back to him. "I don't have all the answers, Zion, and at the moment I don't care. I'm too worried about the impact of what we have brought, and any future immigration. I am afraid for the civilizations of this world. They are right and good, not like those from Earth."

"Which you have told me repeatedly. But surely Earth's survivors aren't all bad, Shandiin; that's a generality I find surprising coming from you. And we can give the people of Hiraeth technology, medicine..."

"And the newcomers can use technology to overwhelm a culture they see as backward," she retorted bitterly.

He regarded her sadly. "You speak as though you are no longer one of us, you know that?"

She had to look away. She didn't answer him.

He shook his head. "You really wanted Hiraeth to block us, didn't you? I can't believe you wanted the magic back, after everything you did to remove it."

"I hate the thought. But magic may be the only thing that can save this world."

"Do you think magic still may exist here? Shandiin...I have to ask you something. Did Hiraeth contact you, just as we were about to enter the wormhole? You told me you saw flashing lights, but passed it off as a headache."

She hesitated. "Wow. I should have remembered how smart you are. I'm sorry I didn't tell you right away. Yes, it was a brief contact...and it scared the hell out of me. I guess I ran away from it instead of telling you, which would have made me confront it."

"What did she say that scared you?" he asked.

She exhaled. "She told me to bring her someone she calls the son. She'd actually said it before. She told me before to bring the son if I came back, but I ignored it then because I was certain I was never going to return."

Her revelation startled him. "Who would that be? Shandiin, you talk about this planet like it's a goddess. I know Earth had legends, its own living goddess called Gaia. I think people made sacrifices to her. Are you planning a sacrifice to this planet, Shandiin? Who is this son?"

"I'm not sure. But I'm terrified that I may know." She swallowed, and confessed the horror she'd carried since Hiraeth's brief contact. "He was born to save this world. I knew it the night he was born. I looked at an infant and saw a spirit brighter than sun or moon or truth itself."

Zion was shocked. His scientific mind had never accepted her interpretation of Khedran's spiritual origin, but he knew who she meant. "You would do this to him? You would sacrifice your High King?"

"I can only hope Hiraeth will give him the magic to defend his world. I can't believe it could be a true sacrifice. Hiraeth isn't evil."

He stared in disbelief. "Not evil? She nearly destroyed the first colony with a tsunami. She put those people into the control of gods and vicious magic, and a thousand years later they don't even have electricity. You are delusional, Shandiin, if you think she is not evil. Now you plan to give her the man you practically worship. And you honestly believe he would go along with it! You think he is a savior, don't you? You have an obsession about him."

"He is what you and your family made him, Zion. Hiraeth's magic only magnified your design. You used genetic engineering to create a bloodline of incorruptible leaders whose entire purpose was caring for their people. Yes, he would sacrifice himself for them. He has no choice when it comes to saving his people. Your design took away his free will. Dammit, Zion, I'm the only one in Khedran's life who understood him. He cares for them all. Half of the High Kings committed suicide because they could no longer carry the burden of every life in their charge."

Zion shook his head. "Suffering depression just proves they are still human, despite anything we did in a laboratory. Your hero is not perfect, Shandiin. You told me magic gave him influence over his people. But I think it affected you, too, or you couldn't believe he was all that wonderful." Frustrated and angry, Zion left her there.

She watched him go, her heart hurting for too many reasons.

Zion knew too much. She had unburdened herself to him, because leaving Hiraeth...and leaving Khedran...had filled her with despair that had to be released. With a heart as great as his brilliant mind, he had somehow accepted her love for another man.

But that was before it became possible that man would be in her life again.

You are wonderful too, she thought as she watched him walk away from her. *You just don't realize you are a genius and a savior in a different way than he is. I do love you. I love you for who you are. And God knows, I do not want you to be hurt.*

But I don't want his world hurt, either.

The new base perimeter lights came on, and she blinked at the brilliance that turned night into more than day could ever be.

Electricity on Hiraeth. She looked up. The familiar stars were lost in that glaring white light, and she grieved.

<h1 style="text-align:center">CHAPTER 6</h1>

The required briefing was held in the hastily erected main structure after a makeshift breakfast. Everyone was tired after working through most of the night, but eager to hear the latest reports on this new planet.

Zion, as Chief Science Officer, brought up the aerial videos taken from the orbiting *Aztlan*.

"This is Cabre," he explained, and they all saw a sprawling medieval city backed against the western ocean and surrounded by open land which had once been a deadly battlefield.

Shandiin tried not to think about the unknown outcome of that battle.

He could be there, she thought. *If he survived.*

With a thrill of joy she saw Chaine ships in the harbor, but said nothing as Zion continued speaking. "Cabre is the capitol of Azlatan, and may still be home to the High King who rules over the seventy-seven Dominions of Azlatan."

"Looks like something out of ancient Rome," said Vice-Premier Ben Canard. "Shouldn't be hard to convince them we can improve their life. They don't even appear to have electricity. Do you think they still have slaves?"

"They never had slavery," Zion said, forestalling Shandiin's angry response. It was apparent that Canard had not read the official report Zion had provided based on Shandiin's knowledge. Shandiin, recognizing intellectual laziness, deduced that he'd expected others to brief him on the written report, so was operating on hearsay and opinion. "It was an agreed-on, rather symbiotic arrangement that lasted a thousand years, but which probably fell apart once the gods were gone."

Canard snorted. "You mean the supposed magic gods? C'mon, Alexander..."

"That's Doctor Alexander," Shandiin cut him off abruptly. "Show some respect. And the gods were quite real."

The arrogant glare she got from Canard was intended to put her in her place. She ignored it, caught Zion's cautionary glance, and subsided in fury while Zion continued the overview of the planet Canard already referred to as Earth Two.

"That western country is pretty well settled, but this is a huge continent," Canard noted smugly. "Plenty of room for more people."

"It's inhabited," Zion reminded him. "Even these wide plains are inhabited by the nomads called the Sundancers. And there is civilization in the mountains south of here. It appears only partially populated, but there are people."

He brought up another picture, and Shandiin sat up alertly, seeing a sprawling unwalled city. "That has to be Xanthe. They were the people who warred against Azlatan. It's looks like they lost."

"Wouldn't take but a few warcraft to take them all out." Canard spoke flatly, and this time it was Zion who turned on him.

"This is a peaceful mission. We are not here to make war or take over these people."

Canard snorted again. "Then why did we bring the military?"

Zion looked over at Roland, Commanding Officer of the military, who said, "I understood we are here for protection and transportation, not to make war."

Canard frowned as though surprised at the response, then waved it away impatiently as he addressed Zion. "Didn't you say you found a second continent?"

"Yes. It's on the opposite side of the planet. It's smaller than this one, and we barely took note of it on our previous expedition here." Zion changed the image, and Shandiin was astonished to see another continent she'd been unaware of. She sat forward, smiling to see golden Chaine ships in a peaceful harbor. When she glanced toward Zion, he surprised her with a wink. "It appears the people called the Chaine have begun settling this one, so it is inhabited as well."

"We'll see," Canard declared. "Now, Commander Bond, when can you be ready to transport us—"

"Our mission statement says we will not use mechanical transport," Zion interrupted, "until my wife and I have made contact with the people here, so they can understand our purpose is peaceful."

"Ridiculous," Canard sneered. "Waste of time, you two tromping around on foot when we can fly." He threw an angry glance toward Roland. "And why we only have one skycraft available on the ground is beyond me."

"Your brother approved the mission statement," Shandiin reminded him. "He's the Premier, not you." She got a glare in response.

"She's right," Zion agreed. "And Shandiin and I plan to tromp around starting this morning."

"You can't be serious. It's leagues to that city on the coast where you said their King lives. By God, we'd be here forever waiting for you."

"We'll be able to give you updates," Zion said comfortably. "We launched communication satellites, remember?"

Canard drummed his fingers on the arm of his chair, his eyes hard on the monitor where Cabre spread. "I'll give you eight weeks," he finally snapped. "That's more than enough time to deal with these natives. If you haven't resolved issues with them by then, I will obtain clearance to go in myself...with the military, to make sure they understand who is in charge."

"Issues?" Shandiin asked. "What issues do you expect us to resolve, Canard?"

"That's Chief Commander Canard to you, Mrs. Show-Some-Respect." He spoke in a falsetto voice meant to mock Shandiin's comment moments before. "And the issue to be resolved is the natives' acceptance of colonization, starting with those empty lands."

"The Sundancers…"

He turned to glare at her openly. "Read your history, girlie. It's what has always happened. It even happened when America was colonized. The natives succumb to those who are stronger."

She stood slowly, wishing for a sword in her hand. "Those were my people. I am one of those native Americans."

"Quit being so dramatic. You couldn't even be a half-breed, not with that red hair." Canard shoved to his feet. "All right, Alexander. You have your orders. Contact the natives and have their agreement within eight weeks. You're all dismissed."

He walked out. Zion and Shandiin looked at each other in dismay while the room emptied.

Aware of listening devices, they were silent as they went to their quarters. They were still uncomfortably silent, gathering their gear for the journey, when the camp alarm sounded. Shandiin was out the door before Zion could react.

"Unidentified personnel, Potential Sector 8 breach," came the thunderous public announcement. *"Stations as assigned."*

Shandiin saw Roland striding out ahead of her, and ran toward him. He turned, apparently hearing her boots on ground already hard-packed, but she didn't give him a chance to speak.

"Don't let them shoot! For god's sake, Commander—these people are not a threat!"

He tapped the communication device he wore. "I've already ordered them to stand down. You think it's your Sundancers?"

"Yes," she said in relief. "Let me go speak to them."

He smiled, and she was reminded that she had liked him when she first met him so long ago. "Of course. As I understand it, that's your job." He looked up as Zion approached, adding, "We will stand sentry while you make contact." Zion only nodded. Shandiin was already headed away, and both men followed in her wake.

A group of armed soldiers stood at the edge of camp, staring out over the grass. "What is that?" Shandiin heard one ask, sounding very young and frightened. "Is it a wild animal, half a man?"

Grew up on a ship, she remembered. "It's a man on horseback," she explained as she strode past.

"What's a horseback?" he asked, but she was already out of earshot, breaking into a dead run through the tall grass.

There was only one "unidentified personnel." He had long sandy hair, bleached almost white by the sun. He wore white buckskin, and dismounted his white horse as she approached.

Varady's continued existence, his beautiful smile, filled her with such gladness it caught her off guard.

He read that emotion as she came flying to him, and held out his arms to take her in. She went willingly, and to her own shock and his surprise she wept against his shoulder.

He kept her in his embrace, watching the other two men approach. His eyes of dark gold widened when he saw Zion, who so resembled the High King.

Shandiin stepped back, scraping tears from her eyes with the heel of her hand. "I'm sorry. I'm just so damned glad to see you. I didn't know if you...if any of you would still be alive."

He returned his attention to her face, and she saw understanding. "You have been gone for a long time. I am very glad to see you as well, Shandiin. And yes, Khedran lives yet, as well as Roinn who is now The Chaine. I have a great many stories to tell you." He looked up at the waiting men. "But I think you have news for me first."

She turned to the others. "This is Varady," she introduced. "He is brother to the High King of Azlatan, and leader of the Sundancer nation. Varady, this is Commander Roland Bond, and Dr. Zion Alexander."

Zion offered a hand in greeting, but glanced at her sidelong. "I am Shandiin's husband," he said bluntly to the handsome man she had run to, and who had embraced her so warmly.

Varady's eyebrows went up, but Shandiin chose to address the greeting. "It's a custom of Zion's people to offer a hand in friendship at meeting," she explained to Varady.

"I see." Varady took the offered hand, and smiled. "Some friendships run deep," he told Zion. "Shandiin and I fought side by side on the ramparts of Cabre, though she is far the better warrior. I am glad to meet her mate. Well come, Zion Alexander." He turned to the man who was much darker than those he had once known as Rioch. "And to you, Commander. You are a soldier?"

"I am." The Commander lifted an eyebrow when Shandiin added, "He is the leader of an army of soldiers brought to your world, Varady."

Varady's warmth cooled. "I see," he repeated, but this time with a different meaning. "And why would you bring an army of soldiers to my world, Commander?"

It was the Commander's turn to look at Shandiin sidelong. "It was determined we were best qualified for a mission to an unknown place."

Varady looked past him to the strange buildings made of metal, the soldiers who stood at attention, the many others who thronged in obvious curiosity. His eyes lifted to the tall array of poles holding things that had blazed with steady lightning throughout the night. "Would you mind if I spoke with Shandiin and her husband alone?" His voice was flat.

Commander Bond looked at Zion, who nodded. "Of course." He walked away.

"He can be trusted." Zion scowled after him. "Shandiin, you made it sound like an invasion."

"He reports to Canard," she retorted. "You heard what Canard intends to do, if we can't get permission for immigration."

Zion ran a hand through his hair. "Yes. He managed to keep that quiet until this morning. But you can trust Roland."

Her eyes flashed doubt before returning to Varady. "We need to get to Cabre. We need to tell you, and Khedran and Roinn, who these people are and what they want."

Varady only nodded, and turned to lay a hand on his horse's arched neck. To Zion's surprise, the white stallion snorted and wheeled to gallop away.

"I asked him to bring horses for the two of you," Varady explained. "I have a small band of Sundancers waiting not far away. But I will be the only Sundancer to accompany you. They will join the rest of my people, who I have sent to Iesse."

Zion was stunned. "You asked him? You can talk to a horse?"

Varady shrugged with a smile. "Sometimes he even listens."

Shandiin softened, taking pity on Zion's confusion. "The Sundancers and their Shalmira...their horses...have always had a symbiotic bond. This means some magic still exists, even without the gods." Her expression went sharp. "Varady, does Khedran still have his gifts?"

Varady nodded. "He still has the gifts of the High Kings." His gaze slid toward the base, the many soldiers. "All but the Star Blade, and I think he may need more than that."

Shandiin put a forestalling hand on Zion's arm, because she knew he had questions but wanted him to wait; they were, she thought, still too near camp for some things to be discussed. He lifted his eyebrows, but waited as she turned back to Varady and asked, "Why have you sent your people to your mountain stronghold?"

"Because my brother Jael still has gifts also. He has visions. He warned me that I would see a bright light on the Admech, and when I did I should send my people to safety and come to Cabre."

"Jael," Zion put in. "He's the child Khedran took in?"

"Our younger brother, yes. But no longer a child. He is now the age I was when we went to war."

Zion frowned, glancing at Shandiin. "Just how long has it been since Shandiin left here?"

"Twenty years."

Zion shook his head. "Then it's verified. I don't understand how it's possible, but the planet is on the same subjective time as you are, Shandiin."

She threw up her hands. "Don't ask me, Zion. Between magic and relativity, I never know what time it is. Varady, is Jael still with Khedran in Penumbra?"

"No. Khedran has titled him High Prince, but he does not answer to it. He lives apart from Penumbra, in what was once the Temple of Liethe. It is yet a place of healing, but without magic it is now based upon Chaine medicine. He is seer and healer and teacher. The people call him the Sage of Cabre."

"Sage? And he has visions? That sounds like Sarnath," Zion said thoughtfully. "I always wondered if his talents were genetic." At Varady's questioning look, he added, "Genetic meaning inherited. It sounds like your brother is psychic."

"I am not familiar with that word. We call him magic. May I ask, who is Sarnath?"

"I guess you could say he is my brother. And an ancestor of yours, as am I."

At Varady's stare, Shandiin shook her head. "I think that's too much too soon," she told Zion. "Look, the Commander's coming back. I think he's bringing our gear."

Commander Bond dropped the backpacks at their feet. "Do you have the second communicator?" he asked Zion.

"Yes."

"Use it if you need to." He nodded politely to Shandiin and Varady, and left.

"What was that about?" she asked.

"Just backup in case we need help. I've told you we can trust him."

She frowned because Zion sounded irritated, and she realized he had enough concerns without her distrust of a man he considered a brother. She was aware of her own distrustful nature, knew it wasn't always warranted, and wondered if she should apologize.

But she set that aside as the horses arrived and their journey to Cabre began.

Varady answered and asked questions in a friendly manner as they journeyed, but he frequently rode ahead to confirm their path. Zion took those moments to talk privately to Shandiin, but it was a long time before he was ready to discuss the High King with her.

Instead he expressed curiosity about Varady's speech.

"It has a certain cadence, and is rather formal," Zion noted. "Is that because he's a Sundancer?"

"The Sundancers have their own patterns. Varady was raised in Azlatan." She tilted her head, thinking. "But I guess it's true of the Chaine as well, that formal way of speaking. I believe that's Khandor's fault."

Zion looked surprised. "Really? Surely a King from a thousand years ago wouldn't have that much influence." He grinned. "That same thousand years didn't make your language less blunt or salty."

She smiled, remembering a long ago journey across the Admech. "Zion, one of the first things I noticed about the men in your family is how unusual you were...not just from being engineered, but because of your decency in a world that had set aside civilized behavior and speech. I told Khandor I hoped that gentility was something he would encourage as he established the land of Azlatan. He said he would, but in return he asked me not to change who I am." She shrugged. "It's like we made a contract. I think Hiraeth heard us, and wove it into the culture of this world."

She tilted her head as she regarded her husband. "So you see, you are the one with the influence on Varady's speech...while I am still riff-raff. No one here ever understood a lot of the words I use, and they never learned them. Hell, I think I kept Khedran confused half the time."

Zion lifted his eyebrows. "So maybe I understand you better than he did?"

"Well," she laughed, "you know what a dickhead is. He never did figure it out."

"And I don't imagine you tried to explain it."

"Do you realize how inane some expressions are if you try to explain them when there is no common reference? Once when he was being very quiet I used the phrase 'Cat got your tongue?' and the look on his face made me laugh for five minutes." She shook her head. "But it's even more bewildering when there's no mutual connotation. No, Zion, I never attempted to explain the filthy things I said. I didn't really want him to know their meaning."

"You wanted him to keep an innocence from that part of our culture."

She looked at him with surprise. "I guess I did. But before that...I had just hoped for them all to be more like you."

Zion was a new rider, but soon settled into his horse's rhythm as the days wore on, and she relaxed into something near peace until she saw a dark cliff's edge on the horizon, and knew it was the eastern boundary of Azlatan. She watched it rise against the sky, highlighted by the setting sun. Her thoughts were far away until she picked up on a discussion the men were having.

"Shandiin has told me the King...your brother...has a gift of presence," Zion was saying.

Varady nodded thoughtfully. "He does. But his connection with people is a greater gift, I think."

"The connection she calls a thrall? Do people actually fall in love with him?"

Shandiin caught Varady's brief hesitation before he answered. "He has an affect, and it varies with each person he encounters. You will understand when you meet him. But he considers it a curse more than a gift. I have seen him patiently waiting while people overcome it. He respects each person's autonomy and right to dignity." Varady was thoughtful, looking for the right words. "But his connection is more than his affect of presence. He is curious about each individual, not in any surface or usual way, but because he truly likes people. He always tries to connect, especially with those who disagree, and even more with those who are afraid of him."

"Are people often afraid of him?" Zion asked.

Varady smiled at that. "Oh, yes. That is something else you will understand when you meet him."

Shandiin wished the simmering dread in her belly would go away when Varady stopped them near the base of the cliff, suggesting they start the climb at first light.

"You've been very quiet," Zion remarked to her as they dismounted and Varady built a campfire. "Are you worried about meeting him again?"

He didn't have to name Khedran. She knew who he meant. "Yes," she admitted.

"It might help if you knew more about what we'll find on our arrival. Ask your questions, Shandiin. You've been honest with me. I'll also be honest and admit I dread you meeting him again. But we both know it has to be. I just...wish things were different. When you started explaining your life here to me, I watched you break down when you spoke of him. You don't break, Shandiin. I found that rather terrifying."

She put a gentle hand on his cheek. "You helped me through what was a very difficult transition. You have a wonderful heart, Zion. It's one of the many reasons I love you."

He smiled at that, and leaned in for a kiss. "Go ahead and ask your questions," he repeated.

"Ok, I will. When I'm ready." They both turned to the mundane chores of making camp.

Varady was curious about the gadget Zion used to start the fire, and intrigued by the MRE's he pulled out of his gear. "There is food in that?" he asked, and when Zion tapped the vacuum sealed packet and it expanded, heating, he grinned in delight.

When he tasted it his delight wasn't as great, but his curiosity remained. "This isn't magic?"

"No," Shandiin smiled. "But Zion is sometimes jokingly called a sorcerer, because technology...science, that is...is very similar to magic, and he is..." she sought for a word, shrugged. "He's like a High Tahmond, but one we can trust."

Varady looked thoughtful, and Zion laughed. "Isn't that a priest?"

"It's a metaphor, Zion, not a religious thing." She drew in a breath. "Varady, I guess I need to know more about what's happened in your world. Were there a lot of losses in the war after I left?"

"No. Because Khedran is the only one who fought."

She sat back, only partly surprised. "So he did it. He challenged the giant Tahmond, didn't he? With the agreement that the armies wouldn't fight...so no one else would be hurt."

"He what?" Zion asked, amazed, and she turned to him with a huge smile.

"It's who he is, Zion. I figured he might try that avenue, so I left him a gift of armor. It's made from the element we call Chaine gold, which is stronger than steel." Her gaze flashed back to Varady. "He won, obviously."

"Not without great injury, even with the armor. It was a terrible battle, Shandiin. The giant hammered him with weapons and armored fists, but Khedran was seething savage, and relentless." He shook his head in grave admiration. "Even your Chaine warriors were amazed at his skill, his tenacity. But he was almost killed. The giant had no honor, and tricked him by stabbing him in the back after he had conceded. The sword pierced the weakened armor, and Khedran couldn't get up to fight back as the giant readied the killing blow. No one was close enough to help because he'd ordered us all to stand down. I thought he was going to die, but Stormwing..." he hesitated, and his pride shone through. "My mate Stormwing shot an arrow through the eye-slit in the giant's armor, and killed him."

Shandiin stared, feeling a wave of cold. "I must thank her."

"She has received much thanks from many," Varady smiled. "And when Khedran was finally able to return to duty...oh yes, Shandiin, he was hurt very badly; Danon told me he didn't know how he'd kept fighting, blackened throughout with bruising beneath the armor, and with cracked ribs. It took some time for him to recover, but when he returned to rule, Khedran decreed that the changes in Azlatan would include more than the integration of the races. He had defended Azlatan, he said, but his defenders had all been women. He named you, Shandiin, and his wife Marre, and my Stormwing. He has since elevated the role of women in Azlatan, and many are taking advantage of it."

At this, Shandiin's eyes in the firelight were suspiciously bright. "You don't know how proud that makes me." She exhaled. "So...he married his betrothed."

"On the steps of Penumbra, in the sunlight, with most of the city as witness." Varady smiled. "No more dark Temple weddings for the High Kings. Cabre celebrated for days after the wedding, and again when Marre gave birth."

"So he has a son. How wonderful...what are you smirking about, Varady?"

"His changes on behalf of women appear to have been prophetic. Khedran has a daughter, Shandiin, and she is named after you. They call her Shandi."

Shandiin went perfectly still. After a moment, she shoved to her feet and walked away. She stopped with her back to them, staring out over the Admech.

Both men watched her, where she stood with her arms crossed at the far edge of firelight.

Zion asked, "Why did his wife allow their child to be named after Shandiin?"

"Shandiin is an icon in this world, Zion. I understand it was Marre's suggestion, not Khedran's."

"So she doesn't know…" Zion's voice trailed off and he bit his lip.

Varady watched him carefully. "I think Marre knows very well what you don't want to say."

Zion was silent. Varady added gently, "Khedran and Shandiin are two of the most honorable people I've ever known."

But Zion was still watching Shandiin stare into the darkness.

When they climbed the twisting road up to Azlatan the next morning, Zion looked around at a young forest with a lush understory of ferns and shrubs. "This is completely unlike the plains below us. It's quite beautiful."

"And I'm surprised," Shandiin added. "The last time I saw this parcel, the only thing left was dust and soot. It seemed the invaders wanted to destroy every living thing they saw."

"Many of the invaders now live under the rule of the High King," Varady explained. "And even those that chose to return to Xanthe asked for what was needed to restore the land they had scourged. They all understood that Khedran had given them not only their continued existence, but freedom to live as they chose…something they had never known under the Law of Phaelon and their giant Tahmonds."

Zion turned around to face Varady. "What does it mean to live under the rule of the High King? What does he require to become a citizen here?"

"An oath." Varady smiled toward Shandiin. "I think he may have based it on Chaine beliefs. Each person must take an oath to respect all things that are part of the world, including their fellow humans."

Zion frowned. "That seems overly simplistic."

Shandiin shook her head in disagreement. "It creates focus on what matters, Zion. Everything else is detail."

CHAPTER 7

Traveling mostly by night, they crossed several Dominions without event before they came to Cabre. When they arrived Varady agreed to enter the city first, going alone to Penumbra to contact Khedran.

He left them at the edge of a forest encircling a broad expanse of barren land ending at Cabre's tall outer wall. Shandiin recognized that stark zone as the last battlefield of the Prophecy War. Varady had explained it was left barren at the High King's command, a memorial of the Prophecy War that had taken so many valiant lives before the gods departed.

Shandiin regarded it thoughtfully. She had taught Khedran well about setting aside assumptions of safety, and about planning. She knew the King almost certainly had other, more tactical reasons for leaving that clearing around the walls of Cabre. Those on the ramparts could see anyone or anything approaching his city.

She and Zion spoke little while they waited. As the day grew late, slanting sunlight gilded the city's great white walls. Shandiin sat cross-legged at her horse's feet, peering at the city where once she had stood and fought. Cabre's great central gates stood open now, and traffic flowed along the central road to which all roads in Azlatan eventually met.

She looked over as Zion settled onto the ground next to her. He brushed a lock of her wayward hair from her face, then trailed his fingers gently down her cheek. "Shandiin, it's been hours. We need to talk about this. You practically forced Varady into going into Cabre without us. Your reasons sounded valid; you wanted to know what to expect after the High King gets the news that outsiders have landed on his world. But I have to ask. Did you also do it because you're still nervous about seeing him again?"

She only nodded, and he sighed.

"Is it because you are still in love with him? Is that why you were so upset when you found out he had named his daughter after you?"

She raked her fingers through her long shaggy hair, and left them there a moment. "My reasons are not what you think, Zion. It's not about what I feel for him. I simply wanted him to forget me. How could he do that with my name on his lips every day?"

"Then help me understand, Shandiin. Varady says you are an icon here. Why, when you saved his world from the gods, would you want him to forget even your name?"

"Because I wanted him to be happy." She dropped her hands and met his eyes, wishing she could make him understand, doubting she ever could. "I'd never have come back here, given a choice. I wanted him to have a wife, and a family, and the peace he deserves, without remembering..." She looked away. "I was so wrong, making love to him. It was so wrong of me, on so many levels. It was selfish."

"It was twenty years ago, Shandiin."

She shook her head. "You have no idea how little that will mean to him. He was disloyal to his betrothed, a woman he told me he loved. He failed his nature because of me, the nature you and science built into him and magic magnified beyond reason. And now I'm back, and because of what Hiraeth said...I may have to take him from his family and everything else he has built and cared for since I've been gone. If what you've warned about sacrifice has any truth, it's possible he may never see them again."

"It's his choice, you know. You can't make him do anything against his will."

Can't I? She thought, but did not say.

He glanced toward the gates of Cabre, and came to his feet. "I think that's Varady."

She stood up beside him to see the white-clad rider who even now seemed a little brighter than the light afforded.

Varady came with two others. One had long red hair, and Shandiin recognized the Chaine woman named Shajii.

The other woman rode a black horse, and wore black.

Zion had his binoculars out, and she heard him exhale loudly. When he looked back at her his eyes were wide. "That has to be the most magnificent woman I have ever seen." He swallowed. "Oops. Sorry."

Shandiin took the offered binoculars and focused in.

Shandi wore a simple black uniform.

Her hair was like black flame blowing around her shoulders.

Her eyes were his.

"My God," she whispered. "She looks like him."

They both waited as the three riders galloped toward them. Shandiin smiled at her old Chaine companion Shajii, smiled again on seeing that the young woman in black rode as well as her father. But the smile faded as they came near.

"She looks angry," Zion noted.

"She looks furious. She's certainly not channeling the Black Wolf."

Zion threw her a curious glance. "You mean the persona Khedran uses to control his feelings? Would he have taught her that?"

Shandiin didn't respond, watching in perplexity as Shandi dismounted before her horse came to a full stop. She strode to Shandiin and faced her with emerald eyes blazing. She stood equal to Shandiin's six feet, and her boots were braced apart as though for battle.

"You don't belong here," Shandi snapped. "Leave now."

Shandiin lifted her eyebrows. "Is this by order of the High King, Princess?"

Shandi's hands fisted at her sides. "No. I don't want him to know you are here."

Shandiin braced, warrior to warrior. "I don't think that's your call."

Varady moved to put a hand on his niece's shoulder. "Shandi, I told you. There is danger to your land. Danger to your whole world, in fact. Khedran has to know, and Shandiin bears the message."

"You told me she didn't come alone. Let her companion come to Penumbra with their message. She stays out." Shandi's eyes never left Shandiin's.

Shandiin frowned, glancing at Shajii, who arrived to place a hand on Shandi's other shoulder. "Respect," Shajii warned. "She was The Chaine, and the goddess who saved Azlatan."

Shandi finally broke eye contact to glare at the two who flanked her. She then returned to confronting Shandiin. "You and I need to talk. Alone."

"Yes," Shandiin frowned. "Apparently we do." She turned and walked away, leaving Shandi to follow.

When she thought they were out of hearing of the others, Shandiin turned to face the angry Princess. "I don't understand your anger, Princess. Can you tell me why?"

"Did you use magic on him?" Shandi demanded.

"What do you mean?"

"You know very well what I mean. I heard my father talking about you to Compatri Danon. He said you had relations with him, and my mother knows because he confessed to her."

Shandiin lifted her hands, palms out. "Wait a minute! Why—"

"My father told Danon he couldn't not love you."

"What?"

Furious, Shandi stepped up to the woman she had been named for, as though to spit in her face. "Don't try to pretend. My father was in love with you, and you left after...you know what you did. Now my mother is..."

Shandiin realized Shandi was choking back tears as well as fury.

Uncomprehending, she just waited.

"So you don't deny what you did." Enraged, Shandi drew back her fist and punched Shandiin in the face.

With no effort at defense, Shandiin dropped like a stone.

The others were there immediately, but Shandiin refused their help. She eyed Shandi warily while reclining with her elbows propped on the ground. "Are you finished?" she asked.

"I don't know. You haven't answered me yet."

"What answer are you looking for, Princess?"

"You *hurt* him! Did you use magic to make him love you?"

"That's enough!" Zion snapped, stepping in front of Shandi. "If he is hurting, it's only what he deserves, because I watched her cry for hours over him. Why don't you punch *him*, Princess, for the mistake they made before you were born? And what gives you the right to bring judgement on them?"

Shocked, Shandi stared into the face that mirrored her beloved father's. "Who are you?"

"My name is Zion Alexander. The woman you just struck is my wife. You may be the High Princess, but you have no right to judge her, much less strike her. I expect you to apologize."

His visage and his reprimand drained her anger even as Varady put his arm around her protectively.

"Her mother is dying," Varady explained. "Her physician, Danon, told me Khedran has fallen into such despair he's concerned for him as well. I think that explains Shandi's behavior."

"Marre?" Shandiin was on her feet and pushing past Zion. "What is wrong with Marre, Princess?"

Shandi blinked hard against tears she had fought for days. "Danon and Jael both say she has cancer and is near death."

Shandiin turned to her husband. "Do you have anything with you?" she asked urgently.

"Not much. I will have to call for help, Shandiin, if you want to save the High Queen."

Shandiin looked from him to Shandi, back again. "No choice. We have to save her, Zion. This world needs them both."

"I agree," Varady put in.

"Save her?" Shandi cried. "You think you can save my mother?"

Zion nodded to Shandi. "We can save her. But this changes our plans. A lot." He pulled out his communicator, then hesitated long enough to touch Shandiin's face tenderly. "That's already bruising."

She smiled at him. "Certainly not the first time I've had a bruise. Call in the skycraft, Zion. Tell him to land by that rock formation away from the road."

He nodded and walked away, speaking into his communicator.

Shandiin turned to Shajii. "Is Roinn The Chaine now?" she asked.

"Yes. Why did you let her strike you, Shandiin?"

"She is Khedran's daughter. Can you help us, Shajii? I need someone to wait for the skycraft and fend off anyone who might see it come in. Also to help the pilot know where to go next."

"Shandi was wrong to strike you. I am glad to have you back. Of course I will help. What is a skycraft? What is a pilot?"

"A machine that flies. The pilot is the person controlling it."

"A flying machine? How fun. How long will I wait?"

Zion had joined them, putting away his communicator. "He'll be here in about an hour." He looked at Shajii curiously. "Doesn't any of that frighten you?"

"I have seen magic nearly destroy an army. This flying machine sounds much better." She went to her horse and took a cloak from her saddle, tossing it to Shandi. "They'll need this if you're taking them to Cabre," she told the Princess. "Those odd clothes they wear are too conspicuous, and the man looks too much like the High King. I'll go wait by the rock."

They watched Shajii mount and ride away. "She is brave," Zion noted.

"She is Chaine." Shandiin spoke with pride, and turned back to the Princess.

Shandi didn't look chagrined but said carefully, "I should apologize for striking you. I have always known you as the heroine of Azlatan, as Shajii pointed out. And Father long ago explained you were once a goddess, and why you left. Then, moments before Varady came to me to tell me you were here, I was caught by surprise to overhear...the other thing about you and him."

When Shandiin said nothing, Shandi lifted her chin. "I am ashamed that I never learned what the danger is. What you came to warn us about."

"Invaders. People from another world, who may want to take yours."

Shandi stared, then grimaced. "Varady was right. You need my father. We should go. I have another hooded cloak so you can both put one on." She was removing it from her saddle as she spoke.

Evening had fallen quickly. When they left the empty fields and reached the road, they had to share it with heavy supply wagons. Shandiin knew they were generally allowed only at night, to leave the roads within Cabre for use by its citizens.

It was windy, but fluttering torchlight shone along Cabre's ramparts and behind the open gate. Varady dropped back to ride beside Zion, but both men were in deep thought and silent.

Shandiin rode beside Shandi, whose hair blew around her like a black flag in the wind. Shandiin asked the question at the top of her mind. "How do you want to handle this? Me meeting your parents, I mean."

Shandi took a deep breath. "You must talk to Compatri Danon first." Shandiin was glad to see she had it through. "He is the one who should tell them about this cure you have promised." She lifted her head to look across at Shandiin, her eyes glittering green fire in the torchlight. "After that...Father has no idea why I left Penumbra, if he has even realized I am gone. News of your arrival came just on the heels of what I had discovered about you and him. He doesn't know I overheard his conversation with Danon, when he admitted everything. I saw him weep, Shandiin. I have never seen my father weep, and it shocked me. Varady came to me just after and told me you were here. I reacted. Father will not understand what I did...striking you, I mean."

"You only need to tell him what's important. What is important at this moment is that you found us, you brought us here, and we are going to save your mother. If you need to tell him anything else, I think it can wait."

Shandi nodded, but waited a moment to speak again. "I do not want to be there when he sees you. I do not want to see his reaction. If he still cares for you…I am afraid it would change him, in my eyes."

Shandiin glared at the Princess, for the first time showing real anger toward her. "So, despite all that he is, all that he's done for Azlatan…caring for me would make him less, to you? Is that the real reason for your anger?"

Shandi's expression was pained upon hearing it so bluntly put, and it took her another moment to respond. "Perhaps it was part of the reason. But not the main reason. Since he has loved you while he loved my mother…and he does love her, Shandiin, very much… I heard him say he feels guilt for it even though she has forgiven him. Maybe even because she forgave him. I saw a side of him I never knew existed, Shandiin, when he spoke with Danon. He was close to broken. I am very afraid that seeing you again when she is so ill could destroy his own self-worth. He would no longer be the man I know." She looked across meaningfully. "I know your history with him. You may be the only one who understands that could be the end of him."

Shandiin grimaced. Knowing the strange truths of the High Kings, especially Khedran, she realized Shandi was right. "Then he must not see me until he knows Marre will be healed. Zion is the healer, Shandi. I will send Zion to him, and stay away."

Their little group blended in with others entering Azlatan's gates. Shandiin kept her hood close but peered around at the city she had helped to defend so long ago. Damage had been repaired, and changes made, but she saw much that was familiar, and her heart clenched in painful memory.

She looked across at Zion, who was also being careful to keep his face hidden under his hood. She thought of Marre.

We are both so lucky, she thought, *to have mates with a heart bigger than they are. I was a selfish fool that night. Of course Khedran carries guilt because of it. If only I could go back and change it...*

But she couldn't. And knew in her heart she probably wouldn't.

Shandiin glanced up at Penumbra as they neared, the beautiful palace that no longer sparkled with moving stars because she had taken away Daimaine's magic. Now it was just an edifice of black obsidian, the home of Azlatan's leaders. She lowered her head as they neared the entrance guarded by Khedran's black-clad soldiers.

The soldiers snapped to attention as Shandi neared. "Send a messenger to the Compatri Danon," the Princess ordered quietly. "Tell him he is to meet me and my companions in the family library as quickly as possible."

Obedience was instant. The group left their horses to the soldiers and walked through the atrium where another guard opened the door to the library.

It was a large room, full of books and scrolls and artifacts. As soon as the door closed behind them, Shandiin threw back her hood and walked to the fireplace, gazing up at the sword displayed above the mantle. It was a silver sword with a black hilt.

"The Star Blade," she breathed.

"It is a replica," Varady said. "The real sword turned to dust when the gods left."

Shandiin turned back. Her eyes were a little wild as they sought Zion. "I don't know if I can do this."

He came to her as she had known he would, and laid his hands gently on her shoulders. "You can. This was your choice, Shandiin."

She searched his eyes, his beautiful emerald eyes, while her own blurred with tears. "So many memories. So much loss and pain."

Varady spoke. "And so much courage. There was also joy, Shandiin, and caring. I am glad you are back."

Shandiin lowered her head. "Thank you, Varady." She pulled up her hood, even as she met Zion's eyes again. "Shandi and I agreed I can't meet Khedran until after you have seen to Marre, until he knows she will be made well. So first contact is up to you, Zion."

He simply nodded and turned as the library door opened.

Danon's eyes went immediately to Shandi; he scarcely noticed the others in the room. "You need to come, Shandi. Your mother is worse."

"Go," Varady said to Shandi. "I will talk to him."

Shandi was gone in an instant.

"I can't stay," Danon said to Varady. "Marre needs...."

Zion stepped in front of him. "You must be Danon."

Danon went mute and stayed that way for a long moment, his eyes wide with shock. "Who are you?"

"I know I resemble your High King, but that is incidental. My name is Zion. Like you, I am a physician. Varady can confirm I have come to help the High Queen."

Danon's mind was on his patient, even through the amazement of seeing Khedran's likeness on a stranger. "I have seen this disease before. It is always fatal."

"I do have a cure. Please take me to your patient, so I can begin treatment."

Danon straightened. "I don't know you, or where you come from. And I will not allow you near her without permission from the High King."

Well, shit. Shandiin dropped her hood. "There isn't time for that, Danon. We have a lot of things to talk about, but Zion must go to Marre immediately. He really can cure her."

Varady quickly nudged a chair behind Danon when he saw him step back, knees buckling. Danon sat down hard, staring at the apparition walking toward him.

Shandiin knelt at his feet, looking into his arctic blue eyes, seeing there was now white at the temples of his black hair and lines on his handsome face. But his wide-eyed expression was still very much Danon, and she had to smile. "Have you behaved while I was gone?"

In answer he pushed to his feet, clutching her arms to lift her with him, his gaze pinned to hers. Then he gathered her in and hugged her fiercely before drawing back to study her face. "I have missed you every day for twenty years. But why would you think I behaved without you to kick my ass?"

She had to laugh. Danon had always been able to make her laugh. "Of course you're right. Danon, this is my husband, Zion. He's a genius and can really cure cancer. Take him to Marre."

Danon drew breath, releasing his hold on her as he turned to Zion. "Because she said so...please come with me. The High King is with the Queen in their chambers."

Zion looked to his wife, who pulled her own communicator out of her pocket. "Let me know when you are ready for me to join you."

When they left, she sat with Varady, wondering how she was going to face Khedran.

Dusk purpled the world when Shajii finally saw the machine she had been watching for. The skycraft landed silently. She walked toward it as a door opened in the side and a man got out.

She stopped dead in her tracks.

The man wore a one-piece black garment with straps and pockets and metal things on it. He was taking off a helmet to reveal a very dark and handsome face, neat curly hair and a beard. He had brilliant dark eyes and white teeth in a big smile. "Hello there," he called. "Were you waiting for me?"

She resumed walking toward him in amazement, and saw something similar come over his features as she drew near. He lifted his hand to aim a light at her, saw her leather armor with gold filigree gleaming, her long hair like fire. Her beautiful face.

After a moment of staring at each other, he blurted "I thought all the goddesses were gone from here."

She had to laugh. "You are trying to flatter me. I am Shajii, of the Chaine."

"Ah. The warrior race. I am Commander..." he hesitated. "Aw, hell, my name is Roland. I apologize for my forwardness, Shajii. I was caught off guard."

"So was I. I've never seen anyone who looks like you."

"In what way?"

"Not as dark, though some in Azlatan are nearly. You are very...exotic."

He regarded her armor, the sword at her hip. "I can surely say the same about you."

She reached out, and when he just smiled permissively, touched his flight suit. "What material is this? It does not feel like leather."

"It's Kevlar. This stuff can stop a bullet."

"What is a bullet?"

He removed his Glock from the holster on his thigh, but held it away from her when she reached for it. "Dangerous," he warned. Ejecting the magazine, he gave her a bullet. "When placed in this," and he held up the gun, "there is a small explosive that makes the bullet fly out faster than you can see. It is very deadly when it strikes its target."

She eyed the gun. "How far does the bullet fly?"

"It can kill someone very far away."

She frowned. "That would be a battle without honor." She unsheathed her sword. "I prefer this."

"Holy shit! Is that gold?"

"It is named Chaine gold. It is stronger than iron or steel."

When he reached for it, she held it away. "It is very dangerous," she warned with a wicked smile. "And it doesn't need bullets."

So began a new friendship.

"Wake up," Shandi was saying as she stroked her mother's still face. "Please wake up, Mother."

Khedran sat on the other side of the bed, almost as still as his Queen. He watched his daughter sadly but could say nothing as Marre slipped away from him. He thought, in fact, that she would not wake, and seemed unable to think beyond that.

He didn't look up when Danon entered and dropped a hand onto his shoulder. It took a moment to register what he heard. "Khedran, I've brought someone who can help. Shandiin told me he can cure Marre."

Khedran lifted his head. He saw Shandi looking past him and realized someone was there. He turned to look.

A man with short black hair in strange clothing stood with his back to him, going through an odd case placed on a small table. "New Chaine medicine?" Khedran asked, puzzled.

The man didn't turn. "No." He was assembling something. "It is not. The medicine I offer is from off-world, Your Highness, and it will make your wife well again. Azlatan had a thousand years of peace, a war, and now faces wonders you can't imagine." Zion turned around, holding an unfamiliar object, and looked for the first time into the High King's emerald eyes.

If Shandiin had been there, she would have understood his abrupt stillness, his stunned expression.

Zion had expected the facial resemblance, the longer hair falling to the shoulders of a plain black uniform over a body more powerful than his own. But the face was not just a mirror; its beauty was magnified. And even though Shandiin had tried to explain the King's commanding presence, he had never expected the impact of Khedran's gaze.

He knew a frisson of fear, followed by awe.

You will understand when you meet him, Varady had said.

Khedran merely waited until the stranger pulled himself together.

Zion swallowed, straightening his shoulders, and lifted a strange apparatus. "Danon says she is not getting enough air. This will help. If you will let me help her. Please."

The High King stood slowly, glanced thoughtfully at Danon, then nodded. The man who was his double stepped to the bed and put something transparent over Marre's face. There was a hissing sound.

"Oxygen," Zion explained. "It's the part of air she needs most, and this device extracts it directly to her. It will help revive her." He reached back, picking up a long tube with a sharp needle on the end. When Khedran moved reflexively to stop him before he slipped the needle into Marre's arm, Danon put a hand on his shoulder.

"Shandiin says he can cure her," Danon repeated.

Zion glanced across at Danon. "How long has she been in coma?"

"It just happened. When the sun went down."

"Damn. While we were on our way here. Well, this should temporarily..."

"Mother!" Shandi exclaimed as Marre's eyes fluttered open. "I'm here, Mother. It's going to be all right."

The High Queen blinked, looked around dazedly and saw Zion. She started to smile, then stopped. Her voice barely carried. "Why did you cut off your hair?"

Khedran had stepped around the bed to stand with his daughter. He took Marre's hand. "I'm here, love."

Her eyes moved from Khedran to Zion and back again. "Why are there two of you?"

"That is a good question." Khedran met Zion's eyes. "But I'd first like to know if what you have done will truly cure her."

Zion shook his head. "She is very ill, Your Highness. This is a temporary respite. I'll need to take her with me to give her the treatment that will save her life. With your permission, of course."

"Take her where? How?" Khedran frowned. "You said you are from off-world."

"Yes. Your realm...your *world* has visitors from another world, and I am one of them. We had planned to have a formal meeting with you, but then your daughter told us about the Queen's illness, so we came without ceremony. I would take her in a skycraft for treatment to the base we have established on the Plain of Admech."

Khedran was silent for a long moment. His expression was neutral when he finally responded. "You say 'we.'" His gaze shifted to Danon. "And you mentioned Shandiin. Is Shandiin with him?"

"Yes. She assured me that this man can cure the High Queen. She is downstairs in the library, with Varady."

"I see." Khedran turned back to Zion. "On the word of Danon and Shandiin, and facing no other choice, I find that I must trust you. Yes, you may take Marre to make her well. But I am coming with you."

"Your Highness," Zion began, but Khedran lifted a hand, palm out, to stop him.

"You are not from Azlatan, so I don't understand why you call me that. I don't even know who you are."

"My apologies. I am Dr. Zion Alexander. Shandiin...my wife...said that the honorific was expected when addressing you."

Khedran's eyes narrowed. "Shandiin is your wife?"

Zion gazed back with the same expression. "Yes."

After a brief moment, Khedran simply nodded. "Tell me what has to be done."

"We need a place for the skycraft to land, and a way to get the Queen to it."

Shandi stood. "We are at the top of the north tower. It's all rocks below, and quite some distance to the beach. The tower roof is flat, but I do not know if it would hold your flying machine."

"If we can get her to the roof, the pilot can hover and drop a rescue basket. He can winch her in, and then he can take us up the same way." Zion looked down at his patient. "I am sorry to speak as though you aren't here," he told her. "Do you think you can do this, Your Highness?"

"I am completely confused, but if Khedran says I should, I can do anything."

Zion blew out a breath. "You are one brave, loyal lady. Shandiin was right about you. Now we just have to figure out how to get you up to the roof."

"That's simple. I will carry her up the stairs." Khedran smiled down at his wife.

"Father, please..." Khedran turned in surprise to his daughter, who went on plaintively. "I must go with her in the flying craft. You cannot leave Azlatan now. You know I do not want to rule...perhaps never, and certainly not now, when your experience is needed." When he scowled, she lifted her hands to his shoulders. "Shandiin has warned me. Me, and Varady, because you were not there yet. She says this is not a reunion or even a rescue mission, that we as leaders must think of our people and what this contact means to them. The world will change forever, Father. It needs you, not me."

He considered her for a long moment, then closed his eyes and rubbed his forehead. "I understand. You go with your mother. I will take care of Azlatan."

Dropping his hand, he looked down at Marre. "I am sorry, my love."

She crooked a finger, and he leaned in so she could touch his face. "It's all right," she whispered. "I will be all right, with Shandi along. You are not choosing between me and Azlatan."

When he drew back they regarded each other. "I am sorry," he repeated. "I have not been strong for you." He exhaled and took her hand in his. "I will do better, when you are well again."

Still holding her hand, he stood to face Zion. "It is very dark out. How will they know where to come?"

Zion lifted his communicator. "I gave the pilot general directions, and there is a Chaine woman to help him navigate. This device has enough light for him to home in on. But he will have to use the skycraft's lights for safety while he hovers, and they are very bright. Your citizens are sure to see it."

Khedran sighed. "Lights over Penumbra. They will think the gods have returned."

"It's very windy," Shandi put in. "Will that be a problem?"

"No. The pilot's an expert."

Khedran looked back at his Queen. "I think you are going to have an adventure," he told her dryly, and she smiled. Then he turned to Danon. "Please go with them."

Danon looked into his King's eyes and saw not a command, but a plea. He simply nodded.

Khedran gathered Marre into his arms, lifting her from the bed. She smiled again as he carried her. "I could get to like this," she whispered.

"Then we will do it often," he answered just as softly, "when you come back to me."

She seemed to weigh nothing as he carried her up the stairs, and then there was an end to whispering as the wind roared at the doorway and a light brighter than the sun exploded over them. Khedran held his Marre close, protecting her while looking up at the strange flying machine, squinting against light and wind.

He didn't notice Zion watching him with an expression nearing anger.

A basket was lowered from the machine, and when it touched the roof Zion signaled him to place Marre inside. Khedran marveled at her courage, weak and sick yet strong enough to face this. But then, he knew better than most that Marre had always been courageous.

The basket was large enough for Shandi to join her mother. It was winched up and, after that was done, a harness dropped for lifting Danon.

As Danon was winched up, Zion touched Khedran's shoulder and motioned him back to the stairs. Once inside on the upper landing, he closed the door against the wind and noise. His face was stony as he faced the High King.

"It's just you and me here at this moment. I promise I will take care of your wife and bring her back to you safely and in good health. But my own wife is downstairs, afraid to face you. I watched her cry for hours when she told me about leaving this world. Leaving *you*. I know she loves you; she told me she does. But you will not hurt her again, regardless of your feelings or hers. She is mine now."

After a moment...during which Zion could read nothing on the King's face...Khedran said, "I think there are more important things to be considered, Zion Alexander. Marre and I have worked hard for twenty years, building a new Azlatan after the war. It's apparent you and those with you are about to disrupt everything we have worked for."

"I'm glad you realize that. Just don't take it out on Shandiin."

Khedran frowned. "Is that what you are concerned about? I would not, and she would not allow such irrational mistreatment if I did. As you should well know, being her husband." He regarded Zion thoughtfully. "I think she told me about you, when I discovered she was from another world, and what she had come here to do. I asked her where she would go when she left, and if anyone waited for her. She told me there was someone who loved her. After she was gone I attempted to be glad of that, for her sake. But my attempt was never successful, and I can surmise how you must feel, knowing she loves me. You probably feel the same way I do at this moment, learning that she is now yours."

With that Khedran turned on his heel and left him there.

CHAPTER 8

Khedran stopped just inside the door of the family library, where Varady and Shandiin sat across from each other in front of the fireplace.

Varady took one look at him and stood up. "I gather the Queen is on her way to their base?"

"Is that what they call it?"

"Yes. They use a lot of strange terms. I'm going to leave you both now, and find Jael. He should be with us when we discuss this in the morning. And what about Xanthe?"

"Xanthe." Khedran sighed. "Yes. They will have to be brought in, too. But the three of us should meet with Shandiin first. And Roinn. Do you know if Roinn is coming?"

"Yes. Shajii told me he will be here in the morning." Varady glanced back at Shandiin. "I will see you both tomorrow." He left abruptly, leaving Khedran and Shandiin alone.

Khedran looked down at her without expression, but she knew him.

She studied him thoughtfully. *He has matured physically and lost the last aspects of youth to male solidity. Still wears the black, probably to continue tradition for the comfort of his people. I bet Marre sees to his hair; he used to just hack it with a knife, and now it is neat, if just a little longer than when it barely brushed his shoulders. Oh, but he is as beautiful as ever, despite that scar on his cheek.*

And dammit, he is looking at me with a wariness I should have expected.

She gestured to the chair Varady had vacated.

Ignoring her invitation, Khedran went to a sideboard, poured them both a drink. He handed Shandiin's to her and sat down across from her, then simply waited.

"Not even a hello?" she ventured after a long minute.

"I just spoke to your husband. I cannot read him. He appears to be immune to my gift, as are you. But it is apparent he is very jealous, Shandiin, and that worries me, if he is the one I must negotiate with about what you have brought here."

"I didn't bring them. I came with them, because they were coming anyway, and I wanted to help you. You don't have to worry about Zion. He has a good heart. It's the others I'm concerned about."

"Why did you weep, telling him about me? I thought we had both accepted our need to say goodbye."

Blindsided, she blinked and looked away. "It wasn't just about you, Khedran. I left behind a life of a thousand years, and went back to being someone I didn't even recognize. Zion helped me through that."

"I see. But his jealousy disturbs me as it relates to your mission here."

"Zion isn't going to be your problem," she repeated flatly.

When she said nothing more, he studied her as she had him, and saw that she had not changed, though her denim clothing was strange to him. Her shaggy red hair bloomed wildly around her head and shoulders. Her grey eyes were almost silver. There were fine lines at their corners, and a strong jaw, and the beauty he had never been able to define even as it made his throat ache.

He lifted an eyebrow. "How did you get that bruise on your face?"

She touched her jaw gingerly. "Your daughter has an amazing right cross. Laid me out flat. She'd just found out about our transgression, Khedran, and she was furious. It seems I showed up right

after she overheard an apparently revealing discussion between you and Danon."

She saw the jolt before he sat back. After a moment he set
aside his glass so precisely she guessed he was controlling the
need to smash it against the wall.

"I'm sorry she found out about us, Khedran. I'm sure there's
never been a reason to tell her about it. But why the hell were
you discussing that ancient business at this late date?"

He was staring at the glass, battling emotions she read as
dismay and grief. "Because Marre asked me if I still loved you,
just before she fell into the sleep presaging death." He closed
his eyes briefly. "It broke me, Shandiin. Danon came to me
in concern, and I told him everything. I had no idea Shandi
overheard."

She winced. "I never thought Marre could be that cruel."

He turned his head to her slowly, frowning. "What do you
mean?"

"To ask you that on her deathbed? She didn't want an answer.
It was payback. She wanted to hurt you."

"I don't believe that. She forgave me, Shandiin, before we
were married. There's no cruelty in her."

Shandiin lifted her eyebrows, sat back and looked away. "All
right," she lied, knowing the truth – and she was sure it was the
truth – would only hurt him. "You certainly know her better
than I do. I'm sorry Shandi found out about us that way. She
had a right to be angry."

"It's not you she should be angry with." He picked up his
drink again, set it down, shoved it aside. "Shandi has never
had a temper, though she's always been more judgmental than
others of our bloodline, something Roinn has tried to help her
with. He has trained her in Chaine ways all her life, as you did
me. She was always proud she was named for you. Striking you
tells me she's been deeply hurt on more than one level." He
sighed. "Now she knows I am no better than my father."

"I thought you'd gotten past judging him."

"Mostly. But Shandi is her own person." He hesitated and met her eyes. His wall was down, and she saw cold, hard pain. "And she isn't wrong to judge me. What am I to do, Shandiin, with you back in my life?"

She lowered her head and scraped her hands through her hair, unable to face that gaze. "I know I'm a complication for you. But when I learned these people were coming to Hiraeth, I thought I could help you. I...did things so I could come with the expedition."

"You are saying we are allies once again. But it is far from the same, Shandiin. I do not know where you have come from or what you have brought with you. I know you have changed, for as The Chaine you would never have married anyone. I no longer know who you are, so how could we again be allies? This time we don't ride openly together against a common enemy. This time I go weaponless and navigating the unknown. I do not know if I want you at my back. I do not know if I can trust you."

She flung up her head and glared at him.

Then she shoved to her feet. He watched her approach, frowning when she placed her hands on the arms of his chair and leaned in. Inches away, she studied his striking face, the emerald eyes, wary now under those thick black lashes. His gaze dropped to her lips, and back to her eyes, and she saw the wariness hid something much deeper, and knew only she could have read him so well.

But her anger welled, born of navigating her own kind of hell. She would not betray Zion by letting her greatest love know the facts behind her marriage.

She drilled a finger into his chest. "Khedran, get off your damned Highness horse and listen to me. Just because I got married – and it's obvious to me that's caused you to be just as jealous as Zion – doesn't mean I'm not me. You know damned well you can trust me. You just don't know what to do with me. Having me back in your life complicates things for you. You still love me, and you can't do that because of who you are. Guess what? I still love you, but I'm loyal to my husband. So we deal with it. We're both grownups, and we just have to fucking deal with it. *It's not about trust.* If I'm wrong, tell me. Just say it, and you can be damned sure you'll never see me again."

She began to shove away.

He caught her wrist.

"No."

It was all he said. The rest lived in his eyes, his acceptance as clear as the truth she had spoken. The truth that he, who never lied, had tried to hide from himself.

Steeling herself against his pain, she tugged her hand free. "Make up your mind, then. What am I going to be to you? Your ally, or your complication?"

He sighed. "You'll be both, I think. And you're right that I need your help in this. So it's time we faced our mutual complication, instead of stepping around it."

She took a deep breath, and just sank to the floor by his chair. "I had to go. You know that. I had no choice but to leave, to take the magic away. You don't know how much I wanted to stay. But I had no choice, if you and your people were to be free."

"I understood. Then you went back to your first love."

She shook her head. "No. I love him, but...no. You are my *amharen.* Still, I almost think it was fate, that you look so much like him. That it had to be."

"Then fate is cruel. We both love someone else, and we have caused them pain. Still...I can't not love you, Shandiin." He sighed, allowing himself to briefly touch her wildfire hair so near his knee. "You understand the many reasons I can never act on that. Never again."

She smiled sadly. "The many reasons including far more than the fact we are both married. I know you've lived under the shadow of your father's adultery all your life, Khedran. He was the only one of your bloodline to betray the veneration held by the people of Azlatan. It almost lost you the Prophecy War before it happened. With what could be coming now, it's even more important that your people have faith in their High King, their paragon." She looked up at him. "But can we be...as we were before that night? As we were before you became so suspicious of me, when I was just The Chaine?”

“You were never 'just' anything, Shandiin. Not to me.”

He hadn’t expected a response, and got none. He sat back, took a deep breath, and was once again the King. “Now, tell me, please, how your Zion can so resemble me, and what I can expect from the people who came with you.”

So, since she’d only told him parts of it before, she began the long story of Earth’s demise, and how she had met four genetically modified people who had saved as many as they could, and their plans to establish a colony with a leader who could be trusted.

“Many of your world’s ancestors were created using genetic modification, though only your bloodline was completely engineered. You are related to Zion because you carry his genes. What you would call the same bloodline.”

“You are saying he is my brother.”

“More like your great grandfather a thousand years removed.”

Khedran looked thoughtful. “You said he is a good man. Now I have learned he saved my people long ago, and is my ancestor.”

“Yes. And he did it while he and the others were considered abominations. Genetically modified people were not considered human.”

“Like the Tahmond said about the Chaine.”

“Yes. But Zion’s family weren’t always able to defend themselves, unlike my Chaine, and I think normal people hated them simply because they were superior to a natural human. Zion is a genius...as I believe you are; you just haven’t been tested by Earth’s standards. Despite the hatred, despite the evil done to them, the four people that are all that remain of Zion’s 'family' have ensured the survival of the last people from Earth. It is their work that has brought humanity back, given it a chance for a future. They developed the science for the starships that, apart from Hiraeth, are now the only home of humanity’s remnants.” She had already explained about the ship still orbiting the Earth.

Khedran was thoughtful. "When will I meet the other three of Zion's family?"

"Sarnath and Egypt are still on the starship orbiting Hiraeth. Roland...I don't know what to think about him. He is currently Commander of the battalion of soldiers that came with us, and reports to Vice-Premier Canard, who I don't trust at all. He and Zion are the ones you'll be negotiating with."

"They brought a battalion of soldiers to a negotiation. That sounds ominous, to say the least. Is that as many as a Legion?"

"Not quite. But the soldiers are why I don't trust Roland. Canard's people are mind-controlled...kind of like the Anzihi were controlled by Phaelon. I'm sure that includes the soldiers."

She looked away for a moment, bit her lip before continuing. "Zion supports a peaceful immigration of those survivors to your planet. But I fear for your world, Khedran. I wish Zion had never told them of Hiraeth's existence."

"A peaceful immigration would be acceptable to me, Shandiin. Why would you not wish to help those people who are left behind, stranded to live on a ship above a destroyed planet?"

She took a deep breath. This, then, was what she had not been able to explain to Zion, and what she feared Khedran would not understand. "Because I'm afraid they will infect what the High Kings have built here. These new people know only a cunning and nefarious code of politics. Beyond an inability to trust, they are certain of evil intent in anyone in authority."

She hesitated before she continued. "I'll admit, it's also personal. My own people lost their land to invaders who called them primitive savages, less than human. My people weren't the only ones who faced that attitude. Earth's civilizations were built on the bones of the conquered, by those who believed themselves lords of everything they surveyed."

She looked up at him again. "My people knew better. The Navajo respected Mother Earth...what you call nature, understanding we are part of it. But they are gone now, with our lost world. Now I fear for your world, Khedran."

He considered her carefully, and she thought with some puzzlement. "Shandiin, I am only the leader of my people, not the owner of this world. It is not my place to tell people not to come here."

Damn his honesty, damn his kindness. It will be the end of him. She scraped her hands through her hair, trying to think of more reasons he should refuse this invasion.

"Khedran, even if they come peacefully, there are practicalities. You must understand they will come with nothing. Unless they can bring food from the ship, they will have no way to feed themselves. They will have no shelter, no home. They won't even have the kind of clothing necessary for a natural world. They've never known weather, or seasons. They will have no understanding of how to live in nature. How could you manage all that?"

He frowned. "You paint them all as bad people. But whatever they are...they are also human beings with needs. I would expect myself, and the people of my realm, to help them. It is not true they would have nothing. Like all the High Kings, I have stores kept to help those in hardship. More importantly, there are people in my realm who would never let them starve, never leave them without a home, never leave them naked in the cold. They would be helped, and then expected to find their way to help themselves, and eventually be able to help others as well."

She just stared at him. "They will take advantage of your people. They can't be trusted. They are liars who will agree to anything and then do whatever they want. In the end, Khedran, I'm afraid your efforts to help them will destroy you...and I don't think I can bear it."

His eyebrows lifted, and he shook his head. "You are describing people with no conscience. I cannot believe what you say is true of every one of those people living on that ship. You know Azlatan well enough to know we also have such miscreants. Azlatan's citizens are not as perfect as you seem to think they are. I've never expected them to be. I will only agree that my people have no tolerance for the behavior of those who have no respect for others. They frequently become violent about it."

He took a deep breath. "Shandiin, you told me before you left that Earth's civilizations fell because they came to accept evil as commonplace, and good as the exception. It sounds as though you have accepted that yourself. And it seems your mistrust of these people is greater than your trust in me." He met her eyes, and she saw sorrow. "I find that that very sad, for too many reasons."

They were interrupted by a buzzing sound, and she broke thankfully from his gaze.

He watched her remove an object from her pocket. She held it up to show him it was lit up, then touched it, and he was surprised to hear Zion's voice. "Shandiin? Is everything okay there?"

"Yes, Zion," she said, her eyes returning to Khedran's as she spoke. "Are you back at base yet? How is Marre doing?"

"She's awake and talking. We just landed. I'm sorry I didn't contact you before we left."

"Things moved quickly. I understand, and I'm alright here, I promise. I will meet with the High King and the other planetary leaders tomorrow morning, but I wish you were here."

"I will join you as soon as I can, but I want to direct the Queen's care. Danon was right; she was very near the end. Delay would have been disastrous."

She saw Khedran point at the device. "Zion, Khedran wants to say something."

"Does he, now?" They heard him sigh. "All right then."

Khedran spoke to Zion while watching Shandiin. "I didn't thank you. The Queen holds my heart, Zion of Earth. I didn't thank you for saving her, and I should have."

There was a brief delay before Zion's response. "You are quite welcome. How is my wife?"

Khedran smiled sadly, never taking his gaze from Shandiin's. "You have no need to worry about her. She has made clear that you support a peaceful immigration of the survivors of your planet. I find myself in agreement with you, despite her apprehensions about the problems they may bring." He lifted an eyebrow when she sighed and lowered her head. "She has also made clear certain things that should ease your more personal concerns."

There was another pause before Zion answered. "That is all good to hear, Your Highness."

"Please. You truly do not need to call me that. I have learned you and I are related. I look forward to our discussions when you return here."

"So do I. I'm sorry, but I must go now. Shandiin...I love you."

"I love you, too, Zion. Goodbye for now."

When the communicator went dark, she put it back in her pocket and lifted her gaze to Khedran. He was very thoughtful, and she knew it wasn't about the discussion they'd had before Zion's call. He'd put that aside to think about, as was his way, and she knew better than to press him further.

Especially when he'd expressed disappointment in her, and in her lack of trust in his leadership.

She was right; he wasn't thinking about that. "You do care for him." His voice was very quiet, and hinted of sadness.

"I do, Khedran. Does that hurt you?"

"It shouldn't. You know I care for Marre. You not only accepted it, but you let me know how foolish I was not to go to her, back then."

"I see things differently than most people. I see no dishonor in loving you while you love your Marre. I will always love both you and Zion, and I see no dishonor in that either. You are both deserving of love." She sighed. "But I understand that neither you, nor Zion, nor Marre, see things the way I do. I'm sorry that I am the cause of pain for any of you." She looked away from those emerald eyes. "Still, *amhara* has outlasted all our years apart, and I don't think it will change because of our differences."

"I agree. Come here, Shandiin." He took her hand, and they both rose to their feet. Her spirit melted when he lifted her hand to his lips, his eyes still on hers, and then held it against his heart.

"I will say this for what must be the last time," he told her. "I love you. I always have, and I always will, even knowing you have him in your heart and your life. It hurts, but you have the right to your love as I do to mine. We will always be *amharen*...and I want you to know I have always treasured the memory of our one time together, even knowing it was wrong."

Her throat ached with the tears she fought. "Thank you for that. I was afraid it was a memory you would learn to hate." She searched his eyes, told him her final truth. "I love you too. But here's a bigger secret about why I can step away from you. It's not only because we have given our oath to others. You see, I understand the honor your people pay you. I share it myself."

CHAPTER 9

Danon was standing on Penumbra's tower roof when the lights exploded over him.

He was braced against the wind, but the light caught him by surprise and took him back to a night twenty years ago when Khedran had called on the goddess Daimaine to alert the country to war. Every star in the sky had flared, and their combined light had turned the earth white.

This was like that, only worse somehow.

He had grown up living with magic, but had been relieved when it left, making the world a place he could understand.

He couldn't understand this at all. He liked the idea of medicine that could cure even cancer, but this flying machine of light without noise was terrifying. He set his jaw against it, refusing to show fear. *The way Shandiin taught me.*

He watched the basket come down, saw Zion go to examine it, then signal Khedran to put Marre in it. Danon watched his King lower his beloved Queen into the strange contraption and tell her something he couldn't hear. She smiled, though she had to be terrified too. Or did she? Marre had withstood Daimaine herself when that dark magic had taken her so long ago.

Khedran turned to his daughter, who embraced him briefly before climbing into the basket to lay down beside her mother, holding her close against the wind. Zion signaled and the basket began to lift.

Khedran turned to Danon and put a hand on his shoulder. "Thank you." Danon read his King's open gratitude. "It's important knowing you will be with them when I cannot."

Then Zion was summoning him, and Danon gritted his teeth to get into the lowered harness and then to be hauled into that monstrous machine. He glanced over once and saw Khedran and Zion go back into the stairwell as he was lifted.

Not sure that is going to go well, he thought.

Then he was inside. "Welcome aboard," said the man at the controls. Danon was astonished to see it was Shajii helping him out of the harness. She gave him a broad grin, glancing back at the pilot who was saying, "Go ahead and winch the harness back down for Zion. It takes all my attention to hover the craft in this wind."

Danon saw Shandi still lying next to her mother, her arms around her protectively. He considered his patient, amazed again that she was awake and coherent. He had been certain she was slipping away from life until this miracle happened.

The stranger who was part of the miracle was winched up, and as soon as he was inside the light went out and the machine moved so swiftly Danon almost fell. He must have shown fear, because the man named Zion...Shandiin's *husband?*...grinned at him reassuringly. "It's just normal inertia," Zion told him. "It will steady as he flies. Sit down..." he pointed to a seat, and when Danon sat he strapped him in.

Once settled, he saw that Marre was doing well with Shandi still with her, and when he looked out he realized Penumbra was already falling away as they soared out over the moonlit ocean.

Zion sat in the narrow seat across from him, buckled himself in, and said, "Shandiin told me a lot about you, Danon. I am glad to finally meet you." When Danon just stared at him, he added, "She told me you could always make her laugh."

"That wasn't always my intent," Danon replied dryly. He swallowed, looked out at the darkness streaming past them as they turned back inland. "I have missed her terribly. I realized that she was my friend all along, and I was sorry I never told her that."

"She will be very happy to hear it, because she spoke of you the same way. She said you were one of her truest friends in this world, and you probably never knew it."

Danon smiled, then saw Shajii had joined the pilot at the controls. "I can't believe Shajii is helping to fly this machine."

Zion followed his gaze. "She's an amazing woman. Shandiin thought she would be The Chaine when we came back, but I see that isn't the case."

"No. Roinn told me Shajii wants no part of becoming leader even though Shandiin had intended her to take her place in time. Shajii refuses even to change her name to Roinn, as all the winners of their strange warrior contests have done in the past. So…Roinn is stuck with being The Chaine until she decides differently. If she does. I don't know if even Shajii knows what she really wants."

He put that aside to regard the man who looked like his King, and asked "Will you be willing to teach me about your medical treatments?"

"That's part of why I am here," Zion smiled.

An hour later the machine landed amidst a perimeter of blazing lights and a jumble of buildings and machinery alien to the people of this world. Roland stood to address Zion. "Military's handled. You just need to handle the politician."

"Thanks, Roland." Zion turned back to Danon and his patient. "People are on their way to take the Queen into the hospital. Are you doing all right, Your Highness?"

Marre nodded weakly. Shandi disentangled herself from the basket where her mother lay and scowled at Zion as she stood. "I am going with her. So is Danon."

"Of course you are." Zion kneeled next to Marre. "I am going to lift you, and take you to the gurney outside. Is that acceptable?"

Marre frowned at him, uneasy. "Perhaps Danon could do that?"

Zion lifted his eyebrows. "Certainly." He watched Danon pick her up, and left the skycraft to make sure of the waiting gurney. Together he and Danon had Marre strapped in and comfortable for the short ride to the building he had referred to as the hospital.

As they walked, Zion made the call to check on Shandiin. He was very thoughtful afterwards, as he replaced the communicator in his pocket. Shandiin hadn't really given him an opportunity to refuse discussion with the High King. To his inner surprise, he had found the King's words...even his voice...reassuring.

Zion wondered if that was one of the King's 'gifts,' and recalled his reaction when the High King had turned around and looked into his eyes.

He was beginning to understand why Shandiin had fallen in love with the man, and he found that a little frightening.

Shajii stepped down from the skycraft, turning to watch Roland disembark. She was surprised to see another soldier run up and salute him, then go scurrying off at Roland's word on some errand.

"You are more than just what you said...a pilot," she observed.

Roland grinned at her, teeth flashing in his dark and handsome face. She watched him unzip the flight suit he wore and step out of it to reveal a tan uniform like the other soldiers wore. "Yeah. I'm the CO of this operation."

"See-oh?"

"CO...it stands for Commanding Officer. Zion is Chief Science Officer. He handles the science. Unfortunately we both answer to the dude they put in charge."

"I gather you do not like the...dude."

"Not particularly. But you didn't hear that. He thinks he has my complete loyalty...for now."

She nodded thoughtfully and turned to follow the others into the building Zion had called a hospital. Roland walked in with her, and she glanced at him sidelong, realizing she was very attracted to him. Roland was full of life and fun. Yet he was a Commander, and she thought that made him like Roinn, like Shandiin before Roinn. She found that mattered to her.

She studied these outworlders, these outsiders. She was not The Chaine and had no desire to be, but like all Chaine she was always concerned for the good of her people and her allies. She watched her best friend Shandi walking ahead of her, knowing the High Princess was the same.

Shajii smirked when they entered the building and a man came quickly toward them, stopping dead in his tracks at the sight of Shandi. His mouth dropped open and he stood gaping at her.

Zion quickly stepped in front of Shandi. "Dr. Sato, my patient is the High Queen of Azlatan. This woman is her daughter, the High Princess of Azlatan. They will be treated with the utmost respect, do you understand?"

The young doctor tore his eyes from Shandi, and swallowed. "Yessir. This way, please..."

"Wow," Roland remarked to Shajii as they walked away. "What are you, chopped liver?"

Shajii, who had long ago become accustomed to Shandiin's odd sayings, guessed his meaning. "I am not cursed with Shandi's beauty or her magic thrall. The thrall has always been a gift of the High Kings, but she is the first woman of the direct bloodline. It seems the gift...or curse, as she calls it...is magnified on her, as men are more affected by it. You just saw its effect on the man Zion called Dok-tar Sato. Shandi told me her father taught her carefully about being respectful of people who are enthralled, to help them keep their pride intact." She shook her head. "I wouldn't want that gift."

They followed the others into a room containing a large, long machine with a glass top and a bed inside. Zion stopped by the High Queen's gurney. "How are you doing?" he asked her.

She regarded him with a frown. "I'm sorry. I can't get used to the fact you look like Khedran. Are you another of his brothers?"

He shook his head. "No. I believe Varady and Jael are his only brothers. I have an extremely distant relationship to your King."

"Did I hear it said that you are married to Shandiin?"

"Yes."

"Is she with you?"

"Yes." He saw worry in her eyes, tried to ignore it. "Well, not at the moment. She's waiting for me back in Cabre. It was important to get you here as soon as possible, and she wasn't able to come. Your Highness, the medication I gave you will start to wear off very soon, and you will become sick again. It's important that we start your treatment before that happens."

He pointed to the glassed enclosure. "We are going to put you in there, and I will insert a needle into your arm. A special serum will drip through the needle, and it is what will make you well. When I close the lid, the chamber will fill with special air that will let you sleep. Your body can then begin the changes that will destroy your cancer and bring you to full health. You will be asleep while this happens, but when you wake up you will be well again." He hesitated before explaining the side effect of her treatment. "And...you will outlive your husband."

She had listened to him wide-eyed, but at this she cried out. "What? How...no!"

Shandi looked as shocked as her mother. "What are you saying?"

"This treatment was created using stem cells taken from a very unusual person whose body regenerates as needed." Zion didn't tell his patient that the donor was Shandiin. "Considering your advanced illness, it is the only thing that will save your life. But it will prolong your life as well."

Marre looked wildly from him to her daughter. "I do not want to outlive my husband or my daughter. Can you please give them the same treatment?"

Zion sighed. "Quite frankly, I don't even have permission to give it to you. But I am doing it anyway, because without it you will die very soon. Do you understand?"

Shandi took her mother's hand. "You have to do it. You must, Mother. For me. And you know Father has...just please."

Marre closed her eyes, and they all saw the tears that escaped them. "He...he would not... accept my death. I was afraid for him."

Danon, standing forgotten behind them, leaned in. "You are correct, Your Highness. He has been devastated. I feared for him too."

The lavender eyes opened, full of grief even as her life was being given back to her. "Then I must agree."

Roland had soldiers stationed outside the door while the treatment began, and Shajii joined him there. "Expecting trouble?" she asked.

"Maybe. Zion's doing this on the down-low. The big honcho is not going to be happy."

Shajii took this to mean the treatment hadn't been authorized by the 'dude' he didn't like. She discovered she was right when a diminutive man came puffing down the hallway, dressed resplendently in scarlet pants and shirt. Protectively, Roland turned his back to her to face this apparition.

"Chief Commander Canard demands an immediate briefing," the man puffed. "You were not authorized to leave the area, and you brought aliens to the base!"

"Dr. Alexander directed my assignment as CSO." Roland's response was cool. "Tell Canard the doctor will brief him as soon as his work here is done."

"What work? What have you done?"

"That is between CC Canard and CSO Alexander, and none of your business. Go away."

The man put his hands on his hips. "You military types think you can order anyone around. You're nobody to me, Mister!"

Shajii had remained standing behind Roland after he turned to meet the newcomer. At those disrespectful words she stepped from behind him to confront the man who stood several inches shorter than she. "No one is nobody." Her sword sang metallically as she unsheathed it. "You should leave."

His eyes went round. He stared up at the redhaired Amazon in leather armor, at the golden sword she held. Then he turned and fled.

She re-sheathed her sword. "What a piss-ant."

Roland was grinning. "What did you say?"

"I called him a piss-ant. They are very tiny things of no conse-quence."

"Perfect," Roland laughed. "But I do believe the piss-ant is going to cause some trouble."

"Does that worry you?"

"Not in the least," he grinned at her, and she saw a difference in his gaze that caused her heart to speed up a little.

Shandi had felt discomfort ever since arriving at this strange place. She'd walked alongside her mother's gurney while gazing around at the towering lights and the unknown soldiers going about their unknown business. The lights, the buildings, even the skycraft were not the magic her people had gladly left behind, but it all made it her uneasy. Were these the tools of the people, or their cage?

She wished for a sword. She had no more protection than the knife always sheathed within her boot, as Roinn had taught her.

Now she and Danon watched as her mother slipped into peace-ful sleep under the glass door of the box Zion had called a stasis chamber. There was a screen attached to it which Zion had explained reported her vital signs. "She's stable," he reported. "She is going to be fine."

He turned as the door opened and Roland walked in with Shajii. "Canard?" he asked.

"Yeah. He already sent one of his...piss-ants to demand a briefing." Roland tilted his head toward Shajii. "She scared him off."

Shandi heard, but paid little attention. She turned from staring at her mother to look at the readings on the screen which she wished she understood. "Zion, you must explain this to me," she demanded.

"I will be glad to, Highness," Zion told her. "But first I must go to see our Chief Commander, and I would like to ask you come along."

She frowned. "Why? My father will handle any formalities."

"I am sure he will. But I think for this first contact you will make a very good first impression." He looked at her meaningfully.

It took a moment for her to realize his intent, and it both surprised and alarmed her. She finally nodded an uncertain assent.

"Dr. Sato will stay with you," Zion said to Danon. "If there is any change at all, he will know what to do, and will notify me. I'll be back as soon as possible."

Shandi stepped outside with Zion, but immediately turned on him with her hands on her hips. "Did Shandiin tell you *everything* about my bloodline? Is that what this is about?"

"Yes. She told me one of your gifts is a charismatic thrall." *Your father's nearly undid me.* "I just saw evidence of yours when young Dr. Sato saw you."

"I see." She sounded disgusted. "I gather you want me to purposely use it on this person we're going to meet. Tell me why."

He began as he led her across the brightly lit, busy compound. "Ben Canard is the Chief Commander of this mission. I felt it was necessary to bypass his authorization to bring your mother here for treatment. To be frank, I don't think he would have authorized it."

"I see. You don't trust him. So why is he the leader of this...mission?"

"He represents the leadership of the people we came in hope of saving. The people live on a ship and have never stepped foot on the soil of a world, because their own was destroyed. The mission is to negotiate the peaceful immigration of those people to live here, Your Highness. I know Shandiin called it an invasion, but that is not our intent. Ben Canard was chosen to lead the mission because he's part of the Premier family. What you would call the royal family, I think, though the head of the family...and leader of all...is ostensibly elected by the people we are trying to save."

"Royalty elected by the people? There is a difference between elections and royalty by inheritance, and this mixture sounds like a bastard offspring. Explain the situation, please. I wish to make no errors that my father will need to correct."

He was a little surprised at her perception, and then remembered her bloodline. "Yes. The Premier's family is not trustworthy, but the mission is meant to save the people trapped under their rule, who live in an artificial environment. I am hoping those people can finally come here, to live as nature intended."

"I can see how that would be a good thing for them. But you said the mission is meant to seek permission, which is not the same as saying it will seek permission. Therein lies your distrust of this Commander Canard."

Zion nodded. "Yes. I am not sure we can trust him to consider the other side of the mission, which is the effect it will have on your people. I am hoping that, meeting you, he will be more...accepting of your viewpoint."

"I see. So I will meet him with that in mind." She hesitated. "But there's something I need to know of a more personal nature. Shandiin seems to have told you everything about her life here. Did she willingly tell you ..."

When she hesitated again, he knew she wanted to ask about the relationship with her father. "Yes," he said gently. "She told me they fell in love. But you think she used magic on him. Did you always know she was a magic goddess?"

"Yes. She was Chaos. Father told me long ago she was feared in Azlatan, and revered by the Sundancers, and deserved neither attitude because she never wielded magic except against magic." Shandi frowned, then sighed. "I guess I forgot that. Please take the lead. I will follow you. But this is a social call only. Only the High King can make decisions affecting our people."

"Understood."

Ben Canard dismissed his dithering assistant in disgust. The man kept going on about a savage woman with a sword, and he wasn't sure what to believe, but he did know this planet was stuck somewhere in the Middle Ages. Anything was possible.

He was shocked at the behavior of Commander Roland Bond, the man he and his brother, the Premier, had trusted implicitly. The man had taken the only skycraft off base without permission and apparently flown back with some of the natives. He recalled that the Commander had been the one to insist only one skycraft was allowed on-planet during negotiations. Canard considered both of these things in light of the Commander's demeanor in this morning's briefing and was now uncertain of Bond's loyalty. Since the plan was to take control of the planet once he was assured the natives had no science and no technology to fight back with, he would have to find a replacement for him.

When Dr. Alexander walked in, he regarded him narrowly. The man was a genius scientist, but no more than a tool to be used. Canard had never believed he belonged on this mission, which was a matter of politics. Certainly his insane wife should never have been allowed. Besides, he hated Alexander's good looks and smug air of confidence.

"I heard about your uninvited guests. What the hell do you think you're doing?" Canard demanded.

"A mission of mercy," Zion replied calmly. "We discovered that the High Queen of Azlatan was on her deathbed with terminal cancer. It appeared politically correct to save her. Commander Bond airlifted her out at my request, and she is now being treated in the medical stasis chamber."

"What?" Canard stood up behind his desk, outraged. "You said there is only one dose of the nostrum for that treatment! I understood it was for use for by our own people!"

"Is that what you thought? Why do our people matter more than those already here?" Zion returned.

Canard's mouth snapped shut on fury.

"I have a guest," Zion continued, "who wishes to meet you. To thank you. It is the High Princess of Azlatan, whose mother we are treating."

"You brought her here? For God's sake, I don't have time for dealing with the natives."

"Please. It's important to the mission that we deal personally with these people, Ben. May I show her in?" He didn't wait for an answer, but bowed as Shandi stepped in.

She barely glanced at him, but walked toward the man standing behind a desk, her chin up, eyes watchful. Having heard the conversation before she entered, she used another gift of her bloodline, and lowered her shield against empathy to determine Canard's true self.

She was immediately flooded by evil without conscience, and knew that this person would not be accepted in Azlatan. Her people were taught how to recognize such, and if he were unable to contain his baser instincts to manipulate others he would likely be a powerless outcast.

Disgusted, she quickly slammed closed her mental shield, and decided to disobey her father's careful instructions about helping people withstand the thrall in dignity. In fact, for the first time in her life she did the opposite, and purposely cast the thrall. Her intent was to make him defenseless against her.

Giving Canard a haughty smile and a smoldering gaze from her emerald eyes, she stepped forward and offered her hand. "Thank you for saving the High Queen. My father will be very grateful, as am I."

The man reached for her hand with both of his, his mesmerized eyes on her face. "My pleasure," he managed. "It was my pleasure to offer our service. Um...Your Majesty."

She smiled again and watched him unhinge into his chair. "My name is Shandi. You are free to use my name, Sir..."

"Ben. Call me Ben, please." He glanced rather wildly at Zion, who kept his face carefully dispassionate. "Can we get some refreshments, Dr. Alexander, for our royal guest?" He locked his eyes back on Shandi. "Anything at all she wants."

She smiled. "I thank you, but I wish to get back to my mother. I hope very much we will have the opportunity to speak again...Ben Canard."

He could only nod, releasing her hand reluctantly, and watch as she turned and walked out. Zion remained, eyebrows raised as Canard stared after her. "Will that be all?" he asked.

Canard didn't respond. Zion took that as dismissal.

Shandi stopped outside the hospital, turning to face Zion. "My father taught me it was my responsibility to help people past the thrall, to act unaware of their response so they could find their equilibrium. I have never used my gift as I did just now with that nasty little man. I hope it makes him malleable to your wishes regarding the treatment of my people."

"I appreciate it, Princess. And I apologize for making you uncomfortable. I didn't realize you had been told not to use it."

"I think Father will understand your intent." She tilted her head, studying him. "You are very much like my father, I think. More than just in looks."

"I believe you just gave me a wonderful compliment."

"Did I? I wouldn't think you would appreciate him, since he was once in love with your wife."

Zion raised an eyebrow. "I can't exactly blame him, can I?"

Shandi was surprised into laughter, and he had to smile. "Do you plan to punch her in the face again?" he asked.

"No. But I am wondering how you had the courage to leave them alone together, in Azlatan."

"That doesn't take courage. It takes trust. I can tell you that she didn't mean to break my trust before, and I don't think she'll do it again. Do you no longer trust your father?"

"He was guilt-ridden over what apparently happened only once. I blamed Shandiin, and that was wrong. As you pointed out, it took both of them to break that trust."

"So you have forgiven him."

She didn't answer.

"Even fathers can make mistakes, Princess."

She met his gaze briefly. "Not mine." She walked away into the hospital.

CHAPTER 10

Camion had once been Duine, a servant bonded by the God of Order to the High King. He hadn't been a servant since the Prophecy War that had released all his people from bondage, but he remained loyal to his King, and was amazed and proud to have been given the title, and the position, as Mayor of the city of Cabre, central to all the Dominions of Azlatan.

He entered Penumbra's smallest meeting room a little nervously, stopping in surprise to see a familiar woman sitting there quietly talking to the King. She wore strange clothing, something like linen in light blue with metal trim. But he was sure she was, or had been, The Chaine.

They both looked up, and she smiled at him.

"Morning bless, Camion."

"And to you," he stammered.

"Did you get word out to the citizens?" Khedran asked him.

"I did, Your Highness. Cabre is being assured that the lights over Penumbra last night were friendly, and nothing to be alarmed about. May I ask...what they were? And...why has The Chaine returned?"

"I'm not The Chaine any longer, Camion. I'm just Shandiin now."

The High King slanted a look at her, then tapped the chair next to him. "Sit down, Camion. Shandiin is back in a new capacity, but she is again working on our behalf as Azlatan starts a new age. She came with visitors who have already..."

He suddenly hesitated, very unlike him, and both Shandiin and Camion watched curiously as he stopped and looked down as though taking control of himself. Then he lifted his gaze and started over. "The lights were visitors who have already taken the High Queen to cure her of the illness that almost took her life. I am more than grateful."

Roinn had just entered, and stopped on hearing the King's words. "That's wonderful news!" he exclaimed. "Varady was telling me about it." He turned to Shandiin, an expression of pure joy on his usually staid face. "And you have returned! You will renew your leadership?"

She just laughed, and stood to go to the man who had been her friend and second in command for more than two centuries. She looked him up and down, this man who stood a full head taller than her, who was powerful as a bear in his leather armor chased with gold, his deep auburn hair falling both loose and braided down his back. "You're as ugly as ever," she announced with the warmth of long fellowship, "and you're stuck being leader until Shajii changes her mind. I thought you'd have either convinced her or made her your *amharen* by now."

"We are not of that persuasion," he said somberly, and there was a flicker in his eyes making her guess that he had someone else in mind...at long last. She would find time to tease him about it, later. "I do wish you would reconsider," he smiled. "We have missed you."

"I am no longer of the Chaine people, Roinn."

He shook his head. "You will always be of the Chaine, even if you no longer wish to lead."

She sighed and led him to a chair. They sat down together.

"Do you really hate being The Chaine?" she asked him.

He shrugged. "I would be happier if it were you. I had thought it would be temporary, but Shajii is like a wild thing, and will have none of it."

"Then it's best she stays wild. You're a solid leader, Roinn, and I am glad it is you I will be dealing with."

Khedran looked toward the door where a tall man stood. "Jael. Please come in."

Shandiin looked over to see the man Varady had called the Sage of Azlatan. He'd only been ten when she left Azlatan, but was now entering his thirties, and shared the male beauty of the bloodline of High Kings; he was Khedran's other half-brother. His eyes were sapphire blue, reflecting light almost as did the King's emerald. His black hair fell in waves to his shoulders. He hesitated at the door, but that ended as Varady pushed in from behind, then laughed and pulled him in for an embrace. Jael's face lit with joy as he looked into his older brother's golden eyes. "I am so glad to see you."

"Your vision led me to Shandiin, so I could bring her here. Great changes are coming, my brother, and we will need you as never before. Come now." Varady led him to a chair. Jael sat, then looked at Shandiin.

"You were The Chaine, before Roinn. Welcome back."

"Apparently you already knew I was coming. Do you know why, Jael?"

"I only know that danger follows on your heels." His gaze shifted to Khedran. "It is you and the High King we will need, despite what Varady said. I am only here to help."

Khedran frowned, then leaned back. "It seems we are all here. Perhaps, Shandiin, you can explain to everyone the danger following on your heels."

She looked around at the expectant men. "For those of you who don't know yet, I come from a place called Earth, a world very far from here. When I was here before, it was my mission to help the High King win a war, and to get rid of the magic that was making it impossible. I didn't expect to come back. However, against my wishes, a decision was made to send representatives to your world. I came with them.

"This isn't the first time people from Earth have come to your world. All of your ancestors originated there, and came here over a thousand years ago. We're all from the same place. But the magic that controlled your world during those thousand years kept Azlatan from being advanced technologically, like Earth was."

"Technologically," Khedran repeated. "Meaning we don't have your craft that fly, or your medicine that can cure cancer, or the communication devices that allow you to talk to each other over distance."

"That's a small part of what they bring. There is a lot more. And you…the leaders of this world…need to be aware that both good and bad can come from this. Starting with the politics." She leaned back. "You need to have a central government. You need to be united in all your dealings with these people. And you dare not show weakness. You do not want to be ruled by them."

"We will not be ruled by anyone," Roinn scowled. "The Chaine are a free people."

Shandiin nodded agreement. "And yet," she explained, "you have a leader. You are a leader. Just as Khedran is. And Varady. You all have your own people; you speak for them. But now you need one leader to speak for everyone, to stand up to these outsiders when it becomes necessary."

She had used the word 'outsiders' purposely. It was what the people had termed their enemies, those who had invaded and almost destroyed Azlatan in the Prophecy War.

"You already told me that we had to be prepared for great change," Varady said. "But you haven't been specific about danger. Do you believe these new people want to take control of our lands?"

"I am afraid so." She watched them all straighten. "I don't know what all their motives are. I don't trust the man in charge, though the mission as explained to me was to be a peaceful negotiation to allow colonization here. But they are all humans, just like us…" she slanted a glance at Khedran. "So they will have the same failings. Selfishness, ego, greed. The quest for power."

"So you didn't all come in peace?" Camion asked.

"That is the stated intent. I am just warning you not to trust them."

"You don't speak as though you are one of them," Roinn noted, and she sighed, remembering Zion had told her the same thing.

"You are exactly right. I don't. I came with them because I lived here for a long time. I know you. I know your ways and...I'll be honest. Except for four others, I trust you more than those who came with me. I will not see you taken over. I will not."

"How could they take over, as you put it?" Varady asked.

"Firstly through politics. Like offering gifts. Like curing the Queen."

Khedran's emerald eyes narrowed, and she nodded at him. "Yes, you are already in a position of gratitude. You know how that works politically. But there are other things they can offer. The life of the High Queen was a given, something neither I nor my husband were willing to barter for. We just did it, without asking permission from our...'government.'" She saw Khedran's eyebrows go up. "That's right. We did not have permission. Zion...my husband...will try to ensure that is seen as a good thing, but they aren't going to be happy about what we did. We'll deal with that."

"They have terrible weapons."

They all looked at Jael, who had spoken quietly but firmly.

Shandiin frowned and nodded. "Yes. They have weapons that could destroy this entire city. I am not saying they would use them. They have no reason to use them. But they have them."

Jael's blue eyes looked haunted. He looked from her to Khedran. "They will use them. I have seen it. She is right; we cannot trust them."

Everyone stared at him while he sat back and waited.

Shandiin's eyes flashed from him to Khedran. "Varady told me he still has magic."

Khedran nodded. "There is still magic here, of a kind. Gifts that were inherent from birth remain with us. Mine were passed on to Shandi. Jael sees things others cannot, sometimes in advance, sometimes as they happen. I don't like this, Shandiin."

"Neither do I. Can you tell me anything," she returned to Jael, "about how or why they use weapons?"

Jael began to speak, then stopped and abruptly looked alarmed. "The Princess!" he exclaimed. "He has taken her away!"

Khedran and Roinn both shoved to their feet even as Shandi-in's communicator alerted.

The others had gone to get some sleep, but Shandi wouldn't leave her mother.

She sat in the chair Zion had placed next to the chamber that held Marre, watching the monitor he had explained to her. She frequently checked Marre's breathing, just for reassurance. Focused on the moment, she didn't hear the door open.

But she sensed it.

She looked up to see that nasty little man she had enthralled. He stood just inside. As he spoke there was an edge to his smile she didn't like.

"Hello, Princess. You must be getting tired. Your mother will be fine, or the others wouldn't have left. I'm going to take you to a better place. I run this show, you know. Everyone here answers to me. Just like everyone in your country answers to your father, as I understand."

She watched him carefully, recognizing danger, deciding to stall until she understood the situation fully. "You are the High King of this place?"

"Yes, like that." His smile became feral. "Do you know how beautiful you are, Princess?"

She lifted her chin. "Do you think so? That is very flattering."

"I've never seen anyone like you. Never in my life." His eyes flicked to the stasis chamber. "I had planned that my life would be much longer. Alexander said that chamber would make a person immortal with the medicine that could only be used once. I planned to be the one who used it. Now they've put your mother in there. I think you owe me for that."

She said nothing, but sat back and crossed an ankle atop her knee. Her hand now rested inches from the knife in her boot.

"Are you coming?" he asked.

"I do not want to leave my mother."

His face hardened. "I'm asking you one more time. Come with me."

"No."

He reached inside his jacket and took out what she realized was probably a weapon.

"You will come with me. If you don't, I will use this…" he wagged the weapon…" and blow a hole in that stasis chamber. Your mother will die."

Shandi stood, knife hidden but in hand now, watching him carefully. "How can that 'blow a hole' in anything?"

In answer he lifted the Glock and fired one shot into the ceiling.

The noise was deafening. Part of the ceiling crashed to the floor.

"You are coming with me. Do you understand now?"

Shandi considered while she slipped the knife up the cuff of her shirt. "Why are you doing this? I thought your people were here to help Azlatan."

"Fuck Azlatan. I came because Alexander had that chamber. I'd have forced him to use it for me once we took over this world, because then we wouldn't need his science anymore. Then I'd have killed him. Now there's no reason to wait. You and I are going to take the skycraft up to the ship, where I will contact my people to explain how dangerous this place is, and order it wiped clean. Some good nukes will take care of it all. Then you and I will become true royalty where it matters…on the starships of Earth."

She thought the man was quite insane, and therefore very dangerous. The courage of her bloodline and Roinn's lifelong training kept her cool, watchful. Wise.

"All right," she agreed, standing. "Let us begin our lives together, Ben Canard."

His eyes narrowed suspiciously.

Insane, she thought, *but not stupid.*

"Don't try anything," he warned. "I would hate to desecrate your beauty, Princess, but I will wound you if I must. Do you understand me?"

"Of course I do. Men like you are rare on my world, but I understand you well. I deserve what is rare."

His eyes brightened. "Yes. You deserve greatness, and I will give it to you. Come." He gestured with the Glock toward the door.

"You don't really need that thing. I'm coming to you."

He didn't lower the gun, which was the most horrible weapon she had ever seen. He just smiled. "I like being in charge. Come."

She walked out the door ahead of him, and knew fury when she saw the soldier who had been standing guard. He lay unconscious or dead, with a pool of blood under his head. When she hesitated she felt hard steel against her back. "Keep moving. He doesn't matter. He's just one of Bond's goons."

She glanced over her shoulder at the man who obviously relied on awful weapons because he had neither strength nor skill. She thought about killing him; she was strong and well-trained. But Roinn's careful training warned her to be certain before chancing her own life or limb.

Shandiin put her communicator on speaker. Zion's voice came through immediately.

"That misbegotten asshole Canard has taken the Princess," was what she heard, along with a lot of background commotion.

"Taken her where?"

"To the ship. He seized the skycraft and is taking her to the *Aztlan*."

"Have you contacted the Captain?"

"Yes. She is aware of the situation. He had a gun to Shandi's head, Shandiin. There was nothing anyone could do."

Roinn's eyes were full of fury and, Shandiin thought in vague surprise, a terrible desperation. "Shandi is a warrior. How could he just take her?" he demanded.

Shandiin held up a hand to forestall further questions. "I knew Canard was an asshole," she told Zion, "but I never expected this."

"It's my fault. He was causing trouble, and I asked Shandi to use her gift…the thrall…to win him over. I did not think this would happen!"

"The Captain will handle it when they arrive, Zion. Just please make sure she knows how important the Princess is."

"Of course she knows. Tell…tell the High King how sorry I am, but that we will get her back."

"What about Marre?" Shandiin flicked a glance at Khedran. He stood very still, but his emerald eyes had gone feral.

"Just a few more hours in the chamber and she will be cured. I saw the camera recording, Shandiin. He got Shandi to go with him by demonstrating a gun and threatening to kill her mother."

Shandiin could barely look at Khedran, because she knew very well there was a painful kind of fear behind his fury. She bit her lip. "Keep us apprised, Zion. Please."

"I will, my love. Goodbye."

The communicator went dark, and Shandiin looked around the room full of very angry men. She swallowed.

"Well," she said. "Shit."

Shandi sat belted in, watching Canard operating controls in front of a screen like the one she had seen at the hospital.

"No windows?" she asked. "How can you see where we are going?"

"I don't have to. I am programming the skycraft to take us to the ship."

"The ship that brought you here from Earth?"

"Yes."

"Can anyone follow us?"

"No. This is the only craft on the planet. They can't stop us."

So I am on my own with this miscreant, she thought while smiling at him warmly. "I see."

Her gaze shifted to the gun he'd set down next to his hand. "Would that thing even 'blow a hole' in this ship?"

"Yes. And then we would both be dead. Now be quiet, I'm about to dock."

"And then we will be inside the big ship, and safe?"

"Yes."

Shandi waited.

Egypt watched as the skycraft docked, and spoke to her crew members as the airlock filled. "Keep the weapons out of sight. He has to think we are going along with his crazy plan until we can be sure the Princess is safe."

"Never did like that bastard," one crewman muttered. Egypt's mouth twitched, but she didn't smile. As soon as there was a green light, she stepped into the skycraft airlock ready to kill the man she had secretly hated since the mission began. She watched as the skycraft door opened.

She blinked when a glorious woman in black stepped out, shaking back her waist-length hair to regard the Captain and her crew with emerald eyes as brilliant as Egypt's own. She stood defiantly, knife in hand, obviously ready for battle if needed. "I hope you are not here to welcome Ben Canard. He is in there, but he is dead." Shandi held up her knife. "This slipped into his eye when he wasn't looking."

Egypt stared, then snorted laughter. She tried to regain her professional composure as she signaled the crew to stand down, and bowed deeply.

"Welcome aboard the *Aztlan*, Your Highness. I am pleased to see that you are no longer a hostage. I am Captain Egypt Alexander."

Shandi tilted her head, studying the beautiful woman even taller than she or her father, but with the same distinctive eyes. "Are you related to Dr. Alexander?" she asked curiously.

"Yes. He called to warn me about your situation, and is now being told you are safe and well. We will get you back to your planet as soon as you wish. But would you be interested in seeing my ship first?"

Shandi considered. *As a leader of Azlatan I should take advantage of this to learn as much as I can. And this very dark woman is...interesting.*

"I would love to," she smiled. "Thank you, Captain."

When the communicator lit up again it was already on the table waiting, and Shandiin had only to touch it to answer. But this time they heard a woman's contralto voice.

"Captain Alexander calling. Is this Shandiin?"

"Yes. Hello, Egypt. Is the Princess safe?"

"Oh, yes. She wishes to let her father know she is fine, and she is coming back to Azlatan with her mother later today."

"What about the man who abducted her?" Khedran demanded.

"He's no longer a problem. The Princess killed him before I could." Egypt's audience thought they heard a snicker. "Apparently he never saw it coming."

Roinn sat back while Khedran exhaled. Shandiin was momentarily puzzled by the look on Roinn's face, but then realized she was seeing heartfelt relief. She slid a look at Khedran and wondered if he knew The Chaine was in love with his daughter.

"Weapons," Jael reminded them quietly.

Shandiin quickly returned her attention to the matter at hand. "Egypt, what did Canard plan to do?"

"That's very concerning. He told the Princess he planned to nuke the planet, without regard even to the people he had brought with him on this mission. That makes me doubly glad she took care of him. Not that I'd have gone along with it, of course. But he has friends in high places, as you know, and if he'd contacted them it may have destroyed any hope of peaceful negotiation."

"Egypt, I know Zion used the *Aztlan's* AI to communicate in real time with the *Earthstar*. Canard could have used it in transit on the skycraft. Do you know if he did?"

There was a brief silence before Egypt responded. "No. I do not. And I had better find out, hadn't I?"

The communicator darkened and silence fell.

"What is a nuke?" Khedran asked, deceptively calm.

She grimaced. "It's a weapon of mass destruction. It would destroy Cabre and much of Azlatan."

She looked around the table. She saw both fear and anger, and in Khedran's case, the final feral transition to the Black Wolf.

She met that emerald fire meaningfully. "This is why I came back to Hiraeth. So you could know all the facts, not just the ones they might feed you."

"The Captain seemed to be trustworthy," Varady put in. "Who are these others in high places that she mentioned?"

"They are still years away in Earth orbit, so are not an immediate concern. And yes, Captain Alexander can be trusted." She continued to hold Khedran's gaze. "She is related to my husband, if you know what I mean." She pointed at her eyes, then his.

He only asked, "There are those from your Earth that would use that weapon on us?"

Jael leaned forward. "They would, and they will. My brother, please believe me. And...Shandiin, you are wrong. They are an immediate concern. They are already on their way."

"What?" Shandiin stiffened. "How can that be?"

"I do not know, Shandiin. I only know what is."

She stared at him, back at Khedran. "I have to talk to Zion. This...this kind of attack and this immediacy are even more than I feared."

"How can we fight a weapon that could destroy Cabre?" Camion cried.

And here it is, she thought. *Damn it to hell. There's no choice.*

"There is only one possibility that I know of, and..." She looked at Khedran, away again, thinking about what she must ask of him. Thinking of Zion's concern about sacrificing him.

When she didn't continue her sentence he frowned, knowing she was never indecisive.

When she finally returned her gaze to Khedran, her expression was unreadable. "Do you have a way to alert your Dominions to danger?"

He turned his head toward Camion, who just nodded.

"Camion's already begun the alert," Khedran told her. "We established a communication plan right after the Prophecy War. The Dominions are always on standby for what we named an Assemblage. We have relayed messengers to every Dominion, with orders to convene in Cabre on the last day of Stareven. I didn't want to delay past that date. It may be too difficult for those farthest from us to get here in time, but messengers will use relay horses and Chaine ships, also part of the plan. Camion initiated the callout last night at my direction."

So, Shandiin thought, *he was working to save Azlatan before he even came to speak to me, with his beloved wife on a strange flying machine going somewhere without him. He hasn't changed. His people have always come first. Please, by all that matters, I don't want to ask more of him...but now it seems I have no choice, if this world is to survive what Jael has seen.*

Khedran continued while she bit her lip in thought. "Varady and Roinn, please join us at the Stareven Assemblage." As they both acknowledged, his gaze returned to Shandiin. "I will need your help notifying and convincing Xanthe of the need for their attendance. They do not acknowledge me as having any authority over them, nor even a liaison. That has never mattered until now." Xanthe was the city where Azlatan's enemies in the Prophecy War had originated; many of its people had become citizens of Azlatan, but the city itself remained sovereign.

"All right, we can help with that. Right now I need to have a private talk with Zion." She stood, and lifted her communicator. "While I am gone, I want all of you to think hard about choosing a succession of leaders for this planet. I understand you will want the High King as your world's central leader. But we need at least two others who can step in...if for any reason he should be absent."

She didn't meet Khedran's eyes before leaving the room.

Shandi confirmed that Canard had communicated with someone while they were in transit to the Aztlan, but she had been blocked from the particulars. Egypt set her people to the task of tracing the communication while she gave her royal guest her full attention.

"I am one of the few having access to Zion's complete report. I read it all the way through." Egypt handed a cup of coffee to Shandi. "I've also talked at length with Shandiin, who lived on your world for so long. I'd like to discuss some of that with you, but first I wanted to show you what your planet Hiraeth looks like from many, many miles above."

She had taken Shandi to what Egypt had termed the "observation room," where they sat facing the giant monitor that looked like a window into space.

Shandi gazed in wonder on her world. It was, as Danon had passed on from what he'd learned from Shandiin, a globe like the moon. It hung brilliant in blue and pearl and green and tan against a black sky spangled with stars.

"It is almost all the sea," she commented almost to herself. "Where is Azlatan, Captain?"

"We should be passing over it shortly, and I will show you. We are in orbit around your planet."

Shandi pointed at a silver object passing under them.

Egypt smiled. "That is one of the satellites which we also put in orbit, so that we could have communication with the ground. One of the things the mission planned on was connecting your planet through the same system."

"Like the communicator Zion was using." Shandi shifted her gaze from the window to regard the strange woman who was watching her from emerald eyes such as she'd seen only in her own bloodline...until now. *She has an uncommon beauty*, Shandi thought. *She is exotic, and striking. And she is built for strength. There is no softness about her.*

Aloud, she said "You were telling me about a report that Zion wrote?"

"Yes. When Shandiin came back from her adventures on your planet, he wrote a complete report on everything that transpired here. I do mean complete...he interviewed her for weeks, months, until he was sure he had all the details."

Shandi sighed. "And she told him everything. Even some things I do not believe my father would have agreed to." Shandi was thinking of the family curse, which Zion had asked her to use when she met the man who had taken her hostage.

"I'm sorry if that is true. But the complete report was only shared with his...family. Only an abbreviated version of the full report was provided to Canard and his minions."

Shandi took a sip of the coffee, which she found she enjoyed. "I gather you are part of that family."

Egypt smiled. Shandi fascinated her on many levels, not least of which was the bright reflection of the two sons she had loved and lost to Hiraeth's history. "Yes, I am part of Zion's family. And you are our distant descendant. Your ancestors, those we called our sons, were part of the colony brought to this world long ago."

"Colony?"

"It's a long history, Shandi. Yes, your planet was colonized by people from Earth, over a thousand years ago. Apparently, there was some sort of...well, Shandiin calls it a hijacking. Your planet has a magic spirit, and it took over everyone immediately, including her. She was the only one who could commune with that spirit, and made a covenant with it to save your people from the gods, including herself. When she returned to us...within minutes of having vanished...a thousand years had gone by on the planet's surface. She took the magic of the gods with her when she was finally able to leave."

Shandi nodded thoughtfully. "I know about Shandiin taking away the gods."

"Yes. She had hoped that the planet's magic would return to hijack the people on my ship as well, so Azlatan would be safe from the Earthers. But it didn't."

Shandi looked at her in surprise. "She wanted to be, what did you call it...hijacked?"

"Yep. To keep your people safe from the Earthers. By the way, they don't believe in the magic. They still don't, since there was no hijacking."

"But you believe?"

"Of course I do. I saw the evidence. And I find magic intriguing."

"You wouldn't, if you had lived through it. I was born after the war, but everything I have learned is not good. People were like slaves to the gods, who mostly only seemed to care about themselves."

"All but Shandiin," Egypt pointed out. "She was secretly a goddess...I see you know that. But she hated the magic influence on the people, and as part of the covenant with the spirit of your world, she made sure that the tribe of colonists who followed her were made immune to it."

"You mean the Chaine. So they are colonists too?"

"Everyone in your world is descended from the original colony."

Shandi sat back, set aside the cup. "Now tell me why Shandiin didn't want anyone but your family to know about us. And who your family is, please."

"The second part of your question is what creates the first part. There are four of us left in our family. Shandiin is the sister of my spirit, but is not of the family. There used to be more of us, but they were murdered before the apocalypse that made our planet uninhabitable. We were hated, you see, for being superior."

Shandi frowned. "Superior in what way?"

"We are a little more than human, Shandi. Like you. Do you honestly think your bloodline is like other humans?"

Shandi lifted an eyebrow. "We are mortal, like all humans."

Egypt regarded her thoughtfully. "I can quote Zion's report, for I have read it several times. It says: 'The rare bloodline of the High Kings has inherent or magical gifts to bolster their purpose, which is to serve their people through their leadership. The gifts include a command voice that is always heard by anyone in sight, and often results in immediate obedience; a presence that causes them to be recognized as the realm's ultimate authority without need of insignia; and charisma that causes a thrall to fall over most anyone who meets them, a thrall of wonder and sometimes love. All of this is in addition to their special beauty and intelligence...and most importantly, the fact that they are completely incorruptible, maintaining standards most humans would find impossible and even unreasonable.'"

Shandi's face hardened. The only thing missing from Egypt's recitation was her bloodline's gift of empathy, the ability to read the emotions, the spiritual truth, of others. It was rarely used, because it was an invasion of privacy, and it affected the user as well as the used. She'd felt sickened by her minute brush with Ben Canard.

"Quite frankly," Egypt continued, "I find those things rather intimidating. I am glad there are so few of you. But I must admit I look forward to meeting your father, the current High King."

"You said 'inherent or magical gifts.' Do you mean these things...which I wish were not such public knowledge, even just to your family...that they come from our heritage, not from magic?"

"Yes. You were engineered to be who you are. But magic intensified everything beyond our greatest expectation. I have wondered if any of these special talents have continued since the gods' magic was taken from your world."

Shandi didn't comment on that. She knew the gifts remained. "Are those of my bloodline the only people that are...as you call it...superior?"

"No. Your bloodline is the only one that began purely through engineering, and it appears it has remained true through several generations, likely because the women chosen to be Queen were linked to it. But there were many who began from different but very special bloodlines, as you would call it. We call it genetics."

Shandi nodded. "I have heard Danon use that word. Shandiin taught him a lot of things we found surprising."

"Yes. She told me he has an amazing intellect, so she gave him knowledge she thought might help the future of Azlatan. However, she gave far more knowledge to your father, as she mentored him to prepare for the war she knew was coming. She believes him to be a true genius, like her husband Zion. But, returning to your original question regarding Shandiin's wish to keep your world's existence from the Earthers, the answer is simple. She doesn't trust them. Her declared purpose as part of this mission is to protect all of you."

Shandi grimaced. "You will probably not be happy to know I punched her in the face."

When there was no response to her admission, Shandi glanced up to see Egypt's emerald eyes were wide with amusement.

"How badly were you hurt?" Egypt asked.

"I wasn't. She wouldn't fight me. Why? Do you think she is a better warrior than I am? I have trained all my life with The Chaine Roinn."

"I wouldn't take on Shandiin without backup, and I'm bigger than she is. Why wouldn't she fight you? That doesn't sound like her at all."

Shandi frowned. "My friend Shajii asked her something like that. Shandiin said it was because I am Khedran's daughter."

"Oh." Egypt looked away. After a moment of thought, Shandi cursed. "He included *that* in his report?" she demanded.

"No. She told Zion the truth because he loves her and she is honorable, and she told me because she is my sister. She told me she had fallen in love with your father."

Egypt turned back to regard Shandi solemnly. "Princess, this is the first time she's ever fallen for anyone. She never wanted it. She told me long ago that the idea was terrifying to her, because it gave another person the power to destroy you." Egypt frowned at Shandi's belligerent expression, and continued relentlessly. "Are you aware that they had made love, the night before she left?"

When Shandi nodded, her anger evident, Egypt sighed. "Shandiin thought she was never coming back, Shandi. She told me everything out of need to share her terrible grief. It wasn't just your father she loved and lost. She loved your world – her world – and she had to give it up to save it."

Shandi grimaced, her anger tangling with shame. "I know I was being judgmental. Maybe I still am, despite everything you just said. I cannot accept that he could have cared for anyone but my mother."

"So you blame her because he is your father. I can understand that."

Shandi shook her head. "You don't. You couldn't...if you don't know him."

"I am really hoping I get the opportunity." Egypt looked up as a crew member came in.

The man saluted his Captain and bowed briefly to Shandi. "The Princess was right. Canard did send a message," he announced. "It appears he had already given the *Earthstar* the coordinates for this planet. He asked when they were expected to arrive in this system. As far as we can determine he didn't receive an answer."

"Dammit," Egypt muttered. "Well, that's not an immediate problem. Even if they had Zion's FTL drive, it would take them ten years to get here from there. But I want to talk to Zion about this face to face. I'll have Sarnath take over the Bridge. I'm going dirtside with the Princess."

CHAPTER 11

S handiin was using the communicator in the family library. She spoke to Zion while looking up at the replica Star Blade, hanging lifelessly over the mantel. She was vaguely surprised to realize she missed the bright glory of the original.

She had learned that Canard's death had not created havoc among his followers at the base camp, but mostly relief; they had quickly agreed to Zion's leadership as well as Roland's. Roland's soldiers were integrated from what had been the rebels of the *Earthstar*. They were loyal to him, as were also the crew members he had left on the *Aztlan* under the command of Egypt and Sarnath.

In return Shandiin asked Zion to make contact with Xanthe, to get them to send a representative to the planned Assemblage.

Then she took a deep breath and placed a calming hand over her heart.

"Zion, there is a place in the eastern mountains where I used to communicate with Hiraeth. We must take Khedran there. That's the only way I can think of to follow her direction about bringing her the son."

"I think that's premature, Shandiin. Hiraeth is under no immediate threat. Egypt just advised that Canard apparently gave the Earthstar our coordinates, but even if they decided to come here before immigration was approved, they don't have my FTL drive...and even using that took us ten years from Earth to Hiraeth."

She responded grimly. "Jael has proved very well that he sees visions that are true. At our meeting this morning he saw Shandi's kidnapping before you called us to report it. And Zion...he has seen them use weapons of mass destruction on Azlatan! He said it will happen sooner than ten or fifty years from now, that they are already on their way."

"I don't see how that's possible."

"You didn't think magic was possible, either."

He exhaled loudly. "That's true. I can't ignore anything now, can I?" It was several seconds before he continued. "What do you think is the source of Jael's visions? He previously had connection with Daimaine and Liethe. We know they're both gone."

"Perhaps it's from Hiraeth herself."

"Then maybe it's Jael you should take to her instead of the High King."

She had an immediate selfish hope that she would not have to ask Khedran to go. Hiraeth had created the goddess Daimaine, who had done the unspeakable to the High Kings. So how could Khedran trust her?

I can't think about that. I'm the only one who will ever know about Daimaine's torment of the High Kings, and I can't think about it.

But a world was at risk. "Maybe you're right, Zion. But I have to cover all the bases. I will take Jael along with Khedran. And Varady. He still has some of his magic as well."

"I still don't like it. You should warn them what could happen, Shandiin. If there is any reality to any of this...hard as that is for me to accept...there could be similarity to the myths of Earth's goddess. Human sacrifice is part of that, and I just don't see how that could be a good thing."

She rubbed her eyes, refusing to argue or agree. "We have to go by skycraft. Going there on horseback would take too long. When will that be available?"

"Not until tomorrow at the earliest. Shandiin, I have to go now. The Princess is on her way back, and Egypt is playing skycraft pilot."

"Why am I not surprised? She never wanted to be stuck in orbit when all the action is down here, as she put it. Bring her too, Zion."

"Are you sure? We're flying the royals and Danon and the Chaine woman this afternoon. Roland and I are also coming. Including Egypt would mean there would be three of us outworlders. That's a lot for Cabre's people to accept. Hell, Egypt alone would be a lot, if she's in a mood."

Shandiin could almost smile, knowing exactly what he meant. "She'll be fine. They accepted me, after all. Zion, I understand now you were right to trust Roland, and with Canard out of the way it's time to connect with this world's leaders. Despite everything I warned him about, Khedran will accept your peaceful immigration, if that's still on the table. I can't stand in his way. I'll try to have everything cleared for you, with some ceremony to alert the populace of your arrival."

"All right." There was a brief hesitation. "It will be good to see you again, my love, even though we don't agree on everything."

The communicator went dark.

Shandiin bit her lip. *It seems neither of my loves agree with me about leaving the* Earthstar's *people where they are. Trouble is, I understand their point of view as well as my own.*

There was a time I'd have been on their side.

She knew in her heart that both Zion and Khedran were in the ethical right. She understood the humane thing was to bring the *Earthstar's* oppressed people to a real planet. But she knew just as fervently that it was sometimes necessary to take the hard road, the hard and unkind choice, in order to save what mattered most.

And what mattered most to her now was the people of Hiraeth.

Returning to the meeting room, she announced, "The High Queen is returning this afternoon, and it's time for Cabre to see the skycraft. I suggest clearing the main concourse and the thoroughfare from Penumbra to the city gates."

Khedran nodded toward Camion. "I'll advise the merchants to shut everything down," Camion responded to the unspoken command. "Your Highness, we should have a presence of the Guard there, and ensure the nobility is aware so they can wear proper attire. We should also plan a banquet. It's appropriate for dignitaries."

Khedran sat back. "A royal entrance, and a celebration. Is that what you want, Shandiin?"

"For several reasons, yes. In addition to the High Queen's return, your people will be getting their first view of the out-worlders. There will be three on the skycraft. My husband Zion Alexander, Commanding Officer Bond, and Starship Captain Egypt Alexander."

"The ship's Captain? Is she landing the ship, then?"

"No. She is bringing the Princess back in a skycraft. The *Aztlan* is meant to stay in space."

Jael, who had remained quiet through most of the conversation, leaned forward with his palms flat on the table. His sapphire gaze was pinned on Shandiin. "I understand the need for ceremony at this time, but I want to know if you have any plans to address what you called a weapon of mass destruction. The weapon I saw them use in a vision."

She read fear on his face, and urgency. "Yes, Jael. I have one plan, or at least one hope. But I can't really explain just yet. I need the four of us...Khedran, Varady, you and I...to take a trip tomorrow. I'll explain when we arrive at our destination."

"Why the secrecy, Shandiin?"

She turned to answer Khedran with her heart hurting. "Please. Trust me? You'll know more tomorrow."

He considered her for a moment, then sighed. "Roinn, it appears you and Marre will be in charge tomorrow, if that's acceptable? I'll bring Marre up to date when she gets here."

Roinn merely nodded.

"Are we going somewhere in the skycraft?" Varady asked.

"I'm afraid so." She smiled at brave Varady who, for once, appeared nervous.

Varady sighed unhappily and sat back.

Shandi strapped into the skycraft with Egypt and watched as the Captain selected a control that opened a window. "I didn't know that window was there! That miscreant just used the little screen."

"He let the computer do the flying, because he wasn't a pilot and trusts machinery more than people. I prefer handling it myself. Hang on..." and they were suddenly outside the *Aztlan*, with the planet hanging below.

Shandi leaned forward, fascinated. "It is so beautiful."

"Yes, it is. I've been hoping to see it from the ground. I just didn't have an excuse. Not that I'm glad you were taken hostage."

"I would experience that again, for the opportunity to see this."

Egypt laughed. "Shandiin told us that the people of your planet stand strong, especially the royalty. And looking at you, I hardly think you need the thrall."

Shandi wrinkled her nose. "It is not something I would have asked for."

Egypt considered. "I can imagine it makes it difficult, wondering if someone really cares for you or if it is magic. But aren't some people immune to it, like Shandiin said she is?"

Shandi nodded. "Some. All of the Chaine are." She sighed and finally looked from the window to magnificent Egypt. "I am sure you would never need a thrall," she added bluntly.

Egypt lifted her eyebrows, amused. "I think we may become friends, Princess."

"In that case, please just call me Shandi."

"Were you named for Shandiin?"

Shandi returned her gaze to the window. "Yes."

"Uh-oh. You don't sound very happy about it. I am sorry you don't like her, Shandi. She's an amazing woman. I owe her my life."

Shandi looked back in surprise. "Your life? How?"

"We were soldiers together, a very long time ago. She saved me. She's got quite a history, Shandi, as a heroine, but she doesn't see it like that. It's a shame her children were so different."

"She has children? Are they Zion's?"

"No. Long before him. There's your country, Shandi."

They were coming in over the ocean, and Shandi watched the shoreline appear. They glided over Cabre, and then the countryside of Azlatan, and then the great grasslands they called the Plain of Admech. The ship slowed to circle over a small city of metal buildings filling a swathe of land where the grasses had been cut or removed.

"How did you get all of this down here from your ship?" she wondered. "It wouldn't fit in this skycraft."

"We have several surprises on the *Aztlan.* It's a starship engineered to carry many things, including several methods of transport. Hang on, we're landing."

They touched down gently, and the exterior doors opened. Zion waited there, with a young woman standing behind him.

He greeted Shandi with concern as she disembarked. "Are you all right, Your Highness?"

"I'm fine. I have had quite an adventure, actually. How is Mother?"

"I'm here," Marre said, stepping from behind Zion.

Shandi saw a lovely woman barely older than herself.

Shandi blinked. Her jaw dropped when she realized it was her mother. Then she gathered her in and hugged her hard, pulling back to stare. "You are gorgeous! Father is going to be so amazed."

"I look the way I did when he met me, and apparently that's how I will look forever. Like Shandiin, I will never change. I am still getting used to it. I don't know how your father will react."

"He'll be thrilled. He was devastated, Mother, thinking we would lose you. I was afraid we were going to lose him too. This is truly miraculous." She turned to Zion, looking into the face so like her father's, and made a decision.

She embraced him. Surprised, Zion laughed and returned the hug gingerly. She drew back and smiled up at him with tears in her eyes, which would have shocked anyone who knew her. "Thank you. I am sorry I was mean to your wife."

"She accepted it, so I must. And...I wasn't very nice to your father, either."

Her eyebrows went up in surprise, and he had to laugh.

"What is this about?" Marre demanded.

"Apparently," Egypt put in as she exited the skycraft after shutdown, "the Princess knocked Shandiin on her ass."

It was Marre's turn to gape. First at her daughter, then at the woman who was taller even than Zion, wearing a white uniform. Her skin was richly dark, her hair a giant sphere of curls, and her eyes were the same emerald as her daughter's.

"Captain Egypt Alexander," Zion said formally, "let me introduce the High Queen of Azlatan."

"Marre. Please, call me Marre. Thank you for rescuing my daughter, Captain."

Egypt bowed with a grin. "She didn't need rescuing. She killed that jackass before I had a chance."

Marre lifted an eyebrow, then nodded in satisfaction before she turned to Shandi. "Now I want to know why you were mean to Shandiin."

Zion cleared his throat. "Perhaps we should take this inside."

"All right." Marre took her daughter's arm as they walked back to the building. "At least you have proper clothing," she observed, glancing down in distaste at the denim jeans she was wearing, though she rather liked the silky white shirt that had also been given to her.

Shandi looked down at her own black uniform, the only thing she had ever worn, and sighed. "At least you are wearing something different. Maybe father will consider changing that tradition now."

When the royals entered the building together, Zion tactfully stopped Egypt outside. A few minutes later they heard a very loud "What?" and he drew the intrigued Captain further from the door.

Inside, Marre stood staring up at her tall daughter. "I cannot believe you did that. You *punched* her? How did your father react to that?"

"I don't know. I don't even know if he knows what I did. He had to stay behind while we brought you here to be cured." Shandi frowned. "With her."

"Shandi, do you truly think that's a problem?"

"Mother, I heard him myself. He told Danon you knew he loved Shandiin, that he told you he made love to her. Mother, I saw him weep from the guilt. I couldn't bear it, and that's why I punched her."

Marre went pale. After a moment she said, "I have always hoped she would never return here. He did admit to me he loved her, and...what he had done." She swallowed. "I had to accept that. She mentored him all his life, to help make him the man he is. She saved Azlatan, when she took away the gods. She saved us all."

Shandi stared. "And for that will you share him with her now?"

Marre shook her head. "No. There is no question of sharing. Your father is the most honorable man in the world. He will never touch her again, Shandi."

"I wish I could be so sure. He's not who I thought he was—"

She didn't finish the sentence before Marre spun back and slapped her. "You will not disrespect your father!"

Shandi put her hand to her stinging cheek and looked down at her mother in shock and despair. "I don't want to. I don't. But I never thought he would do something like that. Not him!"

She ran out before her mother could stop her. Marre came through the door right behind her, but Egypt stepped in front of her. "Let me talk to her. She's very young, Your Highness. I think she just needs some time."

Marre put her hands over her face. "I slapped her. Never once in her life had I ever struck her...until now."

Egypt threw a glance at Zion and went after Shandi.

"I slapped her," Marre repeated, still in shock.

"A lot has happened to both of you in a short time," Zion began. "She was distraught when she punched Shandiin, something she and I both understood. I imagine you're feeling overwhelmed yourself right about now."

Marre looked after her daughter. "Shandi has been everything to Khedran, from the moment I gave birth. His love for her made him vulnerable, I think, for the first time in his life. For her to think less of him for one...mistake, as I think it was..." She shook her head. "He knew Shandiin was leaving this world. He believed he would never see her again." She looked up at Zion. "I gather she told you, just as he told me. They are both honorable people. Even if...even if their love still exists, I cannot believe they will ever act on it."

After a moment he asked, "Does that make it acceptable to you?"

She took a deep breath. "He loves me. He respects me. I have to hold on to that."

He said nothing.

Shajii was walking across the base when she saw Shandi on the ground behind a building, sitting curled over her lap while she sobbed. A stranger, an extremely tall dark woman in a white uniform, was standing over her with arms crossed.

Knowing Shandi had previously been taken hostage by one of these outworlders, Shajii did what came naturally to her. She drew sword and tapped the woman's shoulder with it.

"Step away from the Princess."

The stranger turned, saw the sword, tilted her head. "You are one of the Chaine people."

"I am. Get away from her, I said."

Egypt considered. "Put away the sword first."

"No. Move."

Shandi came quickly to her feet. "Stop, Shajii. Egypt's just trying to help. And she's also my friend." She was surprised to realize it was true even as she said it.

Shajii looked from one to the other. Shandi had ceased that surprising weeping. She sheathed her sword and regarded the tall stranger, noting her coloring was like Roland's, though he didn't have the strange green eyes.

Then she turned back to Shandi. "Why were you crying? Did that piss-ant hurt you?"

"No. I seem able to do that all by myself, lately. Shajii, this is Captain Egypt Alexander. She brought me back from the ship that's going around our planet. She belongs to a family that she says is probably related to us."

Shajii looked up at the woman, down again, up again. "You are almost as tall as our leader The Chaine Roinn, and you look as strong. Do all your family have the green eyes like the High King's bloodline?"

"No," Egypt replied. "Which is good, since they make us easily recognizable. There are some people who do not like my family."

"Why?"

Egypt tilted her head. "I understand not everyone liked the Chaine people. Do you know why?"

"Because we are different from them."

Egypt just nodded meaningfully and looked back at Shandi. "Are you all right now, Princess?"

Shandi wiped her eyes with her sleeve. "I can't believe Mother got so angry. Or how she can be so forgiving!"

Shajii frowned. "Are you still being judgmental about what had nothing to do with you?"

"It has everything to do with me. He is my father!"

Shajii shrugged. "Then it's not your mother you should be talking to. If he hurt you, it was twenty years before you were born, but you should talk about it to him, and let him know how you feel. You already gave Shandiin your message." Shajii lifted her fist. "Perhaps he is the one you should punch."

Shandi's eyes widened. "I couldn't."

"No? So only the woman is to be blamed?" Shajii looked disgusted.

Shandi looked from her to Egypt, who showed no expression. "Am I so wrong? Should I just accept it and forget it?"

Egypt shrugged like Shajii had. "If it bothers you that much, I think you should do what your friend just suggested. Go punch him too, at least figuratively. Get it out of your system."

Shandi threw up her hands and strode away. The two women she left behind eyed each other.

"Is your Princess always so stubborn?"

"Oh, yes. But she's not my Princess. My people do not have royalty. She is just my good friend. But she has been off-balance since she heard of her father's transgression. She has him on such a high pedestal I'm surprised he can breathe."

"I gathered that. He is an unusual man, from what I have heard."

"Yes. He is."

"What do you think of him?"

Shajii considered as they turned together to follow Shandi. "I admire him a great deal. He puts his people first, and he is very brave and wise. He and Shandiin are the same that way. I believe they should be allowed to care for each other without all this outside judgment."

"Is that the way your people see it?" Egypt asked.

"Yes. Those outside the Chaine do not understand *amharen*. That depth of *amhara* is rare, but it is real."

Egypt nodded thoughtfully, remembering Shandiin's explanation of *amharen.* Then she saw the skycraft was being readied. "It looks like we are going to Azlatan. I am really looking forward to meeting this man. This High King."

Cabre's concourse had been cleared while citizens thronged its edges and lined the city's thoroughfare. The air buzzed with celebration of the Queen's reported recovery.

Khedran stood with Camion and his first Compatri Farbet, Master of the Queen's Guard, who had finally turned completely gray in hair and beard. Khedran's brothers, with Roinn and Shandiin, stood aside for now while Khedran looked to the east, hoping to see the machine that would bring his wife back to him.

A distant crowd-roar heralded the approach of the skycraft. Soldiers of the Black Guard stood to keep citizens back as it appeared, glinting metal in the westering sun, to sweep over the city and then hover over the concourse plaza. The observers stepped back in nervous amazement as the silent metal creature settled gently to the plaza floor.

The doors opened and Danon was first out, turning to help Marre from the high doorway. She was a tiny figure in white blouse and jeans, her black hair swirling free down her back, and her expression as she looked around for her King was full of nerves.

Khedran didn't hesitate. He blinked hard, but he knew her immediately, as even her own daughter had not. He strode to meet her and she, seeing him, ran to him.

As he had once before, long years ago but a short distance away at the entrance to Penumbra, he curled her into his arms and kissed the top of her head. He held her close for a long moment, and then they parted to look at each other with such obvious love that some who watched had tears in their eyes.

"I have so much to tell you," Marre told her King. "But we have to get through this ceremony first, according to Dr. Alexander."

"That's Zion Alexander?"

"Yes. I like him, Khedran."

"Is that because he looks like me?"

Surprised by his teasing smile, she smiled back. "Well, he's not nearly as handsome, of course. All right, we should be royalty now."

She turned to the crowd then, lifting her arms in greeting, and laughed happily at the answering cheers. Then Khedran took her hand and they walked together, back to the skycraft where the others were disembarking.

Shajii and Shandi stepped back together to make room for Zion. There were the expected cries from the crowd as they saw his face, but Khedran walked up and offered his hand in greeting as an equal, removing any concern that this was a problem.

Then Egypt alighted. She wore the white uniform that made her dark skin even more apparent, and her brilliant emerald eyes held laughter as she saw shock on the faces of the onlookers.

Her laughter faded to fascination as she turned to the man she had wanted to meet.

She was a fraction taller than the High King, but knew immediately he would seem the greater to anyone who saw them together. The presence he carried struck her immediately, but his smile when she offered both her hands fairly stunned her. She'd later tell Shandiin he'd taken her breath away, and it was a moment before she could speak.

"I am Captain Egypt Alexander. I am so glad to meet you, Your Highness. You are legendary, you know, in certain circles."

He studied her as closely as she did him, and appeared just as fascinated. Marre frowned; Shandiin, watching from a little distance, rolled her eyes. She knew her friend was a blatant flirt.

Khedran noticed neither reaction. "You will have to explain your legends to me, Captain. I'm only beginning to learn some of the pre-history of my world, and I know you are part of it. I look forward to learning more." His gaze lingered a moment before he turned to the others. "Is that everyone?"

"Not quite," came a voice from the skycraft, and then the Commander stepped down. In his black Kevlar jumpsuit, Roland strode to the High King and offered a salute.

His smile vanished when he met Khedran's eyes. He seemed momentarily frozen, but caught himself and stepped back, bowing low to King and Queen. "Commander Roland Bond at your service, Highnesses."

Khedran knew his gift of presence had been his own introduction. "Commander Bond, well come to Azlatan. Well come to all of you, from myself and the City of Cabre. You are our honored guests, and a celebration in your honor is waiting. Please join me in my home Penumbra, where I will introduce you to others also necessary to your mission to our world."

He turned then to his own people, and the outworlders were shocked to hear his command voice, which seemed to originate between their ears. "My thanks to all of you for giving our guests a proper welcome, as well as the High Queen whose life they saved with the medical technology they have brought to our world. My hope is for a bright future for Azlatan and its allies."

His people had long known that magic voice. A soft chorus answered him.

The High King is the Gift to Azlatan.
He is known by the magic of his presence
and his voice that is always heard.
He is incorruptible. He is truth.
The trust and honor of Azlatan live within him.

Shandiin saw Zion's shock as he took it in. "It's an ancient mantra," she explained. "Khedran was sixteen when his father bequeathed a letter requiring him to have faith in himself even when the people turn against him, because his duty is to protect them all. He told his son to accept the homage of those who are loyal, because their faith is necessary to the same purpose. The Kings require no reverence, Zion, but accepting it is part of their duty to the people."

Zion turned his gaze from the crowd to her, then to the High King, who accepted the homage with lowered head. "I'm beginning to understand what you meant about the difference in culture. It's not magic that made this. It's trust."

Khedran held Marre's hand as they led the way into Penumbra. He looked down at her, smiling once more. "You are young again."

"Yes. Just like twenty years ago when I came to be your bride, I got a lot more than I bargained for. But right now my biggest concern is our daughter. She somehow found out about you and Shandiin."

His smile vanished as guilt returned. *Trust and honor*, he thought ruefully. "She wouldn't even look at me."

"She is being impossible. She does not deserve your attention."

Khedran looked at his Queen in surprise, but said nothing more as they walked with their entourage to Penumbra, which had been made ready for festivities.

The banquet hall had once been a Temple to the goddess Daimaine, a dark void with only magic stars and a giant statue for light. Those were gone with the goddess. At Marre's redesign and direction, the black walls were now mirrored and held brightly burning crystal sconces. A hundred candled chandeliers held sway over even more candles on the many tables set around the room, burning in crystal holders that scattered the light until it seemed magic had returned. A feast had been set for the many guests, including the Dominion royalty who were in Cabre on business and therefore lucky enough to attend this unexpected historical celebration of change.

A long table had been erected on the low stage where a statue of the goddess had once stood. Marre and Khedran took their places at the center, with Shandi and Varady on their right flanked by Jael and Roinn. On their left were the outworlders. Khedran noted Captain Alexander was seated next to him, then Zion and Shandiin and the man called Roland, who kept looking at his communication device.

As people filed in and were seated around the room, Marre excused herself and walked to where Shandiin was sitting. "I am sorry I didn't get a chance to greet you outside."

Shandiin leaned back in her chair to look up at the renewed young Queen. "It's good to see you alive and well. Khedran was very worried about you."

Marre glanced from her to Zion. "I'm curious, Doctor Alexander. You said that you used blood from an immortal to heal me. Was it Shandiin's? And how long have you been together?"

Zion nodded. "Shandiin's stem cells have saved a few lucky people. And we were together even before she came to Azlatan."

"So very long. I am glad to know that love lasts, when there is more than a lifetime to live." When Zion looked nonplussed, Shandiin placed her hand over his and responded to the Queen. "You are concerned about the immortality aspect. You know you are going to outlive Khedran now."

"Yes. I wish he had received this treatment rather than me. Will it ever be possible to give him the treatment, so we can be together?" Marre continued addressing Zion.

His gaze slid to Shandiin. "Yes. It's possible."

"Thank you," Marre murmured gratefully, and returned to her chair.

Shandiin regarded her husband. "Really? You think you can give Khedran the treatment? I thought you weren't doing that any more except for emergencies."

"What do you want me to say, Shandiin? That I won't give the treatment to the man you both love?"

At her startled frown he turned from her to Egypt, who was sipping water while she studied the crowd.

"Why did you hijack my seat?" he asked softly. "Are you planning on making moves on the High King?"

"Maybe." Egypt grinned at him, and answered just as quietly. "Perhaps I can replace all his current love interests. Relax, Zion. You and the Princess Shandi are making much ado about nothing."

"You are looking in from the outside."

"Thank God for small favors. Having heard your snarky comment to Shandiin, I think perhaps you should open a door and breathe some of that outside air yourself." She turned her back on him, planning to address the High King.

She noticed he was still looking at his wife and had taken her hand again. Egypt leaned in a little to see Shandi turned away from them both; she was conversing with Varady.

Khedran lifted Marre's hand to his lips before releasing it to pay proper respect to Egypt. "Captain. You pilot a ship between the stars. I find that amazing."

"And you lead a country...perhaps even a world...that came from the stars."

"So I have been told."

"Shandiin explained that this planet was a colony from our world?"

"Yes." He studied her a moment. "You also have the green eyes. Are we related, then?"

She nodded. "Very distantly. A thousand years ago in your pre-history, my genetic factors were part of those contributed to your bloodline."

"Have you always known Shandiin?"

She hid surprise at his abrupt change of subject. "I have known her since we were soldiers together and she saved my life. She disappeared, afterwards, for several years. I was more than glad when my family found her and brought her along to colonize your planet."

"Your family being the superior people created by your science?"

"Yes. Although Shandiin believes you are even more exceptional than one of us."

He shook his head. "I believe I am more different than I am exceptional, and less human than you. How large is your family?"

She was taken aback by his response, tucking it away to discuss with Shandiin later. "There are only four of us left. Not counting the citizens of your world."

"Is everyone on my world related to you, then?"

"It's possible after a millennium of intermarriages, but we can't be sure until we do a DNA test. That's a simple thing, really, and Zion has probably already obtained some samples to start the research."

"I hope to learn more about that. But for now...I have wondered about something Shandiin told me. That you and your family were not born of woman. How is that possible?"

"Your wife will be able to explain the device she was put inside for her cure. Zion...he's the genius, and ostensibly our leader...believes we were grown inside of something like it. Then we were raised in a commune environment and broadly educated before being sent into the world for the first time."

"Who did that to you?"

She hesitated, gazing into his eyes, and saw he was concerned by what she had said. Somehow, she knew curiosity didn't drive his concern. He cared. For a reason she couldn't understand, she felt an unfamiliar ache in her throat.

Is this man magic, then? I thought I was immune!

She shook it off. "I never felt anything was done to me. I felt it was done for me, and I am glad."

"Then who did it for you?...and it seems hardly right, that you had no real childhood."

"People who suffered bad childhoods might disagree. As for who? He was Dr. Damon Alexander, a scientist who believed our kind were humanity's hope for survival. Zion and I took his surname in his honor."

"I understand those not of your family turned against you. Are they still against you, Captain?"

"Yes, Your Highness. There are still many in the remnants of Earth's people who dislike us just because we exist."

"Then I am glad you have come to Azlatan, where such dislike is not condoned. We once had a similar problem with the people called the Chaine. My father, Allasar, passed laws that did not allow discrimination. The Tahmond—I believe you would call them priests—repealed those laws while I was in exile. I reinstated them when I returned to Azlatan and ascended to leadership. Not that the laws are what created change. Human nature is the only thing that can truly do that. The acceptance of change can be a contrary thing, but for the Chaine it came when they fought alongside us in the Prophecy War."

Her smile was as stunning as his own, and Khedran's eyes warmed when she gave it to him.

"I have been told you are a wise King."

"I try to be. Shandiin's Chaine training has helped." He tilted his head slightly to see Shandiin sitting quietly two seats away. "Shandiin is not one of your family?"

"Shandiin is an unusual person in her own right, with her own origin unknown. She and I are very close."

He nodded. "She told me that. I am glad for her, that she has you for a friend. She was my mentor and defender for many years."

Egypt took a deep breath. "I know rather a lot about that."

He went still, his emerald gaze waiting, as Egypt continued. "She did a lot for this world, and wants to do more now, to keep you all safe. I hope you realize how hard it has been for her...leaving, grieving, getting past her grief at last, and now having to come back again."

"I do. She and I had a long discussion about the reasons for her return, one continued with the other leaders of this world. They've appointed me to be the spokesman for everyone."

"I believe that's a wise choice." When a cheerful server chose that moment to offer a glass of wine, she thanked him and lifted it to the King in salute. "A very wise choice. I will watch the proceedings with great interest, though from a distance."

"From your ship?"

"Alas, yes, I should return. Though I wouldn't mind staying right here beside you." Egypt grinned when she saw Marre frown in her direction. "Your King is far too handsome," Egypt told her frankly, "and I would love to know him...better, but I also know he would not allow it. Admirable, this man."

"He is," Marre agreed. "But be very sure I would not allow it either."

Khedran looked at Marre in surprise.

"I am rather forward, aren't I?" Egypt laughed. "Sorry, Your Highnesses. I will try to be more circumspect."

"That would be a treat," Zion said from her other side. "I have never seen you be circumspect about anything, Egypt. You are worse than Shandiin with your mouth. Your Highness, I apologize for the Captain's rudeness."

"No need," Khedran responded. "The Captain seems very...honest."

"Oh, I am," Egypt grinned again. "To a fault." She saw Varady watching her in amusement. "This is your brother, am I right, Highness? He is as attractive as you. God, I love this realm. But I must leave this party for now, hopefully before I have worn out my welcome. Roland is signaling it's time to take me back to the ship." She tossed back the rest of her wine and stood.

Whereby all those at the table stood as well, and she laughed again in delight. "I love it. Such an old fashioned, completely outdated courtesy, right along with the reported traditions of honor, duty, and respect. Not to mention all these gorgeous men. Shandiin, you were right about this world. It must be saved at all costs. Good-bye, all." She bowed briefly, turned, and walked out with Roland.

Everyone sat down, looking a little confused. Shandiin just shook her head while Zion exchanged glances with Khedran. Khedran's lips twitched, and Zion also tried to hide a grin.

Danon, arriving late, dropped into the seat Egypt had vacated. "What did I miss?" he asked, and was answered only with laughter.

The banquet went on cheerfully after that, but Khedran was disturbed by the vacant chair next to Marre, which should have been his daughter's. Shandi had slipped out unseen.

He worried when she didn't return.

When the banquet was over Marre set a hand on his arm, knowing what he intended. "Let her be, Khedran. She needs to grow up, and quit this nonsense."

"It isn't nonsense to her," he responded quietly. "She is hurt, and I am the cause. I have to talk to her."

He searched and finally found his daughter in the library with a book open on her lap. She wasn't reading, but staring into the glowing fireplace.

Shandi looked over as her father entered, then away again.

He sat down in the chair facing her. "You didn't eat your dinner, love. Why did you leave?"

After a moment she closed the book and set it aside. But she didn't look up at him.

He sighed. "Please, Shandi. Talk to me."

She kept her head down. "I heard you tell Uncle Danon about you and Shandiin."

"Shandiin told me you overheard. I am sorry."

She finally looked into his face, and her eyes brimmed with tears. "What is it you are sorry for, Father? For loving Shandiin and hurting my mother? Or are you just sorry that I found out about it?"

He moved to take her hand, something he had always done, but she drew it away.

"Shandi. Can you not forgive me for something that happened so long ago?"

"I meant to try. But our gift of reading others betrays you. The wall against violating another's secrets fails me in this. Your feelings for her burn through it when she is near." She swallowed, and her voice dropped to a whisper. "You still love her, and it is wrong of you."

He turned his face away, unable to say anything for a long moment. When he finally met her eyes again, he made no attempt to deny the truth.

"You are more than disappointed in me, aren't you?"

She nodded miserably.

"What can I do, Shandi, that will let you forgive me? I cannot change the past. Nor can I change what you see is still true. But Shandiin and I will never be together the way we were once. Once," he repeated when she frowned. "Once, Shandi. Never again. I made that promise to your mother, and you know I do not break oath."

She said nothing.

He sighed. "You remind me of myself when I was young. I could not accept that my father was human, that he could have loved anyone but my mother. I took it out on the mother of my brothers. I accused her of sorcery, and worse."

"I took it out on Shandiin, but it was pointed out to me that it takes two to have an affair."

"Is that what you think? That I had an affair, like my father did? Once, Shandi. One time I failed to be what you rightly expect me to be. I understand, even as it hurts me, that you now think less of me." When she didn't deny it, he gazed down at her lowered head for a long moment.

His voice nearly broke. "I have always wondered what I would do if a man ever broke your heart. I never thought it would be me."

When she said nothing, he left her there.

Khedran left his daughter and went to walk alone on Penumbra's beach under the moon, oblivious to the harsh sea-wind that lashed his cloak and his hair. When he turned to regard moonlight shattering upon the fitful sea, Penumbra rose like a shadow against his back. Its dark towers had once been a glorious ladder of stars, but he didn't miss the magic. He had been saved an eternity of torment when Shandiin had taken the magic from Azlatan.

He was aware without seeing when Shandiin came to join him. She stopped by his side, her presence all too familiar from all the years he had known her.

All the years he had loved her.

She shoved her hands in her jean pockets. "I saw you leave. I'm guessing why. I'm sorry about Shandi."

"So am I. She can't understand, Shandiin. Nor can I. It's like I am bewitched. I love Marre, but I've never been able to get you out of my head or my heart. I can hide the truth from everyone but myself...and now from my daughter."

He turned around to look up at Penumbra, at the tower where he and Marre had lived for twenty years. Where Marre waited for him even now.

"Of course Shandi knows," he continued. "She has the same gift of reading emotion that I do, and learning the truth has ripped it open. She now knows I never put you behind me."

He took a deep breath. Shandiin only waited, hurting for him. "During all those years, Shandiin...I missed you at the most unexpected moments. A flash of memory, a quick stab of grief to steal my breath." He lifted his shoulders. "Not that it mattered. Your memory was too precious. I would not have given it up, even if I could."

He closed his eyes and lowered his head to rub his brow. "And of course none of that is important now. Are you here to tell me why we are going away tomorrow? What is it you want of me?"

She swallowed hard. "I didn't want to talk about it in front of everyone. I don't want to ask you at all. It's...hard. I know what Daimaine did to you, Khedran. But...now the one who created Daimaine may be our only hope for Azlatan. For this world."

He turned, finally, to face her. Moonlight fired his emerald eyes. His handsome face was set and hard. "Another secret, Shandiin? There is another god?"

"She is not a god like you have known. She created the gods I took away. She is the world, and I know she's still here, but I think she's asleep."

He regarded her warily. He knew her history on Hiraeth, and he knew her too well to disbelieve her. "What would you have me do, Shandiin?"

"I need you to wake her. I think it must be you to do it. There is a possibility it could be Jael, or Varady. The three of you hold some of her magic yet. But no matter who can do it, she must be awakened. She has the magic that can protect your world. I see no other choice, against what is coming here. I think I know where she sleeps, and that's where I plan to take you tomorrow."

He said nothing for a long time, but returned his gaze to the wind-tossed sea, the star-filled sky. Then he sighed. "This undertaking won't be for my brothers. You know that as well as I." He closed his eyes. "What will she do, Shandiin, if I wake her? Will she take me, as Daimaine took all the Kings?"

She wanted to deny the truth, but said it anyway. "I don't know. I don't know, Khedran. But I don't believe she is an evil goddess. She is the living planet, the source of nature. But I only know what she told me...that I had to bring the son to her."

"The son."

"That is what she said."

Again, he was silent for a long time.

When he finally looked back at her, he seemed to study her face. The moonlit fire of her wind-tossed hair. Her lips.

But he turned away.

"If I must," was all he said, and left to go to Marre.

Chapter 12

The skycraft cleared the great cliffs of Khaibara, the eastern mountain range the Sundancers called the Wall of the World. Its passengers saw a jumble of rocks at its summit.

Varady, who had been the most nervous about flying, was now the most fascinated as his long-time love for exploration came to the surface. Jael, next to him, kept returning his gaze to Khedran.

Khedran sat beside Zion, directly behind the pilot and Shandiin, who was acting as navigator. His mind seemed far away from his first flight, even as he gazed down at the rocky mountain tops below.

Zion tapped his shoulder, and Khedran turned his head to face him. "You seem very troubled." Zion spoke low, though aware Shandiin could probably hear him. "Is it because of what may be waiting for you here? I'll tell you again, you don't have to do this."

"I know." Khedran didn't elaborate.

Zion asked no further. He and Khedran had waited for the skycraft together, and talked for a long while before leaving Cabre. His respect for the High King had grown from that conversation. Khedran's intellect had not been exaggerated by Shandiin, and intelligence was Zion's gauge of humanity, though both Shandiin and Sarnath disagreed that it should be the final measure.

Zion had been surprised to find himself willing to talk to the King about Shandiin.

That conversation began when she'd entered the library where they waited. Seeing them together, she'd lifted her eyebrows, winked, and then simply turned around and left.

Khedran, regarding the door she'd closed behind her, noted dryly that she was a complicated person.

"Not only complicated," Zion agreed, "but unpredictable. I never know what to expect from her."

Khedran turned to him with a thoughtful expression. "Nevertheless, I long ago learned to trust what comes in her wake." He hesitated. "Your ship's captain mentioned that Shandiin's origin is unknown. Can you tell me what she meant?"

Zion's forehead creased as his memory returned to a lost world. He explained that Shandiin had been found at sunrise in a land of primitive people whose faith was tied to nature. When Khedran frowned in question, Zion explained as best he could.

"I guess they were like your Sundancers, here. No cities, no written laws. She lived among them for the first twelve years of her life, and then was taken from them to a more advanced society. I think she turned away from her early beliefs, but never accepted the civilization she was brought to join. She distrusts it. In fact, she's completely independent and stands apart from any culture I've ever known. Egypt said she defied orders even in the military. Frankly, I don't know if she's ever had any lasting allegiance to anything."

"She stood by me," Khedran responded quietly. "Even when she saw her people, the Chaine, falling in battle. She left her beloved people behind to fight and die, to save me." He lowered his head at the memory. "She did it, she told me later, because she believed I was necessary to save the rest of the people in this world. I could see what it cost her, but somehow she bore it, and kept her purpose. She lived a thousand years, Zion, for the single purpose of saving the people here. Now she is back to save us again. I call that an allegiance beyond lasting."

Zion had subsided at that, feeling that he and the King knew two different women...and the feeling was not comfortable.

He wondered still why Khedran had come along on this trip, knowing he might never return to his realm, his life...to the wife and daughter he so clearly loved.

He saw Shandiin lean forward to point something out to Roland, who switched on a speaker to ensure all could hear him. "Change coming up. Everyone hold on."

The world dropped away beneath them, a dizzying effect that faded when they saw the verdant valley floor below. The craft dropped to just above the treetops and followed a broad silver river flowing through its center. They came to a meadow that hugged a cliff wall. A village edged the meadow, low-slung rock dwellings in surprisingly good condition despite centuries of abandonment.

Shandiin spoke on the open microphone. "We called this the Valley of the Chaine. It's where the Chaine lived before we left for our hold in the northwest, a long time ago. We built well, I see. Roland, please land near the rock wall. We'll start from there."

"Do you think the goddess of the world is here?" Varady asked. She had explained their mission during the flight. Zion had expressed his concerns about human sacrifice, but none of the brothers had responded to that. "Where would she be? It's apparent no one has been here since you left."

"Just a little longer, Varady, please."

The skycraft settled to the grass and all six disembarked.

Khedran walked away from the rest to study the buildings, the first homes of the colony's people who would become known as the Chaine. He turned back to watch the others. His eyes followed Shandiin in her strange garb of blue jeans and denim jacket. He missed the leather and gold she had always worn, in her life before she'd taken the gods away. Before she had gone away with them.

But she was still her.

He turned away from that thought and, with Jael trailing him, walked to the front of the skycraft where his brother Varady stood gazing up at the cliff wall with interest.

"We are inside the Khaibara." Varady's voice held wonder. "The Wall of the World. This is where I had planned to go, before I found the Sundancers."

Shandiin walked past them. "It's full of caves. They're why we are here."

Varady frowned at her departing back. "I do not understand what to expect."

"Join the crowd." Zion appeared resigned as he followed his wife toward the cliff. "I'm never sure if she loves drama, or just likes surprises."

Khedran looked back in question at Roland, who waited by the skycraft. The man shook his head, not meeting his eyes. He seemed strangely in awe of the High King, but Khedran had too much on his mind to find out why. "Zion asked me to wait here," Roland explained.

Khedran turned to follow the others.

Shandiin walked into a dark and narrow cleft, not looking back. She turned on her flashlight, continuing to the end of the narrowing fissure. Her stomach clenched on stopping before the plain end-wall, still familiar after all these years. She closed her eyes and swallowed, waiting for the others to join her.

When she turned off her flashlight, they all watched a narrow line of light appear, tracing from the ground up the wall of rock, then across, then down. When it met the ground again, it was a narrow rectangle, the outline of a door. She touched its center.

The rock disappeared into a doorway filled with strange golden light. Three brothers recognized the color from a burning magic sky they had witnessed twenty years before, the day the gods left.

Shandiin walked into the light without comment to any of them. The others looked at each other, and then followed her into an arching cavern. The light emanated from a giant statue of a woman, created of fiery gold. She looked down on them with a familiar wicked smile, a sword in her hand.

Khedran stopped at Shandiin's side, gazing up at the majestic armored figure. "The Annals of Azlatan say there is somewhere in the world a likeness of each of the gods," he remembered aloud. "No one has seen Phaelon's. Daimaine's was destroyed. Liethe's remains at her Temple, but has lost its magic Light. Why is Chaos still here, with her own magic still burning?"

Shandiin shook her head. "I don't know, Khedran. I'm no longer Chaos. The planet...Hiraeth...must have her own reasons to keep the statue and the magic, and I know nothing about that. I came here because it's the place where I came to talk to Hiraeth, centuries ago...before the Chaine left this valley. When we were still mining what became known as Chaine gold."

Zion's voice was cold. "I don't like any of this. I don't like seeing your likeness on that magic statue, Shandiin, and I'm still concerned your goddess may want a human sacrifice."

"I was warned," Varady told him. "We understand the risk, Doctor Alexander. We've dealt with gods before."

Jael just nodded.

Khedran said nothing.

"There must be another way," Zion insisted.

"I wish there were." Shandiin turned to Zion, lifting her open hands. "It has to be one of her own, born here and holding her magic, not an outworlder. She mistrusts, even hates Earthers. We humans destroyed her sister we called Gaia, the spirit of Earth. She will not come to anyone but her own."

"Yet apparently she spoke to you. Why?"

"I don't know, Zion. She changed the reality of all those she believed came to rape and murder her, as they had Gaia. Perhaps she allowed me the truth because she needed a connection to ensure it wouldn't happen here, to her." She took a deep breath. "I never meant to come back. I don't know why she told me before I left, and then on the way back here, to bring the son to her. I am only certain the one she called the son must be one of these three brothers."

Zion was studying her grimly. "Are you sure you won't become Chaos again? I don't like this statue."

"It has to be a son. That is the term she used."

He waited a moment, thinking. "So how do we find her?"

"I think she will wake when the son draws near. I always felt her presence in there." Shandiin pointed to another door, one they hadn't noticed in their awe of the statue. It existed in the shadows of the magic fire, and seemed made of old wood and moss. She turned to the three brothers who watched her silently. "I hate this. I have no way of knowing if she will change you, at least one of you. But this is the only hope I have...to save your world."

Varady glanced at his brothers and began walking toward the door. Shandiin watched him in wonder; his simple courage in the face of need had always amazed her.

He disappeared inside the shadowed door.

Before long, Jael followed in concern.

Shandiin looked at Khedran, who shook his head at her wordlessly.

Shandiin bit her lip. "She isn't Daimaine."

He was silent.

Jael stepped half-out the door, his gaze on the High King. "She wants you."

Khedran turned his back on all of them.

Shandiin circled him, confronted him. "You have to," she pleaded. "It's the only way I can think of to save Azlatan...even more. Your whole *world*, Khedran."

Zion stepped behind her and gripped her shoulder. "Don't do this. Shandiin, stop now. He's done enough for this world already. Just as you have."

She paid no attention to Zion's words or his grasp. Her eyes were on Khedran's. No words passed between her and the High King, but their communion was clear. He was set against her.

Until he turned his head, as though listening to someone only he could hear. His lips parted as he listened, and his eyes widened. When his gaze returned to Shandiin, she saw a hard-won composure...and acquiescence.

He lifted a gentle hand to frame her cheek. "Goodbye, my love."

Then he turned and walked into that room with his brothers.

There was a detonation of brilliant light.

He did not come out again.

Varady and Jael only shook their heads when they returned. "He's gone," Varady told them. "There was a pillar of white light glowing in the center of that room. When he came in he walked into it. It flared, and the light vanished, and he was gone with it."

"Why didn't you follow him?"

"There was nowhere to follow him to." Varady took her shoulders, looked into her eyes. "He just vanished, Shandiin. She took him. He's gone."

She stared, then ran to the door herself.

And found only an empty, lightless room.

She whirled back to Jael. "You said she wanted Khedran. How did she tell you that?"

"It just came into my head. I knew it was her, speaking from the light."

She ran back into the empty room, turned on her flash to stare at every empty wall. "*Where is he?*" she demanded. "Where have you taken him, Hiraeth? Where are you? What are you doing? He was to become magic, *not become part of you!*"

Varady went to where Shandiin paced the empty room, a look of terror on her face. He stopped her gently, again placing his hands on her shoulders. "He is gone," he repeated gently. "I am sorry, Shandiin."

"I'm not leaving until he comes back!"

"I am certain he is not coming back here."

"Is your magic telling you that?"

"Shandiin, she spoke to me too. She said he is hers; he has always been hers, and she is what he needs."

"No." It was a whisper of anguish. "This can't be happening again."

"What do you mean?"

Her eyes were wild. "He never told anyone what Daimaine did to him. She said that too. Daimaine said he belonged to her. She was cruel, Varady. More brutal than you could believe." She pulled away from him and shoved her hands into her hair, turning in a circle, still searching for the one who was no longer there.

Zion had been silent since witnessing Khedran's parting words to Shandiin. He had watched her fall apart. Then he watched the others try to talk her down.

He watched them try over and over again, to no avail.

For hours.

He finally went to her. "Shandiin, calm down. Please. We knew this could happen."

She put her face in her hands to scrape away tears. Then she shook her head in agitation. "*You* thought it could happen. I never believed it, or I wouldn't have brought him here. I would never have just *given* him to her."

"He went willingly, at the end. There must have been a reason. You told me he would do anything to save his people. He must have gone so they could be saved."

Her eyes were wild. "You don't understand what I've done. I taught him to trust me from the time he was a child. He went because he still trusts me." She swallowed hard, and he saw such anguish it shocked him. "I listened to my head instead of my heart, Zion. I knew he would do anything for me, and I pushed him to go to her." She shoved her fingers through her hair, closed her eyes. "You should go. I'm not leaving him here. I'm not leaving without him."

He took a deep breath. "You are sending me away...so that you can wait for him?"

She didn't answer, but turned away to call out to Hiraeth once again.

He put a hand on her shoulder, compelling her to face him. "I'm never going to be enough, am I?"

She shrugged free. "I can't do this right now, Zion."

"I can't do this at all. Not anymore. I've always known I love you more than you love me, Shandiin. I thought I could love hard enough for the both of us. But I know now it's not enough. It will never be enough. You love him so much more, and I can't bear it. He's gone, but...I can't bear it."

He moved to leave. She managed to say "Zion..."

But he just shook his head and walked away.

She put her hands over her eyes, and hated herself, and turned back to call on Hiraeth again.

Jael was the last to give up on her.

Exhausted after her endless circling, Shandiin put her back to the wall and slid to the floor. Jael crouched on his heels in front of her. "Shandiin, I can't sense him. I am sure he is no longer in this world. Won't you come..." he read her continued denial, and sighed. "Do you want one of us to stay here with you?"

She shook her head. "No. I want none of you. Just go."

Her eyes were fierce with grief, and he saw truth. They couldn't make her return without using force. None of them were willing to use force. Not on her.

Sadly, he walked out of the cave to where the others waited by the skycraft.

They left her there alone.

PART III: THE SON OF RHIATHE

Love is strong as death;
jealousy is cruel as the grave.
—*Song of Solomon*

CHAPTER 13

Varady broke the news.

Marre simply sank into a chair, her hands over her face, while Shandi stood in shocked disbelief. "He can't just be gone," the Princess cried.

Varady only looked at her sadly, and she whirled away, then came back to her mother and knelt beside her. "He's not gone," she insisted. "He can't be, Mother. Stop crying!"

"But I knew it." Marre gulped in a breath, looked into her daughter's face with truth in her eyes. "I felt him leave. I have always felt his presence, since...since the day I took the Star Blade from him all those years ago. I have always felt his presence, even when we were apart. He has always been a part of me. But now I can no longer feel him. He is no longer in the world."

Shandi stared in disbelief. Then she stood to face Varady. "Take me there," she demanded.

"The skycraft has already returned to base. And he isn't there, Shandi."

"Shandiin is. I swear she will pay for this."

"Stop it." Varady took her shoulders as he had Shandiin's, looking into emerald eyes so like her father's. "Vengeance will solve nothing. And you know in your heart she didn't force him to go. No one could force your father into something like this, not even Shandiin. He made a choice. For Azlatan."

"How does this help Azlatan? We need him here."

"We don't know yet. But I don't believe he would have gone except to save his people."

Shajii burst in, Roinn following. Shajii ran to Shandi, reached to take her in her arms. "I heard. I saw Roland getting into the skycraft before it left, and he told me. I am so sorry."

But Shandi pushed away from her friend, her face hard. "I am going there. I am going to where he went, where she is. Will you go with me, Shajii?"

"Shandi, we cannot. Roinn says the Valley of the Chaine is very far, and he does not know exactly where. His people left there before he was born."

"No." Shandi turned to Roinn. "We will find it. You will take me."

He looked into her eyes. He started to say something but shook his head. Started over. "I am so sorry, Princess. I cannot." There was grief in his voice, and it was for her.

"Varady, how could you leave Shandiin there all alone?" Danon asked from the doorway.

Shandi spun to him, furious. "You worry about *her?* What about the fate of your High King, Compatri? Traitor!" she shoved past him and ran from the room.

Danon watched her go, then went to Marre.

"Are you going to be all right?" he asked her.

"No. But there is nothing you can do about it." She reached out to Varady. "Please take care of Shandi. She was so angry with Khedran when last they spoke, and he...he was in despair because of it. I think Shandi is using anger to avoid facing her own guilt, and I can't help her with that. Not right now."

Varady bit his lip. Gifted with his bloodline's empathy, he had understood a great truth in that strange cave, when the High King had said goodbye to his greatest love. He couldn't tell that to Marre. "My gift does not work on Shandi," Varady reminded her. "And she refused Shajii."

His gaze turned to Roinn, because he also understood what Roinn had never admitted, even to himself. "I think you are the one to help her, Roinn."

Roinn frowned.

Astute Shajii glared at him for hesitating.

So Roinn went in search of the Princess.

Roinn was familiar with Penumbra, but he had never entered the private chambers of the High Princess.

He halted outside her door. Hearing nothing, seeing the door ajar, he pushed it open tentatively.

She stood at the window with her back to him. "Go away."

"If you wish. But I am concerned for you, Shandi."

When she didn't answer, he continued. "I wasn't there when your father left the others in that cave. But I do not believe he would do anything just because Shandiin told him to. You must know that whatever he chose, he did it for his own reasons."

She turned to face him then, and he winced at the despair in the eyes of the proud Princess. "I'm terrified that this is my fault. I hurt him. He...he must have thought I no longer loved him." She took a step toward him, then covered her face with her hands and sobbed.

Roinn looked at her in disbelief, at the beautiful warrior he had believed cold and contained and far beyond his carefully hidden love for her. After a moment he went to her. "Stop. Please stop this. We are at a crossroads in history right now. Nothing you did, nothing anyone did, would make your father turn his back on his people in the face of that. You know him better than that."

When she shook her head, hands still over her face, he hardened his heart because it was the only way he knew to help her. "You have never been stupid before, Shandi."

She dropped her hands to stare up at him in shock, tears still streaming.

"Your father saw to it you were educated with Chaine logic. Now it seems you have forgotten all of it. How can you think your father has walked away from his people when they need him? I am disappointed in you."

Nothing could have stunned her more. It cut, even through her grief. "You don't understand."

"What is there to understand? Your insane belief that he went off and killed himself because of your judgement of him? Do you really think he is that weak, this wise man who has led Azlatan longer than you have been alive?"

"He...he is not weak. She was a goddess, she used magic..."

"You know better, and I know her well. She never used magic except to fight magic. And apparently you don't understand *amhara*, Shandi. Your people seem to believe love can be changed according to circumstance. The connection of *amhara* is not subject to any outside condition, but only to the people involved, and it is by nature honorable, because respect cannot exist without honor. Shandiin and Khedran are both honorable *amharen;* they will not break oath to cause hurt to others they love."

"But he admitted..."

Roinn shook his head. "Your father is the most honorable man I have ever known. According to Varady, he tread on the edge of oath before it was given; he was betrothed, but not married. Knowing your father, I am sure he has paid for it since...even without your knife in his heart."

She recoiled, grimacing, before she looked away. "But he still loves her, and he is married now."

"He honors your mother, Shandi, and he loves her. That his *amharen* lives yet in his heart has nothing to do with her, or you. What someone feels is not subject to another's demand."

She wiped away the last tears and looked down. He waited her out while she struggled between thought and emotion. She finally shuddered, shoulders dropping. "You are right. About all of it." After a moment she went on, her voice trembling. "I am sorry you are disappointed in me, because I have so badly wanted your respect. I know you must see me as a...a foolish young girl, and I have so badly hoped for...something more."

He waited for her to look up. When she didn't, he gently lifted her chin so he could look into her beautiful eyes. "Shandi, doing one foolish thing does not make you a foolish girl. I have watched you grow up, seen how hard you work to be all you can be. Yes, you are young...especially from my very long point of view...but you are the most wonderful, the most amazing woman I have ever known. I..." he stopped himself and began to turn away. "I should go now."

"Was that really what you started to say, Roinn?"

There was still a tremor in her voice, and he couldn't bear the thought that he had hurt her, even for her own benefit. His eyes told her the truth. "No."

"Please." Her voice was almost a whisper. "Please tell me I am not foolish...for hoping you were going to tell me you care for me. And by all the gods, I don't want you to go."

He opened his arms then, and when she came to him, she filled his heart.

Jael waited until he knew the High Queen was alone before he went to her.

She'd always been good to him. Brought to Penumbra as a child, hated by everyone but his mother and his brother the King, he had found Marre's kindness a great comfort. He understood her love for Khedran as few others could, because he saw things others did not.

His gift was seeing. He wished sometimes he did not.

He found Marre in the chambers she had shared with her husband for more than twenty years. She opened the door to his knock but did not smile. "Jael, I am not fit company right now."

"I have to tell you he is all right."

"What?"

"He's all right, Marre. The others think the worst, but I don't."

"Why can't I feel his presence, then?"

"He is not the same. But he is not dead. He is part of the world now. He will help us fight what is coming, as he always has."

"I don't want him to be part of the world. I want my husband back." She slammed the door in his face.

The moon rose over the canyon wall and filled the valley with silver, but Shandiin didn't see the beauty.

She wandered through the trees to the river, to watch its dark and sparkling mirror beneath the star-filled sky, and saw only emptiness. She sat on the bank for a while, then rose in restless pain to walk back the way she had come.

To the cave. Using her flashlight, which was failing, she went again to the room where she had last seen Khedran. When the light flickered out, she stood in darkness for a long while.

"Give him back," she whispered, because her voice had given out from her demands. "Give him back, Hiraeth."

There was still no answer.

She left and went to lie in the grass. Staring up at the stars netted in the treetops, she wondered if her spirit would find his if she could die.

She was back where she had started, a thousand years before he was even born, before the Earth's ending. She'd had no purpose and no hope before turning to find him smiling at her on a city street corner while strangers passed around them. The memory of that brief meeting had given her an inexplicable sense of hope until her untrusting nature had put it away.

But a thousand years later he'd returned to her in a vision, on a snow-ridden mountaintop under a cathedral of stars. That same night, his mortal being came to the new world that was now her home. She'd allowed herself to believe his birth brought a bright spirit with meaning she could finally accept as truth. She had allowed the return of hope.

For this? For him to simply disappear into the void?

She curled up on the ground while the stars wheeled overhead. She waited.

Captain Egypt Alexander was on the bridge of the *Aztlan* when Zion's call came in. It was flagged private, so she took her device to the observation room where she had once had a conversation with the High Princess.

"You aren't going to believe this," Zion began.

"Try me. Like Carroll's Queen, I've believed many impossible things before breakfast."

"Try this one. This planet that created gods to control the colony is like a goddess herself. She's like mythical Gaia, the goddess of Earth. Shandiin dragged the High King and his brothers to where this goddess was, despite all my warnings against it. The goddess took the High King, Egypt. The goddess literally took him. He has vanished. I believe he was a sacrifice to her."

Egypt was silent for a long moment, staring out the window at the planet below, thinking of the beautiful King who had given her a glimpse of compassion within greatness, a sense of awe that she did not understand, but had hoped mightily to explore. "I am sorry to hear that. But there had to be a good reason for her to take him...and for him to go."

"She thought he would be given some kind of magic to save the world. The King didn't want to go, but at the last he went anyway. He said goodbye to her. He called her his love, and said goodbye. And then he just vanished." Zion took a deep breath. "Shandiin fell apart, Egypt. No one could talk her into leaving that cave where he disappeared." She heard him swallow. "She sent me away."

"You left her there?"

"Dammit, Egypt, don't you get it? She sent me away! It's like I didn't matter. I always knew I loved her more but...that drove home. It's clear he's what she really wants. I can't take it anymore,

Egypt. I told her how I felt. She could have stopped me, but she barely bothered to say my name. It's over."

Zion was her family, one of the very few that were left. She had worried over his marriage to Shandiin, because she had watched Shandiin's valiant battle against the loss of her greater love.

She sighed. "I understand. I am sorry, Zion."

"So am I." She heard his exhale. "The others kept reassuring me she would be alright when they left her behind. But I couldn't even let myself care."

"She can take care of herself."

"I can't…" There was a pause, while he gathered himself. "Egypt, the mission is what we have to concentrate on. Apparently, the King's brother Jael is a psychic. He has visions, and thinks the Earthers will somehow attack Hiraeth with weapons of mass destruction. Shandiin believed him. That's why she took Khedran to the goddess. But I don't see how that's possible. Were you able to decipher the message Canard sent to the *Earthstar?*"

"Yes. He told them he had taken treasure from a planet that needed to be destroyed because it is full of witches. He asked when they were expected to arrive in this system, so I'm sure he'd already given them the coordinates. They've been trying to communicate with him ever since."

"Witches, huh? That's their favorite word for anyone genetically engineered. He figured out the colony's source, then."

"The Princess was a big clue."

"Damn. I'm afraid this is on me. I took her to Ben Canard, thinking she could domesticate him. Instead he went all Jack Sparrow and kidnapped her."

"You couldn't know he was going to do that. Don't start the guilt trip on yourself, Zion. What's your next move?"

"Khedran was supposed to be spokesman for the planet. I don't know who they will choose in his place. Egypt, can you come dirtside and help me? I'm almost afraid to face the High Queen. She didn't like to look at me even before her husband disappeared. I think the resemblance bothers her. I think she will relate better to you."

"Do you? She wasn't happy that I flirted with Khedran."

"I don't think that will matter. She must be used to women falling in love with him. It was part of his...mystique."

"I was not and am not in love with any man, Zion. Not even that one." She considered. "Sarnath would be a better choice to help you."

"Maybe. But I think the Queen will relate better to a woman."

"All right, then. Sarnath can skipper the ship as well as I can. I will come in on the *Good Conduct* in about an hour."

"You're going to use a warcraft?"

"Skycraft are no fun. I want speed and weaponry. I'll tell my crew to have the other warcraft ready for action as well, since Shandiin believes the others are somehow going to show up and attack."

"I don't see how that can happen. Do you really think the Premier will order you to nuke the planet?"

"Do you remember the 'Spectacle of Retribution?' Anything's possible with a hierarchy that believes in punishing their own people by eviscerating them in public. Premier Canard hasn't tried to contact me yet, and he's out of luck if he gives me that order. The key people on my crew are handpicked by Roland, and loyal to our little family. But the Premier is likely to be pissed off about his brother."

"And what will you tell him if he asks about that?"

"I plan to lie and say that I killed him when he abducted the Princess and endangered the mission. But I really don't give a shit about him. I'm sick of our agreement with the Earthers. We have to find a way to get around the Premier and save those people...and I'd like to live in Azlatan myself."

It was a moment before he responded. "Me too. I don't think Shandiin would be happy anywhere else anyway. If she ever is happy again."

"I thought you were done with her."

"Yes. But neither anger nor resolve change the feelings underneath. Only time can do that." He sighed. "I think I understand now how torn Khedran must have felt when she walked back into his life. I hope it doesn't take me twenty years to get over her."

"Do you think his feelings about her return had anything to do with his choice to...sacrifice himself?"

"I don't know. I don't understand his kind of heroism, Egypt. I'm a scientist, not a warrior, not a King born to put his world ahead of himself or those he loves." He exhaled. "It's all too damn complicated. People are too damn complicated. I'll stick to math and science. I'll see you soon, Egypt."

"Yes." She hung up and sat for a moment regarding the planet below her. *A world full of witches, is it? I think it's time we stood up for ourselves...and our descendants. Maybe Shandiin is right about our good intentions being dangerous to them.*

The woman called Kimhi was very tired, but too worried to sleep.

She had spent the day trying to convince the people of Xanthe that they should approach Azlatan for help.

Xanthe had lost most of its population after the Prophecy War twenty years before. Many of those not killed in the fighting had come home thoroughly defeated by the knowledge they had been tricked, that their God of Order was false and was now gone. Many others had become citizens of Azlatan after swearing the required oath to its High King. They now lived under his law and his autonomous rule; the King could override anything. That had sounded like a dangerous kind of authority, but Kimhi had since learned the High King was a man of principles and could be trusted.

The people of Xanthe had been bred for centuries for the purpose of war, under the laws of the God of Order and his Tahmond. The giant Hierarch Tahmond had fallen on the last day of the

Prophecy War, at the hand of the High King himself...who had then freed all who followed him.

There was no more God of Order in Xanthe. But there was no order, either. No leader had come forward to help them rebuild their society. Kimhi did what she could, but she didn't believe she was a true leader. Now they faced a disease that was racing through the population and decimating it even further, and they did not have the medicine to treat it. Kimhi was almost certain Azlatan did.

Staring at the ceiling, she became aware of a strange white light growing in his room. She sat up abruptly, the hair on her neck prickling.

The light was somehow outside of her, and inside of her head. She grabbed at her hair, terrified.

"Don't be afraid," a voice said from the light. "I have come to help you."

Kimhi stared around, gulping fear.

"There is a place not far from here," the voice said, "where you can get the medicine you need to help your people. I will lead you there."

Zion watched the sleek warcraft skate over the base, then wheel in playful circles before Egypt decided to land. The ship dropped smoothly, hovered a moment, then touched down.

The canopy lifted and Egypt climbed out. She wasn't wearing her Captain's uniform this time, which Zion thought was telling. She wore jeans and a tee shirt of plain army green. Both fit her body like a glove, and he had to smile, for her body was amazing. All six feet, three inches of her was curved not with fat but with trained muscle. She generally wore the uniform to hide that gorgeous body, because of reaction from the naturals she served with.

She swaggered over and met his grin with her own.

"Wow. First time I've seen you like this in a long time."

"Get used to it. I might even go after the King's brothers. They are lovely."

"Varady is happily married, Egypt. And Varady told me Jael is a confirmed bachelor, not for lack of women who want him. I don't think even you could penetrate his psychic armor. He's like a saint, and an enigma to everyone who knows him."

"Well, shit. Isn't that just my luck?" She turned to look around. "Where is Roland? Did he hook up with that Chaine woman who confronted me?"

He laughed. "Anyone would think you like soap operas. You've been in space too long."

"You got that right. Way too long for good behavior. Do you have anything to drink?"

"Sure." They turned and walked companionably toward his quarters.

"Have you heard anything about Shandiin?" she asked.

Zion shook his head. "No. And despite everything, I'll admit I'm ashamed of leaving Shandiin alone in the wilderness in that condition."

"She rather demanded it, didn't she? And she'll use the time to get her head straight. You know she never stays down for long."

He said nothing.

She stopped him, and they turned to face each other. "She was really that bad?" she asked.

He nodded. "I've never seen her like that, even when she returned to us from her thousand years there."

She considered. "Then perhaps I will have to go there and straighten her out."

"I can only hope you could. But I need you here more than there."

She frowned, noticing an aura at the corner of her vision, and turned toward it. He followed her gaze to see a light approaching from the desert.

"Egypt...that's like the white light I saw in the cave."

But the light faded as it neared the blazing beams around the base perimeter, and they saw a lone figure on horseback coming toward them.

The horse tried to shy at the strange surroundings, but his rider calmed him and continued to ride toward them. His rider was a woman, her dark blond hair scooped back, wearing rough laborer's clothing. She surveyed the camp in amazement, then showed even more amazement on seeing the two of them.

She halted in front of them. "Hello. I am Kimhi of Xanthe. Are the gods back? I think I have been led here by a god."

Zion took the horse's bridle to keep him still. "You are welcome, Kimhi of Xanthe, but I don't think it's any god you've known that brought you here. I am Zion Alexander, and this is Egypt Alexander. Can we help you?"

Kimhi exhaled gladly. "Yes!" She dismounted, then did a double take at dark and stunning Egypt, who seemed to loom over her, her eerie emerald eyes aglow under the perimeter lighting.

Overwhelmed by her, Kimhi turned to the handsome man with the same strange emerald eyes. She stared. "Are you the High King of Azlatan?"

"No. Just a relative. How can we help you?"

Kimhi glanced from one to the other, calling on her innate courage and her people's need. "My people are dying of a terrible disease. The god in the light said to come to you."

Zion merely nodded. "How far is Xanthe?"

Kimhi looked behind her. "I do not know. It is that way, as the bird flies..." she pointed, then turned back, her brown eyes wide. "But I think I covered too much ground to be possible. I think it was magic."

Zion sighed, still coming to terms with magic. "Please come with me. I am sure you are tired after your journey, and I can give you refreshment. Egypt?"

"Yeah. I'll round up Roland and Dr. Sato, and we'll join you in a minute."

Zion gestured for their visitor to come along. "You can tell me about the disease. Once I know the symptoms, I will know what medicines to send. Are you the leader of Xanthe?"

Kimhi frowned nervously. "That is what the light said. So I guess so."

Zion remembered Shandiin's request for contact with Xanthe. "Then perhaps you can help us, too. I will explain how."

Chapter 14

The High Queen awaited the skycraft when it landed again in Cabre. She stood in a black uniform with a phalanx of her Guard at her back.

"I'm going to leave you here," Roland reminded his passengers, "because I have things to manage on base. Call if you need me before tomorrow."

"Thanks." Zion spoke off-handedly. His eyes were on the Queen; he noted that the Princess was not present. "Here we go," he muttered as though steeling himself, and followed Egypt from the skycraft.

The skycraft had drawn a crowd. He and Egypt made sure to acknowledge the people with a smile and a wave as they walked to the Queen, where Zion bowed low. "Your Highness," he greeted her, and looked into the lovely lavender eyes that held pain behind their schooled poise.

She nodded to him, and he saw that her gaze rested more comfortably when she turned to Egypt. "Well come to you both. Please join me in Penumbra."

Curious, they followed through Penumbra's first floor to the sea-walk, a long hall level with the sea that crashed just below its windows. From there they were led to a room that made Egypt exclaim in delight. "It's like a greenhouse!"

"My King's design," Marre explained. "There is a glass roof above." Marre glanced around at the trees, at the flowers, and led them to a table set for a meal. "This was his favorite place, because it is always bright."

"Unlike your banquet hall," Zion noted.

"At least that room now has light, though the candles and lanterns there are not as bright as Daimaine's starlight could sometimes be." She looked down for a moment, sighed. "How he hated that place."

But the High Queen quickly brought herself back to her duties. "Please be seated. I know we are here to talk business, but I would like to get to know you both."

"Will the Princess be joining us?" Egypt asked.

"I do not think so. I have not seen her since yesterday. Would you care for some tea?"

They sat down and the outworlders watched Marre dutifully fulfill her role as hostess with tea and food, until Egypt couldn't stay quiet another minute.

"I'm sorry about your husband," she said in her forthright manner. "He was...he is a great man."

Marre hesitated as she regarded the beautiful woman across from her, then set down her cup. "Like you, I do not know how to speak of him, present tense or past. I do not know if he is alive or dead." Her attention moved to Zion. "You did not come back to Cabre with Varady and Jael yesterday. Why not, Zion? Did you go back for Shandiin?"

"No. I did not."

"I'll check on her later," Egypt added.

But Marre's eyes were still fastened on Zion. "Why did you leave her there?"

"That was her choice. She refused to leave."

Marre thought for a moment. "Do you think she was waiting for him to return from that cave where he disappeared?"

"Yes."

"Do you think he will?"

"I don't know, Your Highness. I am sorry, I cannot even guess. I am not familiar with magic."

Marre just nodded and picked up a spoon to stir her tea. "He hated magic, and it finally took him." Suddenly her hand trembled, and she dropped the spoon. "It took him. Forgive me, I need a moment."

They watched uncomfortably as she took a shuddering breath, lifting her napkin to her eyes. When she replaced it in her lap, the High Queen had returned.

"I have not told anyone about his disappearance," she said then. "The only people who know are those we consider family. I am unsure what or when to tell Azlatan."

Zion took point. "You are wise to realize it would be premature to tell Azlatan anything. There are too many questions that are unanswered. It would cause instability in a time when it's most needed. Azlatan's government has become important to me, and I am hopeful that Egypt and I can help you moving forward."

He saw Egypt's questioning look, and addressed both women. "I had a long talk with the High King in the hours before we took that recent journey. I learned much from him." He turned to the Queen, "I'm sure you already know everything about the King's policies, but I would like to summarize for Egypt, if I may?"

At the Queen's permissive nod, he continued. "Education is the High King's first tenet. It starts young where it focuses on the gifts of free will, reason, and personal accountability. The goal is teach youth responsibility for their own actions and their resultant impact on others. To my surprise, they are also taught how to recognize and bypass manipulative or self-aggrandizing behaviors." At Egypt's lifted eyebrow, he added, "Study of topics more familiar to us, Egypt, come later and within that same frame of reference."

He thought a moment before continuing. "Second priority is government. Khedran's belief is the only purpose for government is to serve the people. His Dominion royalty are bureaucratic servants of the people overseeing operations with the assistance of the Black Guard. The Guard comes from the people as specially trained leaders and defenders, not controllers. Young people see them as heroes they want to emulate." Zion smiled a little. "He said frankly he saw that as another way to unify Azlatan."

Egypt was frowning. "So what is the High King? Is he just the ultimate bureaucrat?"

He glanced at Marre, who gestured for him to answer.

Zion nodded respectfully and turned back to Egypt. "No. He is the ultimate lawmaker and judge, and in that capacity has made the people of Azlatan far more powerful than any warrior or member of royalty. They are given guidance by laws kept purposely few, and can go to any member of the Guard if there is suspicion of corruption at any level. The High King's most common judgment is against those who think they are in power instead of in service. Dominion royalty is respected but dares not overstep the law for all people lest they be brought before him."

He turned back to the High Queen. "He also told me, Your Highness, that you helped him build this government, and he had faith in your ability to govern...if he could no longer do so."

Marre stared in shock. "He knew he was leaving?"

"He knew it was possible he wouldn't be coming back."

She seemed to take this in, shock and sorrow clearly visible. Zion's heart went out to her, and he placed a tentative hand over hers. "I would like to help you face this, Your Highness, if I may."

She withdrew her hand and looked away. "I don't want to refuse your help. But I am completely unsure of the people you have brought with you."

Egypt leaned forward and tapped the table in front of her. "Zion and I are not like the people you are very right to be unsure about."

Zion frowned at her. "You shouldn't..."

Egypt turned on him. "Don't tell me what I shouldn't. You wanted my help, and this is it. Zion, you have tried so hard to cooperate with the Earther government, but I know you don't trust them any more than I do. One of them abducted the Princess Shandi. He wanted to destroy this planet. I find that disturbing, don't you?"

She turned back to Marre. "I plan to ask asylum here when we have resolved the immigration issue...or the war issue. I understand your sage has prophesied that those of Earth will attack your world."

"But you are Captain of the starship. You would leave your command?" Marre asked in surprise.

"No." Egypt glanced from Marre to Zion, then back. "My people were carefully chosen, as were Commander Bond's soldiers, and they will follow me. I told them my intent before I left the ship. If there is war as your sage predicts, you may consider the *Aztlan* your weapon." She lifted her chin. "A very valuable and powerful weapon."

Zion leaned back. "Egypt, are you turning against the people of your home planet?"

"Against their leader, yes. You should too, Zion. After everything you agreed to, Canard went behind your back. You can't trust them."

Marre looked from one to the other. "You are both welcome in Azlatan. We would make a home for you, here."

"Would Khedran have done that?" Zion asked her.

"Yes. Especially since you are forming an alliance with us. I very much agree we need your help against this threat that only you understand."

"You have it," Egypt said. "That includes the soldiers we brought with us." She turned to Zion. "Zion, I made my own decision about breaking our agreement after meeting Shandi. I knew immediately Shandi is one of us." She looked back at Marre. "As are you, Your Highness. We all share a family tree of strength and courage, a family that believes in honor and justice. Your High King...and by God, I hope he comes back...your High King epitomizes what a leader should be. I would follow him through hell. And I will follow the Queen he trusted to rule in his absence."

Marre's eyes were too bright, but she managed a smile. "Thank you. This would be best addressed at the Assemblage that Khedran has already ordered. You bring me hope, Captain Alexander. But you only met my King once. How could you..."

"Please call me Egypt. I know a lot about your King because Shandiin told me. And I trust her, and her wisdom. It only took one meeting for me to accept everything she told me about him." She turned to Zion. "What say you?"

After a moment he nodded agreement. "Shandiin tried to explain about the High King, but I'd thought she was exaggerating, or that she had been taken over by this planet's magic. But after everything I have learned since our arrival, I feel the same as Egypt."

"It took him some time and a lot of hard work," Marre agreed, "to arrange these things to everyone's satisfaction. He learned before the war that the Dominion Kings could be a threat to the security of Azlatan. He uses the people themselves to keep that in check. They know they can call on him for justice." She looked away. "I don't know what we will do without him."

Egypt sat back. "You will follow his strategy. You know it best."

"You said has already called an Assemblage of the Dominion Kings?" Zion asked.

"Yes. Although now the general reference is Dominion royalty; since the Prophecy War, Khedran has designated Queens as well as Kings. It will be held here, at Stareven."

"That's the beginning of your warm season, am I right?"

"Yes." Marre watched curiously as Zion reached into his pocket for a communication device and held it to his ear. He listened for a moment, looked at Egypt and handed it to her. "Did you leave yours behind?" he asked.

"I'm always losing that thing. Hey, Sarnath, what's up?" Listening through a long explanation, she sat up straight. "Shit. Okay, okay. Roland's guess was true, then. Tell Magdalena to stay on it, and tell her she's a damn good spy." She handed the device back to Zion with a grimace.

"They were cannibalizing the *Earthstar* to build transports just as Roland suspected," she told Zion. "They weren't going to Earth, though, but to the back of the moon. One of the ass-headed governments had a secret base there, and apparently an accident killed all its personnel, but left behind plenty of usable equipment…along with nuclear weapons. They've been building warcraft on that base. Zion, are you positive they don't have your FTL drive?"

He shook his head. "I don't see how. It's a quantum tunnel drive, and they don't have that capacity…" his voice trailed off and he frowned as though a new thought had occurred to him. "They do have an AI, but it's a long shot that it would have developed FTL like ours did. I'll have Sarnath look into that further, though I still don't think it's possible."

"Is Sarnath more of the family Shandiin told us about?" Marre asked Egypt.

"Sarnath is, yes. There are only four of us left."

"I am sorry that you have lost family members." She slid a glance at Zion. "Now I understand why you seem very sad."

"We lost our family members a very long time ago," Egypt noted. "Zion's concerns are more recent. It's hard not to be sad when you end a marriage."

Zion scowled. "Damn it, Egypt, that's no one's else's business."

Marre sighed. "That is true," she agreed softly. "But I believe I understand your loss, Dr. Alexander."

Their eyes met briefly. This time Egypt kept her thoughts to herself.

Shajii was surprised to find Shandi's door locked, and pounded on it impatiently. "C'mon," she yelled. "The sun has been up for hours. That's enough sadness, Shandi. Come out."

"Go away, Shajii."

Shajii frowned. She'd seen her friend devastated by the apparent loss of her father, and she was determined to help her through it. "Nope. Not going, Shandi." She pounded some more.

The door opened a crack, and Shandi peered out. "I am all right," she hissed. "Go away, Shajii."

"You need to come out. You need to be cheered up."

"No, I don't. Truly. Roinn came and convinced me that Father did what he felt was right and necessary. We think he'll be back. Now go away."

"You should know I am not leaving you alone like this." Shajii put her shoulder into the door and was inside the room before Shandi could stop her.

Where she halted dead in her tracks.

Roinn stood glaring down at her, wearing only breeches. He pointed a finger in her face. "If you say one word of this to anyone, I will personally cut off your head and shove it up your behind. Do you understand that, Shajii?"

Shajii stared at him, then at Shandi, who wore only a robe; she peered through a bedroom doorway and saw Shandi's bed, in disarray.

She started laughing and couldn't stop.

Shandi picked up a vase, yanked out the flowers and dumped the water over Shajii's head, then huffed off to get dressed.

Shajii was laughing even harder while she pushed her wet hair back from her face. "It's about time, Roinn! I've been watching you two give soulful looks to each other's backs for ages."

"Not a word," he warned her again.

She stepped back, grinning up at him. "Oh, you know I won't tell anyone. But you'll have to marry her now. She is the High Princess, and you can't just hop into bed with royalty without repercussions."

Shandi stalked back in her black uniform. "Why not? Shandiin did."

Shajii's laughter renewed. "Ouch. You just can't trust these wild Chaine, can you?"

Shandi shook her head. "He does not have to marry me. I know the Chaine don't believe in marriage. He is my *amharen,* and that is enough."

She looked up in surprise when Roinn pulled her to him, his eyes on hers so full of love it made Shajii catch her breath. "Shandi, I would marry you in a heartbeat. I know your realm would expect it for us to be together. But yes, we are *amharen* even though I would not be an acceptable husband. You should only marry royalty."

Shandi sniffed. "Azlatan's royalty is no more than a duty of leadership. The only leadership I would ever marry happens to be The Chaine."

They didn't notice when Shajii left, so they didn't see the happy tears in her eyes as she closed the door behind her.

Dominion royalty began arriving within the week, too curious about the summons from Penumbra to wait until the actual meeting date.

They were surprised to find the High Queen with two others constantly beside her: the outworlders who, she said, were going to help them against a possible invasion. One looked like the High King but was not mistaken for him, as those of Azlatan had always recognized the true King's presence.

Magnificent Egypt had most of them reeling almost as much as the magical High Princess did. But while entertaining important men at dinner each evening, Shandi played her part with great care, exactly as her father had taught her.

If Marre wondered at her daughter's return of equilibrium, she watched her with Roinn attentively at her side, and also drew her own conclusions.

No one noticed Egypt's reaction when first she met the man named Roinn. She had frozen for a moment, seeing his height, his long auburn hair braided with leather and gold. She'd remembered a vision she'd had when her ship had first passed through the wormhole many years before. But she had quickly realized two things: that he was not the man she had dreamed of, and that he belonged to Shandi. Once again, she set that dream aside.

Egypt was pleased that there were now Queens among the Dominion royalty, not only the Kings Shandiin had reported from her tenure. Marre explained the illusion of male supremacy had begun to wane when The Chaine came to Azlatan, and had fallen the day she herself took the Star Blade to become High Queen more than twenty years before. Khedran's deliberate stand on the issue had cemented the change in Azlatan.

Brend, Dominion King of Ordhold since Khedran had removed his brother for treason twenty years before, walked into Penumbra a full week before he was expected, with a great snowcat at his side.

The royal family and the outworlders were busily in discussion in the atrium, so Danon saw him first. He greeted the Dominion King and kneeled to honor the white cat that came nearly to Brend's waist. "Majia, is it really you?"

The cat's golden eyes blinked and he purred in answer, a deep rumble heard by all those who had followed him to greet Brend.

Shandi, having known Brend all her life, greeted him with a kiss on the cheek. He blushed and she laughed. "It's just me, Brend."

"I think you do that to me on purpose," he retorted. "My father always said I blush like a girl. Hello, Roinn. I hear Shandiin is back. Is she here?"

"No." Roinn frowned, puzzled.

"I expect she'll come in with Khedran, then. He caught me by surprise. I don't know why he told me to bring Majia."

Silence fell like a stone. Brend looked around, obviously confused.

"Where did you see Khedran?" Danon demanded.

"In Ordhold, of course. I left immediately, as he asked. I thought he would be back by now, though he said he had some stops to make."

Marre came, to look up at him almost desperately. "He was in Ordhold? He is well?"

"Yes and yes." Brend looked around in confusion. "What is going on?"

At first Shandiin thought she was dreaming.

The forest was washed in emerald light. She sat up blinking and saw a woman who had died more than fifty years before.

High Queen Rhiathe, wife of Allasar, mother of Khedran, stood in that magic light watching her.

The light dwindled to become a soft aura around Rhiathe, who wore a long gown of forest green. Her long earth-dark hair was plaited with gold and crystal, leaf and shell. Her moss-green eyes were full of magic.

"Hello, Shandiin." Her voice was that of the beloved Navajo grandmother Shandiin had lost so very long ago.

It took a moment of realization. Then Shandiin shoved to her feet. "Hiraeth? Is it you?"

The goddess, if that's what she was, just smiled. "Yes. I am also Rhiathe."

"Where is Khedran?" Shandiin demanded. "What have you done?"

Rhiathe lifted her hands, and a shimmer of green followed them. "I am sorry you were left to grieve. The son has been on a journey to the world from which you came, to witness its ending and learn the cause. It has been hard on him, Shandiin. He has changed, carrying those innumerable deaths. For everything that is behind him, and what remains ahead, he will need you. I knew you would wait, and that you would help him. I told you long ago you are necessary to the son."

Shandiin stared. Khedran was an empath. She could imagine his agony, experiencing the extinction of billions. "How could you do that to him? Why did you do it?"

When Rhiathe only gazed at her sadly, Shandiin exploded. "Damn you! You didn't need to tear out his heart! Why didn't you just stop the Earthers from coming here? What is it you expect him to do…me to do? For God's sake…why the hell are you posing as his mother?"

"I am not posing. You knew me once as Rhiathe, and I knew you as my friend. I came, born as a mortal woman, to bear the son. Being mortal was difficult and grim. My death was a relief, but I had to rest for a time and could only follow you in dreams." She smiled. "I depended on you in my absence, and you did not fail me. You did not fail him."

Shandiin was stunned, her thinking still fogged. She drew a deep breath, battling useless fury. "So…you've been asleep. But you're awake now. You can stop them. You can stop the Earthers who are coming now."

"I cannot stop their technology. It is a threat. It is up to you and Khedran to stop it."

"Dammit, how?" But Shandiin could see that Rhiathe's magic light was fading, and she cried out from the heaviness of her heart. "Rhiathe…you sent him to a dying world, and made him suffer the death of billions. How could you put such a burden on your own son?"

"He is not just my son. He is also the son of those who came before, and they saw the necessity." She lifted a warning hand when Shandiin began to speak again. "He needs you, Shandiin. You have another hard road ahead, and it will not be easy for you. He has been changed with knowledge that has brought him darkness. You are his light. Promise me you will not leave him again."

Shandiin scowled. "I damned well won't leave him again as long as he needs me. Where is he?"

Rhiathe tilted her head as she faded away. "He is where he left you. Go to him, Shandiin."

The cave.

She was running as soon as she thought it, through the moonlit forest, into the cleft in the cliff, and through the door of golden light.

She found him sitting hard against the statue's base. His legs were drawn against his chest, arms wrapped around them, his forehead on his knees.

She knelt in front of him and placed her hands over his. "Khedran, it's me. Look at me."

He lifted his head slowly, his fall of black hair tangled around his face. His eyes were stunned and dulled to jade. He stared at her for a very long time. Recognition came slowly, gradually.

When he finally spoke, it was only one soft word.

"Shandiin."

Her name held the return of hope, and such love it was a physical presence.

Then he blinked, and all of that was shuttered. It wounded her to see tears brimming in his eyes. She realized she hadn't seen him weep since he was sixteen, when he had finally broken down at the death of his father.

One tear fell free when he asked, "How did you bear what happened to your world?"

Because she knew him, she understood the question wasn't just rhetorical. She drew in a shaking breath, hating the memories that came. Then she tightened her grip on his hands and sought for words. "I felt an unspeakable horror, a terrible sorrow for the end of everything and everyone that had been. For all that would never be again. But Khedran, I think human emotions are sheltered from the loss of strangers. The true agony of grief is personal, and comes hardest for those we know and love." She swallowed. "I know you are different. Your gift of empathy made you suffer for every life that ended. Knowing what you have experienced hurts my heart. I could damn Hiraeth to hell for what she has done to you. I wish I could help you."

He shook his head. "I know you met my mother, Rhiathe, who embodies this world you named Hiraeth. She did what she had to, Shandiin. And you already helped me." He took a deep breath. Puzzled, she waited while he fought despair.

Slowly, the ghost of hope returned, and with it his visible love for her. His eyes, still wet from the tears he fought, met hers. "You have already helped me," he repeated. "I searched for you, among all those desperate lives. I needed you, so I could survive the darkness I knew was coming. And I saw you, just for a few seconds. You saved me, Shandiin, and never knew it."

Her eyes widened. "On a street corner, with a crowd around us. You said my name and confused the hell out of me. That was really you."

She saw the ghost of a smile. "So you remember. I am glad."

She curved a hand against his cheek, noticing the scar that had been there was gone. "I have never forgotten, and now I finally know why it happened. Your mother is a goddess, and sent you to that hell. I don't understand why she did that to you."

He covered the hand on his cheek with his own, and sighed deeply. "I do. I understand now what really happened on your world, and therefore what I must guard against here. It wasn't technology that caused the end of your world. It was what came before technology, and what never ended. Everything seemed to divide people. Even their search for enlightenment divided them. Rules for the spirit were created, and people were threatened with an eternity of horror for noncompliance. They imposed rules instead of honoring their own gift of free will."

"Um. Gift? Khedran, free will is chaos."

"You should know," he responded. "But it needn't be, you see. The will to divide is only one use. When that will is used to accept differences, it creates harmony."

"*Hozho*," she murmured, and smiled at his lifted eyebrows. "It's a Navajo word that means 'walking in beauty,' to live in accordance with oneself, others and nature."

"Yes. Your purportedly uncivilized people could have saved Earth's civilizations. Shandiin, giving technology to the people of your world was like giving fire to a child. I cannot let that happen again."

His eyes, bright emerald returning, searched Shandiin's as if seeking her understanding. "Rhiathe is the spirit of this world, and everything in it except for the people. Rhiathe needs me to take care of the people. To keep them safe. To keep her safe." He gently drew her hand away from his cheek, and released it. "There is too much depending on me."

She read his meaning in his gesture, in the sadness of his gaze on hers. His need to deny his love for her had not changed. She understood that because she understood him.

She stood up when he did, but her mind was racing. "I understand, but I am puzzled. Rhiathe seems to think I am necessary to you. She's told me that more than once. It seems in opposition to what you and I believe. Do you think...did she use magic to make you love me? Is...is what you feel for me even real?"

She watched him begin to reach for her, stop, and step back. She waited while he fought again for the control she had taught him, that had served him all his life. When he finally met her eyes again, she knew he was barely holding on.

"Shandiin, I cannot believe my love for you isn't real. With what I now know, you are all that stands between me and the darkness. But we have important work to do, you and I, and...we cannot be lovers. You understand why."

She heaved a sigh as he turned away from her. She could only be sure of her own reality, and it had to be enough.

But she was terribly afraid the Black Wolf had been mortally wounded, and would no longer be enough to keep him sane.

CHAPTER 15

Penumbra welcomed many from the farthest reaches of Azlatan as they arrived for the Assemblage sooner than expected. The stories of Khedran's appearance grew with each new arrival, until it became obvious to all who gathered that magic had returned to Azlatan.

Marre became increasingly silent.

Many beasts came with the arrivals, as Khedran had directed in his visits throughout Azlatan. Ordhold's Majia was only the first. The King of far Dominion Vanhold brought another cat, the great black panther he had raised from a cub; his wild kin answered his call as though understanding their relationship. The Queen of the inner Dominion of Denori brought with her a wolf she called Star. It was the same color as her silver hair, and never left her side. Other canines came as well, both wild and domestic.

Only when all were gathered at noon on the appointed day of Assemblage did the labeled Black Wolf of Azlatan make his silent appearance.

No one saw him enter, but Marre saw him first. He wore his plain black leather uniform, and his cloak was thrown back from one shoulder as was his habit. He looked commanding, as he had more than twenty years before when she had seen him facing the loss of his realm, of his life. When she had seen the great spirit that lived within that powerful body. When she had fallen in love with him.

Before he had left her behind to vanish with Shandiin, and broken her heart.

Now she watched her King walking through the crowd toward her, stopping frequently to speak to his people.

Kimhi of Xanthe was stunned when Khedran came directly to her. "I thank you for agreeing to represent your people," the High King told her.

"Was it you in the light that spoke to me, that led me to the outworlders for help, Your Highness?"

Khedran only smiled. "Are your people doing better, with the new outworlder medicine?"

"They are. Thank you so much."

"It wasn't my medicine, Kimhi, but you are well come."

The room fell silent as others realized the High King was somehow among them.

Shandi and Roinn sat together at the head table. When Shandi saw her father she moved to go to him, but Roinn took her hand to hold her there.

"I must apologize to him. I hurt him, Roinn."

"Not yet, I think." He put a steadying arm around her as they waited, his eyes on the High King. He had seen a difference in him. It would take nervous Shandi little longer.

Khedran walked up to see their locked hands and half embrace, and nodded to Roinn with a raised eyebrow. He met Shandi's anxious gaze briefly but said nothing.

Then he took his place beside the High Queen.

"Hello, my love." He spoke for her ears only. There was sadness in his regard of her, for he recognized her pain and simmering anger. "I am sorry to have been gone so long."

Unshed tears brightened her lavender eyes. "I thought you were gone forever. Why didn't you come back to me when you could go to all these others?"

"We will talk," he promised her.

But she didn't smile, didn't touch him. He watched her fight back the tears, draw herself up proudly, and turn away with her expression masked for their audience.

After a moment Khedran took a deep breath and surveyed the room, where sat Dominion royalty, his Compatris and Legion Masters, and others he had invited for his own strategic reasons.

The outworlders had brought lighting and set up the room for sound and visual, but Marre never got to make the presentation she had planned in Khedran's absence.

The room dimmed to darkness. On a wall where Daimaine's statue had once stood, a screen lit up. Displayed in living glory was a beautiful scene of blue sky, blue sea, white beach, and strange tall fronded trees swaying in the wind. A sigh of amazement went through the room, followed by murmurs as the scene changed to something unrecognizable: impossibly tall buildings stretching to the sky, crowded together over streets flowing with metal creatures. Another scene followed, this one of a great forest reflected in a perfectly blue lake, with majestic mountains rising in the background.

"This was a planet like ours, a world called Earth," Khedran said to the room. "It was home to more people than any of us could imagine."

The last scene shrank as though they were watching it through the eyes of an ascending bird. They saw a lush forest below, stretching out to become surrounded by hills, and then fields. Next there were buildings in the distance, but the view kept shrinking, until they could see the curve of the world and darkness beginning to creep over the land. The unseen bird flew the viewers into night.

Where they saw the lights.

They were looking at a world where all the dark land glittered with lights. Chains of light connected clusters netted with geometric patterns.

"There were cities," Khedran explained. "Those clusters of light are cities where most of the people lived. The tall buildings you just saw were central to these great cities. The bright lines between them are mostly roads, where people rode in the vehicles you saw on the city streets."

They watched the world turn beneath them, saw moonlight reflected on a great sea where giant ships traveled. They saw amazing flying machines pass in many directions.

But when the world turned toward daylight again it was hazed like a dirty window. Now there were wildfires on what had been the verdant land. A storm came riding over the sea, and drowned what had been left behind. Finally there was a barren desert, cracked and empty of any kind of life.

When next a city appeared, they saw it falling into ruin, and many of the wheeled metal creatures stranded everywhere.

Then came the worst of all, as they saw death in too many forms. Dead animals were strewn grotesquely, pitifully, on infertile plains abandoned by humans as useless.

There were people trapped forever in the metal creatures on roads that were blocked and impassable.

Mass graves were filled with skeletal bodies.

"Stop," someone cried. "Please stop! I can't look anymore!"

The screen went dark for a blessed moment.

But Khedran warned them. "There is yet this."

And this time they saw a city still living, people masked against the dirty air that filled it. People who disappeared in a brilliant bloom of fire that grew and grew until there was nothing left to see of the world at all.

The screen faded and the lights came up.

Khedran looked out at the devastated faces of his people. His brother Varady, next to him, had his face in his hands. Jael sat with tears tracing his cheeks.

Zion was staring at him in shock. "Where did you get those videos?"

"Those are not videos," Khedran answered quietly. "They are memories." He didn't take his eyes from the audience, watching as they turned to each other in fear and dismay, unsure what they had seen, knowing only that it was horrible.

When they calmed and returned their attention to him, Khedran spoke again. "That was the planet called Earth, which was destroyed by the people who are on their way here."

There were immediate questions.

"How could people do that?"

"What did they do to make that happen?"

"What was that last thing? *What was that fire?*"

Khedran answered the man who had asked the last question. "It is called a nuclear weapon. It would destroy all of Cabre and most of Azlatan. And when the fire goes out, the land is poisoned for years beyond count."

Some began to stand, terror in their manner. Khedran watched closely as others drew them back to their seats. He measured those who showed courage and control in the terrifying face of what they had witnessed.

And those who met fear with meaningless fury.

"Is this true?" someone shouted to the outworlders at the King's table. "Is this what you are bringing to us?"

Responding cries built until it seemed the threat against the outworlders present was becoming real. Until Khedran's command voice came like a fist to the throat.

"Know the facts before you rush to judgement."

There was immediate silence.

Then another voice filled the room, a woman's voice that some recognized.

"I, too, come from the place called Earth. But no one lives there anymore, because it can no longer sustain life. So, now they live on ships."

The screen lit up again, and they saw a metal orb floating in a sea of stars. It took a moment to see the smaller ships coming and going around it like bees around a beehive. It took a moment more to realize the smaller ships contained people, and then the size of the *Earthstar* became apparent and there were gasps.

Shandiin walked in front of the screen, microphone in hand. "There are two starships, and they are able to hold many other craft, as you see. Some are transport only, but some carry weapons...including the kind of fire you just saw destroy an entire city. The kind of fire that made my world uninhabitable.

"For those of you who were doubtful that people could have caused a world's destruction, I can tell you it is true. There were billions of people, and most thought of their world only as a resource to be used. They used it up, even though it was their only home. They fought over what was left, until there came the final insanity. There came war."

After a moment she looked up again. She waited a beat before continuing. "I lived through the end of my world. I am a survivor. Of the others who survived, there were a special few who should be known as the Heroes of Earth. These heroes labored without recognition to save what was left of humanity. Two of them are sitting at the table with your High King. The one who resembles the King is Zion. He designed the ships that have carried Earth's survivors. He also directed the people who built and repaired them. He and his fellow heroes – Egypt, who is here with him, and Sarnath, and Roland – have worked tirelessly to help those who have neither appreciated their efforts, nor honored them for the saviors they are. I am asking them now to give up their devotion to those people. I would ask all of us off-worlders, we who have lost our world, to change allegiance. I am asking the two who are here now...Zion and Egypt...to join me in asking for asylum in Azlatan, to become citizens under the rule of your High King."

She turned toward Zion and Egypt, awaiting their answer.

They both stood slowly and walked to Shandiin, turning then to face Khedran, who simply nodded toward the audience, indicating he would leave the choice to his people.

"So be it," Shandiin said then, and turned back to the room. "We are here to become part of your world, and to help you fight those who are coming to take it from you."

With that she lowered the microphone and waited.

Khedran's command voice needed no microphone. "What say you?" he asked his people.

The crowd rose as one, and no voice said nay.

That day the leaders of Azlatan saw their High King as they never had before.

He had once created an army to save Azlatan.

Now he was creating leaders to save their world.

He chose those with courage and control to lead others for him, to help them in strategies he knew would be needed. Once these assignments were made, the screen behind him brightened with more visions.

These were of warfare, and they were as terrifying to their audience as the bomb had been. The weapons carried by a single soldier could destroy many enemies and the buildings where they sheltered. He showed them those weapons, and behemoths called tanks that rolled over anything in their path; he showed them flying machines bringing fire to the land.

And all of his people wondered how they could possibly withstand any of it.

Brave Dominion King Brend finally stood, challenging his High King for the truth. "Your Highness, many of us stood with you on Cabre's ramparts, fighting by your side. But no matter how valiant, we cannot overcome the things you have just shown us. What use is our army here?"

Khedran nodded understanding. "We fought magic then, but we need magic now, and it has been given to us."

They waited raptly. He stood then, and walked around the table to stand before it, boots set apart and arms crossed. Looking downward, he seemed to be waiting for something.

Majia rose. The great cat stalked to stand at his right.

The wolf called Star came to stand at his left.

One by one the beasts of Azlatan came to the High King and lined up with him to face the leaders of the Dominions, the Chaine that Roinn had selected to attend, the Congress of the Sundancers, the Masters of the Black Guard, and the new leader of Xanthe.

They were all astonished to find themselves in a grassy meadow. It sloped gently to the edge of a forest, thick trees lining the banks of a wide and gentle river. The land rose again beyond it, a jumble of living green broken occasionally by golden rock, climbing to misty distance where rose the great eastern mountains named Khaibara. By the river grazed horses, the valiant Shalmira who were the partners of Khedran's Black Guard and of the great people known as the Sundancers.

Khedran, with Shandiin's help, had led his people into understanding things that were frightening but necessary. Now they would see he held dominion unlike the gods they had known. As he lifted his head to look out on his leaders, a sense of awe settled over them all.

Once more his voice reached everywhere in that world, as it had one night long ago when he had called on Daimaine to warn his people of war. That power was now his own.

"This planet is our home and our mother," the High King told all of Hiraeth's inhabitants, and even the people on the starship above. "For a mother provides everything needed for life. In return it is our duty to love and protect her. If we are true to that, she will help us against those who would harm us. But the rules are clear and simple. We must respect her. We must respect all living things that are part of her, never forgetting that includes us. So we must, despite whatever differences we may have, also respect each other."

His eyes held an unholy emerald fire as they swept his witnesses while his voice swept the world. "The spirit of our world of Hiraeth is alive, embodied in the goddess Rhiathe, who came to us in mortal form to be my mother. Rhiathe has given me the magic and authority to help protect all who live here. If any would deny my rule, speak now."

The valley disappeared; they were all back in the meeting room, and an outworlders' communication device was sounding loudly.

Khedran, still standing with the beasts that were his, smiled a little. "Answer it."

Egypt obeyed immediately, putting her communicator on speaker by her microphone.

"What is it?" she asked the caller.

"We heard." Roland spoke from the outworlder base in the Plain of Admech. "We heard the High King. So did those aboard the *Aztlan*. We stand for the world. None here will deny the High King's rule. We stand for Rhiathe."

Khedran answered. "Well come to all of you. I will be there tomorrow, Roland."

"Yes, Your Highness." The communicator went dark, and Egypt put it away with fingers that had rarely trembled before.

The High King sighed, reaching down to stroke the snowcat's white head. "Yes," he said, as though answering Majia. "We are all exhausted, I think, from everything we have seen here. Let us stand apart, for a while."

It was a clear dismissal. The animals returned to those they'd come with, who were rising gladly to seek soothing sunlight and fresh air.

Khedran remained where he was. Crossing his arms again, he stood alone, in deep thought.

Varady came to him, to put a gentle hand on his shoulder. "You have taken on a heavier burden than ever, my brother. I don't know what I can do, but I am here."

Varady had always touched Khedran's heart, never more than in that moment. The King met his eyes gratefully. "You and Jael will be my right hand and my left in what comes, my brother. Because in warfare there is pain and death, and both your gift and Jael's vision will be sorely needed." He looked across the stage to where Shandiin stood in conversation with Egypt.

He frowned. "Rhiathe has determined that Shandiin will serve as my conscience. Rhiathe did this even though I refused much of her special magic, in fear of becoming a tyrant like two of the gods that once controlled us. Rhiathe reminded me that Shandiin fought those gods when she was Chaos. I trust her to ensure my actions in the coming war will be just."

Varady lifted his eyebrows. "I hardly think *you* need anyone to be your conscience."

Khedran shook his head. "Rhiathe believes I do. For that reason alone I fear that what is coming will be more heinous than we can know."

CHAPTER 16

After Varady left, Khedran glanced over to see that Shandi and Roinn were gone. He took a deep breath and turned to walk back to his Queen.

Marre remained seated at the head table. As he neared she only watched him, waiting.

He turned his chair sideways and sat to face her. "I am sad that you are angry with me."

"You left me. I have mourned you terribly, Khedran, not knowing if you were alive or dead. I do not understand why you went to others, and not to me."

"I have had much work to do, Marre."

She waved that away. "I understand the work. I have always come second to your duty." She looked toward Shandiin. "But you went with her that day, while you left me here, and disappeared from my world. I know she stayed behind when the others came back without you. Now she has returned with you. You have been with her, while I mourned you." Her eyes cut back to him. "I've always known you love her. You told me that, the day that she left and took the gods and the magic with her. It hurt, but I could accept it because she was gone. But now...now she is back, and you have been with her again. What am I to think?"

He frowned in surprise, understanding the implication. "Marre, you are my wife. You know I do not break oath."

"I do not trust her, Khedran. She brought you to her bed once when I was already carrying your child. I do not believe our marriage would make any difference to her."

Stunned, he could only lift his open hands. "No, that isn't true. Neither she nor I would break our marriage vows. And...Marre, You know I have always loved you. What we have shared all these years has nothing to do with Shandiin."

"So you say. But you still love her, don't you?" When he hesitated she slapped her hand on the table. "Answer me!"

He couldn't answer her, because he couldn't give her the answer she needed.

His silence held the truth that wounded them both.

Marre's lavender eyes brimmed with tears. When one sparkled free on her cheek, he reached to touch her, but she slapped his hand away.

"No." Her rejection was fierce.

She shoved to her feet, and left him.

He watched her walk away, his heart heavy.

After a few minutes he stood, turning to see Egypt approach, her steady emerald gaze on his. He carefully set aside what was personal to give her his full attention.

"What do you need of me, Captain?"

"Your Highness, Shandiin has told me many admirable things about you. But I have some questions."

He only nodded, waiting.

"First, do you really want those strangers to colonize your planet?"

"Apparently we have been colonized before. This world is large enough to allow many more to live in nature instead of on those ships. As long as they agree to my law and my rule, they will be welcome."

"Your law?"

"You have heard it. It is required to respect all living things, including each other."

"What about your rule? It is autonomous, isn't it? What would you restrict?"

"Very little, as all human actions fall under my primary law. Your Earth had many rules. Most were wrongheaded, as they invaded what should have been personal rights. Others would have become unnecessary if the law of respect had been invoked."

She frowned. "That still leaves a big question. Shandiin told me that you will not condone evil. How do you define evil? I know you have exceedingly high moral standards. Do you believe those with different standards are evil?"

"No, Captain. Morality is a subjective thing. I saw in my time on Earth that morals varied between cultures and from person to person. They were often imposed by laws that ignored human rights. Morals and laws can change. Evil does not."

"Then what do you think is evil?"

"The Chaine teach that all evil is human. I agree. Humanity is part of nature, but it has gifts that require a higher standard than nature's other inhabitants. Those higher standards are imposed by a human conscience. Evil is achieved when a failure of conscience allows a living thing to be treated as an object."

When her eyes questioned, he smiled at her. "You recognize it with your gut, whenever you see purposeless harm to the defenseless. You know what evil is, Captain. So does everyone with a working conscience."

She stared at him for a moment, then took a deep breath. "I need a sword," she grumbled. "Laying a firearm at your feet doesn't really cut it, but it's all I have." She knelt and set the mentioned weapon between them. "I would swear to your service, and be accepted as one of your Black Guard."

He touched her shoulder. "You are far more than that, Egypt. Please stand."

She obeyed and faced him. "You shall be Compatri," he told her. "That is the highest rank in the Guard, and they are few. You will have complete access to me whenever you need it, and I will rely on your absolute loyalty to see me through what comes. You are also Legion Master, for you command many in that starship circling our world."

"Roland said the people of my ship also heard your words, Your Highness. It will be as you wish."

"With my thanks." He took her hand and lifted it to his lips.

Egypt grinned. "Damn. I'm going to flop at your feet if you ever do that again."

His expression lightened at her humor. "You remind me of Shandiin."

"I consider that a compliment."

They both looked over at Shandiin, who was approaching Zion. They saw her reach to touch him. Zion stepped back abruptly, shook his head, and strode away.

Egypt grimaced. "Ouch. That had to hurt." At Khedran's frown, she sighed. "Apparently she hasn't told you they broke up."

His gaze remained on Shandiin for a moment before he returned his attention to Egypt. "No."

When he hesitated after that single word, she sighed again and told him the rest.

"Shandiin has been my dearest friend for a very long time. We share things we would share with no one else. I have always known she loves you. She was honest with Zion, so he's known it too. But he never really understood the depth of your connection until you disappeared, and she sent him away while she waited for you. It was more than he could take. My heart breaks for them both, because I love them both."

He regarded her carefully. "I am glad she has you for a confidant. You must know I cannot help her through this."

"I do. So does she, or she would have told you. Your Highness..."

"With what you just told me I rather think we are past honorifics, Egypt."

She smiled sadly. "I disagree. You will always be my liege, an ideal I have searched for all my life. I just wanted to tell you my heart breaks for you, too. Because I know you love her."

He lowered his head to rub his brow, then looked away. "For that reason among others, I do not believe your ideal merits your heartbreak. I must go now, Compatri. I trust your discretion in this matter."

"Of course."

She watched him glance back at Shandiin before he left.

It had been a long day of meeting with his leaders, and the High King wasn't done yet. He met next with the Congress of the Sundancers, who were integral to his plans. Varady joined him there with his wife, Stormwing, who was now part of the Congress.

When that meeting ended, Khedran hesitated at the stairs leading to his chambers. He stood there a moment before beginning the climb.

He opened the door quietly, and found Marre at the window looking out over the sea, as he had once long ago.

She kept her back to him as he closed the door behind him.

"Would you make me beg?" he asked her quietly.

"You can just go to her now. It doesn't matter anymore."

"Marre. Please. I love you. I need you. Don't leave me."

She spun to him at that, and he saw rage. "How could I leave you? I am High Queen of Azlatan. I am *your* Queen. I have no other place or purpose in life, because I made you my purpose!"

"Do you think I don't know that? But you are leaving me, Marre, in the only way that matters, and it is tearing me apart."

"You have already torn me apart, Khedran." She put her face in her hands, and her shoulders shook.

He went to her. When she tried to refuse his embrace, he took her gently into his arms anyway. She finally set her cheek against his chest and wept while he fought his own pain. He wrapped her in closer. "Marre, please forgive me for what I have done to hurt you."

She pushed back to peer up at him from the circle of his arms, her fists clenched against his chest. "All these years I have wondered if you still love her. I have wondered if you would have come back to me, if you would have married me, if she had not left Azlatan that day. Yes, Khedran, you have hurt me. If you truly want my forgiveness, *send her back*. She does not belong here. Don't let her destroy what we have. Send her back to where she came from, away from our world."

He was stunned by her revelation more than her demand. How had he never guessed the pain Marre had felt, being so unsure of him? But all he could answer was her demand. "Marre, how can I send her back to the Earthers, when she has pledged allegiance to us? Would you have her executed as a traitor?"

Marre shook her head angrily. "I do not believe that would happen. She left this world to go back to them. She is one of them. Would you rather keep her here...and destroy *me?*"

Desperately she watched him absorb what she had said.

His beautiful eyes on hers became so full of sorrow it almost broke her. He had always commanded her heart. But she stood fast, even when he released his embrace and drew away.

"I have loved you more than you could know," he told her finally. "But you are justifying what you want by choosing disbelief over truth. Since her return Shandiin has only helped me with preparing for a possible invasion. She has done nothing wrong, Marre. I cannot cause the death of any innocent person. It would be evil of me."

"You just want to keep her here. You have made your choice."

"No. I am not choosing her love over yours. I could not and I will not. You are my wife. You are the mother of our daughter. You were the one who has made my life worth living these many years. I have loved you. But I cannot do the evil thing you demand of me. You are distraught...and you are wrong."

He searched her eyes for a long time, but she didn't relent.

She didn't move, even when he left her.

He saw Roinn when he walked back down the stairs. The big man was leaning against the wall, obviously waiting for him. Khedran stopped in front of him. "Is this about Shandi?" he asked.

"Partly. I did not hear your plans for the Chaine today."

"Only because I know I can depend on your people. Those who are Chaine will not stand down from what is coming. I planned to discuss strategy with you after I accomplish a few other things."

Roinn nodded. "Will you let Shandiin return to us?"

"You can ask her if she would prefer that to being my Compatri. She asked asylum to Azlatan, Roinn. She is a citizen here now."

"It feels wrong. She is the soul of my people. She built the Chaine. She is more than just one of us, she is all of us."

"Then talk to her. Please. I am willing if she is." He looked away. "It might even be best."

"To get her away from you?"

Khedran looked back in surprise. "Yes," he admitted. "Though I need her help right now, Roinn."

"Then what Shandi told me is true."

"I don't know what she told you. She seems to think Shandiin and I had an affair. We did not."

"That is not my concern. What I have long understood is that you and she are *amharen.* That is difficult, in your narrow world that believes such a sacred thing should meet the requirements of those who are not a part of it. Shandi was wrong to judge you, Khedran, and I have let her know that is my belief. She has accepted that she was wrong to judge you, but she still hurts for her mother."

Khedran looked away. "As do I."

Roinn grimaced. "I am sorry for that. But Shandi wants to apologize for hurting you with her judgment."

Khedran turned to face Roinn fully. "Tell me, my friend – are you certain her judgment is gone?"

Roinn frowned. "I do not understand."

"Do you believe she wants to apologize only out of love for me, or to appease you? Or has she truly realized her error, and made a free and personal choice?"

Roinn looked puzzled. "She was rife was guilt over things she had said and done, to the point of fear that you had died because of it. I encouraged her to use the logic you raised her by. In doing so she realized that you would not leave Azlatan when it needed you. She further recognized the source of her guilt...the fact she never had the right to judge you in the first place."

"So she no longer judges me, despite the constraints of our bloodline against our own immorality. That is a relief to me."

"May I ask why?"

"It means she is human, and so is better than I am. Roinn, why isn't she here to apologize in person?"

"She asked me to speak for her. You seemed to look through her, today, and it hurt her badly. She thinks so much of you, as her father. She loves you deeply."

Khedran sighed. "I am sorry if that hurt her. I hope she will realize I am more than her father. I am also her King, and she is part of a royal family that has duties and responsibilities more important than assuaging hurt feelings, right or wrong. I did something wrong, something that hurt her mother...and then Shandi, when she learned of it. I apologized to Shandi, but she seemed to want more when there was no more to give. If I seemed cold, that is why. I have had to set aside some difficult personal matters to focus on my duties. Please tell her that I have never stopped loving her, and I am glad to know I no longer disappoint her."

Roinn nodded. "She's an amazing woman, but I think she just needed to finish growing up."

Khedran could almost smile. "I love the Chaine way of seeing truth. Are you going to marry my daughter, Roinn?"

"With your permission."

"You do not need my permission. She is a free woman. My Marre..." here Roinn saw him hesitate before revising his words. "Her mother and I made sure many years ago that arranged marriages were no longer lawful. That allows unarranged marriages, I believe."

"I would still want your blessing."

"I perceived, upon seeing you together, that you are *amharen*."

"We are."

"In that case, be assured you have my unnecessary blessing, and I am glad for both of you. I must go now, Roinn."

Roinn watched him walk away and thought of the kind boy he had once helped to teach, and wondered how the noble man could think he was less than human.

The bridge of Egypt's starship *Aztlan* awaited the arrival of their Captain, Zion, and Shandiin...and their new King.

The crew was confused. They had received communication that those personages were on their way, but no skycraft had launched from the planet. Sarnath was the only one who was unsurprised when four people appeared from nowhere.

Shandiin was first to recover, having made similar transitions as the goddess Chaos, called also the Sunqueen. Egypt took a moment longer, but her reaction was delight. Zion looked a little dizzy.

Khedran hesitated like an animal scenting danger. Very slowly, he turned to face Sarnath. "Who are you?" he demanded.

Those who knew Sarnath were shocked to see him tremble under Khedran's gaze. "Don't you know me?" he asked.

Khedran lifted his chin to study the big man. Though Sarnath was taller, the King's power was greater in what appeared to be a confrontation. "I have some form of knowledge, but it is like sound muted by distance. I only know you are with the engineered Heroes of Earth, but you are not one of them."

Sarnath nodded slowly. He seemed mesmerized. "No, I am not. Just as you are not one of the humans you protect and serve."

Shandiin saw Khedran flinch, and was immediately at his side. "Have you lost your damned mind, Sarnath? He's as human as any of us...more than most!"

Egypt's reaction was just as fierce. "You are speaking to the High King, who has our sworn allegiance."

The big man blinked, and they watched him visibly calm himself. "My apologies, Your Highness. I seem to have had a vision that is not helpful."

Egypt was still glaring. "Get your shit together, Sarnath. You were supposed to be gathering information on the warcraft and AI."

Khedran had stood silently during all of this, thoughtfully studying Sarnath. He intervened by turning back to Egypt. "Give me a moment, Compatri. I was distracted, and have been neglectful of your people." He moved from his companions to the bridge crew.

Already stunned by the sudden appearance and the sense of presence Khedran brought with him, some who met the King's eyes went to their knees. He didn't remark on this but studied each person respectfully before speaking. "I thank each of you for your allegiance and welcome you to the citizenship of Azlatan. I hope you will not again be alarmed by my method of arrival. It is expedient, and expedience has become necessary."

He came back to Egypt. "Would you now explain, please, about these warcraft and AI?"

Egypt glanced from her recovering crew back to the High King. "The High Queen may have already told you what we've learned. The leaders aboard the Earthstar have been building warcraft, small ships designed for attack. It appears Shandiin's suspicions are right: they want to take your planet. But their warcraft are not Zion's design. Ours are superior. Our spies tell me we are faster. And our weapons are better. We just don't have as many."

"I don't believe that's a problem at this point," Zion put in. "They are lightyears away. It took us ten years to return from Earth's orbit to Hiraeth, and they don't have the quantum tunnel drive used by the *Aztlan*."

"How many years would have passed on the *Earthstar* in those ten years, considering the effects of relativity?" Khedran asked.

Zion was shocked. "How do you know about relativity?"

"The same way I was able to share the memories of Earth at the Assemblage, which you also questioned." Khedran regarded Zion reflectively. "It seems science has always been your religion, Zion, so perhaps it would help to remember your idol's own words. Einstein said, 'everything is connected. The greatest tragedy of human existence is the illusion of separateness.' Our worlds were never as far apart as you thought." He smiled at Zion's lifted eyebrows. "Now, can you answer my question regarding the amount of time that has passed on the *Earthstar* while you traveled here?"

Zion swallowed. "Fifty years to our ten."

"Yet I understand the man who took Shandi was able to communicate with them."

"Yes. Real-time communication is possible through the entanglement inherent in the quantum communication systems between the *Aztlan* and the *Earthstar.* I used it after I received the call that the *Earthstar* was in trouble, which came in at the same time Shandiin returned to us from the surface of Hiraeth. It took us ten years to return to Earth's orbit, and during that time I gave them instruction for the repairs they could make until I got there."

"So you used quantum entanglement for real-time communication. Your computers are connected by it?" Khedran asked.

"Yes. The artificial intelligence of their quantum computer developed the communication system. Ours developed the tunnel drive for FTL travel." As soon as the words were out, Zion's eyes widened and he spun back to Sarnath. "Did you look into the ability of their AI?"

Sarnath looked resigned. "Yes. I apologize; I was distracted or I would have mentioned it sooner. It appears the *Earthstar* and the *Aztlan* have entangled their AI. They may have the quantum tunnel drive, and the warcraft may already be on their way."

Zion swore and turned aside.

Egypt was scowling. "Your Highness, if they left within a month after we did...and I will try to find that out...they could be here very soon. We have superior warcraft but we will be outnumbered in a one-on-one battle. Unless you happen to have any fire-breathing dragons to help?"

Khedran lifted his eyebrows in question, apparently knowing less about mythology than science. Shandiin stepped in. "A dragon is a mythical creature. Khedran, can Rhiathe create anything like ChanDethe that could fight the warships?"

"No." Khedran rubbed his forehead, and Shandiin realized he was exhausted. "So it seems the possibility of war is nearer than we thought, as my brother Jael insisted. I have another question. As I understand it, artificial intelligence is emergent from a computer. Computers are programmed with parameters. Is it possible for an AI to exceed its parameters?"

"No," Zion answered distractedly. "It may appear so to the observer, but it isn't an entity like a human. It has no free will."

"I see. Thank you. Now it's necessary that I leave while you gather more information regarding the status of the *Earthstar*. Shandiin and I will return tomorrow."

Shandiin opened her mouth, but she was gone before her words formed.

CHAPTER 17

"What the hell?" Shandiin looked around at the empty Valley of the Chaine where Khedran had first found her. He was walking away from her toward one of the ancient cottages among the trees. "You could have warned me we were transitioning," she finished, striding to catch up.

"I apologize, Shandiin."

"Why are we here, Khedran?"

"Because I am mortally weary. I need to rest."

She frowned at him, realizing it was true, so went ahead to open the door of the old cabin that was the only structure handy. She expected it to be dilapidated.

Instead the door opened smoothly to a comfortable room. Bright rugs warmed the stone floor, and a cozy sofa was centered before a fireplace already glowing in welcome.

Khedran went directly to the sofa, flinging his cloak over the back as he sat down.

Shandiin looked around approvingly. "Looks like your mother is taking care of you. I'm betting there's food in the kitchen, too." She went in search and returned moments later with a repast to find Khedran already asleep in front of the fire.

She set the tray down and went to him where he was slumped. After a moment she picked up his feet and put them on the sofa, then wrestled off his boots and pulled his body straight. She tucked a handy pillow under his head and drew his cloak over him. He slept through the entire process.

Then she stood a long moment and watched him sleep. Momentarily giving in to her heart, she lowered to the floor to watch him and found herself brushing the hair back from that handsome face.

"I am glad to see you love him still."

Annoyed, Shandiin lifted her gaze to the goddess who was the spirit of the world. Rhiathe sat on the arm of the couch by her son's head, smiling at her.

"You've put him through hell and loaded him with too much. He's so tired. Can't you help him with that?"

"He is mortal yet, Shandiin, because he required it. I would have given him much more, but he refused to become a god. I ensure therefore that he cares for his mortal form. He needs to rest and will not, so I have forced it on him. I am glad you came with him."

"I told you I'd stay with him as long as he needs me." Shandiin tucked his cloak closer to him, letting her fingers drift over his stubbled cheek. "I do love him still," she admitted. "But you have changed him, Rhiathe. He has a darkness he never had before, even under siege in the Prophecy War. I'm worried about him."

"I know. I have concern for him too, Shandiin, but I know you will help him. When he was taken from you in the cave, you stayed and waited for him out of love, out of hope. I want him to have that in his life." Rhiathe set a gentle hand on her son's hair. "His Queen appears to see only her own needs. I would prefer he have you as his mate."

"You can't make that decision for him. He loves Marre. I would never take that joy from him."

"I know. Because your love is true and unselfish. No, I will not take anything away from him, Shandiin; you have my word on that."

"What about the bad things? Can't you take away the things that hurt him?"

"Regretfully, no. He required that he remain mortal, not too different from his people."

Shandiin sighed. "Of course he did. Shit. He deserves happiness and he's had so little of it. Partly because of me, I guess."

"Because of love. He could not let go of you although he believed you were gone forever."

"I shouldn't have…"

"You know better than saying 'should' or 'shouldn't have.' You taught him better than that. And it would have made no difference, if the two of you had not made love. He would still have mourned your loss. Sleep now, Shandiin. You are tired, too."

When Khedran awoke, he was surprised to find himself wrapped around Shandiin on the sofa, her head tucked under his chin, her bottom warm against the male part of him that was very much awake.

He thought about this for a moment, and realized it was Rhiathe's doing. The mother he had missed as a child, the goddess Mother he now loved.

The Mother who appeared to have a wicked sense of humor, because he knew Shandiin's integrity. She would not have put herself where she was.

He moved his hand carefully from the swell of her breast, remembering its silk under his lips. Closing his eyes, he wrestled that memory into submission, and touched her hair gently…that unruly fiery hair he forever longed to bury his hands in.

"Shandiin," he whispered. "Wake up, please."

She stirred with a murmur, a soft wriggle that was almost his undoing. He felt her brace when she realized where she was, and then she was gone from him.

He sat up to rub his neck, then looked up at her where she stood against the windowed dawn, staring down at him almost wildly.

It made him smile. "I don't believe I have ever seen you embarrassed before."

"I don't know how I got there!"

"Rhiathe, I am sure. She appears to have your outrageous sense of humor. But I am sorry she did that to you."

Shandiin took a deep breath and didn't tell him how right it had felt, waking in his arms...despite everything. Instead she walked to the window to peer out.

"It snowed!" she cried in delight.

"Then I had best build up the fire. You have seen snow before, Shandiin."

"Not since I left Hiraeth. I've been on a damned ship for twenty years. Oh, this is so beautiful! It makes me feel like I've come home."

He joined her at the window, ducking to look out at the valley cloaked in white. Then he lifted an eyebrow and smiled at her. "You have. You are home in my world, where you belong." He moved away from her to rebuild the fire.

She turned to watch him for a moment, where he knelt lit by fire's glow. *That's home*, she thought. Then she went to get the food they hadn't eaten the night before and called him to the little table already set.

When they sat down she scooped up a strawberry and pointed it toward the bowl of flowers. "Food and flowers. Rhiathe is good to you." She looked up to see Khedran wasn't eating. "What's wrong?"

He sighed, shoving the plate away. "Even in the face of war, personal things won't leave my mind."

Assuming the obvious, Shandiin scowled. "Quite frankly, I think Shandi's too smart not to get over that shit."

"You speak so eloquently. I do not know how I resist you."

She looked up warily to see him smiling at her.

"Well, crap. You learned sarcasm, and I can't imagine from where."

"Your sarcasm, your humor, have helped me through so much in my life." He shook his head. "But now...Shandiin, I am very much afraid Jael's visions will come true. I cannot allow personal concerns to get in the way of preparing for it. I still feel the horror of your world's destruction, and… I can't bear the thought it could happen here."

"Personal feelings just mean you're human, Khedran. Rhiathe told me you refused to become a god. And you're carrying a lot of stress. It's worried me because it shows, as it never did when I was here before."

"I'm not fully human. You know that. And there wasn't as much for me to lose, when you were here before."

Her throat filled with an ache she couldn't swallow. "That nonsense again. You and Sarnath are both full of shit. Why in the name of God don't you think you are human? You understand humanity better than anyone I've ever heard of."

He didn't look up. "You are missing the obvious. I do not fit, Shandiin. I do not have the gift of free will."

"No! You care. You love. That is your choice. That is free will, Khedran."

He sighed. "I never chose to love you, Shandiin." He pushed away from the table. "Enough of this. We should go."

She wanted to tear her hair out. She wanted to know things she didn't want to know.

Instead she respected his need to return to duty.

"Why can't Rhiathe just stop them from invading, Khedran?" she asked, rising to follow him.

"She said she knew it was wrong to attack with magic when your colony first came, but she was angry and terrified. She knew you were from Earth. She knew what had happened to Earth. But she now realizes the potential of good in humans, and would not again take their free will."

"But she could stop the technology…"

"No. She cannot. That is why Earth was lost. She is nature; even her magic has no power over the destructive technology humans can build. I showed my people only a small part of what had been done on your home planet. It haunts me."

She saw the truth of his words, and knew his horror also lived in the potential for Hiraeth's destruction. Even after a good night of sleep, his eyes were shadowed, weary with that weight.

She scowled. "Are you sure about that fire-breathing dragon?"

"There is no magic creature to fight anything made through technology. You know she did not destroy the technology of your first colony, but used nature...a tsunami...to take it out to sea and beyond your reach." He sighed. "We must get back to work."

"We just found out they're all coming," Zion announced when Khedran and Shandiin appeared again on the starship bridge. "He's breaking our agreement, bringing the *Earthstar* and endangering everyone on it."

"How many people are on the *Earthstar?*" Khedran asked, and scowled when Zion gave the estimate. "So many to risk. Exactly how is he endangering them?"

"He's bringing nuclear weapons, and that's never safe. And if he's figured out that we might fight him, he knows we carry nukes as well. Your Highness, that starship contains all that's left of Earth's humanity. It was intended that it stay safely in Earth's orbit. The agreement was that we would return after negotiating with you, to pick up those people who chose to immigrate to your planet."

"Apparently he's breaking your agreement, as you said. Is this Premier Canard like a king to these people?"

"He pretends that he acts at the people's directives, which is nonsense. His family took over the *Earthstar* a century ago by their relative time. There's no one else to vote for but those of his family, but he's supposedly an elected leader who serves his people, not a ruler like you."

Khedran lifted an eyebrow. "While I do not take directives from my people, I serve their needs through my rule. I thought you understood that."

Zion flushed. "Yes, Your Highness."

Khedran regarded him a moment, then turned to Egypt. "Will the two starships fight, or just the warcraft?"

"As Zion said, we both have formidable weaponry. I don't intend to attack the *Earthstar* unless you order me to. Which you may have to, if they attack my ship. Our loss would leave your world defenseless."

Egypt read the King's despair at her words and shared an understanding glance with Shandiin. She turned to Sarnath, who had remained silent since the King's arrival.

"How long until they get to the wormhole?"

"Apparently they left Earth's orbit soon after we did, and will soon arrive at the other side of the wormhole."

She grimaced. "Okay. Once they're through, it's only a matter of days before they reach Hiraeth's orbit. I'll have my warcraft on standby. I have an idea, though. We are nearing a large asteroid belt..."

"The Starfall belt." Shandiin looked up in understanding. "This planet passes the edge of that belt every year, and it's an impressive display in the night sky. It's also the herald of winter. We...they call it Starfall."

Egypt nodded, her attention still on the King. "I am thinking of putting my craft among those asteroids."

"To hide them from those who are coming," Khedran agreed. "So you can take them by surprise. I like that strategy, Captain. Has the *Earthstar* tried communicating with you?"

"No. I am guessing they don't know that we know they're coming. We know because we have friends...spies...hidden among them."

While they continued discussing details and strategies, Shandiin watched Zion leave the bridge. Her heart heavy with guilt, she followed him.

He turned to her as she approached him in the hallway, his expression wary.

"Zion...I just want to tell you how sorry I am."

"For what? For loving the man everyone so obviously idolizes?"

"He didn't hurt you, Zion. I did, and I'm sorry for it." When he looked away, she kept herself from reaching to touch him. "I told you I would love you the best that I can, and I have. I do. I'm sorry that my best isn't good enough."

"I don't buy that line anymore. You discarded me like an afterthought. All you could think of was him, and now you are with him constantly. He's always had your best. I was just a substitute."

When he took a step away, she spoke from her heart. "You've never been a substitute for anything, but I always knew you deserve better than me. That's on me. You can't blame him for any of it."

He stopped. "God damn it, Shandiin. You don't have to defend him to me." When he turned back to her, his eyes were suspiciously bright. "I don't blame him, and I can hardly blame you for loving him. He's far more than we bargained for, all those years ago in a laboratory. But you're right, I did deserve better than what you did to me, and it's going to be a long time before I can think about forgiving you. So go be as sorry as you want. Just leave me alone."

She watched him walk away, unable to swallow what was lodged in her throat.

"Please let Roland know we will be there next," Khedran told Egypt.

"You'll probably be there before he gets my message. And how am I to contact you, Highness?"

"I will know if you need me. Just send a mental call. Are you ready to go, Shandiin?"

She nodded as she stopped beside him.

A moment later they were standing by the skycraft on the outworlder's base, and Khedran was regarding her in concern. "Are you alright?" he asked.

"I am exactly as alright as you are. Probably a little better, actually, considering your family problems. I only have one daughter left, and I hope she's French-frying in hell."

Her words were strange, as they often were to him, but he caught the meaning. "That must be difficult for you. I did not know you had children."

"New revelation, Khedran. I had two. You knew them as Liethe...and Daimaine."

She saw his eyes widen in shock.

"I'm surprised Rhiathe didn't tell you. And I'm now apologizing to you for what Diane...Daimaine did."

"It was not your fault. Our children are not required to follow our rule when grown."

"Except yours."

He sighed. "Not even her. But I was not asking about children, Shandiin. I should not be asking, but...I was talking about you and your Zion."

"He's not my Zion anymore. I think he stopped being that as soon as he met you, though he tried. He's a good man, but his heart isn't as big as Marre's. He can't accept what I feel for you, and I've hurt him badly." She shook her head. "I can't talk about it with you. It feels disloyal."

He looked into her eyes for a long moment, then nodded in understanding and turned away without sharing his own truth about Marre.

When he began to step away she routinely fell into the position she'd used for years as his Defender, on his left and slightly behind.

He stopped. "No."

"What?"

"Please don't walk behind me, Shandiin. I no longer need you at my back, but by my side."

He didn't look at her when he said it. After a moment's hesitation, she stepped forward and they walked together.

Roland had his soldiers ready for review, but Shandiin was surprised to see Shajii waiting beside him.

Roland stood at attention, saluting as they walked up. Khedran returned the salute after a moment's study.

"Egypt has told me to expect ground troops," Khedran told him.

Roland nodded, still at attention. "We have been preparing for that, but there are too few of us."

Shajii nodded in agreement. "We need more soldiers. There is an armory of off-world weapons for use by the Black Guard and the Chaine, but they will not know how to use them."

"I see. Give me a moment, Shajii, to attend to an important matter before we go on to your important matter." He turned to the troops.

As he had on the bridge of the *Aztlan*, Khedran walked through the assembled soldiers and studied each person individually, in fact getting to know them without words. Shandiin watched their reactions and wondered as their faces changed. Some almost seemed near tears.

Khedran next stepped back to address these soldiers of Earth as a group. "You have my gratitude and that of this world. I know that none of you have dealt with magic before. I understand your trepidation. I can only promise that it will not be used against you, but only on your behalf." He smiled at their acceptance and turned back to Roland.

"Several people will be arriving here shortly. I suggest that you dismiss your troops for now. I thank you for bringing them to me."

Roland, still at attention, said loudly "Dismissed!"

As the soldiers walked away, many casting awe-filled glances back at the King, Khedran frowned while studying Roland. "You do not have to remain at attention, Commander."

"I think I do, Your Highness. I haven't the vaguest idea what else to do in your presence. I admit I am overwhelmed. And...I believe we met before, on Earth...which I know is impossible."

Khedran hesitated while Shandiin held her breath. She had forgotten that Roland had also met a man who looked like Zion, a man with an "overwhelming aura of authority." She realized Khedran's magic journey to Earth must have connected with Roland as it had with her.

Khedran spoke carefully. "Our previous meeting is not as impossible as you believe, Roland. I remember you as well, though we only met in passing. I know you are one of the engineered Heroes of Earth, who saved so many from your world's destruction. I can only give you my condolences for the loss of your family."

Roland looked surprised. "Do...do you mean Lilith?"

"Not just her. I mean all of them. There were so many of you, and then only five, and with the loss of Lilith you are now only four. Your family was murdered. Yet those of you who survived set about to save people that included their killers."

Khedran set a hand on Roland's shoulder and held that nervous gaze respectfully. "When the *Aztlan* had to leave you behind, you carried on alone to save those who were being subjugated on the *Earthstar*. You shrewdly hid them and yourself among the subjugators, winning the confidence of tyrants so you could come on this mission. Now you are a leader of soldiers for my world. You are marvelous, dedicated and clever, Roland. I am very honored to know you."

Roland's eyes widened in shock. "How do you know all that?"

"I just do. You have already pledged to serve this world, and you are now a Legion Master of the Black Guard. You and your soldiers are mine, in the best meaning of the word."

Khedran dropped his hand, and Roland looked down in astonishment at his new black uniform. It was twin to the King's except for the emerald bars on his shoulders. He heard exclamations from his soldiers that told him they had also been reoutfitted for service in Khedran's Black Guard.

"Good God Almighty!" Roland gasped.

"I have never claimed that title," Khedran said solemnly, but his eyes were amused.

Shandiin snorted a laugh despite herself, and Roland relaxed visibly. Giving him time to recover fully from everything, Khedran turned to Shajii, who was eying Roland's new uniform, or possibly the man himself.

"Where are the weapons you spoke of?" he asked her.

"We will take you." She signaled Roland and walked away with him, leading toward one of the buildings.

Shandiin dropped in beside Khedran as they walked behind them. "I knew you had met Roland before. Zion told me. But Sarnath obviously knows something about you that he's not explaining. And I saw you on that street-corner on Earth, but there is more. I also saw you in a dream, in a vision when I first came through the wormhole, and again on a mountain-top here on Hiraeth on the night you were born. Can you explain any of that?"

He was quiet for a moment. "No. But the answer may lie in something I recalled in my strange meeting with Sarnath. There were terrible shadows in my mind when I journeyed through time to your Earth. There were ancient memories in those shadows, and they frighten me, Shandiin. My very spirit quakes. I cannot face them. Not now, when my world is under attack. My people have to come first. Please just let those mysteries go, at least for now."

Surprised, she watched him step away and join Roland. It was unlike him not to seek answers. Never before had he feared the truth.

But she understood his people came first, and always would. He had never been given a choice in that.

She did have choices, and her choice now was to let him be. If a shadow of memory frightened him, it horrified her.

She'd been curious about the strange meeting between him and Sarnath. She'd planned to corner Sarnath and uncover what he knew. Now she wondered if she should.

Having caught up both mentally and physically, Roland led Khedran toward the weapons room while the women stopped momentarily.

"Why are you here?" Shandiin asked Shajii.

"First, because I know what's coming. Roland told me. I also heard the King's words, as everyone did. I want to help with the defense of my world."

"And second?"

Shajii glanced back at Roland. "I like him. I don't know how far it will go, but I really want to find out. So I have been staying here with him, since Shandi now has Roinn to help her find herself."

"No more Danon?"

"I will always care for Danon as a friend, but I couldn't wait forever for him to feel for me as I once did for him." Shajii grinned. "Besides, you were always too much competition."

"He got past that nonsense. But I'm sorry, Shajii, that he didn't see you as you wanted."

Shajii looked from her toward Khedran. "I am fine with that now. But I am sorry about you. Neither Roinn nor I are blind. We always knew who was your *amharen*."

"Don't be sorry. I don't need more than what I have."

"But you must want more."

Shandiin smiled. "I want very little. Being back in this world is already more. I'm home again. I have missed it so much in all those years I was gone. I finally feel a rightness, even with what we are facing."

"I believe the High King will save us."

"Do you, now? Why are you so sure?"

"You taught him." Shajii shrugged. "As you did us, the Chaine. And he is now magic. Good magic. That combination? I believe in him."

Shandiin smiled, warmed by her words. They started toward the armory where the men were discussing weapons. As they came in, Roland took a rifle from a rack on the wall and offered it to Khedran.

They saw him shake his head in refusal and turn toward a table full of handguns.

"I feel the same about the long guns," Shajii noted. "Roland tried to show them to me, but I feel they are weapons without honor. When you cannot see the eyes of your enemy, and they cannot see you at all, there is no honor in battle."

"But they can save lives in the warfare that is coming," Shandiin pointed out.

"I know. I just don't like them."

The people Khedran was expecting turned out to include his long-time master builder, Pharmond, and many others, several who had worked with him in reconstructing Cabre before the Prophecy War.

They arrived in the armory full of nerves from their magic conveyance. Khedran reassured them and thanked them for accepting his invitation.

"But we need soldiers," Shajii pointed out with typical Chaine directness. "These are not soldiers."

Pharmond agreed. "We are not soldiers, Your Highness, though we are willing to serve as best we can."

Khedran nodded understanding. "Nevertheless, you are far ahead of most of my people. You set aside magic long ago, choosing instead to use your own minds and skills to rebuild my city. From that, I believe you can learn how to use these weapons." He gestured around him.

His gesture included all of the men and women who stood with Pharmond. "I have chosen you because you found your home in Chaine philosophy before others even recognized it. You do not have military training, but you have the kind of minds necessary to understand and use these weapons and teach others as Pharmond may recommend."

"That will take time, Your Highness," Roland put in. "How much time do you think we have?"

"A very few days. But we have an advantage now. A new kind of magic has been given to us by our mother world, and she will use it to support our needs. I can guarantee that it will take no more than an hour for them to learn this new skill, because they already have the natural talent her magic can build upon."

He turned back to the nervous group. "You must of course be receptive. I know many of you abhorred magic, and that is why you turned to Chaine ways. If you do not want to accept the help of Rhiathe, I understand, and you will be asked for no more than you can give."

He seemed surprised when, after a moment's contemplation, each of them lowered to their knees before him. He threw a glance at Shandiin before completing the ritual of service, touching the shoulder of each before he walked back to her.

"Is this wrong, Shandiin?" His voice was low, his face troubled. "Neither of us liked it when the bloodline's thrall helped to build the Black Guard."

"I don't think that's what this is. I think this is deference not just to you, but to Rhiathe. The goddess is always with you, isn't she?"

He smiled a little. "Yes. Despite all my restrictions on changing me, she manages to provide a wisp of comfort."

Shandiin looked away, feeling gratitude that he was given even that much.

The rest of another long day was spent visiting the other leaders and, with Jael as visionary, planning their part in the coming war. Shandiin was amazed at their creativity within the common magic that was nature.

When he told her he wanted to meet with Roinn in Cabre, she pointed that out to him. "Roinn's Chaine can't use even rudimentary magic, unless you've talked Rhiathe out of the agreement she and I made in the beginning."

"I would not do that."

224

"Even if they could, you said magic couldn't stop technology. I am concerned for your city, Khedran. It will be a target. They know it is your home; they may expect you to be there."

"I am aware of that. Which is another reason we are going to Cabre. I want to evacuate Penumbra." He hesitated. "Jael saw it fall. He saw it destroyed, Shandiin."

His voice held misery. She fought the instinct to comfort him. It wasn't her place.

He said nothing more, but a moment later they were walking up Penumbra's broad entry stairs.

His Guard snapped to attention as they approached. Shandiin thought she was the only one who saw the High King's expression as he glanced up at his ancestral home, the only home he had ever known. He quickly looked back to his soldiers.

Farbet gave salute. He was the first of Khedran's rare Compatris, and had gone gray with age. But his stance was proud and strong yet, and his uniform carried the emerald bars and sickle moon that disclosed he was Legion Master of the Queen's Guard.

"Welcome, Your Highness."

"Thank you, Farbet. I wish to see the High Queen. Will you let her know I am in the library, please?"

"She is in your chambers, Highness," Farbet pointed out.

"The library, please." Khedran walked past him.

When the library door closed behind them, Shandiin asked "What is it, Khedran? Why are you meeting her here instead of where you belong?"

The look he gave her said it all, and her heart dropped. "I should go. It's about me, isn't it?"

"I want you to stay, Shandiin."

"Why? That will just make it worse."

"Marre has already made up her mind. I don't believe it can get worse. Please!" He lifted his hands when she started to say something. "Please. Just stay. I need you for this. I cannot do it without you, do you understand?"

She didn't understand at all, but she'd made a promise to stay with him. She muttered, but she stayed.

When the door opened it was Shandi who entered, not Marre.

Khedran turned toward his daughter, waiting.

She looked at him, at Shandiin, and back again.

"Mother won't come down. I am sorry, Father. She does not want to see you."

"Then this is for you to manage, Shandi. I am giving orders that Penumbra is to be evacuated. The war is coming. Penumbra will fall. Do you understand me?"

She swallowed hard and nodded. After a moment, she walked to him, and rested her hands on his arms as she gazed up at him. "Are you all right, Father?"

He didn't break his gaze on hers, but Shandiin saw his hesitation. "No," he said finally. "You know I am not. But you must also realize it can make no difference. Is Roinn with you?"

"Yes. He is waiting outside."

He looked across the room. "Shandiin, please ask him to come in."

While she went to do as he requested, Shandi's eyes remained on her father's. "Mother loves you. She is just in pain, Father."

"It is by her own choice, Shandi. Nothing has changed except her."

"I know that. But she believes you have a love that replaces her."

"I cannot change what she perceives, and I cannot meet her demand."

Shandi frowned. "She made a demand of you?"

Roinn stopped inside the door. He looked at Shandi and her father, and down at Shandiin, who shook her head in disgust.

"What demand did she make?" Shandi asked.

"She required me to send Shandiin to the Earthers. I will not make Shandiin an outcast from both worlds...nor send her to a certain execution."

"Damn it!" Shandiin cried. "Khedran, you never told me about this. And I damned well shouldn't be here with you; it's like a slap in her face."

"I need you here, Shandiin. Rhiathe told me you had to be by my side for this."

"That is bullshit. Rhiathe wants us together for some reason. She wants me for your mate instead of Marre. Even if you wanted it, I wouldn't. And you sure as hell don't need me to save the planet. I'm just unnecessary moral support, which became obvious to me today while I followed you around like a pet dog. Well, fuck it. I'm going upstairs to talk some sense to Marre. Don't try to stop me."

He moved to follow, but she shoved a hand toward him, palm out. "Don't."

She found Farbet at the foot of the stairs, with two other Guardsmen.

"Let me pass," she demanded.

"I cannot, Shandiin. I have orders from the Queen."

"This one time, you will disobey your Queen."

"No."

She lifted her chin and stood tall, ready to fight. "Do you remember who I am, Farbet?"

He and his men drew sword. "Don't do this," he pleaded.

Shandi appeared beside her. "Let her by, Compatri."

Farbet regarded the Princess, nodded grimly and stood aside. Shandi looked at Shandiin. "It was wrong of me to judge. I apologize."

Wordlessly, Shandiin left Shandi behind and climbed the stairs.

She didn't bother knocking, but slammed open the chamber door and strode in. Marre had been sitting by the fireplace; she immediately came to her feet in alarm.

"You are the biggest goddamn fool I ever saw," Shandiin began. "You are breaking his heart for *no reason*, do you hear me? He loves you. You are the only one who can destroy his love for you. This is *your* failure, not Khedran's. Further, I promise you'll have your wish to have me gone. I have a duty now, but once this war is over I swear that you will never see me again, and neither will he."

Marre drew breath, lifted her chin. "Do you love him?"

"I have always loved him, and it had nothing to do with you until I selfishly acted on it, and you only know about that because he told you out of honor. It means nothing. Nothing, do you hear? Because he is more than that. *He has always been more than that, and you should know it.*"

"He was with you while I mourned him, thinking him dead."

"You've got that wrong too, Your idiot Highness. I was alone in that damned valley. He was not with me. He was doing the bidding of the goddess he now serves."

Shandiin didn't look around when Khedran stopped in the doorway behind her. She'd known he would follow. She knew he loved his Queen. "Stop being a fool, Marre," she finished coldly.

Marre looked from her to Khedran, who waited, having overheard it all.

Marre narrowed her eyes at Shandiin. "You just gave oath to me. You swore you will go and neither Khedran nor I will ever see you again. Do you hold to that promise, with him here to witness it?"

"I do." Shandiin turned and began to brush past Khedran. When he tried to stop her, she glared into his face. "You should have told me."

When his eyes held hers, when he didn't let go of her arm, she jerked free, steeled herself, and slapped him.

His expression was thoughtful as he rubbed his cheek and watched Shandiin storm down the stairs.

Then he turned back to Marre. "She said nothing but the truth. Why did you demand that she leave anyway?"

"Because she has come between us. I was wrong to let you go, Khedran. I should have fought for you. I want you back. But I cannot trust that she will ever leave you willingly. She just admitted to me that she loves you. You need to send her away."

He looked into her furious eyes, finally accepting that what they'd had was broken.

She hadn't suddenly lost faith in him because Shandiin had returned. She'd admitted that faith had never been there. Despite her words on that long ago day when she had pledged her love and her hand in marriage, she had never truly forgiven him for Shandiin.

Shandiin had known. She had known why, on her deathbed, Marre had asked whether he still loved Shandiin. *It was payback*, Shandiin had told him. *She wanted to hurt you.*

For once he had dismissed Shandiin's wisdom. He should have listened.

He had never guessed the injury hidden inside of Marre's heart. He had believed in what they had together, and never used his gift of reading a spirit's truth after the first time they'd made love.

He took a deep breath against a new kind of pain. "You are blaming Shandiin for what has hurt you, but it was I who caused the hurt. It is me you distrust. And Marre...can't you see? You cannot respect who you cannot trust. No love is true without respect. It is not *amhara*."

"That's her Chaine teaching!" she cried. "How dare you use that against me? I have never given you reason to doubt my love!"

He held up a hand, shook his head. "It is not a matter of doubt, but a matter of difference. I am using nothing against you, because you are not the one at fault. I have hurt you badly. I came to you with a heart not whole, and that was wrong of me. Thinking myself forgiven, I gave you my love, and I will never regret it. But I know now that I had already destroyed what should have been yours."

"What? What are you saying, Khedran?" She stepped forward with hands outstretched as he began to turn away. "Just wait! The things she said—she has twisted everything! She's taking advantage of how you feel, don't you see? She thinks you belong to her. Otherwise, she would not have dared to slap you!"

He stopped. "That slap was for your benefit. She was hoping it would soften your heart toward me so that you would take me back."

"I don't believe that. Why would she do that? And how could you possibly even know such a thing?"

He sighed. "Because underneath it all, Marre, she has always been my friend."

It was Danon who found Shandiin hours later, where he had found her once before when they had faced a battle they were certain they would lose.

She was sitting with her back against Cabre's outer wall, looking out over the barren battlefield. When he walked up to her, she remembered what she had said to him back then, and repeated it.

"You shouldn't have come."

He dropped to the ground next to her, and leaning against the wall, drew up a knee to rest an arm on. He looked across at her with a lifted eyebrow. "Roinn sent me. You've left the whole place in an uproar."

"Did you know about Marre?" she asked.

"That she basically threw him out? Yes. There has been no reasoning with her. She is convinced that he belongs to you, now. As though he could belong to anyone, even you."

She managed a smile. "You know him well. But I think he comes closer to belonging to Marre than even he would like."

"Is that why you are out here?"

"I have to stay away from Penumbra. I never meant to cause this shit, Danon."

"Of course you didn't. It isn't in you, no matter what she thinks."

She took a breath and shook her head. "What did I ever do to deserve you? I know I hurt you, all those years ago. Yet here you are, still my friend."

"You did not hurt me. I was obsessed with you once, like a foolish teenager, but I've grown up and learned to love you simply because you are you. I am fine. Really. I have missed you terribly, and now you are back, and my world is right again."

She looked into his eyes. "That simple?"

"Yes. That simple, Shandiin. Will you no longer be his Compatri, alongside of me? Roinn wants you back with the Chaine."

She thought for a long moment. "That would be an ultimate rejection of Khedran. I can't do that. Not yet." She exhaled. "Shit. I slapped him, Danon."

Danon lifted both eyebrows. "Then perhaps he will decide you shouldn't be Compatri anymore. I believe that may be insubordination."

Danon had always been able to make her laugh.

CHAPTER 18

Farbet and Camion were charged with the evacuation of Penumbra under Shandi's direction. This included more than the people. The crypts of the High Kings would be moved as well, along with many artifacts of historical significance.

All was to be stored in the Temple of Liethe, as it was still known although it served now as a hospital using Chaine medical expertise. Liethe's Temple was part of the cliffs that marched to the great Rammorth Range; it was built into the natural terraces that rose like a giant's stairway from the city. Much of the Temple was built into the mountain, and so Khedran had believed it the safest place for those he loved most...those who had refused to seek safety in a place distant from Cabre, as he wished they would.

Those he loved were among the people that he left without further word, once he knew Penumbra's evacuation was well under way. If the citizens closest to him saw anger or sadness when he turned to leave, they were careful not to remark on it. He was the High King. His personal business was none of theirs.

Except, apparently, for Danon.

Khedran walked up to the pair sitting close together against Cabre's outer wall, and regarded them inquisitively.

Danon immediately clambered to his feet. Shandiin followed more coolly and faced the High King with arms crossed. "I'm not going anywhere with you, Khedran. You should have told me what the hell was going on instead of blindsiding me with that shit."

Khedran turned his gaze to Danon, who swallowed. "I'll go now. This isn't what it looks like." He glanced at Shandiin nervously.

She immediately embraced him and planted a kiss on his cheek. "He knows better, idiot." She gave him a little push to be on his way, and he went gladly.

Danon looked back after a minute to see them confronting each other.

Then they were gone.

"Damn it!" Shandiin exclaimed. "I told you I wasn't going anywhere with you."

"I must rest, and I need to talk to you. This seemed like the best place for both."

She scowled at the cabin they had left early that morning, then turned on him. "Why the hell didn't you tell me Marre wanted me gone? And then why the hell did you drag me into that damned soap opera?"

"That what? Never mind. Rhiathe told me to take you to Penumbra." He dragged a hand through his hair, an unusual gesture for him, and his expression was almost pleading. "And you are not a pet dog, Shandiin. Please do not believe you are of no worth to me. My need for you is...more than you know."

She frowned at him, her anger draining into uneasiness at his behavior. "Why would Rhiathe want that awful scene to happen? It was demeaning to you."

"I think Rhiathe wanted me to know the truth, Shandiin. Your concern that I was somehow demeaned is part of the truth she wanted me to see. You never mentioned your own feelings, and I know you too well. Your anger was born of pain, of worry for me."

"You love Marre. You belong with her."

He searched her eyes. "Do I?"

She stared at him in disbelief. "You love her. I know how much you care."

"She has been my heart and center, for many years. You? Shandiin...you have always been my universe."

She knew he wanted to say more, but she turned away so he couldn't read the pain his words gave her. *How can I fix this?* She wondered. *He can't love us both. It isn't right for him to be torn like this. Allasar died because of that division in his universe.*

"We have to go," he warned suddenly. "Egypt is calling me."

And they were back on the bridge of the Aztlan.

"This is starting to piss me off," Shandiin muttered. "Hello, Egypt."

"Hi yourself, Sunshine. Your Highness, the *Earthstar* has arrived on this side of the wormhole. I have new intel, and I have received a recorded message from Premier Canard." She nodded to her Second Mate, and a voice filled the bridge.

"This is Premier Dick Canard. I am sending this message to the Aztlan, *in orbit around Earth Two. Captain Egypt Alexander, as you are probably now aware, the people of the* Earthstar *have directed me to come here, rather than waiting decades for your return. Please acknowledge."*

"Have you responded?" Khedran asked.

"Not yet. I wanted your direction."

"How far away are they?"

She explained. "It's a matter of days, as the starships can't use tunnel drive too near a star. Your sun, I mean."

He smiled a little. "I know that our sun is a star, Egypt. Well, they are too far for me to personally transition there; this orbit is at the outer edge of Rhiathe's magic as it is. So I believe I shall give him a return message. Are you ready to transmit?"

At her acknowledgement, he stood for a moment in thought. When he spoke it was with his rarely used command voice.

Everyone on the bridge snapped to attention, but he didn't know if it would come through as such on the other end.

"Greetings to Premier Canard. I am Khedran, seventh High King of Azlatan. I have been chosen to speak for all the people of my planet. We welcome those who come in peace."

He signaled the end, and returned his attention to Egypt. "Have you already deployed your warcraft to the asteroid belt?"

"Most of them, as planned. Your Highness...he's going to wonder about you being aboard this starship. They know you have no technology. It could be to our advantage that they not realize your wisdom. They are so narrow-minded they probably don't believe the people of this planet smart enough to even use technology. I'm not sure you should have been the one to answer that message."

"I am just smart enough to ride in one of your craft and speak into a microphone. He will know the rest of it soon enough, assuming he makes it necessary." He shook his head. "I wish he had not brought the *Earthstar*. I do not want to see harm to the rest of Earth's surviving descendants, but it appears they are at his mercy."

Egypt began to respond when her Communications Officer signaled, and Canard's voice filled the room again, this time not pre-recorded.

"I return your greetings, um...King Khedran. I am glad to hear you are prepared to accept the colonization of your world. Where is Captain Alexander? I want to know what has become of my brother Ben, who is not answering our attempts at communication."

Egypt looked at the King in question. Khedran began his response, again using his command voice.

"I am with the Captain, as she has been kind enough to allow me aboard her ship. But your brother is dead, Premier Canard. He wrongfully abducted my daughter. She responded by killing him at the first opportunity. I cannot say I am sorry for the death of your brother; I approve of it. My rule has always represented justice. We are a peaceful people, but I will not tolerate evil."

Egypt grimaced as he finished. "I was going to tell him I killed his brother. I thought that might avert any unnecessary anger against your people."

"I do not lie, Egypt."

Shandiin rolled her eyes. "He really doesn't. But there are times I wish he'd just kept his mouth shut."

Khedran threw her an annoyed glance.

Canard came back. *"I am horribly shocked, as I was not aware of my brother's misconduct. I hope this will not interfere with the immigration of my citizens. We had hoped to begin transport of colonists to your planet soon."*

"As I said," Khedran responded, "we are a peaceful people. When can you and I meet in person to discuss details, Premier Canard?"

"It will be some time before we are in range. We will speak again, um, Your Majesty. I will contact you through Captain Alexander."

"Thank you. I will await notification." Khedran ended the transmission. "He is apparently unaware that his brother's last transmission was intercepted."

Egypt nodded in agreement. "Our hidden people will let us know if those transports he mentioned contain colonists or soldiers."

The Communications Officer spoke up. "Another message, Captain. I think it's the Earthstar's Captain this time. It's on a private band."

"Put it on speaker anyway," Egypt directed.

"Greetings to the Aztlan *from the* Earthstar. *This is Captain John Garcia. Egypt, what's going on? Why did you let one of the natives respond to the Premier instead of answering him directly?"*

Egypt returned attention to the High King. "I bet Canard is standing right behind him. His ego has been pricked." With Khedran's nod to her, she answered.

"Hello, John. What a surprise to find you here in my sector of space. Frankly, I didn't dare to insult the man by refusing his request to speak. He isn't just any native. He's the High King here. The whole damn planet answers to him. He's got more power than our Premier." She grinned wickedly as she ended her message. "That will send Canard's temperature up several degrees."

"A strategy, Captain?"

"Yes. An angry mind, a jealous mind, is not as likely to think with any intelligence. Not that Canard ever had any, anyway." She scowled. "I've also learned that he has remarried, and even his own family is concerned that he has become unbalanced by his wife's manipulation. Which is odd, considering their exploitation of women."

The Communications Officer turned toward them again. "This one's on our Purr band," he said, and she gestured for him to play it.

"That's our secret channel," she told Khedran. "It's one of Roland's people."

"Egypt, this is Magdalena. I heard the King's transmission. I have never heard a voice like that. It seemed to arrive in my head, and that should have been scary, but was somehow comforting. Is he anything like the way he sounds?"

Egypt chuckled. "Yes, Magdalena. The High King is one of the good people, and much more. I believe we have all found a home, though he is too smart to allow entrance without scrutiny."

Egypt smiled at Khedran as she ended transmission. "I was hoping your command voice went through, Your Highness. That had to make a lot of people sit up and take notice, which had to make Canard furious. But tell me...why do you want to meet him in person? He'll lie to you there as well as from a distance."

"I have ways of influencing people when in person. Captain, are Roland's people on that other ship in any danger?"

"Only if someone realizes who they are," Egypt replied. "And I don't think that's likely. They've long been part of Roland's underground. Magdalena says Canard's people started plotting as soon as they found out about your habitable planet. My latest intel says they find its current occupation a minor and easily rectified inconvenience. Thanks to Roland's work, though, we had already put our own people...his soldiers, my crew...into place even before we were sure of their intent. Sarnath's had a lot of good influence on them as well. He has some of your...mystique."

Khedran lifted an eyebrow. "From what Shandiin has told me, Sarnath is one of my ancestors, like the rest of your family. Where is he?"

Egypt glanced toward Shandiin. "He's with Zion on a personal matter."

Khedran dropped the subject. "Is there any chance you can coax the Premier into bringing his starship closer before he begins sending transports or warcraft? I would like our meeting to be near Rhiathe's magic perimeter. My personal influence may not be enough to sway him. With Rhiathe's help I can rectify any harmful intent."

She frowned thoughtfully. "I could advise him the stupid King is eager to accept immigration, leading him to believe there's no hurry to launch his attack. It would be much more efficient for them to hold off on launching transports until they are closer to the planet."

"Are you certain the first transports won't have peaceful colonists aboard?"

"I am. They're going to send armed soldiers to displace, even to destroy what they call the natives. In the secret message we intercepted, VP Ben Canard called this a 'planet full of witches.' The word 'witches' is their code for the genetically engineered. He let them know the people of your planet are related to my family, and they do not believe we are human. They will not hesitate to bring violence to your world."

Khedran nodded grimly. "Let me know when your people verify the ships coming to us contain armed soldiers and not promised colonists. I am arranging ground forces to address transports with soldiers. Keep your warcraft hidden in the asteroid belt unless they send Earther warcraft carrying nuclear weapons. Don't wait to seek my direction if that happens. You are my world's only defense against them. My trust is in you, Captain."

Shandiin saw Egypt take on that weight, and elevate her posture to bear it. Her eyes on the King's were steady and bright.

"Thank you for that honor," was her only response.

Shandiin was only able to give her friend a supportive smile before Rhiathe's magic transition took her again...

...and she found herself back in their snowy valley cabin.

She almost growled in exasperation. "Dammit! Khedran, this isn't where you belong. You belong with Marre, and I don't belong with you."

To her surprise he turned his back on her and, shoving his hands through his hair, held them there. "Stop. Please, Shandiin."

The atypical frustration in his action and his voice made her swallow further words. After a moment he dropped his hands and turned back to face her, and she saw his eyes were bright with unshed tears.

Zion's had been the same, the last time she saw him, and that had stunned and shamed her. But seeing Khedran like this crushed her soul.

"I'm sorry." His voice was thick with the emotion he was fighting. "For all of it. For what's been done to you, and Marre, and Zion. It's all my fault."

She realized he was carrying the onerous burden of a world under attack, the loss of his family, and now an unreasonable guilt because it was simply his nature to be accountable. She was, for the first time, seeing him overwhelmed.

That frightened her, and fear always made her angry.

"Well," she snarled, "that's a crock of bullshit. I'm the selfish bitch who started it. I seduced you instead of leaving when I should have. I hurt Zion terribly because I couldn't love him the way he needs. If anyone's to blame, Khedran, it's me. And I can't bear seeing you like this. You don't deserve any of it. Do what you have to do to save your world. You don't *need* me."

He began to speak, then stopped. Shook his head. "I cannot need you. I cannot love you. But Shandiin...I do anyway, and there is no way to change that...even if I wanted to."

Unable to manage anything else, she held on to anger. "Rhiathe did this, damn her. She used magic to make you love me."

"No. I am broken, Shandiin, but it isn't Rhiathe who broke me. She did not make me love you. I am no better than a computer, programmed to do what I am required to do. You are the anomaly."

She stared at him. "You've lost your freaking mind. You think you're an AI?"

"If so, I am obviously not a very good one." He settled on the couch and shook his head. "I wish I could make you understand. I've always relied on you to understand, but this seems impossible. If you don't want to try, if you want to leave me here, the next cabin has been prepared for you. Is that what you want?"

When he lifted his face to her in question, it held the same emptiness she'd seen when he'd come back from Earth. That finished her.

"No, Khedran. I'm not leaving you until I understand what the hell is going on. Where did all this AI nonsense come from?"

He rubbed his eyes, and she could tell he was fighting exhaustion again. "Shandiin, I was simply trying to explain how I see myself. I'm not a normal human. I am programmed to do and accept only certain things. Yet by some miracle my soul reached for yours the instant I was born. That miracle is the only thing that makes me think I might have a soul at all."

He lost the battle against fatigue and just laid down. "I cannot be sorry for loving you." He closed his eyes. "I am just sorry for what it has caused."

"Khedran..."

But he was already asleep.

She covered him again with his cloak, lowering herself to the floor to watch him while she waited for Rhiathe.

"I am here, Shandiin."

She glared up at the beautiful goddess. "You have corrupted him. You made him love me and he can't. He's in total misery. You have to fix this!"

Rhiathe leaned back to study her. "So you think love is corrupt? Do you think I corrupted Allasar, by giving Mia to him when he was married to me?"

"Yes, dammit! Allasar never got past what he had done. He gave up and waited for the Anzihi to kill him. Just because you were temporarily human obviously didn't make you understand them. Especially not a human like a High King."

"If love is corrupt, Shandiin, you corrupted my son when you sent him to Marre."

"I did nothing of the kind. He was already betrothed to Marre."

"They were betrothed on the order of a false god. He loved you first, Shandiin, and not by my doing. Why are you turning away from him?"

Shandiin shoved to her feet, fists clenched at her sides. "You just don't get it, do you? *He doesn't have a choice.* He married his betrothed; that was allowed. But leaving her is not allowed. Loving anyone but her is not allowed."

"Humans do that sort of thing all the time."

"And apparently your short time being human has made you as stupid as we are. You should know damned well that kind of behavior is not true of the High Kings. They are held to a higher standard. By themselves...always, by God, held to it by themselves. But this is beyond even that. Their purpose is their people, and they are held to a higher standard by their people. Do you think it was only guilt that led to Allasar's death? He was a failure, Rhiathe. When he committed adultery he failed his people's expectations, and he lived with that shame long before he was found out. Khedran has always lived under the shadow of his father's dishonor. It's one of the reasons his people almost turned against him before the Prophecy War."

When Rhiathe looked away, Shandiin knew she had struck home, and she continued relentlessly. "This isn't about love. He can't leave his High Queen. He serves his people, and they would never accept it if he left his Queen for anyone. The High Kings are revered for their nobility, and they need that reverence to meet their purpose of leadership. If he fails his purpose, it will destroy him."

When the goddess made no response, Shandiin sat down on the edge of the couch, her gaze on Khedran's sleeping face. She blinked back the tears she hated. "I beg you, Rhiathe, to take this cup from him. Make him not love me. Let him have some peace."

"I cannot, Shandiin. I cannot take his memories, his joy, or his pain. I would have made it otherwise, but he would not allow it." She looked down on her son with pride and sorrow. "What are you going to do?"

"I don't belong in his world. But I can't leave him yet. I'm worried about his mental state—and I think I do have a role to play in helping him defend his people. But as soon as this war is over I plan to disappear from his life, just as I promised Marre today."

Rhiathe regarded her sadly. "You will break his heart."

Shandiin shook her head. "He loves Marre, and she loves him. They had a solid marriage until I showed up again. With me gone, I believe they can work things out."

"In this case I think it is you who doesn't understand him, Shandiin. He loves you deeply and always has." Rhiathe laid a gentle hand on Khedran's hair, preparatory to leaving him. "I wish I could take away his pain. I wish he had accepted all my gifts, because I know too much of what is yet in store for him."

When Shandiin tried to ask what that meant, Rhiathe was gone. She looked back at Khedran. *I won't think about what is still in store. What use is worrying even more than I am already? I just won't think about it.*

When Khedran woke it was morning, and he was alone. Puzzled, he looked around until he saw Shandiin through the window.

It was snowing. She was playing in the snow.

Making snowballs. Piling them up. Occasionally splattering one against a tree. She stopped to throw her head back and catch the flakes on her tongue, and he could tell she was laughing.

He had tried to look past her in the darkness of these days. But how could he ignore Shandiin? He had marveled all his life at her contrary nature. She found amusement in the strangest things, even in what vexed her, and tossed joy at him when he least expected it. She was outrageously flippant when she should have been serious. She was, in fact, frequently just outrageous. She never spoke of her own heart. She was almost impossible to know. Yet, for all her unpredictability, she was steadfast and true as the sunrise.

His soul yearned for her.

He donned boots and cloak and went to join her.

She saw him approaching and immediately reached into her armory of snowballs and threw one at him. He put up an arm to protect his face, but the next one got him square in the chest, and he enjoyed her amusement. He kept advancing through her barrage until his black garb was splattered with white.

When he stopped in front of her, he caught her arm before she could plaster his face. Instead of fighting, she threw herself backward into a drift and began flailing her arms and legs. "I'm making a snow angel!" she laughed.

"You don't even have on a cloak." He smiled down at her. "You will freeze."

"I don't care. It's been so long since I have felt snow. Since I have even been cold. This is amazing."

"Shandiin. Get up now, or you are going to be wet as well as cold."

She accepted his reaching hand, and he pulled her to her feet. Shaking snow from her wild red mane, she smiled at seeing her

High King with snow in his hair, on his black attire. "I saw you play in the snow when we were in Ordhold," she reminded him.

"I was little more than a boy then."

"So what? Aren't you allowed a simple joy, the kind of joy you want to give those people on the ship?"

"A lot else must happen before that could. We have work to attend to, Shandiin."

She huffed, her shoulders dropping. "I know."

She turned to start toward the cabin, and a snowball smacked the back of her head. When she turned around in surprise, the next one splattered in her face. She squealed when he continued to pummel her with snowballs while she scrambled to return fire, until finally she laughed, "Uncle! Uncle! Hey, that means stop, Khedran! I give up!"

She stilled as she watched him come to her, laughter on his lips. She looked into those beautiful emerald eyes and saw the unfailing love he had for her. His complete joy in her.

Watched him remember who he was, and what was not his.

Watched die the laughter. Watched die the joy.

"We should go," he said, and started back to the cabin.

Suddenly realizing she was cold, she followed him.

Roland had finally recovered from his awe of Khedran's presence, and his avid personality had returned.

They were on the busy shooting range. "Your builders are not only learning how to use these weapons," he told his King, "they are amazing marksmen and teachers. I have flown them to the other places you directed, to train your Black Guard and Chaine warriors. But they tell me many of the Chaine refuse the rifles."

"They believe them dishonorable," Khedran explained. "It is a rare exception for them to refuse reason, but honor is even more important."

Shandiin sighed. "For some, reason is lost when personal standards are involved. But I wish Roinn would bend on this."

"It isn't Roinn's order. It's his people, including Shajii." Roland glanced over to where the redhead was practicing with her Bond and Wesson 500. She hadn't yet missed a target, and he was still amazed she could handle its recoil. "By the way," he told the King, "Shajii tells me your daughter was the quickest to learn, and she has no qualm about using a rifle."

There was a definite hesitation before Khedran responded. "Is Shandi planning to fight alongside the Chaine, then?"

"That's what I understand."

Khedran fell silent.

Shandiin understood. "Roinn won't let anything happen to her, Khedran."

He shook his head. "I should have known she would do this. She has trained hard to be a warrior."

"She's your daughter, with your fighting spirit. You should expect no less."

But I'd be worried too, she thought. *You're engaging the Chaine where magic is useless against modern weaponry, for the front line ground defense of Cabre. She will be in the direct line of fire.*

Roland pulled out his communicator, turning it to speaker as soon as he identified the caller as Egypt.

She was brusque. "Canard is moving the Starship closer, but they have already deployed the transports. Advise the King, Roland. It's verified they're carrying armed soldiers, not colonists. Canard is lying to everyone on the starship, telling them colonization has begun and it will be peaceful until he sees how the natives react. He also transmitted the same message to me. Apparently he doesn't trust me to know the truth."

"That's what you get for being a witch," Roland responded. "The King is with me now, so he heard your message. How long before the transports pass your orbit?"

"Less than a day. They've marked the King's city as their priority destination, I am told."

"How long before the starship comes into orbit?" Khedran asked.

"That will be a few days more, Your Highness. I was really hoping they'd hold the transports until they are close enough for your magic."

"How do you know what he is telling his people?"

"Canard uses television for everything, not just to show their horrid Spectacle of Retribution. He likes to make speeches at the people and thinks his face is important. Magdalena streams it to me." There was a moment before she continued. "I saw their Spectacle yesterday. They pulled out a prisoner's guts while he was still alive and very much aware. Canard and his regime are pure evil, Your Highness."

Khedran and everyone in hearing grimaced. "I have to agree," Khedran responded. "Continue to hold your warcraft for now, Captain. We have plans for ground defense. As we discussed, your role is to stop their warcraft if they are deployed."

While Roland put the communicator away, Khedran turned to Shandiin. "Would you come with me to Cabre, or would you prefer to stay here?" he asked.

"Oh, so I have a choice?"

"You always have a choice. Surely you have known that."

She sighed. "Yes. I guess I do. I'll come along, Khedran."

With a brief goodbye, they walked away. Roland looked after them as Shajii came up. "That's strange," he frowned.

"What?"

"They are so careful with each other. It's like they've just argued about something."

The pair went around a corner and were gone.

Shajii sighed. "I think their argument lies within their own hearts. That is a sorry battle."

The ramparts of Cabre were once again geared for war.

But this time its defenders had guns.

Shandi turned to see her father walking toward her along the rampart's fighting platform. She waited, wearing full Black Guard regalia with sidearms strapped at hip and thigh, and a strange weapon behind her. Khedran frowned at it as he approached. "What is that?" he asked, dispensing with awkward greetings.

"Roland says it is a grenade machine gun with smart shell and can fire 260 rounds per minute. We have five. His plan is to use them to destroy any warcraft or vehicles at a distance from these walls, but it can kill a person far away. It's also light enough for me to use, he says, but I could handle far heavier."

Khedran considered the weapon and then his daughter. "Are you wearing Kevlar? I am told it will stop a bullet."

"I am wearing under-armor of Chaine gold. It will serve, Father."

They regarded each other for a long moment.

"I wish you would not be...here," he said finally.

"You know it is where I belong. To serve Azlatan. To fight alongside the man I will marry."

He sighed. "Of course. I would expect no less of you, but I will still worry."

"Of course you will. But I know you will not hesitate to put yourself in danger, either. Do you think I don't worry about you? Do you think I no longer love you, just because I was stupid and angry?"

"You were not stupid. You were hurt. For that I am sorry."

She shook her head. "You have already apologized when you had done no harm to me. Please forgive me, Father. I was being a foolish girl, not the strong woman you raised me to be."

He opened his arms to her then, and she went to him gladly.

Shandiin watched from her near vantage where she stood next to Danon, and breathed a sigh of relief. "That's one down. Now where's Marre?"

"In the Temple." Danon was strapping on his own weapon. "She is busy helping Jael and Zion prepare the hospital with the new equipment Zion just brought in, along with people that know how to use it. If Khedran wants to see her, he will have to go there."

"Zion is here?"

"Yes. Uh-oh. You didn't know?"

"Stop guessing. Yes, we have separated. Permanently."

He said nothing for a long moment. "You can still have me," he joked.

She turned to him, surprising herself with sincerity. "If I were smart, you would be my first choice, Danon. Over anyone in this world or another. I am seriously sorry I am not smart."

"Um..."

"I see you still have that amazing vocabulary."

He grinned.

She saw Roinn climbing up to the fighting platform where they stood in wait. Before she went to meet him she gave Danon a fierce hug. "Please take care of yourself. I need you, Danon. I need your friendship, and everything else that is you. I love you dearly, even if it isn't a romantic love, which I wish at this moment I knew nothing about. Do you understand *amhara*?"

"Yes." They stood eye to eye atop the rampart, a morning wind stirring his dark hair, the sun firing her wild red with broken gold. "It is what I feel for you, Shandiin."

She blinked. "Thank you for that gift. Thank you so much."

In answer he cupped her chin gently and kissed her lips as she had one time kissed his. When he drew back, he smiled at her look of amazement. "I am a little braver," he said, "than I used to be."

"Yes. You are." She grinned and shifted away before she could show how much that kiss had moved her heart.

"Roinn," she called as she approached the big man. "What is this I hear about you and Shandi? You're marrying outside the Chaine? Shit, you're getting *married*?"

He beamed down at her. "You are already taken, and I have to admit...even if you were not, Shandi has my heart."

"That's good. That's more than good. You deserve no less."

He looked over to where Shandi stood with her father. "She is far more than I could ever deserve, Shandiin."

She saw the way he looked at his Princess, and knew his truth. "You are *amharen*. Never mind weddings and love stories. You are *amharen*."

"Yes. She is my universe."

The words Khedran had also used were a blow to her gut. She turned away before he could see it, to catch her breath. "Do you think your heart and your universe could ever be separate?" she asked, trying to sound light.

"I don't see how."

After a moment, she sighed. "Neither do I."

PART IV. A KINGDOM TOO SMALL

When that this body did contain a spirit,
A kingdom for it was too small a bound;
But now two paces of the vilest earth
Is room enough...
– William Shakespeare
Henry IV, Part 1, Act 5, Scene 4

The beast in me is caged by frail and fragile bars.
"The Beast in Me,"
song and lyrics by Nick Lowe

CHAPTER 19

T he man called only 'PT' smiled as he landed his tiny craft on the outskirts of Cabre.

He'd been careful to avoid any possibility of surveillance when he left the *Aztlan*. His truth as a faithful subject of the *Earthstar's* regime had been invisible to all of the traitors on board that ship, traitors he had worked beside, cooking and cleaning for them while he observed. He had planned to report it all when he was finally contacted by his superiors. He'd been surprised to receive new orders instead.

PT was proud that he could maintain his loyalty even without the drugging gifts that had kept him happy and unstressed aboard the *Earthstar.* Indeed, he rather liked the new feelings of excitement that had come with his undercover assignment.

And the natives had no technology, so he was invisible to them as he landed in darkness.

He left the craft in a forest edging a barren field at the entrance to a medieval city. *They call it Cabre, the King's City*, he thought. *They talk about the King like he's a god or something. But he's just a lab experiment. He isn't a real human.*

He settled into the forest's dark boundary, watching the traffic around the city's entrance. There were people in wagons drawn by animals going in and out of the gates in the city's surprisingly high wall.

Dawn was nearing when he spotted what he wanted. He left the cover of the forest and stepped onto the road in front of the horseman in black.

The man reined in, frowning down at him. "What service do you require, sir?"

"I need help. Please. My friend is injured and cannot walk. I hear there is a hospital in the city. Can you help me?" PT didn't have a problem sounding nervous; the creature the man rode was very near and very large.

The soldier dismounted. "Show me where. He can ride my horse."

"He's in the forest, not too far from here. There's some heavy brush though, and I've hurt my leg. Can you and your horse go ahead, and break a path for me? It's that way." He pointed to an opening in the trees.

The man looked surprised but turned in the direction indicated.

PT lifted the dart gun he'd held out of sight and fired. The man went down but the horse turned on him immediately, ears flat and eyes blazing. A second silent dart lodged in the horse's neck. It staggered, then fell.

You could almost believe it could think. It was well trained to react when his rider falls. Horrifying creature.

So far everything was going according to plan. He didn't bother checking either body for breath; the silent gun was loaded with a paralytic lethal against anything with a nervous system. He glanced back to ensure they were far enough from the road that they would not be noticed in the darkness, grinning at how easy this had been.

He swiftly exchanged his clothing for the black uniform, noting curiously the emerald sickle moon which was apparently some kind of insignia. He tossed the black cloak over his shoulders with a grin, thinking of an old vid he'd seen. *Now I am Darth Vader. Look out, you animals, here I come.*

He secured the dart gun in case of future need and made sure his preferred and fully loaded .44 Magnum was discreetly strapped at his waist and covered by the uniform's tunic. Joining the road traffic, he walked without challenge into Cabre.

While Cabre prepared for war and Zion and Jael worked to turn the Temple of Liethe into a modern hospital, Khedran and Shandiin were back aboard the *Aztlan*.

They were watching a monitor that tracked the *Earthstar*.

"I've confirmed that they will send only the transports first," Egypt explained to them. "The warcraft will delay, awaiting results of the ground attack. They believe their soldiers won't meet any hostility, but it won't take the warcraft long to deploy once they learn there is a defense."

Khedran frowned. "Are you monitoring their communications, Egypt?"

"Yes. But I can't block them; I tried."

"Have you talked to their Premier?"

"He has not seen fit to communicate with me."

"Then you must contact him. Tell him I want to meet with him right away to discuss the colonization." He considered. "I will need a pilot."

Egypt's face went to stone. "As you wish, Your Highness."

"Bullshit!" Shandiin exclaimed. "Dammit, Khedran, you can't put yourself in their hands without your magic. He'll kill you or take you hostage."

He didn't take his eyes from the monitor. "I am aware of the danger. My concern is my world and my people. As soon as he learns his ground troops are meeting our defense, he will order the warcraft with nuclear weapons to strike. I cannot stop him from making that order by sending messages. I have to meet him in person."

When she began to argue he spun around, seizing her shoulders. "Shandiin, that is my daughter standing on the ramparts of

Cabre with my people and your Chaine. That is my world. Look at me," he demanded. "*Look* at me, Shandiin."

She closed her mouth and met his gaze. "If I can delay them long enough," he told her, "the starship will be close enough for Rhiathe's magic to help me take out their leader and his supporters. With them gone we have a chance to handle this peacefully. I have prepared my world for war the best way I can, but this is a better option, and you know it."

"Holy cartwheeling Jesus. I should have known you'd do something like this. But what about Jael's visions?"

"I am hoping to make them wrong. I cannot believe that there is no way to keep that horror from happening."

She thought quickly. "At least take Varady."

He sighed, dropping his hands as stepped back, and looked at her in question.

"If anyone can get to this man," she explained, "he can. He may be able to stop him with his gift. You know he can make people see themselves truly."

"I do not believe Varady's gift will work on a sociopath. Don't look so surprised; my journey to Earth educated me in many things, and I have known Canard's kind before without knowing the word. I will not endanger my brother without surety."

She glared at him. "Are you so sure of your own outcome, then? Or are you planning to be a martyr? Damn it to hell, Khedran—"

"I will take the risk, but I am not a martyr. You know me better than that. I will always fight to my last breath."

"How close will they have to be before you can use magic?" Egypt asked.

"How long until they reach the moon's orbit?"

"That's going to be at least a day, maybe more. Can't you give it a little more time? Give yourself a better chance?"

Khedran shook his head. "I must go before he sends in the warcraft."

Shandiin crossed her arms, scowling. "Then I'm going with you. If you don't let me pilot, I will take one of Egypt's craft and follow you. But I'll be there if you insist on..."

She never had a chance to finish her sentence. Khedran shot her a look she had never before seen on his face.

It was sheer terror.

They both vanished.

Morning had come, and PT needed to ask directions before he could fulfill his mission.

The city came alive with the sun. People moved briskly about, though he was surprised to see no merchants set up as surveillance had shown was normal.

He'd watched from orbit, from Egypt's starship. He had watched the monitors, and while his subordinate position kept him away from decisions made on the bridge, he had learned much.

He'd been surprised when he received the order to go to the planet instead of simply giving his report, but he didn't question his superior.

He looked around at all the people who would shortly be dead. That thought made him smile, because he planned to be gone long before that happened. And he hated them all. *Witches. Not human.*

He walked boldly among them in his black uniform and saw the few citizens out and about step respectfully out of his way. There were a lot of soldiers, which puzzled him. When he saw one of them with an emerald star on his collar but no sickle moon, he went to ask him for directions, believing it unlikely that someone from a different unit would question his identity. He was also sure a green insignia couldn't designate any rank of importance. He had carefully avoided those with silver or gold showing.

He walked up to the man, who was leading a horse into the stables. "I am told I must find the High Princess," he said to the soldier. "Would you happen to know her whereabouts?"

Danon stopped and frowned at him. "You must be newly assigned to the Queen's Guard. I would expect a more appropriate greeting, soldier, to a Compatri of the High King."

Oops. He paid immediate obeisance. "My deepest apologies, sir. I am new here, and only wish to deliver a message as ordered."

Danon studied him for a long moment. "The Princess is at the rampart." He signaled to another soldier. "Take this horse in for me, Sergeant. I'll show this man where to go."

Danon turned away. With a breath of relief, PT followed him through the crowd that got out of the Compatri's way very quickly. *I think I will kill this one too,* he thought. *Pompous ass.*

As they climbed up toward the parapet, PT was surprised to see order and discipline...and weapons. *Where did they get firearms? I may have a little more trouble getting out of here than I thought. But nothing will stop me because I am in the right.*

When they reached the platform below the parapet, Danon gestured for him to walk ahead of him. PT was concerned to see soldiers lined up atop a ledge below the crenellation, sitting low where they would not be visible atop the wall. The lower platform held many of the people he knew were called Chaine. One redhaired beauty turned to consider him as they passed, which made him nervous until he realized she was looking at the man behind her.

Shajii gave Danon a friendly nod before turning back to her post.

They know we are coming, PT realized in shock. *They are lying in wait. I must get word out...as soon as I finish my assignment.*

Danon put a hand on his shoulder, and PT turned back, startled, to look into Danon's cool blue eyes. Danon gestured toward Shandi. "She's over there." PT again gave obeisance before turning to follow his gesture.

Danon frowned. Nobody every bowed to him, but this man had done it twice. He'd planned to return to his duties but decided to follow this odd stranger.

Shandi stood with Roinn, deep in conversation. She looked up at the stranger's approach and smiled when she saw Danon behind him.

The smile stopped PT in his tracks.

He had never seen a woman so beautiful. Her eyes were truly emerald. Her black hair swept the long curve of her back. She was all curves. He felt heat and...

I am a righteous soldier, he reminded himself. *I cannot be put aside by temptation. She is a witch. This is proof she is a witch!*

Roinn had also seen the man approach and noticed that Danon was frowning at his back.

The Chaine had a long history of battles fought, enemies defeated; he had trained all his life to recognize danger. Quick as the chill of instinct, Roinn was moving to protect Shandi.

"Greetings!" PT cried. *"I bring a message from Premier Canard. You should not have killed his brother, witch."*

He had the Magnum out, aiming at Shandi's center mass, before he finished his little speech...and was already pulling the trigger.

Roinn took the bullets point blank. They went through him to take the love of his life while PT laughed.

PT spun to shoot Danon next, continuing to fire indiscriminately as he rotated to make his escape.

But he came against blazing emerald eyes in the face of a man who had not been there a second before. Khedran caught the weapon with one hand and PT's throat with the other.

The last thing PT ever saw was the fury in the eyes of the High King before he was thrown screaming over the rampart wall to his death several stories below.

Shandiin was already kneeling in blood, wrestling Roinn's body aside, when Khedran dropped to his knees beside her. She'd known immediately Roinn was lost, so she sought the Princess he'd so obviously tried to protect.

She couldn't tell if the blood covering Shandi belonged to her or if it was Roinn's, but she found a thready pulse. "Alive! Get her to the hospital!"

Khedran gathered Shandi into his arms and vanished. Shandiin clambered to her feet, her body quaking with reaction as she looked around at the carnage.

And then she saw Danon.

He lay on his back, his black hair spilled about his head, blood flooding around him. She ran to him, shucking off her denim jacket to use as a compress. Even as she jammed it against the wound in his chest, she was choking on hopelessness. "No! Danon, stay with me!"

His eyes fluttered open and shifted to meet hers.

She watched the light in their blue dim, then disappear.

And she wept.

Khedran flashed into existence beside Jael, his daughter wrapped in his arms.

Jael had envisioned this, and had frozen in wait. He didn't hesitate. "Put her on this gurney, Khedran. Zion! I need your help!"

Zion pushed past Khedran to the gurney. He started giving orders to the healers he had been so carefully training.

The High King stumbled backwards, and someone shoved a chair behind him before he fell. "Is she dead?" he asked.

"No," Zion said. "Let me work, Khedran."

The High King sat like a thing of stone for a long minute, watching them cut open Shandi's clothing to reveal the broken Chaine armor beneath.

She said it would serve, but Chaine gold did not stop the bullets.

"It must have slowed them," Zion replied, and Khedran realized he had spoken aloud. "With all that blood I thought it even worse than it is. Jael, we need the operating room. Is it ready?"

"Yes," came the immediate response. Jael threw a harried glance at Khedran, who was unable to see anything but his daughter. "We will try to save her, but you have to stay here, understand?" Then he was gone with Zion, rolling the gurney away with Shandi on it.

"What happened?" came a voice almost unknown to Khedran through the strange roaring in his ears.

"She was shot," Khedran heard himself say. "She was on the ramparts, and someone shot her." He leaned forward to stand, but Marre shoved him back into the chair.

"Where were you?" she demanded.

He blinked up at her. "Too far away. I was on the starship, and I knew what was going to happen. I had a vision, a flash...but I was a second too late, and she...she..."

His eyes met hers and filled with tears. Her mouth worked, but no words came out.

She sagged into his lap, into his arms, and they wept together while the world fell apart around them.

Shandiin gently closed Danon's eyes and turned back to her other great loss.

Her Roinn, the man she had known as her ally and friend for near two centuries. The Chaine, first leader to follow her, steadfast and true. And so in love. So happy, when last she'd seen him.

She wept over him as she had for Danon, and wondered if she could ever stop. "You wanted me back with my people." She stroked the auburn hair. "I will do as you wanted, Roinn. I should have done that already. That's where I belong, and you always knew it, didn't you?"

"Should-haves serve no purpose but pain," a familiar voice said. *"You taught him that, Shandiin."*

Hearing the voice of the world-goddess, she was torn between hope and fury. "Bring them back," she demanded. "Bring them back, Rhiathe!"

"I cannot return the dead, Shandiin. Death is intrinsic to nature."

Staggered by grief, Shandiin looked down on Roinn and Danon. "I can't bear it, Rhiathe. These great men can't have died for no reason."

"Many others died the same way, on your world. Many others suffered the same needless loss you now feel, on your world."

"That is not my world. I'm not sure it ever was. This is my world, and I will not have this here."

She didn't care that their conversation had only been mental. She stood up, bloody fists clenched at her sides, and screamed it to the sky. *"I will not have this in my world!"*

She didn't care that those around her stared, some moving away in fear from this madwoman standing and screaming over Roinn's body. She didn't even see Shajii, who knelt weeping at her feet.

When there was no response, Shandiin closed her eyes against everything around her, against anything but her grief and fury at the murder of those who were brave and good, committed by fools who were not.

Reclaiming the control she knew was necessary to her purpose, she returned to speaking to the goddess in her mind only, from the place of her despair. "Rhiathe, is Khedran the only one who can stop this depravity from happening here? Is that why it's so important to you that I be with him?"

"The son may lead the people to be what they need to be. I don't know if he will. This terrible thing is a turning point for him, and he needs you to pass beyond it. If you can help him now, he may persevere. This and what will yet come are what I have dreaded, because my promise to him takes so much from my control. I know you also made a promise, telling his Queen that you would leave him. But he needs you now, Shandiin. He will not abide without

your help. What would you ask of me, to help him through this crossroad?"

Before she made her deal with the goddess, before she sealed her own fate, Shandiin looked down on her two dead beloveds, and made a simple request from her heart. "Will you take care of them, Rhiathe? Roinn...and my sweet Danon?"

"They are beyond me now. They are with your High Kings, and all of the others you guarded against the gods for a thousand years. The many that you have loved and lost before, in all that time. Now what would you have me do?"

Shandiin told her, and in Rhiathe's response had the biggest shock since she had left Earth a thousand years before.

Chapter 20

When Shandiin walked into the hospital, Varady was holding Marre cradled against his chest while she sobbed. He looked at Shandiin over the Queen's head, his golden eyes filled with grief. But he recognized who she was now.

He'd once seen the face of the goddess Chaos. Known by the Sundancers as the Sunqueen, she had answered his call, rising into the sky in a cloak of flame. Though her fire was once again banked within a legendary mortal, he realized Chaos had returned as The Chaine.

"Where is Khedran?" Shandiin asked.

"He is with Shandi. She is dying, Shandiin. I had to take Marre out of there to calm her and give Khedran a chance to come to terms with this. I am not sure he can. I can give him no solace. I think...maybe you can help?"

Shandiin only nodded and turned in the direction Varady indicated. Hospital staff moved aside with wide eyes as The Chaine strode past in leather and gold, her presence unmistakably that of the warrior of legend—even with a Glock strapped to her hip instead of a sword.

She was once more the champion revered by her people and idolized by Danon.

Shandiin paused in the doorway to see Shandi's still form, her bed surrounded by Zion's modern medical equipment. The dying young beauty seemed to be plugged into all of it.

She looked down at her assigned responsibility, the High King of a continent, the leader of a world. On the edge of a chair by his daughter's bed, Khedran leaned with his forehead resting next to hers on the pillow. His face was face curtained by the black tangle of his hair. He held Shandi's hand tightly, as though he could hold onto her life by sheer will.

He's been on the edge for so long, she thought. *But this has finally broken him. Even if I save her, he may never come back.*

She knew he'd be conflicted about her deal with the goddess, because he would understand what it had cost her. But, seeing him there, she knew she had done the right thing.

Zion stood on the other side of the bed, staring at Shandiin in shock.

When her cold silver gaze had passed over him, he'd realized he had never really known this woman. She had spent half of twenty years trying to tell him about this world, but he had never understood the reality of The Chaine, who carried the goddess Chaos within her being.

He saw the years of his own blindness and recognized a force even greater than the son of Rhiathe.

Khedran lifted his head when the beeping machines fell silent.

Shandiin was pulling the plugs, turning off the switches.

And Shandi sat up. Without intubation, without needles in her arms.

Without her deadly wounds.

Seeing her father's ravaged face, Shandi reached for him in reflex. He rose so quickly he knocked his chair over, and gathered her to him as though she were a child again.

Marre rushed into the room. She froze in the doorway, seeing a miracle.

After a very long moment Khedran drew back, gazing at his daughter in wonder. His eyes finally tracked over to The Chaine. She contemplated him without expression.

"Did you do this?" he asked.

"Yes."

Marre ran to the bed, but Shandi broke away from Khedran and fended her mother off, turning to Shandiin with terror in her eyes. "Roinn?" his name was a plea on her lips. "My Roinn?"

I can't allow myself to feel her pain, Shandiin thought. *She's lost her* amharen, *her love beyond words; her Roinn, who told me she was his universe. If I allow myself to empathize with her terrible loss or give in to my own, I'll go as mad as her father will, very shortly. He's already on the verge. I have to stay lucid, or I can't help him.*

So when she looked down at Shandi there was no warmth in her eyes, or her voice. "Roinn is gone. He died saving you." She lifted her gaze to Khedran. "Premier Canard sent an assassin to kill your daughter, Khedran, because you told him she had killed his brother. The assassin killed several of your most loyal on the ramparts before you stopped him. Roinn was one. Your Compatri Danon was another."

Khedran stumbled back as though she had struck him. He just stared at her.

Until his emerald eyes fired wild with rage, and his command voice filled the room. "Canard will die. Everyone on the *Earthstar* will die. If Egypt won't do it, I will put one of her bombs in a warcraft and take it to them myself."

He vanished. A second later, so did she.

Egypt had been trying frantically to reach the High King, to let him know the transports were being launched. Her officers were hard at work, communicating with pilots preparing for battle in the next wave.

But suddenly the High King was on the bridge, and he gave an order that stunned her soul.

"Kill the *Earthstar*."

She fixated on him, horrified. Khedran was covered in blood, and his eyes were not sane. Fury and magic pulsed from him. Everyone on the bridge froze in fear.

"Captain, I gave you an order!"

Shandiin flashed into being, not three feet in front of him, glaring back at the raging fire in those emerald eyes. "There are innocent people on that ship, Khedran."

"The people of my world are innocent, and I have put them all in danger. I have killed Danon, and Roinn, and nearly killed my own daughter. Get away from me, Shandiin. Captain, do as you were told."

Shandiin crowded Khedran even closer. "Stop this," she warned him. "I know where you are; I've been there. But you can't do this. Not you. *Listen to me.*"

He shoved her viciously in response.

She spun back with a hard elbow to the jaw. It caught him by surprise, but he didn't go down as she'd hoped. His eyes were still blazing when he came after her, and she backpedaled quickly with a yelp to Egypt. "Some help here?"

Egypt had been momentarily frozen, but her rebound was quick. She slipped behind Khedran and caught his arms behind him in a wrist lock. Shandiin knew even Egypt's strength wouldn't hold him, but it gave her a simple option.

When he leaned forward to break free, she stepped to him, pulled her Glock, and jammed the muzzle against his forehead.

His eyes widened in shock.

"Khedran, you are not thinking clearly. This isn't you. If Egypt turns her weapons on that starship, it will be the end of Earth's last survivors, and they are innocent of what has hurt you. They are innocent of the threat to your people. It would be evil. If you're that far gone, I *will* pull this trigger."

Seeing he was still furious, she thumped the muzzle against his forehead. "First you." She thumped it again. "Then me."

He saw truth in her cold silver eyes. The eyes of Chaos.

When he continued to stare, unmoving but silent, Egypt spoke up. "Please listen to her. I'm in her line of fire back here, and unlike her, I'm not ready to die yet."

He blinked, and his body finally relaxed. "Please let me go, Egypt."

She released him carefully, stepping away as he straightened to rub his wrists while his eyes stayed on the woman who still held a gun to his face.

Shandiin studied him a moment longer, nodded, holstered the gun. She crossed her arms while his gaze remained locked on hers.

"First me," he repeated. "Then yourself."

"Do you think you're the only one who's suffered a loss?"

He closed his eyes briefly. "No. Egypt, belay that order."

They were all surprised to hear a deep male voice. "You handled that well, Shandiin."

White-haired Sarnath stood near, his dark eyes focused on the High King though he continued speaking to Shandiin. "Threatening to kill him wasn't enough. It was the threat to yourself that broke through his madness."

Khedran frowned at Sarnath before turning back to Egypt. "Have you contacted the Premier as I had asked?"

"Yes. He was surprised but quickly accepted your decision to come to him. They will be waiting for you." She hesitated. "Your Highness..."

He just shook his head slightly before she could continue her plea. She sighed and shifted her gaze to Shandiin. "Obviously you couldn't talk him out of it either. And you're going with him."

"I'm his pilot. Do we have transport?"

"Yes. Sarnath will take you to it. I won't." Egypt was looking at the floor, her fists clenched at her sides.

Shandiin watched as Khedran cupped Egypt's chin and lifted her face. "Hope is not gone, Egypt, unless you let it be. As reason is also necessary, I am telling you Jael is next in line. Shandi told me long ago she will not rule, and Marre will need his help. Do you understand?"

Her lips tightened. "Yes. But I'll damn you both to hell if I have to relay that order."

She crossed her arms and turned her back on him.

Sarnath gestured, and Khedran and Shandiin walked with him as they traversed the ship.

"I understand your magic will not be available on the *Earthstar*," Sarnath said to Khedran as they neared their destination.

"Rhiathe is the source of my magic. There are some inherent gifts of my bloodline that may not be the same kind of magic, as they remained even after Shandiin took the gods from my world. I am hoping those things will stay with me beyond Rhiathe's connection."

"Rhiathe being the spirit of your world...and your mother."

Khedran just nodded.

Sarnath looked to Shandiin. "What about your magic?"

"My magic has the same source as Khedran's." She frowned. "At least I think so."

His gaze went sharp and he halted abruptly. They both stopped with him. "You've learned something." His statement carried a demand.

Shandiin sighed. "When I told Rhiathe to make me a goddess again, she said she could only give me leave to be what I have always been. She said I have always been Chaos, which is ridiculous."

Sarnath lifted his eyebrows. "Is it? That would explain why you were required to go physically to the planet all those years ago, while she built constructs for the other gods to inhabit."

She shook her head in denial. "I couldn't do anything magic until I was on the surface of Hiraeth. What she told me must have been some sort of allegory."

"I think not. Nonetheless you are again Chaos, after everything you did to remove the magic before. Why did you want to be a goddess again?"

"I wanted to stop the evil that could destroy everything good about Hiraeth. To do that I need the power of Chaos, and the freedom to use it as I see fit. Khedran put limits on his magic. Rhiathe never put restrictions on her gods...as he and I both know too well."

Seeing Khedran's scowl, she glared at him. "I am free to act as needed, when magic is available, and I plan to do so. Chaos has no boundaries...and Khedran, I'm warning you that I'll do what I believe is necessary. I am neither as honorable nor as compassionate as you."

Sarnath stepped between them before Khedran could respond. "Both of you, be advised that if we do not quickly have news from you, Egypt will be coming to you. You should know she will not simply stand and wait if she cannot reach you while knowing you are both in danger."

Khedran shook his head. "I am doing this to save people, not risk more of you."

"You may find that Egypt can be as pigheaded as Shandiin." Sarnath pointed to the elevator Shandiin remembered. "The skycraft is in slot 1016."

Khedran slanted a dark glance at Shandiin and walked away to the elevator.

Shandiin frowned after him, then took the opportunity to speak privately to Sarnath. "I'm not expecting a future where I can communicate with Zion, even if he'd let me. I should have listened to your warning about marrying him. I hope you can help him understand that he was never a substitute for anyone. I've always cared for him, for who *he* is. I treated him badly, in that cave, and I am ashamed. I don't deserve his forgiveness, but I am deeply sorry. I need to know he will hear that."

"Your promise was to love him the best that you could, and I believe you did. I've already told him he should have paid attention to that instead of expecting more. But I will give him your message, Shandiin."

He held out his arms. Shandiin went to him and briefly laid her cheek on his chest. "Thank you." She drew back to look up into his face. "When next I see you, if I am so lucky, I want to know who you really are. You already know all my secrets."

He smiled at her sadly, glanced toward Khedran's back, and left them there as the elevator opened.

Khedran didn't acknowledge her when she stopped beside him but merely waited for the elevator doors to open and stepped inside. They rode silently down in the elevator, and he followed her through what had once seemed to be no more than a parking lot beneath an unknowing city.

They found the skycraft behind a metal door labeled 1016. Still wordless, he took Shandiin's direction inside the craft, strapping in while she checked instruments and set them in motion. They were in space seconds later, dropping out of the starship with beautiful Hiraeth below. She set course for the *Earthstar*, away from the system's sun.

She realized he was watching her instead of the wonders of the universe around them. She knew him too well to break silence first; the High Kings all knew silence was the stronger part of an argument.

He finally exhaled in frustration. "I do not understand your defiance toward me. Nor do I understand why you had to become Chaos again. In the past, you have only used magic to fight magic. I cannot believe you would use magic to destroy humans. So why have you done this?"

"I had to. What happened to..." she stopped, mention of Roinn and Danon trapped behind pain. Swallowing, she started over. "I realized I needed magic to stand against what is coming. If you thought what I said was only defiance, you misunderstood. I want the same thing you do, to protect your world. I am not defying you. I just don't have your constraints."

"I know you don't. I've always known that, but I have trusted your wisdom if not your temper. And you taught me well where my constraints had to be set aside. Perhaps I learned too well. Rhiathe told me you would be my conscience, and she was right."

She frowned at a panel, made an adjustment, and sat back to look directly at him. "Conscience isn't the word I would use. A short time ago I held a gun to your face. That's the hardest thing I have ever done, Khedran. Because I knew if you destroyed innocent people, who you are would die with them." Her lower lip trembled. "I knew I would have to kill you because that other death would have been worse."

He studied her, thinking how well she understood him, thinking of *amhara*. "I was out of my head. You were right to stop me, and I give you my thanks."

She had to look away. "I don't want your thanks. I want to apologize for what I said to you. I had to force you to release the fury created by your own guilt, so I threw it in your face. I told you what you had guessed, that the Premier sent an assassin for Shandi because you told him she had killed his brother. I hurt you, to make you face your fear that what happened today was your fault just because you wouldn't lie."

She returned an unquiet gaze to meet his. "I knew where your mind was going about all of that, and since there was no way to stop it, I had to get you past it. So I bludgeoned you through. You were already foundering because of everything you're already carrying. What happened to Shandi broke you. You were already gone, Khedran. I had to get you back."

He didn't argue. After a moment he said, "Rhiathe was right. I needed a conscience, and I had you. But what have you done, Shandiin? What have you agreed to do, to become Chaos again?"

"I honestly don't know, so I can't tell you."

She broke off and tapped her ear, indicating an incoming communication before she responded to it. "This is the *Aztlan Lareta*, in transit with the High King of Azlatan."

"This is the Communications Officer of the *Earthstar*. We have your trajectory and will signal when you are to release control of your craft so we can bring you to dock. You'll arrive at dock 2416. The Premier is expecting you."

"Thank you." She signed off and looked over at Khedran. "We have some time before I give them control of the craft for docking. This is our last chance to change our mind, or even talk in privacy. Once I transfer control, they can monitor everything we say. Are you sure..."

At his set face and steady gaze, she just sighed. "All right, we're going in. But Khedran, while I understand your intent, I'm afraid your command voice and your thrall won't be enough to stop them. We'll likely need to stall until we come into Rhiathe's magic range."

"I realize that." He lowered his head to rub his brow. "While I have the opportunity to speak privately, I must thank you for saving Shandi. It places me forever in your debt. As if I haven't been, all my life."

"You owe me nothing, Khedran. Life shouldn't be a damned bartering system." She shook her head. "Not that I know what it should be. Tell me what you're planning."

"My greatest concern is those warcraft which are not susceptible to Rhiathe's magic. I must find a way to stop Canard, to stop them." He scowled suddenly. "By all the gods! Who is leading the battle at Cabre with both Danon and Roinn gone?"

"Well, it seems your brain has fully returned. Shajii and Roland are running the show back there. I gave them orders before I left."

"You gave orders to my Legion Master?"

"I did. I am, after all, a goddess. I could even order you around."

He looked across to see her smirk. "Like you ever stopped," he said wryly, and her smirk became laughter.

Until he caught her by surprise. "You have no idea how amazing you are, do you? With or without magic, you are so alive, so brave. Your laughter goes straight to my heart, Shandiin."

She squeezed her eyes closed. "Don't do that. We can't do that."

"I know. But using this time to plan what comes next is no more than useless speculation. And I may never have another chance to say what I want to."

"That sounds too much like goodbye, Khedran. Knock it off."

He lifted his eyebrows. "That isn't my intent. I just want to say I wish that...in all our time together...I had taken the opportunity to know more about you, about the life you led before you came to my world. I had never even known you had children."

"I don't, really. Leah is dead, and I hope Diane is."

"Why? Because she was also Daimaine?"

"Mostly. But she was always a sociopath. As Daimaine, she also became an evil psychopath." She frowned. "The Kings educated the people to curtail Azlatan's sociopaths. How will you deal with the Earther sociopaths, Khedran? Now that you have magic, will you use it to control people like that?"

"No. I will not use magic to control even them. It is wrong to take a human's free will."

"I knew you'd say that. Khedran, I want to tell you..."

She stopped, signaling an incoming communication, and opened the comm. "*Control to the* Aztlan Lareta. *Transfer for entry.*"

"Acknowledged," Shandiin said in response. She bit her lip. "This is it."

He caught her hand before she could reach for the control panel. "What were you going to say to me, Shandiin?"

She took a deep breath and looked into his beautiful eyes. "When I first returned to your life, I questioned your ability to help these people. I was wrong. You were meant for nothing less. I hope Sarnath's awareness, his vision of you, means there is more to your path than having it end here. And...I will always love you, Khedran. But your purpose matters more than anything you and I could have had together."

The docking went smoothly. But when they stepped out of the skycraft, they faced eight armed soldiers wearing white body armor, their weapons trained on Khedran and Shandiin. She recognized the ancient regalia of Earth's Warriors of God, soldiers of the defunct Right Church.

One gestured with his gun. "On your knees."

Khedran sensed Shandiin stiffen and touched her arm briefly in a plea to stand down. "I don't understand," he said quietly, but his command voice carried. "We have come in peace, to speak with Premier Canard."

Their leader was unconvinced. "We know the truth. You have somehow hidden the bomb from our scanners, but we will find it. I repeat: get on your knees."

"Why do you think there is a bomb?" Khedran asked.

"We were warned by our ally, Dr. Alexander." The speaker gestured to his soldiers. "You five, take him into custody. Cuff him. You two, take the woman."

With no recourse available, Khedran allowed the soldiers to pull his arms behind his back and snap metal cuffs on his wrists. He was watching Shandiin worriedly as the last two men approached her.

"Zion Alexander?" Shandiin demanded. "He contacted you?"

"Yes," said their leader. "Men, put them both on their knees. They may not stand in presence of the goddess."

Khedran's gaze flashed to the doorway where a woman stepped through. A woman he knew too well.

Daimaine wore a flowing black gown. Her long hair was partially braided with interwoven diamonds. A strange near-invisible aura glowed around her.

His body turned to ice.

And Shandiin detonated with fury.

CHAPTER 21

Their mistake had been assigning only two men to control her. She punched one in the throat and sent him flying into the other. Before the second caught his balance she was forcing them both into a backward stumble against their leader, yanking his weapon free. She fired on Diane.

Diane laughed.

"Use the taser," her daughter ordered.

Khedran had been shoved off his feet when Shandiin fired, and five men held him down. He watched in horror as electricity crackled and Shandiin fell backwards, her body seizing violently as she slammed into the floor.

Diane's strange surrounding aura was gone when she strode over to kick Shandiin in the ribs. "Cuffs and chains," she ordered, and turned toward Khedran.

"Get him up," she commanded as she walked to Khedran.

They used the handcuffs on Khedran's wrists to drag him from the floor onto his knees. He glared up at her as she leaned down to smile into his eyes. "Hello, my love. So good to see you again. Especially in such a desirably defenseless position."

When she slipped her fingers through his hair he jerked his head away, and she laughed again. "You won't be so rebellious for long." She glanced sidelong at Shandiin, who was being wrapped in chains. "Not if you want her alive."

He watched Shandiin hauled to her feet, hobbled and dazed.

"You know where to take her," Diane told her mother's captors.

They dragged Shandiin away before Khedran was finally allowed to stand. He braced his boots apart, his wrists still cuffed behind him, and glared down into Daimaine's face.

No, he reminded himself fiercely. *She is Diane. She is Shandiin's hated daughter, and she is only human. She has no magic. Remember the difference.*

But his skin crawled as she stepped so close he felt her body heat. Smirking, she looked up into his eyes. She came barely to his shoulder, but he remembered the goddess she'd been was as tall as Shandiin, and hauntingly beautiful. The smaller woman she was now had tried to recapture that beauty with paint and powder, but it didn't hit the mark.

He eyed her coldly as she lifted a hand to his cheek. "How I've missed you," she murmured, then turned away. "Bring him," she ordered.

Herded along behind her, he looked around but didn't see Shandiin while they traversed a long hallway. He did see signs of the starship's degradation, even in dim lighting.

But when they entered Diane's quarters, there was only luxury and comfort. He saw a fake fireplace, with imitation fire flickering. There were soft fabrics in brilliant colors. A long wooden table held flowers spiking from a tall vase. A painting of Diane hung over the mantel, and in that image, she wore a gown the color of sapphires, and a crown of diamonds.

She yanked a straight chair away from the table, turning it to face another made for comfort. "Uncuff him and put him here."

"Please," one of the men pleaded. "Reconsider, Morgana. He could harm you."

She threw the man a disdainful glance and touched the diamond bracelet on her wrist. The near-transparent aura reappeared briefly. "A fired projectile didn't reach me through this energy field," she reminded. "And he's too smart to run. There's nowhere to go. You will be outside the only door, and if he did somehow overpower me, you are ordered to kill him and the slut he brought with him. Do as I say."

The cuffs were unkeyed, and Khedran was unceremoniously shoved into the hard and armless chair by a glaring soldier. He rubbed his wrists while he watched Diane (*Morgana?*) cross to a table and pour wine into crystal cups.

She brought one to him, but he just held her gaze when she offered it, unmoving.

She shrugged and settled into the soft chair across from him, crossed her legs, and sipped as she studied him. "You've matured," she observed. "It quite suits you."

When he said nothing, she smiled. "You are older. That's right. The High Kings are mortal, aren't they? Three of you even committed suicide rather than face what I can give. You should know they found it barely more comfortable after, when their spirits came to me." She tilted her head. "Have you no questions?"

When he still didn't respond, she frowned slightly. "Well, you will speak to me when I require it. But first I'll tell you about myself. I came to this place where women are stupid and homely nothings. I am the only woman of great beauty and great intellectual power the leader has ever known. I have ruled great men..." she smiled wickedly as she continued, "and though that rule required magic, I nevertheless learned much about their mortal weaknesses. So there was little to stand in my way when I came here. These people had no defense against me, least of all the man they call the Premier, who married me to enjoy my...unusual methods of giving him pleasure."

She waited for a reaction, but continued when Khedran allowed no change in his expression. "I have been accepted as a living legend, an ideal, even a goddess. When they asked how to address me I chose the title Morgana. Earth was always so full of wonderful myths, and Morgana is a name from more than one. She is a goddess of death, prophecy, and war. Fitting, don't you think?"

She leaned forward. "You made a great error in coming here, Khedran. Premier Canard is no longer the one in charge. He is my puppet. And I certainly don't care about a peaceful immigration. I plan to rule your world...and you with it." She waited.

He watched anger fire in her dark eyes when he remained silent, and her lips twisted. "All right then. I can play harder. Tell me, did my assassin manage to kill your daughter?"

The horror on Cabre's ramparts was still too near. But he kept his voice level. "No. I killed him."

She smiled in amusement, sat back and set her drink aside. "I told the truth when I said I missed you. You'll be a lovely challenge; there is no one to try me, here."

She rose, moved, stood over him.

He looked up at her without expression. "You are lying."

"Why do you say that?" she asked cheerfully.

"Because you never want a challenge. You only want obedience."

"You know me so well." She slid the hem of her gown up her thighs and straddled him, settling her weight onto his lap with her hands framing his face.

He fought a waking nightmare when her lips met his. But they were no longer cold with the magic she had once carried. He focused on that.

She drew back and regarded him archly. "Now, that is an unacceptable defiance. You will kiss me back. You'll do what I want, Your Highness, if you want your companion alive."

"No."

"What?" She laughed in surprise. "You'd rather I kill her?"

"I know you could do whatever you want to her. But your threat will not make me do your will, and you no longer have magic. So be aware that if she is harmed in any way, there is no power in the universe than can stop me from killing you at the first opportunity."

He saw the flicker of shock before she could hide it. "You have no control here. That's just bravado."

"Think again. You know me well, too. Here's the rest of my requirement. You must let me go to her, to assure myself she is alive and well. You must allow this on my demand. If you refuse, you will have no choice but to kill me."

With that he shoved to his feet and dropped her into the chair she had vacated. There was a thrill of cold joy when he saw a flicker of fear before she touched her bracelet, activating her aura of safety.

"Your decision," he finished, his eyes hard on hers.

She glared up at him. "Get back. I'll call in the guards."

"Go ahead. Have them chain me. Have them kill me, if that's what you really want. I think you want something else. You'll get nothing if you do not accede to my demands. Nothing but my death, by your hand or theirs."

She pushed up and shoved him back. He allowed her to force that single step and waited.

"I can hurt you," she snarled. "You know what I can do."

"Yes. But you taught me too well for too many years. You can't cause enough pain to break my will."

He saw another flicker in her eyes, and knew he had scored. She had tried to make him weep. He had screamed, but he had never broken under her torture. She had never heard him beg, never seen his tears.

She studied him. "I'll do what I wish, so mind your step. But yes, I have plans for you, so..." She looked around as if considering, then shrugged. "She's in a cell. I can show you on the monitor."

"No. I must see her in person. I will believe no imagery. And I want to see her now."

She shrugged again, but he saw her annoyance. "Briefly, then."

"And again, before tomorrow morning. You can't expect me to trust you."

She sighed impatiently and touched an earring. "Come in," she said.

The door opened immediately, and her guard came in. "Take him to the woman," she told him. "He may stay for one minute. Then bring him back here."

It was a short walk to a steel door that opened onto a row of chain-link cages.

Shandiin had been sitting on a cot with her back against the wall, but stood up immediately on seeing him, and came to stand against the cage door. Her silver eyes were anxious...and still furious. "What has she done?"

"Far less than was done to you."

She waved that away. "That taser was only temporary incapacitation. She'll use me to manipulate you, Khedran. Don't you dare let her, do you understand me? You have a purpose here, and it isn't to keep me alive. Stay in control, or I'll find you in hell and kick your ass."

He could almost smile. "I see you are undamaged, body or spirit. I cannot stay, Shandiin. But I will return."

He left reassured she was still very much herself.

Diane was pacing when he was pushed back into the room with her. When the door was closed at his back she stopped to face him, arms crossed. The monitor still transmitting Shandiin's image was behind her.

"I heard what she said to you. But she is the manipulator, Khedran. I watched her manipulate you, making you into the Black Wolf, taking from you any chance to be free of her. You think she is your savior, but she is nothing but your jailer. You have always been her hostage. Your love for her isn't natural. She bought it with magic."

His only avenue was to stall. "Prove it."

"I don't have to. Your own logic will make you see it, if you will just think. She's always been there, training you like a dog. And you didn't know she was a goddess, did you? You couldn't see her magic."

"I saw yours."

She smiled. "Mine was open and honest. Hers was hidden and a lie." She glanced toward the door. "The Premier will be here soon. Do you want to be introduced as an emissary, or a hostage? He'll know by now there was no bomb on your ship as Zion warned."

"I thought you didn't care about a peaceful immigration."

She shrugged. "I don't. But I care about politics. I rule here, but Canard is an important figurehead. I plan to maintain control of him and the people on this ship...and then rule your world." Her gaze roamed down his body, slowly up again to his striking face. "You could rule it with me, if you are smart enough to cooperate."

He kept his silence.

"Stubbornness will get you nothing. I have another option, Khedran, one that surpasses any action by you or that woman, dead or alive. And you won't like it at all."

The door opened, and they both watched Premier Dick Canard enter.

The man was shorter than Khedran, but there was command in his bearing. He nodded respectfully to his wife before facing Khedran.

Khedran watched the Premier take a step back on meeting his gaze. It was a familiar reaction. His presence always registered, especially on first meeting. He'd even seen it happen to Zion.

But Canard rallied well. "I did not appreciate being told about my brother's death with such disdain. I hope my emissary gave him justice."

Khedran responded just as coolly. "He failed in his attempt to kill my daughter, if that's what you mean." He slid a glance at Diane. "I thought the emissary was your wife's."

"She suggested it. My wife encourages me, stands behind me in all things." Canard's gaze upon his wife was adoring. "She is my all."

Diane smiled and went to her husband, giving him a cheerful kiss. "Thank you, dear. I trust things are going well?"

"Yes. The transports will land in under eight hours, and if they meet aggression, the warcraft will immediately follow." He turned to face Khedran again. "I trust they will meet no hostility. You probably aren't aware what nuclear weapons can do, but I'd prefer not to deploy them. Any area where they are used would be uninhabitable for a period of time, by your people or mine."

Khedran fought down nausea to respond mildly. "My people have no orders to take action against new colonists."

"So you say."

"You can believe him," Diane put in. "He's famous for always telling the truth."

Canard snorted. "There's not a human being alive that doesn't lie."

"You are assuming I am a human being," Khedran put in.

Canard cocked his head, considering. "That's right. You are genetically engineered, from what I understand...so only a facsimile of a human being." He lifted his eyebrows. "So...your programming does not allow you to lie?"

"That is correct."

Canard considered, and this time it was his gaze that roamed down his body and up again. "Does it restrict...other things?"

Diane laughed gaily. "We're going to find out, my love. I have entertainment planned, and the drugs to make him compliant, if not consenting." She smirked at Khedran once again. "Why, it's almost like magic."

Shandiin knew hours had passed, but the lights were still on. They would probably remain on, but she didn't plan to sleep. She only waited.

She rose from her cot when the door opened and Khedran was brought in. He wasn't restrained, but walked into the cage next to hers and waited for it to be locked.

He stood unmoving for a long moment after their captors left, seeming to be in deep thought. Then he lifted his gaze to where she stood against the cage with her fingers gripping the steel latticework. "How are you?" he asked.

"They haven't touched me. What have they done to you?"

"I've made no headway with Canard. Apparently the transports will land in a few hours. He said if they meet any hostility the warcraft will be launched immediately."

"Don't deflect, Khedran. I want the truth. Did you let her get to you by threatening me?"

"No." He sat down on his cot, ran his hands through his hair. "I'm just playing a waiting game, Shandiin. My only goal is to keep Canard from using nuclear weapons against my world."

She took a deep breath. His flat "no" in response to her question was reassuring, because she knew he didn't lie.

She watched him lean back against the wall and prop a boot atop the cot. He rested a forearm over his upraised knee and closed his eyes.

He knows we're being monitored, she thought, *and he's exhausted from events and worry and his phobia of nuclear warfare that killed billions of people on another planet.*

The only way she could help was to get his mind away from those things. "I think I figured out why Zion told them we had a bomb. The last thing he heard you say before we left the hospital was that you were going to bomb the *Earthstar* because they sent an assassin to kill your daughter. He was trying to save the people on this ship."

Khedran sighed. "I was out of my mind with grief when I said that. The people on this ship don't deserve to die, even to save those of my world." He rubbed his forehead. "I hate this. These poor people don't even know they are being lied to, that their leaders are sending soldiers to destroy the innocent, peaceful inhabitants of my planet for absolutely no reason. It's all so senseless, Shandiin. Everyone on this ship could live comfortably among my people. I would never turn away anyone needing what should be theirs by nature. Fighting, killing...all of it so unnecessary, when a beautiful home is waiting for them with open arms."

"It's about power, Khedran. Something you wouldn't understand. As King you've never governed through domination. Your rule is respected because it's dedicated to the welfare of your people, and your people know that through consequence, not propaganda. Their Premier just wants to be the only boss, and he has no scruples in getting there."

"Well, as of now he's no more than Diane's puppet. She called him a figurehead. She's the driving force behind this war, Shandiin. They call her the Morgana, and treat her like a goddess."

Shandiin tightened her fingers, almost bending the cage's steel lattice. "Just remember she's not. Not anymore. She's just a damned psychopath, and she has no power over you that you don't allow."

He took a deep breath and turned his head to gaze up at her.

He hated terribly to see his lioness in a cage. In that moment he wanted more than anything to go to her, to gently loosen those clenched fingers, to touch his lips to hers through the small space the steel allowed.

But she would never know that.

His eyes reflected only green in the overhead light. "I am quite aware of that, Shandiin."

She scowled in helpless fury, guessing he was hiding something from her...and afraid she didn't want to know what it was.

So she dropped her hands, crossed her arms. "I hate this as much as you do, Khedran. Hiraeth is my world now, and I want it to stay clean. You and your bloodline have built a world based on honor and respect, and we can't let that change. Hold onto that. We'll find a way out of here. We'll find a way to release all the people on this starship and give them a decent home. We'll keep Hiraeth safe for everyone who lives there."

"I wish I could tell Canard's people that. I'm going to lie down now, Shandiin."

When he did just that, and turned to the wall with his back to her, Shandiin fought her own despair.

The explosion woke them both from a thin sleep.

It was muffled, but the sound was unmistakable...and aboard a ship in space, extremely dangerous no matter where it came from.

They listened to distant shouts, muffled pops like gunshots, and, closer by, the sound of running feet on the floor outside their room.

The door to their room of cages slammed open, and armored soldiers crowded in, all armed with tasers.

They went to Khedran's cage first, led by a young soldier bearing chains. Khedran stepped to meet him, holding his hands up in compliance. The soldier lifted his gaze to meet the King's emerald eyes, and Shandiin watched his face change to wonder. But her flash of hope was lost when the young man did, after all, chain together the hands of the man who would have accepted him into a world of freedom.

The one who chained her was far less timid. They were taken roughly and wordlessly from their prison while hearing more muffled explosions. The sounds of battle grew nearer.

The Premier himself waited outside their room, fury reddening his face. At sight of Khedran, he stepped up and slapped him, causing Khedran to lift his eyebrows. "You'll pay for this," Canard snarled. "It wasn't enough to make my wife obsess over you, was it? I should have known better than...than...oh, damn you. But now she's realized her error in keeping you alive, and we're ending this. I don't know how you caused my own people to turn against me, but you will pay for all of it."

They could hear the sound of battle continuing as they were dragged behind Canard to another room. There they were shoved to the floor, where he finished his diatribe. "You'll be executed here. No more bargaining, no more manipulation. My transports are not responding to our communications, so it's obvious they've been disabled. I've already sent the warcraft to bomb your city."

The door was slammed shut as their captors left. Silence fell, and Khedran and Shandiin were, at least momentarily, alone.

Shandiin looked around at the barren and utilitarian room, and was chilled with a memory from her days as a cop. She had witnessed autopsies and so recognized the steel table at the room's center. It was built with channels and drains for bodily fluids. A smaller table nearby held the blades and saws the work required.

The restraints added to the autopsy table said it was meant to hold the living instead of the dead.

Roland called it the Spectacle of Retribution, she remembered. *People are drawn and quartered, the most horrifying kind of execution ever contemplated. They have only modernized it.*

She looked up at the cameras mounted above the table, then shifted her gaze to Khedran. She was prone, but he had managed to pull himself into a sitting position with his chained hands hooked over his updrawn knees. "This metal is not like Chaine gold," he told her.

She realized he was letting her know it wasn't as strong. He flexed his wrists, but it held, and she was afraid to hope.

She also knew she had to say something before they met their end. "Khedran, I'm sorry. I don't know what happened to you before you came back last night, but judging from Canard's speech I know it had to be hell."

His eyes were on his hands as he worked at the chains. "I bought what time I could until we are closer to Hiraeth." He heard her sharp intake of breath. "I don't want your pity, Shandiin."

Her eyes filled and her throat hurt; she couldn't respond until she could swallow. "Pity? My God, no. You have a kind of courage I never imagined."

He said nothing to that, so she dropped it. She stared at the waiting table. "You know what they're going to do, don't you?"

"I believe I know what they have planned." His gaze moved to her, and his voice softened. "Don't give up now. You have never given up on me, and even during all the years before the Prophecy War, when you hid your truth, I knew your heart. It was your faith in me that kept me strong."

Her vision blurred, gazing up at him. She couldn't speak.

He didn't need to say more. She could see the love, the determination.

And the yet unbroken spirit. His eyes were full of contempt as he watched Diane enter with her entourage of seven soldiers.

They could see the aura of Diane's protective energy field as she walked over to glare down at them. "I don't know how you started this insurrection, but your part in it ends now, along with your city. The warcraft are carrying nukes to destroy it all, and the Premier has already let your realm know you and your slut are dead. Your people will die without hope. I only have to decide which of you to kill first."

Even chained and sitting at Diane's feet, the High King was not the supplicant.

"You know who you have to kill first," he said quietly. "We made our own kind of agreement, didn't we?"

She regarded him steadily, tapping her fingers on her hips, then slid a glance at Shandiin. "Yes, I guess we did. And I think killing you first and making her watch will be rewarding in several ways." She turned to a soldier. "Keep the chains on him until he's restrained to the table." She pointed to another soldier. "Stand her up so she can see it all."

Shandiin scarcely paid attention to the soldier who came and pulled her upright. She watched in horror as Khedran was dragged over to stand against the autopsy table, a man on each side of him. They forced him to turn around preparatory to laying him on the metal surface.

Diane stepped close to gloat. Khedran's beautiful black hair fell loose about his handsome face as he gazed down into her eyes.

Even through her terror for him, Shandiin was mesmerized. She had never seen Khedran purposely use his bloodline's thrall on anyone, but she knew he was doing it now. The impact was clearly displayed in Diane's softened posture as she stared up at him.

He added his mysterious command voice, speaking softly to her. "I can't believe you would do this without allowing one last kiss. Your lips on mine."

Gazing raptly into his eyes, she touched her bracelet to key off her energy field.

Khedran immediately snapped free of the weakened chain, using his trained strength to simultaneously shove away the men on each side of him. He seized Diane's wrist, snatched a scalpel from the table behind her and had it at her throat, glaring into her eyes. "Release the woman," he ordered those watching, "or I start cutting pieces off your Morgana. Now!"

The soldiers froze momentarily, seeing the knife at Diane's throat.

There were shouts and thumps outside the door, and Diane snarled triumphantly into his face. "Do you hear that commotion in the hall, Khedran? These and the other soldiers coming will tear you and your bitch to pieces. My husband has already sent the warcraft with the nukes...and I am the only one with the codes to call them back. You don't dare use that knife, and you're outnumbered. Give up."

Shandiin's chains had been partially removed. She shed the last of them, back-fisted her captor in the crotch, and from his reactive position slammed him facedown into the floor. She stepped quickly behind Diane, who was still struggling to free her defensive bracelet from Khedran's grasp. Shandiin seized another scalpel from the table and jerked Diane's head back by the hair. "You're now reacquainted with the best of all bitches," she growled from behind her, and spiked the scalpel into Diane's forearm. She used it to pin Diane's arm in place while she wrestled the bracelet free.

The outer door slammed open. Shandiin flicked a glance that way and smiled as Egypt spun in, launching one soldier into another and hammering a third while her companions took down the rest of the men rushing for the door.

"Well," Shandiin amended, "maybe it's a tie for best bitch."

Diane was screaming in pain and outrage when Egypt stopped next to Khedran, eying all the blood. "Well, shit. I guess we got here too late to rescue you."

"We have to get her to the bridge," Shandiin told her. "Diane is the only one who has the codes to stop the warcraft."

Diane turned livid with fury. She stopped screaming and glared up at Khedran, who studied her closely.

"It's no use," he told them after a moment.

Diane sneered up at him, held in place by Shandiin's hand still viciously twisted into her hair. "Oh, you are so right. It's no use to take me to the bridge, because I will do nothing to stop them from bombing your city, your people, your beloved daughter. And my death will not save them, or you. Didn't I warn you I have an option? I still have the trump that will destroy you. Our son will be the next High King, and greater than any before him."

Khedran's eyes were deadly. "Woman, you have lied until you believe your own fantasies. We have no son."

"Oh, but we do. You will remember, and know that your wrongful love was the seed of your own destruction."

"No. There is no truth in you...except that you will not give up the codes." His gaze moved to Shandiin. "I have read her. There is nothing we can do to make her stop the warcraft. Shandiin, she is your daughter, but..."

"She is nothing but evil." Shandiin's heart had gone to ice. "Do as you will. It is your justice."

She held Diane's head while Khedran cut her throat.

CHAPTER 22

The city of Xanthe had once been a breeding ground for the enemies of Azlatan. They had invaded Azlatan and found defeat twenty years before, but the city's inhabitants had known peace ever since.

Until now. Having been warned of what would come, Xanthe's leader, Kimhi, watched a strange craft descend silently into what had once been a central park, but which over the years had grown deep with weeds. Kimhi signaled her own untested troop of new patriots to stay back, although they all held swords and pikes. She had received clear direction about this while in Cabre.

Standing at the edges of the park, they all had a clear view of the craft as it settled to the ground. Its sides opened to release soldiers such as they had never seen. The invaders wore strange white armor and carried unrecognizable weapons at the ready.

There were many. Kimhi swallowed but stood bravely ready to fight.

The soldiers began an advance in all directions, looking around and up for any danger.

They should have looked down.

A scream shattered the air, and then another, and then such noise as Xanthe had never known.

Many soldiers were firing wildly at the ground while others scrambled back to the craft, where came more screams, more gunshots.

Kimhi's people looked at each other in confusion as this insane behavior continued for several minutes, until the soldiers began dropping their weapons and their screams became pleas for help.

Kimhi and her followers moved in cautiously, while the strangers held up their arms in surrender.

"Make them stop," one of them cried to Kimhi, who realized there were multitudes of snakes, coiled and writhing, surrounding each soldier. Hordes of spiders crawled upon the intruders, their weapons and the landing craft.

Kimhi grinned. She picked up one of the weapons that made such loud noise, and the spiders jumped off as she did. She signaled her followers to do the same, and they took the strange men prisoner without a drop of blood spilled.

Except from the snake bites, that is, and most weren't even poisonous. But how could people raised within the walls of a sterile ship have known about any of what had attacked them?

The visions of Jael, who was titled High Prince and Sage of Cabre, had also given the necessary advance warning for Khedran's trusted Black Guard and Dominion royalty. Many Dominions of Azlatan saw similar almost bloodless victories, though Ordhold's protective great cats were far more lethal than most of nature's allies, and human intervention was frequently necessary to convince them when to stop.

Jael had also given warning to his brother's people. In Iesse, the inner lands of the Khaibara Range, Varady's Sundancers sat upon the horses known as Shalmira. They waited in a circle around a great meadow. Golden rock rose all about, the familiar cliffs known to their ancestors. They waited patiently, in communion with the nature they cared for as the Sunqueen had taught them.

When the strange craft appeared above, they watched it knowingly with spears and bows at hand. They held the horns they still used to sing up the sun in honor of their Sunqueen. It didn't matter that their goddess no longer walked among them; they would always honor the sun goddess who had helped to save the world.

The transport's pilot looked out the window in disbelief as he brought it to ground. "It's like an old western vid," he told the many young and barely trained men who were ready to disembark. "Like Indians circling a wagon train. Horses and bows and arrows, for God's sake."

"Maybe they'll just give up," one soldier said hopefully, "if we fire a shot in the air."

"Yeah," another agreed. "They only have bows and arrows; they can't have seen guns before. Let's just scare them into submission."

"We have our orders," their Commanding Officer snapped. "We are to take out anyone showing any kind of defense, or we'll be facing guerilla warfare instead of a peaceful new home. These barbarians think they own the whole damn planet. They need to die."

The ship landed. The transport doors opened, and the soldiers looked out on something they had never seen in their lives: a green and growing world under a blue sky. As they disembarked, weapons at the ready, they felt a breeze, smelled the freshness of real unrecycled air; they felt the warmth of a sun on their faces. They felt the existence of a natural world for the first time and gazed about in wonder. Some were in tears.

None fired a weapon, though their commander exhorted them.

No arrows were loosed against them.

The horns began: a single pure golden note.

They were joined by a major third, and a perfect fifth above the first note.

More horns joined in harmony that increased, swelling until the cliffs of Iesse sent it back, again and again.

The echoes built the sound until a sea of harmonics filled the canyon to its brim. It was beautiful...and it was terrible.

The soldiers at the center of it went to their knees in the deep cool grass, arms protecting their ears, even their thoughts disrupted by sound. Nature used the music of the Sundancers, those who had honored her always, against those who invaded their home.

The invaders were helpless against their music, and it did not stop until their weapons and their freedom to kill were taken from them.

But what was coming to Cabre could not be reduced by magic or nature. The High King had known that, but he wasn't there to lead his people.

For the first time in a thousand years, a High King was not there for his people.

"I'm out of ammunition," Shajii told Roland as the noise of battle fell away around them.

"I'm not surprised. You're the last one still shooting. I think they're done, Shajii."

She frowned and reloaded while trying to see the action below the rampart where she stood. "It does look like they are standing down."

One outworlder transport lay in smoking ruins in the plaza behind her. It's occupants probably hadn't guessed there was a rocket launcher available to the natives. Several more of the transports had landed outside the city walls and were now surrounded by dead soldiers. Those who had thought better of their mission were hiding behind what was left of their transports. She could see hands raised as the firing stopped, and soldiers stepping out in obvious surrender.

"Open the gates," Shajii shouted down to her people. "Take them prisoner."

Roland lifted an eyebrow. "So you're The Chaine now."

"Just until Shandiin comes back."

"Shajii, I just learned..." he hesitated, looked over to one of his soldiers who had just joined them. "Are you sure?" he asked him.

The soldier nodded, keeping an eye on what was happening outside the gate. "The High Queen just made the announcement. She's pretty broken up."

Roland turned back to Shajii. "I'm sorry. The High King was killed trying to stop the warcraft. Shandiin was with him."

A bright flash drew their attention to the sky. There was a remnant of something left behind, then nothing.

"I hope that wasn't one of Egypt's," Roland said. "But I think we are now in for an aerial attack, and we had better get down from here and find some cover."

Shajii set her weapon down for the first time in hours. "I heard about the visions of Earth the High King shared with his people." She looked up at Roland. "I know we've just been buying time. If their ships bring the nuclear fire, there will be nowhere to hide."

After a moment Roland nodded grimly. "I was hoping you didn't know that. At least it will be quick." His eyes met hers with sadness. "But I wish we had more time, you and I."

She looked at him, felt her heart's loss for Roinn, and Danon, and Shandiin who had surely died with her secretly beloved High King...and now for her own new love. She fought tears, stepped over, and kissed him.

He set down his rifle and gathered her in.

"We still need to go to the bridge," Shandiin said. "Surely someone else has the codes."

Egypt nodded agreement. "My crew should have taken it over by now. Sarnath is skippering the *Aztlan*, Your Highness, and the warcraft are engaged as we had strategized but I am concerned. If even one gets through..."

He just shook his head, too aware of the consequences, and fell into step with her. "How did you cause this uprising?" he asked.

"It was our spy Magdalena, not me. She hacked into the security cameras, and your conversation last night was transmitted over the ship's public address system. Several times, I understand." She glanced back toward the carnage-filled room they left behind. "Diane wasn't as revered as she must have thought, and they no longer had any faith in the Premier. Your words were the last straw. I believe you will have many new and grateful subjects…"

Egypt quit walking mid-sentence and tapped her ear, and Khedran realized she was wearing a communication device. He stopped and waited.

Her eyes met his, and tragedy distorted her face. "Damn. Thanks, Sarnath."

She tapped her ear again. "I am so sorry. One got through. It's headed for Cabre, and it's carrying a nuke. My ships can't catch it in time."

"You mean it carries an atomic bomb."

"Yes."

After a moment he turned and walked on. Shandiin and Egypt shared glances and fell in on either side of him.

The bridge of the *Earthstar* was similar to the *Aztlan*, Khedran saw, and its crew was currently in restraints on the floor while those he assumed were rebels or Egypt's team were manning the controls. The Premier stood with his hands cuffed behind him. Khedran went to him immediately, and the man shrank back from his emerald glare.

"Do you or any of your people have the codes to call back the warcraft?"

"No," Canard responded nervously. "Where is my wife? She has them. She felt that ensured security."

"No. She only felt it gave her control. And she is dead."

Saying nothing more, the High King walked to the observation window, where he could see his world floating in the sea of stars the outworlders called "space." To him it was a dark heaven spangled with living lights, with beauty and wonder beyond imagining.

His world was his center, but Khedran's soul reached for infinity.

Especially at this moment.

His people. His brother. His wife. His daughter. The purpose of his life was in Cabre.

He was about to lose it all.

Someone spoke tersely. "I have visual, but I can't reach him through audio, and he's almost on target."

The screen was suddenly filled with movement. The warcraft hurtling toward Cabre was online, and they watched from the pilot's onboard camera as he sped over fertile outer Azlatan, then over the inner Dominions surrounding Cabre.

An eerie silence fell over the bridge.

Khedran watched his city rise ahead, watched it grow on the screen. His vision blurred, but he didn't need his eyes to see. He knew every part of it. He knew the ramparts so painstakingly built to protect it. He knew every step of the crooked inner streets, which held so many of the people he would have died to protect. He knew the dark towers that were Penumbra's, his ancestral home on the south by the sea.

He waited for the end.

There came a soundless light so brilliant that it forced everyone on the bridge to turn away.

His name was Vladimir. Coming in from the east, the young pilot of the warcraft named *Redeemer* watched the wild grasslands flowing under his craft, and then an impossibly high cliff climbing to a plateau of forests and rivers and pastoral scenes of farms and roads and towns.

He thought what a beautiful world this was, and wished greatly that he did not have to destroy a part of it so his people could live here. He'd been promised that taking out the King's city would stop the killing of innocent settlers, but looking down on the verdant land, the homely settlements, he thought also of those he would be killing.

He swallowed hard and reminded himself he had a duty, a responsibility to do what was right. Earth's history taught that war always required good people to kill, and to die.

When the walls of the target city became visible in the distance, he made ready to arm the bomb he would launch as soon as he was near enough. Once launched, he'd been told, he could fly his ship clear of the devastation he brought.

But the person who told him had shifted his eyes for just a moment, and Vladimir doubted that was true.

His jaw set bravely as the city neared, Vladimir moved to arm the bomb. He gasped as light filled his cockpit, light bright enough to burn his eyes. He threw up a shielding hand but saw, instead of a city on the horizon, a goddess wreathed in a cloak of fire, rising into the sky ahead with the sun like a jewel on her forehead. When she lifted a flaming hand toward him, he screamed in terror and reflexively veered his ship away from her.

The ship careened over Cabre's airspace like an object thrown, and shattered against the towers of Penumbra. Its fiery remains sprayed over the sea beyond it, sinking without further harm under the waves.

Vladimir sat up on the wide steps of Penumbra and stared around in disbelief.

CHAPTER 23

Varady had joined the others below the ramparts, and was the first to react. "We have to see if anyone was hurt."

The others followed him as he raced toward Penumbra. The streets filled as citizens began leaving their shelter. The people they passed looked hopeful; there was no longer the terrible thunder of that new kind of battle.

A young man in a flight suit stood up as they came to the broad fan of stairs at Penumbra's entrance. Roland recognized him immediately. "Vlad? How did you get here?"

"I don't know." Dazed, Vladimir looked from Roland to Shajii. "I was on the ship one minute, and then here. It makes no sense!"

"Magic rarely does," Shandiin said as she walked down the steps toward them. She smiled as they stared up at her. She was resplendent in Chaine gold over leather, her hair a fiery corona around her head and shoulders.

She turned back to look up at Penumbra. "Daimaine's magic created Penumbra better than I thought. The towers don't even look damaged."

"Where did you come from?" Roland asked in amazement.

She grinned. "I just dropped in."

Varady followed her gaze to Penumbra's towers with a glad smile. "This is not like Jael's vision."

Shandiin nodded. "It's always been obvious to me that every choice creates a different future. When there are so many possibilities, I think the veil of reality can be very thin."

"Yes," said Roland. "I understand all his other visions were right on the mark, and the invasion was stopped with minimal bloodshed everywhere but in Cabre."

"Invasion?" Vlad asked.

Roland turned to him grimly. "You were lied to. Your leaders didn't send settlers. They sent soldiers, to kill everyone here before settlement by your people would begin. They did that even knowing the High King has already opened his world to you."

"But why?" Vlad cried. "Why would they do something so horrible?"

"That's the kind of thing decent people are never able to understand," Varady put in. He was watching Shandiin thoughtfully. "It was you, wasn't it?" he asked her. "You stopped the warcraft. I saw you once before, long ago with the sunrise. Just now I glimpsed you briefly through that storm of light."

"It was necessary to deflect the ship before the bomb was armed. It worked. Why are you here, Varady, and not Jael?"

"Jael is next in line as King. Khedran sent him far from Cabre, even though he protested." Varady straightened with realization. "We were told you were dead! Is Khedran also alive?"

"I imagine he'll be along any minute now."

"You imagine correctly." Khedran walked down the steps behind her, Egypt close behind.

Shandiin turned to see him in beautifully armored black leather regalia, not overstated but not plain as he'd always worn. A cloak was thrown back from one broad shoulder, freeing his hand for the ceremonial sword at his hip. *He has never looked more like the High King,* Shandiin thought to herself. *That's Rhiathe's doing.*

He stopped just above her, one boot on a higher stair as he also gazed up at the unbroken towers before turning to Shandiin. "You found your magic first. I am grateful, Shandiin. I truly thought all was lost."

She studied him thoughtfully. She could tell he was still reeling. Even with the salvation of his realm, he seemed darkened.

She hated what she had to do.

All of it.

"Khedran," she began, "you have added to your flock, and I congratulate you. But I must advise you I'm renouncing my Azlatan citizenship. I should not have accepted it. I am The Chaine, and my people have only one leader. You will not rule the Chaine."

She saw his surprise, then his understanding, before she shifted her attention to Egypt. "You also have a choice. There is an alternative to being a subject of the High King. You may join my people instead. But be aware that the Chaine are leaving this continent, which is now entirely under his rule." She slid her gaze to meet Khedran's stunned eyes. "We will not be ruled by the High King," she repeated. "Some Chaine may choose to stay here, but it will be as guests, not as citizens."

Their gazes locked, and she saw the dramatic shift that took him away from pain.

But this time she could see the Black Wolf was wounded.

Khedran drew himself up, then nodded. "So be it. Of course, the Chaine are a sovereign nation outside of my rule, as ever." He looked back at Egypt. "What say you?"

"I have pledged my oath to you, Your Highness," Egypt responded. "I don't believe any of my family will dissolve their oath to you. I think we should go to the hospital now, to help Zion with the wounded."

Khedran nodded to her. "Roland and Varady can show you the way. Shandiin, may I request you remain so we can speak privately?"

"Yes. In a moment." She held out a hand to stop Shajii from leaving with the others. "Are you alright?"

Shajii nodded. "I will be. The loss of Roinn...it is heartbreaking in too many ways, but he would be so glad you have taken your rightful place. As would Danon, I am sure." Shajii's eyes followed Roland, and she took a deep breath. "I won't be going with you. I know Roland will not want to leave his family or his soldiers."

"Then go with him, Shajii, with my blessing. And know that you are still Chaine, wherever you may be."

Shajii bowed her head briefly before she walked away.

When Shandiin turned back Khedran was waiting, his face set. "Why?"

"Why what? I never accepted the rule of the High Kings, Khedran. You know we only came to be Azlatan's allies."

He shook his head. "No. I don't care about the politics. Surely you know I would never think of ruling the Chaine. Why are you leaving Azlatan?"

"To get my people free of all this. You'll be very busy, you and Marre, sorting out your new flock. You have your Black Guard, which will grow with the new citizens coming to your realm. Egypt and her family can help you understand the cultural differences of the Earthers you are taking in. You have a long road ahead of you, Khedran, but you no longer need the Chaine, and you must travel that road without us. My people will finally have a home of our own, and the peace that should come with it."

Her eyes stayed steady on his face, refusing the bigger question harbored in those jeweled eyes. "You don't need us," she repeated, and then she lied, because she could, and knew he could not. "I don't need you, and you don't need me. We're done with that. If you will excuse me, I am going to go and check on my people. I don't even know if any were lost in this last battle."

He watched her go, her hair like living flame over the Chaine garb she wore once again.

She had saved his world for him, with a last-second miracle. He felt its foundation crumbling, as she walked away from him.

"Khedran is alive," Varady told Marre and Shandi. "Zion was lied to."

Marre rose slowly from her chair, her expression mingling hope and despair. "Where is he? Is he with *her*?"

Varady scowled. "Stop it. Shandiin saved Cabre from a nuclear weapon. Now she is again The Chaine, and she has refused Khedran's rule. She is leaving Azlatan, taking her people to a new continent on the other side of the world."

Marre blinked, startled by Varady's rare show of temper as he continued. "Your jealousy, your unforgiving and unreasonable mistrust of Khedran, came at the worst possible time. Your husband deserved your support, not your anger."

The High Queen was aghast. Her daughter's hand on hers stopped her retort.

"He's right, Mother."

Marre stared at her daughter in shock, but Shandi didn't relent. "Neither of us gave Father the support he needed while he was facing a war that could have destroyed us all. He could have died believing we do not love him. I have lost Roinn, and I will never be the same. I am grateful I did not lose my father as well."

She spun to Varady. "Please...where is he? I want to go to him."

"He is at the hospital, checking on the wounded."

"I should have known." Shandi left without looking back.

Marre bit her lip. "You truly believe I was wrong, Varady?"

"I do, Marre."

She put her hands over her face, then pushed back her hair. "Then I will wait for him. If it is truly me he wants...he just has to come to me. Please let him know I am waiting."

Varady frowned, but he nodded and followed Shandi to find Khedran.

Shandi saw her father across a great room where many were being treated for their wounds. She could see his sadness as he turned, but upon seeing her it was replaced by his beautiful smile.

Forgetting even sorrow, momentarily forgetting everything but love, she ran to him and threw herself into his arms.

He held her close. Closer, when he realized she was weeping. "I am so sorry about Roinn," he murmured. "But I have never been more grateful to any mortal being in my entire life, because he saved you."

She swallowed hard, leaning back to look up at him from the arms that had given her comfort since childhood. "I will never be the same. I will love him forever. But like you he would expect my strength, so I will be strong."

He smiled in bittersweet understanding. "I'm very proud of you, Shandi." Then he tilted his head as though listening. His expression changed to wonder.

To joy.

"The goddess just spoke to me, Shandi. Roinn has given you a son. Rhiathe says his name is Ravinn. You carry the eighth High King."

When Varady located them, Khedran and Shandi were together helping a young man in Earther uniform to a chair where he could wait until his wounds were treated.

The soldier gazed after them as they walked away, his face filled with worshipful wonder.

Varady had to smile, glancing back. "It's almost mean, both of you helping. He is twice smitten."

"Where is Shandiin?" Shandi asked.

"Over at the ramparts, checking on her own people, who seem to prefer their own physicians." Khedran frowned. "I am not sure what is going on with The Chaine or her people. I plan to find out, before she takes them all away from here."

"Where is Mother?" Shandi asked Varady.

Varady's eyes remained on his brother. "She is ready for reconciliation, and waiting for Khedran to come to her."

Khedran lifted an eyebrow. "I see." After a moment he added, "It will be some time. I have much to do."

"Camion is already beginning the move back to Penumbra," Shandi put in. "I will go to her, and she and I can help with that. It will give her something to do while she waits."

Khedran cupped her chin, kissed her cheek. "Tell her your news, Shandi. It will make the wait for me much shorter."

He and Varady watched her walk away. "Her news?" Varady asked.

"She is with child, Varady. I have a grandson on the way, and he will be the eighth High King. The goddess told me, when I touched my daughter."

"That is wonderful news after such a very sad day. But what about you, my brother? How do you fare? I saw you hesitate, about Marre, but I am hopeful she is over her nonsense about Shandiin."

"Always the mediator." Khedran sighed. "You always want to make people feel better, Varady."

"Yes. Especially you, because you deserve it."

"Do I?" Khedran looked around at the wounded, thought of his dead. "I have a lot to make up for, in my own mind, and it won't be done overnight. There are some things even you can't make better, Varady."

He turned back to helping in the hospital, and the day wore on.

But Khedran sought out Egypt at his first opportunity.

"I am going to ask you to do something for me."

Egypt waited in surprise, for this careful opening to a command was not his way. He looked down a moment, then met her emerald eyes with his own. "You have sworn allegiance to me, but I know you are loyal to Shandiin as well. I would never ask you to tread on that friendship, but I need you to take a message to her, and I do not think she wants to receive it."

"I will take a message to her gladly, Your Highness. I can't guarantee her response."

He smiled grimly. "No one can ever guarantee her response. That is who she is. She is a wild thing, is Shandiin."

And you love her so, Egypt thought sadly, but did not say.

He took a deep breath. "Please ask her to meet me in Penumbra, in the library, at sundown. Tell her I will wait for her, and for all that she and I have overcome together, I would hope she would honor me one last time and not make me wait until the dawn. Because I will. I will put everyone and everything aside and I will wait for her." When he saw Egypt's understanding, he nodded and turned away. "Thank you," he added very softly.

"You can't do this." Egypt stopped in the entry to Penumbra and almost hissed at Shandiin. "It's wrong, and you know it."

"It would be wrong not to do this." Shandiin sighed. "I wanted to do it without telling him, but that would be even more wrong."

"Using your magic to rip out his memory? Taking part of his very mind? Taking the memory from everyone else who knows he loves you? Shandiin, you told me once you feared being a goddess would corrupt you. I think it has."

"Believe me, it's not something I want to do. But I can't let him love me, Egypt. It's tearing him apart, and he doesn't deserve that while he's trying to help all these people...while he's still reeling from what Rhiathe showed him about Earth's destruction, and his terrible fear it would happen here."

"But to take his memory..."

"Egypt, I will forever hate myself for doing this to him. But I have to do it. I'm afraid for him. He's always been so bright inside, so beautiful. But all of this is taking him into darkness. That includes his love for me. It is dangerous—not just to him, but to the people who are his purpose. He has to be a paragon to do what he has to do. His people have a traditional mantra about the High King, and they sing it out of reverence. It comes from their heart. *'He is incorruptible,'* they sing. *'He is truth; the trust and honor of Azlatan live within him.'* Egypt...I can't take that from him, or from them."

She lowered her head, rubbed her eyes. "Please understand, I would sacrifice my very soul to save him." She shuddered. "And I'm pretty sure that's what I'm doing."

Egypt saw the misery in her friend's face, even in her posture, and knew she was hearing truth. "All right," she agreed softly. "All right, Shandiin."

Shandiin looked up in gratitude and scraped away tears with the heel of her hand. "I have to pull myself together, or I'll never get through this. It's so much harder than when I left him before." She took a deep breath, straightened. "I'm going to need you, Egypt. I won't touch your mind, I promise. Please...will you just wait for me here, until I'm done with...this?"

Egypt simply nodded, and watched Shandiin walk through the door to Penumbra's family library.

Shandiin found Khedran standing by the empty fireplace.

He turned to face her as she closed the door. He still wore his new black regalia, and was cloaked against the room's chill. He was every inch a King, except for the pain in his proud eyes.

She stopped just inside, and held up a hand to keep him in place.

"Don't come to me, Khedran. It will just make all this even harder, because you're going to learn to hate me at last. I'm going to use my goddess magic. I'm going to take your memory of what never should have been between us. I will take yours, and your family's, and that of everyone else who ever thought of the scandal I have created for you. No one will remember any of it. Both you and Marre will finally be free of your pain."

He was stunned. After a moment he ignored her warning, moving to put his hands on her shoulders. "Please don't." For once the love in his eyes was open...and full of fear. "You are again Chaos; don't you know I feel your power, just as I knew Daimaine's? I know you can do this to me. I beg you not to. Shandiin, you would be taking the part of me that is more precious than you understand."

"You aren't going to remember any of this, but I'll explain it to you anyway. You believe the memory of this love we share is precious, but it's personal to you. Now think of the things that you stand for that are not personal. Your rule. Your people. Your purpose."

Her voice was strong, but as she spoke, she lifted her hands to cover his upon her shoulders. "Weigh those things, Khedran, and you'll see clearly that what is personal to you, no matter how precious, isn't as important as what you are meant to do. Who you are meant to be." She carried one of his hands to her lips, kissed it, let it go. "There can be no hint of wrongdoing in your role in this new world. You must be the paragon of Azlatan."

"No. We are *amharen.* Do you truly believe that is wrong?"

"No. But you know the Chaine way is not that of your people. What your people believe is all that matters, and that will be even more important as they integrate the Earthers among them. Your integrity is the most important block in your foundation, my love. I repeat: you must be the paragon."

"If you leave me free and just make others forget...no, I see. Your intent is not to create a lie, but only truth. Will you be part of that truth, Shandiin? Will you forget *me?*"

"What I do will make no difference to you."

He closed his eyes, but she saw such anguish she spontaneously moved toward him. To her shock he shoved her away and turned his back on her. "Don't do this, Shandiin. I can uphold a higher standard without you taking my memory." His voice was broken.

"You could. You're the Black Wolf; you've hidden your true self from the world all your life. But then you wouldn't be free, would you? You told me Marre is your heart, but you can't get me out of your head, and it makes you feel like you're bewitched. *You told me that.* Khedran, I've watched you battle your feelings for me since I came back to this world. I can't leave you with such a division in your spirit. I love you too much."

He turned back to her, and for only the second time since his youth she saw tears flooding his beautiful eyes. She placed her fingers gently over his lips to keep him from speaking what she knew was in his heart.

"You are too important to this world," she finished. "And to me."

She framed his beloved face with her hands and met those emerald eyes for the last time before she took his memory. She kissed him, savoring the taste of his lips, his nearness, his presence.

With her kiss she took from him the burden of his love for her, and its memory from all others who mattered to him. All who mattered to his duty.

When she stepped back he seemed confused for a long time, and stood looking down. When he finally lifted his gaze all confusion was gone; he regarded her with confidence and pride. The High King he was meant to be had returned.

She faced him formally, unemotionally, as one leader to another...presenting exactly what she wanted him to see. "Thank you for everything, Your Highness. I appreciate your farewell, but I must leave now. We sail with the tide."

"Have a safe journey to your new continent. The Chaine deserve a permanent home at last, and I am glad for you. Good-bye, Shandiin."

He stepped past, opening the door for her. He gave her and Egypt a respectful nod, and left to go to his Marre.

He didn't look back.

Egypt took Shandiin in her arms and rocked her like a child while she wept.

PART V. ROINNDA

There are places I'll remember
All my life, though some have changed
Some forever, not for better
Some have gone and some remain
All these places have their moments
With loves and friends I still recall
Some are dead and some are living
In my life, I've loved them all
—*by John Lennon and*
Paul McCartney, 1965

CHAPTER 24

S handiin named the new continent, the new home of the Chaine, Roinnda. The name was in memory of the seventh and last heroic Roinn of the Chaine, and of her friend Danon, who had cared for her more, she believed, than she had ever deserved.

She brought home all but a few of the Chaine who had lived on the larger continent now named Azlatan, since it was all now under the rule of the High King. Egypt visited her frequently in the early years of her exile. Shandiin had carefully disconnected from the life she had left behind, but she trusted Egypt, and admitted to herself she needed her.

She had purposely spared Egypt's memory when she worked her awful magic. She was only partially surprised to learn Sarnath's memory was also unaffected. She knew he was different (and somehow more) than the other Heroes of Earth, and she trusted him. But she didn't invite him or visit him. She knew he would see more truth than she could face.

The motives she had given to Khedran about moving her people were true. The Chaine people had in effect wandered in the wilderness far too long; she believed it right they would finally have a home that was more than a byway on a road not their own.

Chaine settlements grew in a broad realm as beautiful as her dreams of a lost home near a different sun. Roinnda was heavily forested, with rugged mountains and wide and fertile valleys. It was also graced with rivers and streams and and lakes, with grasslands and marshes, and wildlife oddly similar to that of Earth.

Because the Chaine were lovers of freedom and nature, they didn't all collect in one central city. Rather, they settled in the wildlands they preferred, singly and in loose societies. Planned gatherings kept them connected, and over the years these became traditional holidays throughout their anarchistic and productive nation.

For the purpose of those joyful unions they built a central, rambling structure of wood and stone and glass. It rose like a part of the forest overlooking the harbor where their golden ships waited on the sea reflecting the commonly azure sky. The magnificent edifice included living quarters, but was only home to the caretakers who donated their time with the seasons, and the merchants who used it for commercial trade with the land of Azlatan. Otherwise it was meant only for their gatherings, and receiving the occasional dignitary from the other side of the world.

For a few years Shandi came often, both before and after giving birth to her son Ravinn. He was half Chaine, she said, and she wanted him to know his people. Shandiin was glad of that, and the friendship Shandi now offered freely, unaware of any disagreements of the past.

She asked Shandi once if her father seemed happy.

The Princess had hesitated. "It is always hard to tell, as he is much more the Black Wolf than he was when I was growing up. Rhiathe's magic blocks me from reading him as I was once able to do. He has a lot on his mind, with new Azlatan. It has changed, not always for the better, and he is constantly busy among the Dominions."

Shandiin found herself alarmed at this, and regretted asking. She had determined that she would never again interfere with the High King. She had done enough to him, and would not forgive herself for most of it.

Rhiathe didn't come to Roinnda. Shandiin knew she was unhappy with what she had done to Khedran, and Shandiin had made it clear to the goddess that tampering with Khedran's memory, even inadvertently, could be dangerous to him.

"I'm gone from his life and his mind," Shandiin had told her. "You know why I did this to him. Don't tamper with it. Don't speak of me to him, even if he asks. I'm afraid his mind wasn't stable even before I messed with it. Touching any memory of me could destroy him, Rhiathe, and even you couldn't put him back together."

Rhiathe had given an angry oath of silence, and withdrawn.

Shandiin's first years were spent building her own home with her own hands. She had forsworn magic for any purpose, haunted by her last undertaking as the goddess Chaos. Even knowing it had been necessary, she believed magic had corrupted her.

Nor would she ask for help except when her two hands weren't enough, so the construction took time. Her cottage came together slowly at a forest's edge, fronted by a beach and a lake reflecting white-shouldered mountains and crystal blue skies. The view from her covered porch was similar to what she'd seen once, through a door that led to dreams.

Her home was simple and looked much like another cottage in the Valley of the Chaine, where she had once spent precious moments with the King who had tried to so hard not to love her.

It gave her comfort through the years. Except at the first snow of winter.

She couldn't stay indoors when the snow came. Every year she went out into the sifting snow under the cold grey sky, and she made snowballs. She threw them into the muffled silence the snow brought, while laughter ghosted through her memory.

She stopped to close her eyes sometimes, glimpsing happiness along with the vision of white flakes in his black fall of hair. She saw again his emerald eyes, so alive with his love for her, his joy in her.

But the memory always ended the same.

She saw the death of the laughter, the joy. She saw him turn away from her as he remembered what could not be.

She threw snowballs while tears froze on her cheeks.

Wildlife abounded around her home. Bears fished the rushing stream that fed the lake, and she enjoyed watching them from her covered porch while she rocked and petted the white cat that had found her by some means known only to cats. She was joined later by a silver wolf that somehow decided she was a friend.

Cat and wolf and memories were her companions instead of people. She lived a solitary life, finding peace after too many years of struggle. If her mind occasionally drifted to Azlatan, she pulled it carefully back, and this became easier as the years went by. But she allowed herself the news that Egypt's visits brought.

The visits were frequent at first, and the reports were, as expected, about the practicalities of taking in Azlatan's new citizens. As Khedran had anticipated, many people took the newcomers into their homes, and he used his stores to supplement needed goods. Those who still needed shelter were given temporary housing inside the walls of Cabre, in the emptied buildings which had once held citizens displaced by the Prophecy War.

Some of the stories were heartbreaking. Few members of the oppressive regime had survived the civil war in the last days aboard the *Earthstar*, and many others had died with them. Shandi took over the task of finding homes for the children who had been orphaned by that conflict.

The immigrants were slowly integrated into the economy of Azlatan, and found their own homes. A few years in, Egypt reported that some of the people who began their citizenship in Cabre chose to cross the cliff that bordered the Plain of Admech, and from there joined their counterparts in Xanthe. "It's like the neighborhoods in the cities where new immigrants clung to their old culture, remember? We would go there for unique shopping or ethnic food or whatever. I guess it's to be expected."

Wherever they settled, the newcomers found that the King's Law of Respect was honored. Those who believed it inconsequential quickly learned otherwise; the people of Azlatan simply didn't accept rudeness, harshly confronted liars, and were outraged by behavior encroaching on the personal rights their High Kings had protected for a thousand years. The Black Guard was rarely involved in the resulting skirmishes, as the community stood as one against transgressors.

Nor were the King's citizens easily conned, having been educated from childhood about the need to recognize manipulative personalities. Sociopaths, Egypt noted with a smirk, learned early to blend in...or they were left with no community support, and went hungry until they understood their new reality.

Shandiin was glad her Chaine were spared the uncomfortable growing pains of new Azlatan, as were the Sundancers. Varady's nomads were now ostensibly part of Khedran's broadened realm, but were untouched by its politics. Khedran recognized them as sovereign, and they maintained their traditional lands on the eastern Admech and the inner mountains of Iesse. Encroachment without Sundancer permission was against the King's law.

It was some time before Shandiin could bring herself to ask about Zion. She was glad to learn his bitterness and hurt was gone. He remembered their parting as being amicable because he understood her need to return to her life as The Chaine.

This nevertheless resolved none of her guilt about invading his mind with magic. She would never fully believe the end justified the means. She had failed her own code of honor, and it burned more deeply than Egypt could guess.

Shajii came home after a few years, bringing Roland, who was rather nervous at first since he was so obviously different than the redhaired Chaine. But he soon realized the Chaine understood the difficulty of being different in a strange land, and their easy acceptance made him relax until he was as comfortable with them as he had been in Azlatan. Perhaps more so, since their (to him) strange culture didn't support the politics Azlatan had come to know.

Seeing how much happier Shajii was with her own people, he came to the woman they still called The Chaine even in her almost constant absence as a leader. He asked her if he could make Roinnda his permanent home.

"Are you asking to join the Chaine, Roland? You would be the first to become a Chaine without having been born to it."

"Is it possible? What would I have to do?"

She considered him carefully. She knew he was more than worthy of belonging. Her anarchistic heart wouldn't have required him to do anything, but she understood the need for closure, and ritual for a new beginning.

"You would have to give up your citizenship in Azlatan, and your oath to its High King. But not until after you have learned our ways, our philosophy."

"Shajii has been teaching me. That is one reason I want to join. I would like to become her *amharen*."

"You don't have to change allegiance to do that, Roland. That's a personal thing having nothing to do with politics."

"That wasn't true for you." He met her eyes, and she saw his sadness for her. "Egypt told me you gave up your *amharen* because of politics."

Surprised Egypt had said even that much, and realizing that clever Roland had surmised the truth, she looked away. "No. I didn't give him up, Roland. I set him free. There is a difference."

Shandi stopped visiting after her child grew into his teen years, and Shandiin finally asked Egypt if she knew why.

They sat together by her fireplace, each with a glass of wine from Roinnda's own vineyards, and Egypt took a thoughtful sip before she answered.

"Shandi said coming here had always made her sad, because she felt Roinn deserved to be here. She made certain Ravinn would know and respect his father's people, but now she's turned everything over to his grandfather. Khedran has taken Ravinn to Ordhold and beyond, to the northern pass to see the old ruins. He takes him all over Azlatan with him. I think these journeys are teaching not only Ravinn, but the people who doubted him because of his Chaine blood. Ravinn is young, but he's already nearly as impressive as his grandfather."

Shandiin frowned. "So he's teaching him as Allasar and I taught him, and letting the people see his value at the same time. What is this nonsense about doubting Ravinn because of his Chaine blood?"

Egypt was silent, scowling into her glass.

"Uh-oh. It's time to talk, Egypt. I think I need to know the truth."

Egypt looked up, leaned back with a long exhale. "Are you sure?"

"Start with Ravinn."

"Azlatan was shocked when it was learned their next King would have Chaine blood. At first the old-timers were hesitant, but the old-timers are also the ones who accepted the Chaine after they served in the Prophecy War."

"As Khedran often said, laws don't change attitudes. Only human nature can do that, and it can go either way."

Egypt smiled grimly. "Truth. Ravinn can hold his own, I think. What bothers me more is the Earthers who don't accept the High King's ultimate authority."

Shandiin set down her wine, crossed her arms. "What is Khedran doing about that?"

"Nothing. He pointed out to me that most of them have fully accepted his law of respect, and that was his main concern." She took a deep breath. "But there are a lot of Earthers...Khedran prefers to call them immigrants…who don't like his restrictions on technology. They don't understand why they aren't allowed the simple conveniences and entertainments they had on the *Earthstar.* It seemed like a small thing at first, but it's escalated. There's a faction that denies the King should have the right to deny what they want. That's spiraled into extremists claiming he's an attempted replacement for God. They're introducing the concept of religion to the other immigrants. You and I know how dangerous that can be."

"If they want technology so badly, why doesn't he send them back to the *Earthstar*?"

"If they want technology bad enough to give up nature, they are returned there and left to their own devices. The ship has been stripped of weaponry, and there is no transport to bring them back."

Shandiin eyed her friend. "You think he should do more?"

Egypt shook her head. Shandiin realized she wouldn't openly disagree with the High King's policy, not even to her most trusted friend. "My worry is the dissenting immigrants who chose to stay. I wish…"

But she stopped herself and, having finished her wine, stood to leave. "It doesn't matter what I wish. Khedran is dealing with it, Shandiin. He believes they will come around, and I believe in him."

Egypt didn't offer any more bad news during several visits that followed. Shandiin wondered privately whether Egypt still believed in her High King, but she didn't question her.

Egypt reported instead on the evolution of Shandi's school for orphans.

Many war-orphans had never been adopted, so Shandi had long ago established both home and school in what had once been Phaelon's Temple. Left barren when the god vanished, the building had been reconstructed, and was now an establishment of higher learning known as the Cabre Institute. Jael was the headmaster. He had been Zion's disciple, but the roles were almost reversed once Jael began gleaning knowledge brought with the two starships, and he was bringing that knowledge home to his world.

Shandiin wasn't completely surprised at this news. "I knew something about the Institute, as several of my Chaine have gone there to learn and to teach. I am glad Jael is the Institute's head. He's from the King's bloodline, and Khedran was his first mentor. He'll require wisdom, not just knowledge." She considered. "Egypt, does the curriculum include Earth history? I hope not. It's history was always written by the conquerors, and generally overlooked what had been taken from those who came before."

"There's actually an Earther teacher, Mary Ellena, who agrees with your point of view; Roland taught his rebel followers about Earth's real history on the *Earthstar,* and his legacy of truth continued even after he was gone. Sarnath has mentored Mary since the war. Khedran spent a lot of time meeting with her when she was given the post. He told me her insight reminded him of you."

"Me?" Shandiin asked in alarm.

"Yes," Egypt said. "Khedran remembers you, Shandiin, just as his people do. You are honored, in Azlatan, as the heroine you are. You are part of the history that is taught in the Cabre Institute."

"Then its good they are also teaching Chaine philosophy," she grumbled. "Reason and skepticism are necessary to see history with any clarity."

Egypt's visits became farther between as another decade passed, and her concerns more disturbing. The immigrants weren't all as grateful as they should be, she complained, and there were now more pockets of resistance against Khedran's policy against technology, many of them related to the growing religion that somehow equated technology with human rights and spirituality.

Egypt also explained, from her seat on the porch stairs, that it was harder for her to get away for their visits. "I've become really busy. I've given over Captaincy of the *Aztlan* to Sarnath. Khedran had already assigned me as central coordinator for the

Black Guard's enforcement of Azlatan's laws. Now he has asked me to be Defender to his family, the same way you served him before the Prophecy War. Cabre is no longer as safe as it should be, Shandiin. There have been attempts at assassination. Khedran worries...particularly about Ravinn."

Shandiin felt her heart drop. "I was so sure he would find a way to integrate the Earthers peacefully. I know he won't do it, but I wish he'd just send them all back to their ship."

"He isn't about to do that. He said he can't punish all of them for the actions of a few, and it isn't that easy to locate the few." Egypt frowned, looking around at Shandiin's peaceful scenery as she thought. She had declined her usual glass of wine, as she had to return to duty shortly. "It's really kind of strange that we can't find them. Khedran and his family can read people with that empath gift they have. But somehow things slip past all of them."

"Things? What things? You can't mean people are being assassinated."

"I'm not sure. A couple of key people have just disappeared, people who were important to the smooth operation of Cabre and the Dominions. Jael was almost abducted walking out of the Temple of Liethe, where he prefers to keep his quarters. He sensed what was going to happen and got away, but then no one could find his attackers. If I didn't know very well that Jael is psychic, I wouldn't have believed any of it had even happened. That's how secretive they are...whoever they are."

"That almost sounds like magic."

"I know." Egypt's eyes were on the distant mountains, but Shandiin could almost feel the distress radiating from her. "But Khedran can't locate any magic being used, even with Rhiathe's help."

Egypt didn't want to discuss it further, and Shandiin watched her go thoughtfully.

If Rhiathe couldn't locate magic being used, she told herself, then it wasn't there. Azlatan was dealing with unknown enemies, but they were human, not gods.

The next visit alarmed Shandiin.

Egypt's confidence seemed diminished as she reported that the Earther's strange religion was creating fabrications intended to undermine Khedran's government. "They preach there's a savior coming who will replace the High King," she said bitterly. "I think that's treason. Khedran just tells me to gather intel...probably because he knows I will anyway...but to stay out of it. He says he won't try to 'own their minds.' I don't think he understands the danger that can come from the mind of a true believer."

Egypt's faith in the man she idealized was cracking.

Her next visit threatened the foundation of their friendship.

Shandiin saw the change as soon as she arrived. Egypt wouldn't meet her eyes, and for a long time wouldn't even speak. When finally she did, there was fury behind every word.

"It's working. They're undermining him." Egypt stood stiffly on the porch with her back to Shandiin, gazing out at her skycraft and the lake beyond. "He won't address the faithful. He won't even go to Xanthe where it's fermenting. And the intel says they're infiltrating Cabre now. They are purposely seeking out the last generation of the original citizens to preach their nonsense to."

She finally turned to face Shandiin, and her emerald eyes were too bright, too fierce. "He still says he won't try to own their minds. Shandiin, he won't listen to me, but he always listened to you. You need to go and tell him. You need to use magic on him if necessary. You have to!"

It was the first time Egypt had ever asked for help.

And Shandiin had to let her go with "no" as her only answer.

After that visit Shandiin feared she would never see her friend again, so when one day she looked out her kitchen window to see

Egypt's familiar skycraft landing, hope gave her wings. Shoving open her screen door, she ran onto the porch.

But it was Sarnath who emerged and came up the path toward her.

Taking a deep breath, Shandiin waited at the top of her porch stairs and watched him come. She noted his white linen tunic and loose pants, his long white hair in a thick braid, and thought he hadn't changed at all.

But when he lifted his dark eyes to meet her gaze, she saw concern, and she straightened. "Is Egypt alright?" she demanded.

"Yes. No one is dead or injured." He stopped and looked around at the lake, the forest. "You have a beautiful home here."

"Thank you. Um…I'm sorry. I've forgotten my manners. Shall I make us some tea?"

He smiled as he came up the wooden porch stairs and took her hand. "No. At least not yet. I have news I want to discuss with you, and Egypt agreed I should be the one to come."

"That sounds ominous."

He lowered himself to sit at the top of the short porch stairway, and patted the space next to him in invitation, still holding her hand.

She settled next to him, and he kissed her hand briefly before releasing it. "It is good to see you again, Shandiin. I would have come sooner, but I didn't think you wanted to see me yet."

She scowled. "I'm not sure I want to see you now. Tell me the damned news."

"The High Queen has abdicated and returned to her home Dominion."

It took her a moment, and her heart sledged once, hard, against her ribs. "Marre has left Khedran?"

"Yes."

Anxious, she moved to get up. Sarnath caught her hand again. "Are you going to go to him?"

She stared, then sat back down. "No. Of course not. Why are you telling me about this instead of Egypt?"

"Because Egypt wants to demand that you come back and undo your magic spell, and I am not sure that would be wise even if you could. He still has work to do, Shandiin."

"What, she thinks I should go running to Khedran because his wife left him? That's tacky to say the least."

He smiled. "You haven't changed a bit. Aren't you at all tempted?"

"I can't undo the magic, Sarnath. It's one of this planet's laws that once magic is done it can't be undone. It cost me a thousand years of hiding in wait because of a magic prophecy. And even if I could...no. Just no."

He only patted her hand, looking out to the horizon beyond the lake, where the snow-topped mountains rose.

"Egypt told me you disagreed with her before, when she wanted you to come and talk to him about the current immigrant situation."

"Yeah. I guess she's pretty mad at me."

"I don't believe she is. She understands your situation, and has recently been directing anger toward everyone. It manifests from her worry about Khedran. He's become different, darker in spirit. The loss of his wife is only the latest in the burdens he carries. And he has memories, Shandiin, that he cannot or will not share."

"About me?" she asked in alarm.

He frowned and returned his gaze to her. "He has not spoken of you, no. But he has memories of a different lifetime. He admitted that to me once, but he will not speak of it again. I fear he is haunted by it, and that is one reason he immerses himself in his work. Rhiathe has gifted much magic to him, but the only magic he will use is transitioning to wherever he is needed. That traveling is almost constant. He is rarely in Penumbra, and has always left much of Cabre's needs to his Queen...and now to his daughter. On Earth we would say he is spreading himself too thin."

"He's always worked for his people, and now there are more of them with more and different needs. But what do you mean about memories of another lifetime?" When he didn't answer, she continued. "Is that what your visions are? Is that where you saw him before, and why you acted so strange when you met him on the starship?"

He nodded. "Yes. He and I knew each other once."

"I don't know about previous lifetimes, but it's time you told me who you are in this one. I know you aren't one of the engineered family. You came before them, you told me once. How long before?"

"Longer than even you can imagine. Before science, I was called a shaman. Then I was a metaphysicist. My field was meant to explain the features of reality existing beyond the physical world and our immediate senses. Even that was mostly considered supernatural nonsense until there came proof of quantum mechanics, and the knowledge that all things are connected, all things are energy." He smiled. "However, when Earth's sciences finally arrived at the point where it was possible, I changed my field to genetic engineering."

She considered. "I see. Let me make a wild guess. Were you behind the government program that genetically engineered Zion and all his kin?"

"Yes. I had waited several centuries to finally have the opportunity. Don't look so surprised, Shandiin. You spent several centuries waiting for your own purposes."

"What the hell was your purpose, Sarnath? What exactly were you waiting for?"

"Basically, the same thing you were. I was waiting for Khedran." He regarded her gravely. "I can't explain about that previous life. But everything in me knew and still knows he is essential to a critical purpose. Shandiin, reincarnation is part of a natural cycle. There is, in my understanding, only one very rare permanent escape from living. But he didn't come back while I waited through all those centuries. It was as though his spirit had disappeared along with his physical likeness, so different from the ordinary human. When Earth's science caught up to the possibility, I thought to draw him back by starting from the physical end, to create a genetic copy of the being I remembered."

He hesitated before he continued. "Zion was my first success, my best hope. That's why I named him Zion...that word is used in more than one religion in reference to a paradise, and I guess I was too hopeful. I soon realized that he had the likeness and the intelligence, but not the spirit. I had almost given up when you walked up to me that day, and I took your hand, and saw that you had met him, somewhere on a street corner on Earth."

"And a thousand years later, he finally shows up."

He took a deep breath. "Yes. Have you spoken to his mother, the goddess Rhiathe?"

"She hasn't had anything to do with me since I left Azlatan. She's angry about what I did to him. What has that got to do with...." Her voice trailed off as she thought. "He's the son of a planet. Or the goddess who is its spirit. Is that tied in to that previous life, the reason you—you? —brought him back?"

"I'm not sure." He waited. "You don't seem completely certain I'm insane."

"Only partly. Too much has happened to make me disbelieve anything. And I know there has to be some truth in reincarnation. Varady is my Verity, from Earth. But this is more, isn't it? And...I know Khedran has memories that frighten him. He told me."

"I think you have a hidden memory of your own, Shandiin. You know I was there, when you woke on the *Aztlan* the first time. You came back from near death, having regenerated in the stasis chamber, and you were devastated to still be alive."

"It wasn't a memory," she muttered. "It was more like an echo. An awful feeling of loss that hurt beyond understanding."

He nodded. "I think it came from a previous life. You lived before, just as Khedran did. You told me the constellation called the Bridle burned red at his birth. Well, you had a sign at your birth as well. It was the star that turned out to be the wormhole that took us to Hiraeth."

"Zion told me about that. But I'm not the subject of any religious prophecy. It's a wormhole, not the Star of Bethlehem. I make my own destiny. You know how I feel about that."

"I do. But you'll know this Earth saying: 'Where there's smoke, there's fire.' I don't believe all religions have all the facts, but there is truth within each, nevertheless. What's the other axiom, about babies and bathwater?"

"You think I have thrown out the truths along with the myths?"

"You are astute, as always. Shandiin, there's a purpose for Khedran's return at this time, at this place. And you are tied to it, though you have exiled yourself from him."

"And I plan to stay that way. I am not tied to him, Sarnath. Nor will I ever use magic again, for any purpose. I don't trust it. For all its own internal laws, magic doesn't even make sense to itself."

"What do you mean?"

"I've had time to think about it. Rhiathe's magic only extends outward as far as the moon. Khedran told me that, when we went to the *Earthstar* to try to stop their attack. Yet she sent him to Earth, through space...and backward in time! How is that possible?"

He smiled. "I told you I knew him before. Rhiathe couldn't have done that. But he could."

She stared at him for a long moment. Then she shoved to her feet and walked a few feet away to look out on her lake. "So he's really another magic being reincarnated. He went on a trip that damned near destroyed him, and doesn't even know he sent himself." She spun back, the picture of discouraged fury. "Dammit, Sarnath, I am done with this. I'm tired of being used by magic. You said Khedran won't use the gifts Rhiathe gave him except to travel. I understand why, even if you don't. Magic isn't the answer to the problems humans make for themselves. Like technology, it only brings more problems that have to be faced and solved."

"You sound like him," Sarnath said quietly, and she crossed her arms and scowled.

"What do you mean?"

"Egypt is concerned because he will do nothing about the Earther's religion that would replace him. He is, in fact, even turning away from the honor that his own people have historically bestowed on his bloodline. He says he is not a god, and will not be worshipped like one. Egypt thinks he is wrong, though she tries to keep that thought hidden even from herself." He sighed. "She believes, Shandiin, that he could save everyone. He, on the other hand, has come to believe they must save themselves."

She closed her eyes, and wished she knew none of this. "What do you think is going to happen now, Sarnath?"

"I don't know. Neither I nor Jael have had any foresight. We can only wait and see." He stood up. "I'm going to leave now. I've given you much to think about, and am sorry I found it necessary to disturb you here."

"You came because you're worried about Khedran. Because Marre left."

"Yes. But unlike Egypt, I know you aren't the one to help him, not with this. I needed to be sure you understand that. He still has work to do, and you left him to allow that, didn't you?"

She nodded. "And...I had hoped...to give him some peace. But it doesn't sound like that worked." She fought an ache in her throat. "I did a terrible thing to him, Sarnath. If there's a hell, that's where I'm going."

"At the very least, you have allowed him to be the paragon of Azlatan, so he could continue his work."

"But you think he is meant to be even more."

"That is my greatest expectation." He stood and went to her, kissed her cheek. "I will be back. In the meantime, take care of yourself. Enjoy your peace while you can, because whether or not you want it, I believe you are yet the daughter of prophecy."

CHAPTER 25

Thirty years after she had left Azlatan she was summoned to the harbor meeting place, because Azlatan's High Prince Ravinn had requested a public "audience" as though she were a queen.

Her people, she found to her recent disgust, had begun to treat her like an important personage. They insisted she change out of her habitual jeans into leather and Chaine gold, that she wear her golden sword, that she sit in a chair that looked too much, she complained, "like a frigging throne."

The chair faced the long room, and she thought the benches lined up on each side before her looked like church pews. Sunlight poured through the skylights to warm the wood and the stone floor, and her people filing in to take their places on the benches.

Shandiin crossed her legs, propped her chin on her fist, and nodded to those Chaine who greeted her. She glared at the youngsters who dared to openly gawk at her. They were quickly corrected by their elders, but looked back at her with awe as they were dragged to their places.

It's time for me to step down. Shajii will make them stop this cosseting nonsense. And I know she's expecting it; she's had to take over most of my duties anyway.

When people began turning from her to look back at the entrance, she realized the High Prince was near. She uncrossed her legs and sat back with a sigh, wishing for this to be over.

She smiled a little when her friend Egypt stepped in to stand guard at one side of the entrance. Another tall soldier of the King's Black Guard came with her and stood on the other side. She saw he had curly black hair that brushed his shoulders, and mist-grey eyes, and could be any one of the many people once called Rioch. The Prince apparently traveled with two Defenders.

When the High Prince walked in, when he walked toward her down that long aisle, she sat up again.

Sunlight fired the long auburn hair, partially drawn back, partially braided, as Roinn had often worn his. He was as tall as his father had been but built like Khedran, neither burly nor rangy, but sculpted by good genes and hard training.

He had Khedran's emerald eyes. Khedran's presence. Khedran's male beauty.

But he wore Chaine leather and gold, not black, and his father's traditional golden sword at his hip.

High Prince Ravinn strode down that long aisle toward The Chaine and knelt to her briefly. When he stood, he met her gaze with Khedran's proud and commanding intelligence.

And his beautiful smile.

She was furious when she stood to face him. "You will be the High King of Azlatan. You should kneel to no one but your High Queen, do you hear me?"

His smile broadened. "He told me to do it, because it would anger you, and remove the ice."

She was surprised at first. Then she had to laugh. "That's called an icebreaker, Ravinn. Your grandfather was exactly right. What would you ask of me, that made you come all this way?"

"First, an alliance that has long been missing. When I ascend to rule, I would like to have Roinnda known as a friend of Azlatan."

"The Chaine have never been anything but friends of Azlatan."

He nodded respectfully. "Truth. But I would remove all question by making it formal and public."

She lifted a hand and circled it. He raised his eyebrows but followed her direction, turning to face the room.

"What say you?" she asked her people. "Shall we make formal an alliance with Azlatan's eighth High King?"

She saw his sidelong glance at her wording, but he said nothing.

Their audience stood and as one chorused "Aye!"

His emerald gaze swept the room gladly. "I thank you." He turned to look down at Shandiin. She wished briefly for something to stand on; she wasn't used to being that much shorter than anyone neither Egypt nor one of her Chaine.

Ravinn spoke very politely. "I thank you as well and ask if we could speak privately."

"Of course. Okay, everyone, meeting's over. We'll gather back here for a little celebration with the Prince in about an hour." She crooked a finger at Ravinn. "Come with me. We'll talk while we walk."

He signaled his Defenders to wait, and they set themselves watchfully at a little distance. Then she walked with the Prince to the edge of the sea, where they began a stroll down the sand. Hands clasped at her back, she looked him over, still surprised at his leather attire. "I never expected you to dress in anything but black. Do you dress the same in Azlatan?"

"I often do. I do not deny my heritage from either side. Will you sign the formal alliance, or must I rely on what I just heard?"

She sighed. "Tell you what. I've been planning to give over leadership to Shajii, and I'll do it immediately. She can sign it. She'll be easier to get along with than I am, anyway."

He frowned. "I would like to know..." he stopped, looking vaguely distressed. "How am I to address you?"

"We have no royal honorifics. I am Shandiin."

"Thank you, Shandiin. I would like to know why you would swear your people's allegiance to me, but not to the seventh High King."

"Because he knows damned well that we're allies, and we don't need all the formality. I guess things are changing, in Azlatan."

"Yes. Politics abound. Not all good. The old ways are not acceptable to some, nor the new ways to others."

"What will change, when you take power?"

He eyebrows lifted in apparent surprise. "You mean when I take leadership. I'm sure you know the difference; my grandfather made sure I do, using your own Chaine teachings for clarity. And in answer to your question, the law of respect will remain central to all."

She frowned. "That's great. But you're deflecting instead of answering the question."

He stopped then, turning to face her directly. She was surprised to see a hint of amusement in the emerald eyes framed by dark auburn brows and lashes. "You are straightforward, as my grandfather warned. Yes, there have been changes during your absence from Azlatan. There are competing instincts of compassion and prejudice among the people, as there were once for the inhuman Chaine and the enemy Outsiders. There is only one solution to that division. The King will not direct who is right or who is wrong, but lead toward inclusion in the circle of compassion."

"You're still deflecting. I know its more than bigotry."

This time he laughed outright. "Not just straightforward, but challenging. Of course there is no simple answer to a complexity of humans. My grandfather is addressing many problems in multiple ways, and I am working with him as best I can. It would take several hours to explain everything, I'm afraid."

She waved that away, realizing she had overstepped and he was gently putting her off, as was his right. This wasn't like talking to Khedran. He didn't know her, and none of it was her business anymore—if it ever had been.

"A different question, then. Ravinn, isn't your mother next in line for ascension?"

"She has no desire to rule, and has stepped aside for me...when the time comes. I would rather the seventh High King stay forever, so I would never have to ascend." He sighed. "But he is mortal, and the day will come. I will follow his teaching and his example, but I know I will never be him."

She said nothing to that, but bit her lip and started walking again.

"Why have you never visited Azlatan?" he continued as they strolled. "That is one reason I asked for a formal alliance. There are rumors of dissent, because you have been absent from Azlatan all these years."

"Then the alliance should help. I'm sure Shajii will be glad to visit."

"Why won't you come to Azlatan, Shandiin?"

She perceived more than his words. She walked a few more steps, then stopped to look up at this beautiful Prince. He stopped and waited.

"How is he? Is Khedran all right, Ravinn?"

He exhaled. "No. He is not. I am very worried about him."

"Why?"

"Because he has changed, since his wife left him." Shandiin saw a surprising flash of anger in the Prince who, surely trained by his grandfather, had schooled himself to be unreadable. "He has drawn away more every year, until now there seems little left of the King I knew. All he has done is work, then work some more. He has a list of things he says must be done, and I have seen that the list is almost finished. He is almost finished with his life's work, Shandiin." He hesitated, looked at her pleadingly. "Will you come?"

"Do you have some misbegotten idea that I can help him?"

"You were friends, once. More than friends. You were his mentor, as he has been mine."

She looked out over the harbor, at the golden Chaine ship waiting to take him home. The ship that could take her back to Azlatan, without use of the hated magic.

"I would only remind him of what he has lost, Ravinn. I talked him into accepting Marre, back then. He'd been so lonely before that. I thought their love would last. It seemed strong. I can't tell you how sorry I am that it didn't."

"Hers did not, anyway," he said bitterly. "And he was so good to her. He treated her with care and respect, always. She...she broke his heart, Shandiin."

With that, she heard sorrow for the man he loved completely.

She was silent for a long time, and then she took a deep breath. "I hope that will be a lesson for you, Ravinn."

"What? Not to love? I have seen the heartbreak it brings. I want none of it."

"No. Just the opposite. Never fear giving your heart to someone who deserves it. Marre deserved it, back then, more than you can guess. But sometimes love just dies." She swallowed hard, and forced herself to gaze up into his emerald eyes.

"Ravinn, foregoing love because it might die is cowardly. Love takes courage. That's the lesson you should take from this. Love fully, love bravely. It's the magic that makes life worth living. When it dies, it's as painful as any death of importance. It is grieved beyond measure. But it shouldn't be denied while living."

And sometimes it's the only thing that keeps you alive. Khedran, what will be left of me without you in the world?

When the Prince went to speak to Shajii, Shandiin took the opportunity to look for Egypt. She was glad to see a welcoming smile upon her approach, but thought she read sadness behind it.

Stopping beside Egypt, she glanced over at the dark Guardsman who appeared to be Ravinn's second Defender. The soldier nodded to her courteously before walking away, apparently to follow Ravinn.

She pointed in his direction. "Who is that?"

"He is Ravinn's other Defender and his close friend. His name is Mordred. And believe it or not, he's an Earther."

"No kidding. He looks like one of the old Rioch line. How did an Earther get to such a position?"

"Kind of a long story. He's one of Shandi's orphans that didn't get adopted. But he was lucky enough to meet Ravinn when Shandi brought him along to their boarding school. They've been friends since early childhood, went to the Cabre Institute together, and Mordred trained with the Chaine right along with Ravinn. He's a skilled fighter and loyal as the day is long. Seems to look up to Ravinn the way you said Danon did with Khedran."

"So he'll undoubtedly be his Compatri when the day comes for him to be King."

When Egypt didn't respond, Shandiin looked over, and saw her blinking back tears.

"Shit. Ravinn is worried about Khedran. Are you?"

Her friend nodded miserably. "It's like he's fading in front of my eyes, and there's nothing anyone can do. He's not even making a lot of sense, as he still won't send the Guard into Xanthe when it's obvious there is trouble there. He hasn't even officially made Xanthe a Dominion, after thirty years. He says he's giving it time. Time for what? To become a rebellion?"

Shandiin studied her. She refused to step into Azlatan's politics again, but she couldn't ignore Egypt's concern about the man. "You love him, don't you?"

"Since the day I met him." Egypt scrubbed tears away with the back of her hand. "Shit. I hate crying, even in front of you." Then she sighed. "It's not a love like yours. He is my liege, and I respect him more than I could have ever imagined. Of course, I fantasize about him..." here she smiled a little "Even while I am enjoying someone that is not him. But I cherish this, the first pure love I have ever known. I would not endanger that for anything."

Shandiin looked at her friend in surprise, then saw Ravinn approaching. She realized they were about to leave and found herself sorry.

"I'm actually sad to see you go," she told him.

"I will return," Ravinn promised. "I will drag most of Azlatan with me, if I must, but I will see you again, Shandiin."

Then he astonished her by taking her into his arms and whispering in her ear. "You taught him well. He is the greatest High King Azlatan has ever known, and I believe you are a good part of the reason why."

Then he kissed her cheek and walked away.

Egypt hung back a moment as his other Defender fell into step with him, and they watched together as they left.

Shandiin blew out a breath. "Audacious, isn't he? I never expected that. Shit, no one kisses The Chaine; it's unheard of...or was. What do you think of him, Egypt?"

"He's everything. I watched him grow up, but he's turned into more than I ever expected."

"I understand. The same thing happened in front of my eyes with Khedran. Will you serve him, as you have Khedran?"

"Yes. I've already learned to love him in the same way."

Shandiin smiled. "The High Kings have a gift, you know, that puts people in their thrall."

"I've seen it work," Egypt responded dryly. "It's scary. But I'm immune to it and intend to stay that way."

"Be sure you do. I think loving Azlatan's High King is the hardest thing a woman could ever do. I probably understand Marre better than anyone else."

"You may understand, but everyone else just hates her now. I have to go. Are you going to be all right?"

"Sure."

"I don't understand why you don't have a communication device. I'd like to be able to call you."

"I hate those things. If you need me that badly and can't come, just call Shajii, and I'll use hers. She's basically next door."

Egypt looked away. "Shandiin, we're going to lose Khedran. I hope it won't be soon, but we have all seen the change in him. You have to be prepared."

Shandiin didn't try to respond, and Egypt walked away without elaborating.

She stood alone for a long time, watching the golden ship begin its long journey home.

Shortly after that visit, Shajii became The Chaine.

To her disgust, Shandiin was immediately and without her permission awarded the new title of First Chaine. It appeared her people didn't want to let her go.

CHAPTER 26

K hedran was less than one hundred years of age, barely a third of the way into the normal life span of his bloodline, but he knew he was dying...because the once brilliant light of his spirit was fading. It had faded almost to darkness.

His bloodline had been scientifically created, then magically gifted, for one purpose only: to lead and care for the people of his realm. His creation had included an incorruptible and compassionate nature that only the closest to him recognized, and only one had understood. But even Shandiin hadn't guessed the depth of darkness that had filled his soul since his return from Earth, where he had been sent to witness its destruction. Since then that darkness had grown until it filled his being, and without her light he was losing his battle against it.

Shandiin had left him as soon as she believed Azlatan was safe under his rule. She left wrongly believing he would not remember their love.

He missed her almost beyond bearing. Especially today.

It was snowing.

He locked himself away from the snow, and from his beloved daughter and grandson, who worried about him but could not understand what was wrong.

There was no way they could know.

He sat on the side of his bed, and could almost hear her laughter as she caught snowflakes on her tongue. His memory saw again the beauty of her smile and the snow in her wildfire hair and the love in her silver-grey eyes.

Snowfall always brought Shandiin's memory back. On such a morning long ago he had, for just a few moments, forgotten his reality, and so had come alive in his love for her, in the pure joy she brought him.

He put his face in his hands against another remembrance: her final kiss, her good-bye more than thirty years before. She had meant to remove all knowledge of their love with that kiss, but somehow her magic had failed while it worked on everyone else. Understanding her purpose, and recognizing that she had sacrificed her own heart on his behalf, he had never let her know the truth.

Shandiin had understood he could not set aside his duty for her. His life's work was to care for his people. He'd had to set right a realm wounded by war and flooded with need. He could not do it with her by his side, because he had a Queen who deserved his respect and that of their people. His Queen was his family, though his once deep love for her had failed the test of her jealousy and mistrust.

High Queen Marre remembered none of it. Shandiin's magic had erased the memories that had caused her jealousy. Despite that, she had finally left him anyway. Khedran knew he had driven her to it, and that shamed him. He'd given Marre his respect and a deep and tender affection, but his heart was absent to her greater need, and she was not a stupid woman.

Now his loneliness and his life's work had become a burden he could no longer lift, because darkness had made him weak.

He heard a knock at his door and knew he could not stay hidden away much longer. He straightened, determined to bring himself back to who he was.

And who am I, without Shandiin? Without her I am missing the part of myself that made me alive. Long before I knew she loved me, she brought her light when darkness threatened.

"Father? It's nearly time for dinner. Are you alright?"

His daughter was concerned, but his nature did not allow even the simplest of lies, even for her sake. "Please wait for me downstairs, Shandi."

He knew she hesitated by the door. He knew he should go to her, reassure her that her world was still safe.

He loved her dearly, his daughter Shandi, but even she could not comprehend the emptiness in his heart and spirit. She could not give him ease as she wanted so desperately to do.

Does Shandiin remember? Did she remove her own memories, her own painful love for me, before she exiled herself to a continent on the other side of the world?

And there an even greater fear. He didn't know if it was a darkly hidden memory, or a looming terrible anticipation. But there was more, a torrent of pain either behind or before him, and he couldn't face it. His courage was gone.

When he tried to set those familiar fears aside and stand, he went to his knees instead. A new flood of tears caused him to gasp in shock. *It's all gone. All of who I was, what I was. The pride, the strength and courage of my bloodline...all gone, stripped away until all that is left is pain.*

"You have to stop this." He heard the words and felt the hand of his goddess mother Rhiathe on his shoulder. She had given him magic, but he had refused most of what she offered. Nor could she bypass the barriers he had set in his mind, though he knew she wanted to...especially now.

When he didn't answer her, she could only plead with him. "My son, you are destroying yourself. Please, just step down. Give the burden of your realm to Ravinn. Give yourself some peace."

"There is no peace," he told her brokenly. "There is no end to the needs of my people, and I cannot abdicate. My duty does not end until I die, Mother."

She knelt next to him, her cheek warm against the cool tears on his own. "What can I do, my son? How can I help you?"

"Does Shandiin remember our love, Mother? Did she remove her own memories, her own painful love for me, before she exiled herself to the other side of the world?"

Rhiathe did not answer, as he had known she would not, because he had asked her so many times.

This time he knew rage, and threw it at her before he could stop himself, screaming in mind and heart: *Then just leave me!*

He'd ordered her gone. With shock he recognized his own intent in doing so.

He'd made her unable to stop his only escape.

Accepting his final purpose, even his anger died.

Shandi looked up in relief when her father stepped into their family library. "There you are," she smiled.

He smiled back, but she saw the emerald of his eyes was dulled to jade, and there was exhaustion on his fine face. She rose and went to him, put her arms around him and her head on his shoulder.

"I am sorry if I worried you." He stroked her hair, black silk like his own. Shandi had all the beauty and power of their bloodline, but did not have the driving purpose of leadership. He was grateful for that, for her sake.

"Don't be sorry for it, Father. Just please let me know how I can help."

"What makes you think I need help?" He took her shoulders and gazed with love into her face. "You worry too much, Shandi." He turned away. "Have you been out today?"

"Not in this snow, not until it is melted."

"Did it snow?" he asked as he went to the sideboard and poured them both a drink.

She took the drink without saying what she thought: *You know it has, Father. You always disappear at the first snow.* She had no idea why this was true, but she hated the emptiness in his eyes.

She knew he would not tell her his truth even if she asked. He would not lie, but he would change into that unreadable state his people called the Black Wolf. While his emerald eyes appeared feral with that change, his family knew he always had the most caring heart in the realm. They called him 'wolf' but he was the people's devoted shepherd.

When the Black Wolf persona showed up, though, no one could read him.

Which was, she understood, the reason the Wolf existed.

"Has Ravinn returned from Roinnda?" He asked casually as he sat down across from her.

"He was back hours ago, but you were apparently resting, so he didn't want to bother you." *Ravinn knows about the snow, too*, she thought.

They both looked up at Ravinn's entrance. He wore the leather and gold of his Chaine father, as he often did. Khedran approved, but it too often reminded him of the woman he missed.

Ravinn leaned down to kiss his mother and dropped a big hand on Khedran's shoulder as he passed to get his own drink. "You were right," he said over his shoulder. "Shandiin was furious that I knelt to her, and that broke the ice."

"Is she well?"

"She asked the same about you. I do not understand why the two of you have never visited in all these years. She is an amazing woman, Grandfather. She has the aura of a queen but refuses any attempt at reverence toward her."

"Then she hasn't changed." Khedran spoke almost softly.

"She is passing her leadership to Shajii. She no longer wants to be The Chaine."

Khedran looked away in apparent disinterest. "Did she agree to your request?"

"In a strange way. She pledged alliance to the eighth High King of Azlatan, not to you."

"We never thought the formality necessary."

"That's exactly what she said. Grandfather, she seems very lonely. Why don't you go and visit her?"

"If she wanted me to visit, she would let me know. No, Ravinn, don't push it. She has always been a prickly, solitary sort. I'm sure she is fine as she is. Is it still snowing?"

"No." Ravinn studied his grandfather thoughtfully. "It stopped some time ago and has melted off."

"Good. I would like to go for a walk on the beach, after dinner."

"Would you like company on your walk?"

Khedran smiled at his daughter. "No, Shandi. I need to do some thinking. You know me."

She smiled back. "You've done that as far back as I can remember. Gone off by yourself, to think. Even when Mother was still here."

Khedran surprised them both when he asked, "Have you seen your mother at all since she left, Shandi?"

"No." Shandi shook her head, her eyes fierce. "Why do you even ask? No one has forgiven her for what she did to you."

"That's very unfair of you." He glanced over at Ravinn. "Of all of you, really."

They were surprised at the irritation in his voice, of the fact that he spoke of Marre at all.

"She left us!" Shandi snapped.

Khedran shook his head. "She left *me*. I don't believe she ever wanted to leave either of you, but only me. Because I hurt her with my absence while I was still present. That's nothing she should be blamed for, and I hope you both come to realize it and quit ostracizing her for doing the only thing she could. She had no joy in her life, because I had stopped caring enough. She was lonely, so she went back to her childhood home, to her family and friends. She had a right to seek solace, and I hope she found it."

He set his glass down and rose. "I believe it is time for dinner," he finished, closing the subject he had never before allowed open.

The three had dinner, then Shandi kissed her father goodnight and left while the men were having coffee. Ravinn studied his grandfather for a long moment before deciding to risk inviting Khedran's Black Wolf persona.

"Shandiin told me I should take a lesson from your breakup with my grandmother. Hearing what you said helps me understand it a little more."

"That's a very private matter, and I wish you hadn't spoken of it with her." When Ravinn didn't respond, Khedran sighed and looked away. "So what did she tell you, Ravinn?"

"She said what happened should be a lesson to me. When I asked if the lesson was about avoiding the pain that comes with love, she disagreed with me. She said love can just die, and is grieved like any death of importance, but it is cowardly to deny love just because it might die. Is that what happened, Grandfather? Did the love you shared just die?"

Khedran couldn't speak for a long time. He seemed to study something Ravinn couldn't see, finally took a deep breath. "I don't know what to tell you, Ravinn."

"I am sorry to bring you bad memories. But despite what she told me, I don't think I want to love anyone, having seen the pain it causes."

Khedran closed his eyes momentarily. "Sometimes there's no question of wanting it. It just happens to you." He hesitated, thinking briefly of a truth he would never tell anyone but the one who would have understood...if she remembered him.

He added instead: "When Shandi was born...then you...love happened to me that way." He smiled a little. "I spent so many years...until I was your age, actually...denying that love was necessary at all. But Shandiin pushed me to realize my feelings for Marre. And she was right. Marre's love, and what I felt for her, gave me the first true joy I had ever known. And it gave me Shandi, and then you. I will never regret what Marre and I shared. The only thing I regret..."

No. I cannot tell him I shared the last many years out of guilt and duty, no longer for love, and that is the truth that broke my Marre's heart. And finally...my own.

He didn't finish his sentence, and Ravinn looked up in surprise as Khedran set down his cup and rose abruptly. "I'm going to take that walk on the beach."

"What is it you regret, Grandfather? I know something has been bothering you for a long time. Perhaps you will feel better if you talk about it."

"I've never adhered to that theory," Khedran smiled wryly. "As you well know, Ravinn. Let it be. But know this: Shandiin is the wisest person I have ever known. And if she said it is cowardly to deny love just because you might lose it, then you should believe it is true." He looked away then. "I'm going to take that walk now." After a moment he added, "Forgive me for not staying longer."

"There is nothing to forgive you for," Ravinn frowned. "There never has been, and there never will be."

Khedran looked up, and Ravinn was puzzled at the sorrow in those dulled green eyes. "I wish that were true," he said softly, and he left.

He walked on the empty beach behind the dark palace named Penumbra, home to all of his bloodline. He hadn't bothered to wear his cloak, and the gale was cold as he looked out over the wind-shattered sea. Moonlight shimmered erratically through ghostly streamers of clouds under a black, star-studded sky.

He thought of another night long ago when Shandiin had joined him on this beach, to tell him about the goddess he later learned was his mother. He remembered the moonlit fire of Shandiin's hair, her beautiful face, those silver eyes. He remembered the pain he had felt, having her so near yet so out of reach.

The pain of her loss had melded with the nightmares of darkness he could never understand and the burdens he had borne and buried all his life. He could no longer carry any of it.

He believed in Ravinn. Ravinn was not like him, he knew; he was different from the High Kings that had come before. His grandson had compassion, but was able to set it aside for duty without the need to bury his pain inside a cold and hated version of himself.

Khedran was glad the Black Wolf would die with him.

He had explained carefully to Ravinn what he thought should happen for the future of Azlatan. He had faith that Ravinn was wise enough, strong enough to do what needed to be done.

Beyond that, he hoped that Ravinn's life would be different than his, that he would step out of the glass cage of the High Kings and learn to reach for joy even through the inherent obligation of his rule.

He hoped that Ravinn could be human.

His thoughts moved to Shandi, with the deep hope she could at last find her own way to happiness after the loss of Roinn...and now him. He thought of his brothers Jael and Varady, and his once-loved Queen Marre. He thought of his own father, and the many others he had loved, friends who were now gone from him. He thought of his cherished Azlatan, the people he had cared for all of his life.

He tried not to think of Shandiin. She had said goodbye already, and gone to live on the other side of the world. She had surely sacrificed even her memory of him.

He could not say goodbye to those he loved. His selfish act denied him the right to that closure. They would know pain because of what he was going to do.

Instead he asked their forgiveness, believing he had no right to that either.

His mother wept as he walked into the sea. Azlatan had never known such rain.

Shandiin knew.

On the other side of the world, the sun was up, and she had just stepped onto her porch stairway when it hit her.

She sank to the steps, all strength gone along with the spirit that had joined her on a night long ago, when the Bridle constellation had shone red as blood in the sky.

Being who she was, she fought it.

Just a premonition. Just a bad feeling. Egypt put it in my head with her warnings.

After a long moment, she stood and returned to her cabin, busying herself with mindless chores to keep occupied during that long day.

Shajii showed up at her door in the dusk, grief and worry in her eyes.

Shandiin almost didn't answer.

"What?" she asked through the screen door. "What has happened, Shajii?"

"Egypt called. She said that Khedran walked into the sea behind Penumbra. They could see him from the towers, but no one was near enough to save him. I am so sorry, Shandiin."

Shandiin set a hand over her heart, trying to still its sudden erratic tumble. Denial was no longer possible.

Shajii put a hand on the screen that remained closed against her. "I'm leaving immediately. Are you sure you don't want to go with me to honor him? They've been searching, and haven't yet recovered his body, but Ravinn announced the goddess Rhiathe has confirmed his death. They will hold a memorial when everyone has arrived in Cabre."

"Just go. Please. Just go. Tell the Prince..." She lowered her head while Shajii waited.

Shandiin struggled against a sharp and heavy weight in her throat, finally managing to finish what had to be said. "Tell the new High King I am sorry I can't be there."

Unseeing, she closed the door in Shajii's worried face. Then she went to light the fireplace, and settled into her chair with the cat in her lap.

And wept.

The tears continued to fall even when she finally fell asleep.

She woke with the dawn, heavy with grief and guilt.

What have I done? Would he have had a chance at happiness, if I had left his memory clean?

Would he have done the unthinkable, if I had been there for him?

She had refused Egypt's plea to convince Khedran he was wrong. She wouldn't doubt his judgment; she'd done it once, and realized her error. The High Kings had worked for a thousand years to create a culture of trust, respect and accountability. He was their legacy.

She had told him he was made for what he needed to do. She had left him so he could do it.

She still believed he could have kept the ideal of Azlatan alive.

Was that loss her fault?

Did he die because I wasn't there?

She got up stiffly, walked out of the house and down the steps, not knowing where she was going, not caring.

Morning sunlight glinted from her lake. She stopped at the edge, looking out toward its center where a mountain was reflected, thinking how deep the water was.

Was drowning a hard way to die?

Did he suffer?

She took a step into the lake. Then another. Closed her eyes. Took another. The water was clean and cold, creeping up her body as she walked.

Cold, so cold.

Once again she remembered a cold morning in a valley far away.

He turned to her with snow in his black hair and laughter on his lips.

She looked into those beautiful emerald eyes and saw his joy in her.

The love he had for her.

She felt his arms around her, and for the first time did not have to remember that he had turned away from her.

Chapter 27

K hedran stood on a stone threshold with a tall wooden door in front of him. Its many-paned window reflected a beautiful sunrise, and he turned to look behind him for the reality.

The sky was a living sea of light with clouds of golden surf hanging above the flat horizon of an endless savannah. Sunbeams just reached the short fan of steps at his feet. Oddly, there was no path through the high grass that rippled under an unseen wind.

He had the feeling that this was eternally the case, as he knew the concept of the building behind him was eternally existent.

With some trepidation, he rounded back to face it. He put his hand on the curved brass handle, and the door immediately yielded.

He stepped into the odd entry and closed the door behind him. To his left were laden bookcases behind a massive wooden desk. Immediately to his right was an expansive glass door, shrouded by fog on the other side. A hallway opened directly ahead. It was so long he could only see darkness at the end.

A man looked up from the desk, setting aside his pen to lean back and consider him balefully. He wore a plain black shirt in Earther style, with the cuffs folded back from his wrists. His black hair just brushed his shoulders, and his eyes were brilliant emerald.

"You are a coward," his likeness told himself. "And a fool. It took so much to restore your shattered soul, and you have tried to throw away your miracle. You cannot destroy the body it took so long to find again, and you have no right to deny the spirit that finally inhabits it."

"Who are you?"

"That question would better be asked of yourself."

Stunned, Khedran looked toward the long hallway. "Where am I?"

"In a version of reality drawn from your imagination. The construct allows you to interact with a truth that is yet beyond your understanding."

"I had hoped for an end, for peace."

"A coward, as I said. Your kind was not meant for peace."

"My kind?"

"You've always known you aren't human. You are a different thing, created by humans."

"I've heard that before. My ancestors were engineered, and magic gave my bloodline special gifts to lead the survivors of Earth."

The other Khedran laughed harshly. "There is no magic. Your history was the evolution necessary to bring back what existed before."

"None of that is true. I have seen and been used by magic, and I use it. Evolution isn't engineered. Humans are not artificial beings."

"Is evolution coincidence, or engineering? Think of the innumerable circumstances necessary to create life from a lifeless universe. Everything that exists is connected." The man leaned back, and crossed his arms. "You have a purpose. You failed before, in your purpose. The lifeless darkness came, and took what should have lived. Your soul was shattered into pieces. Now you have again reached a crossroads, and you have a choice. You can remain and return to nothingness like the coward you are. Or you can have the courage to live, and so allow what matters to live."

When Khedran balked, his likeness stood to glare at him. "You don't care about the consequences? Are you too weak to face what may come? Then consider this, since you have become so selfish. If you choose death instead of returning to life, you will also nullify her. Her spirit was lost when you failed your purpose before, in the universe you shared. Her existence in this one hinges on yours."

He trembled, because he knew he spoke of Shandiin. "Where is she?"

The stranger who was himself gestured toward the exterior door through which he'd come. "She is out there, but almost beyond your reach now. What a fool you are."

"She doesn't remember me."

His double shook his head. "She's lost all memory of your lives in the universe of the past. But she remembers the life you've led in the now. She never let you go, even though she's spent the last thirty years believing you had forgotten her. She couldn't know you are immune to what she did because of what you are."

"And what am I?" Khedran's cry held rage and fear. "Am I no more than an artificial intelligence, with only a mission and no right to know love?"

"Listen, you fool, and you will know."

A chorus filled the strange and endless chambers of the unreal edifice in which he stood.

It was a word with meaning beyond human knowledge, but was translatable by him; he heard it spoken simultaneously in the many languages of Shandiin's home world. Out of that complex sound came a word with the nearest meaning: *Paladin.*

And he knew.

He was a created being with carefully designed purposes. He was the legacy of humans evolved to their highest level before they moved on.

Humans, as he now understood them, were any species of life that had the power of choice, and thus the potential for greatness.

His design allowed him to connect with all life forms, for it was necessary that he understand and be understood. As a philosopher of Earth had once said, even if a lion could speak, no human would know what it meant. The meaning of language is deeply embedded and intertwined with the internal experience of each species.

But the Paladins would understand both the lion and the human. Understanding was necessary to their own purpose, which was to help each developing race of humans whenever possible. Acceptance was also necessary, so each Paladin was made in the image of the species they were made to help. Many Paladins had an exquisite appearance. Unevolved humans of every species were notoriously chauvinistic about differences perceived as strange or ugly, and all too respectful of beauty.

Humanity's histories always included a period of belief in their own importance as the purpose of creation. This belief was commonly destroyed upon achieving knowledge of the cosmos and their own insignificance within that scope. The Paladins found this part of their evolution heartbreaking. Humans had to understand the true significance of life, or they would...and often did...destroy themselves, everything they had created, and even that part of the universe that had given them life.

A Paladin offered alternatives to annihilation without restricting the power of choice, the potential for greatness. Humanity had to be its own savior.

Khedran finally knew his truth. He was not truly *homo sapiens*, but he was human. He, too, was a child of the universe.

And therefore knew what it was to love, and be loved.

"She stayed behind," the other being said. "She waited for you, while the darkness came. And you left her there."

"To find our son," he gasped. "And I failed that, too."

"So you did. You lost them, and yourself. Now you can die as you wished, or face loss again. Will you stay here, ending your sad existence — and leaving her behind forever? Or will you take an opportunity to keep who she is now, and possibly lose her in the future? You can, only in this moment, return to the before, when she still waited for you as the darkness took her. Choose now."

Terrified, Khedran turned to look behind him, where his other self was pointing.

The fog was gone. She was beyond the glass door.

His goddess of fire and light.

She hung in a sky where darkness invaded. The last embers of her light were dimming. Her unquenchable spirit had finally failed. There was death in her silver eyes. Even as he charged the door, she was dissolving.

He didn't bother to open the door, but smashed through it, desperately reaching for her.

His fists closed on nothing.

"No!"

His denial rang through time, because he was a Paladin, and his kind could travel the eternal chronometer.

His fists held all possibility, like the box that held Schrödinger's Cat. She was both alive and dead, until he opened them.

He spun back through the entry where his double no longer waited and began the race down the long hallway: past all the doors that had closed in this life, then in the eons before this life, to the hated vision at the end.

Daimaine's Temple doors, where his nightmares had always been real.

With a scream of defiance against the forces of fate and darkness, he slammed through the Temple doors and fell into eternity.

Lily Haskie practiced a profession rare among women of the Diné people, named by others as Navajo. She was a medicine woman. Her people sought her out to bless their lives between Yádiłhił Shitaá (Father Sky) and Shimá Nahasdzáán (Mother Earth). Her personal philosophy, shared by her family, was the belief in harmony between all entities of the universe...human, animal, plant, and the sustaining earth.

Sunrise was the time she felt closest to the spirits, believing that was when they came to walk the world. So she stood not in fear, but in wonder, as she watched a spirit passing through the strangely shimmering light of a singular morning to step onto the desert sands in front of her.

He did not seem to notice her, but she watched him with her heart beating fast. He was beautiful beyond words, with black hair tumbled loose around his striking face. He wore strange black clothing, but stranger yet were his eyes of emerald fire. He was staring down at his clenched fists.

He went to his knees in the dirt, and put his upturned wrists together. He slowly opened his hands, freeing his palms to the sun.

She saw upon his hands a small, edged radiance of sunlight, and curls of hair the color of flame, and then a child.

A baby girl, barely larger than the man's two hands, her golden skin bejeweled by his tears of joy. He kissed the baby's forehead, then lifted his gaze as Lily's shepherd dog came to him. The dog put his nose against the infant, then lay down and looked up at him in question.

In answer, the spirit-man laid the child gently in the protective curve of its furry body.

He looked up at Lily at last and smiled through his tears. "Will you take care of her?" he asked in her native tongue, for Khedran of the Paladin knew all languages as his duty required. "I cannot stay here with her. She cannot know about me. But she is my sunlight, and she is needed by a world."

"She will be my granddaughter Shándíín," Lily promised.

He stood, and kissed Lily's cheek in thanks even as he faded from her sight.

She thought she heard him whisper "Bless you, Stormwing," but was never sure.

He couldn't stay with her, but he watched her through the current of time that pulled him inexorably back to where he'd been. His heart clenched at the hardships she faced when she was taken from the Diné, when she walked the edges of humanity while all around her crumbled into chaos. He recognized the courage he had always known in her, and visited her for encouragement in a dream when her world teetered on the edge of ending.

He couldn't face that ending, not again. So he found himself back in the hallway which began upon her first arrival on the planet they called Hiraeth. The hallway was a thousand years long. He followed her on that long journey, though she never knew it. He saw her with her people called the Chaine, giving them her wisdom and foresight while her heart broke for them, because they had been cut off from the rest of humanity's survivors. She knew she was making them different than others of this world. She knew they would not be accepted when she took them back to those others. Nevertheless she trained them to be the allies and saviors of the people of Azlatan.

He followed her when she occasionally visited the nomads who came to call themselves the Sundancers. They gave themselves that name after meeting her in her truest form, as the Sunqueen who was part of all that lived. She never asked them for love, for respect, or even honor. They gave it to her anyway, and not just because they learned from her that she stood between them and the evil gods who ruled a distant land. They saw her for herself, and loved her for herself.

As did he.

He continued to follow her when she made her forays into Azlatan disguised as a young man, Shan the Wanderer. He couldn't resist visiting her in that guise, though she never knew it. He had disguises of his own. He wondered if he would ever tell her about those connections.

Finally he was at the end of that hallway, at that time just before he would be born to his life in the new universe, descended from a line of High Kings and a goddess who was a world. He gave Shandiin a last vision, meeting her on a mountaintop under a cathedral of stars, and tried to warn her about what was coming...about the dangers of the love which would cause them both such pain.

With his birth into her world, time turned back on itself. It had taken away his eternal memory until his death closed the loop he had created.

He was snapped back to now, the timeline of his final existence, in a hallway that existed between somewhere between life and death.

His perspective shifted. He became an observer of the past and the likely future. As Paladin he understood problems rarely had a single cause and there was more than one path to a solution. A leader was not the answer, but only a steward until the people found the path right for them...or not. He had glimpsed this simple truth before, but now saw its wholeness. He was determined to hold onto that wisdom when he returned to the world.

When he returned to *her*. He realized sadly that she'd be both broken and angry, and that was part of his penance.

Then he smiled to himself. She had never been a peaceful sort.

He'd not be able to remember everything when he passed back through that door to life. True clarity was lost in the filter of biology, even for him. But he was determined that he would remember he loved her before, though she would not know that; he'd remember it was his choice to continue their existence together in Hiraeth, the world that he had just left.

And, he realized, his son was part of that world. Diane hadn't lied after all. He had a son who was broken, and therefore dangerous, almost certainly evil. A son with power equal to or surpassing his own. He existed somewhere on Hiraeth.

Khedran hesitated, momentarily unsure if his path was the right one. Was he doing the right thing, continuing a world with the potential of evil? Was nonexistence better than permitting evil to exist?

He turned his head to read the writing on the hallway's last door. He realized his father, Allasar, existed somewhere beyond. As did all the High Kings who had come before him.

He had seen all of them in the Prophecy War, he remembered, when they had been freed from the captivity of Daimaine's magic. He had seen them, and felt power shift from them to him before they vanished.

Now he knew the six High Kings had each given a gift to the seventh.

They had served their purpose valiantly and built Azlatan for their people while they suffered torment unknown to anyone but themselves.

Each had carried a part of his shattered spirit, and returned it to him when they had been made free at last.

Their gift had made him whole.

Truth flooded through him in that moment. He knew joy in understanding that the door between him and his father was no more than an artifice, like all material things known to the living world. There was no wall between him and the other High Kings, or the many he had loved and lost in this new life.

How could he deny anyone their existence here? Life, even in its imperfections, was what gave meaning to everything.

CHAPTER 28

"Shandiin. Please hear me."

She realized he'd been speaking to her for several minutes while she stood trapped against him.

They were both waist-deep in the water of her lake. She'd not recognized the reality because her despair was too deep for sanity.

She looked down to see his arms locked around her waist, holding her firmly against the warmth of his body. He didn't relax that embrace until she began to turn in the circle of his arms. She put her hands on his chest, felt his heart beating, and looked up into his beautiful emerald eyes.

Eyes full of love and wonder. "I just learned you remember me." His voice was broken. "I am so sorry for your pain, Shandiin. I should have come to you before. I thought you had forgotten me."

When she said nothing, he recognized the grief in her eyes...grief and disbelief approaching madness. "Shandiin, I am real. I am here. And I have never stopped loving you. Your magic worked on everyone but me."

He was stunned when she shoved him back, breaking his embrace. "No. I won't allow this insanity. My Khedran is dead. I knew it when it happened, before I was even told he walked into the sea. You aren't real."

He caught her as she tried to turn away from him. She fought him like a wildcat, and for the first time he used his superior strength against hers. "Stop," he begged. "Just stop, Shandiin. I am real. Yes, I walked into the sea. I crossed into death. But I am here now. I am real."

She subsided, apparently accepting his truth. She turned again, very slowly, within his embrace. She lifted her gaze to his, and he was shocked at the fury he saw there. "Rhiathe allowed you to suicide? And then brought you back?"

"No. She had nothing to do with any of this. I sent her away so she couldn't stop me."

She struck swifter than a snake and would have shattered the jaw of a lesser being. He stumbled back as she broke away, and caught her wrists before she struck again. He had known her anger often, but never this vehemence against him.

"You *bastard!* How could you? How could you do that...to me? Shit...to everyone who loves you?" She broke his hold and shoved him again, viciously pushing past him to stride through the water, to the beach.

He could only follow, and when she kept walking he seized her wrist, forcing her to stop.

She stood facing away from him, vibrating with rage. His heart sank. She had never been so far from him as she was in that moment.

But oh, she was magnificent in her fury. He knew it well, though never before against himself.

She was everything he remembered. And he had to win her back.

"Shandiin. Please. I know what I did was wrong. I knew it when I did it. It was cowardly of me, but the pain was more than I could bear. I didn't know you remembered me, Shandiin..."

She spun back, wrenching her hand free. "Are you blaming this on *me?* Did I cause you to be a suicidal coward?"

He saw it then, the guilt driving her fury. It was directed at her own self.

"No." He said it softly. "None of it was your fault. All the reasons you gave that last night, all those years ago? You were right. I had a job to do. Everyone who forgot…it gave me the room to do what I had to do. What you did was right."

Her fists were clenched at her sides. "But *you* didn't forget me. And that's your excuse for what you did?"

He shook his head. "No. I missed you, but there were memories trying to come through. Memories worse than those from my visit to your lost Earth. There was no light left in me, Shandiin. There was nothing left of me." He felt renewed pain, recalling his last hours.

"Don't do that," she demanded. "You look like you did when you came back from Earth. I can't bear to see you like that again. I *won't* bear it, do you hear me?"

He blinked, surprised at how well she read him. He had almost forgotten she could do that. And he didn't like the fear that had crept into her eyes. Was it fear for him? Or something else?

"It's all right, Shandiin. I remembered what came before, and I have some distance from that now. I had to die to learn the truth about myself."

"Is this about reincarnation? You and Sarnath lived before, he told me, but what does it matter? It's just more magic. It just gets in the way of the life you have now. The life you've come back to." She scowled. "Rhiathe told me she couldn't return people to life. How the hell are you here, Khedran?"

"Rhiathe's magic isn't what it seems. There is more to the universe, Shandiin, than you know."

She looked down, and he knew she was thinking. "I've always understood that. But get this clear, Khedran. I've never forgiven myself for using magic on you. I want nothing more to do with magic. So don't answer my question about how you came back. When I die I just want to die, and never do any of this again. I want no more of what life brings."

He was stunned. This wasn't the woman he knew. "Not even love, Shandiin? Would you give love away?"

She flung up her head to glare at him. Her lips were trembling and her voice was full of tears. "I already did, you bastard. I gave it away when I left Hiraeth so you could live free. I did it again when I used magic so you could lead Azlatan. I tore out my heart twice to save you, Khedran. But I held on, because I believed in you...until I knew you'd killed yourself. That was it. I couldn't hold on any more. I almost did the same thing I'm so angry with you for doing. So I guess I understand, but I can't trust you now, and I just...*I just can't do this again.*"

He had never known such shame. Everything she'd said was truth. Her magnificent spirit had burned low because of him. He'd rather she had put a knife through his heart than look at him with such anger, such misery.

He lifted a tentative hand to curve against her cheek. "I can only beg for your forgiveness. As for trust? I gave mine to you all my life, even when I knew I shouldn't. Can you try to do the same for me? Oh, my Shandiin...can you trust me enough to forgive me?"

She looked into his loving eyes and felt the last of her anger drain away. Yes, she had required his impossible trust, and he had given it to her.

He saw the anger go, but he could see that her spirit remained at war; she was suspicious of what he would say next.

He understood. She had never had it easy, when it came to love. He planned to change that, if it took an eternity.

To her surprise he sank to the sand of the beach and pulled her down into his lap. A dawn breeze mingled their hair, bright and dark, as he leaned his forehead against hers, thinking of what he had always wanted to tell her. When he drew back, he saw that her full lower lip still trembled slightly as she searched his eyes, waiting. Sunlight swam around them while he revealed his truth.

"All my life, you have given me everything I ever needed, to be who I had to be. You have always been the one who understood my needs, and you always put them ahead of your own." He drew a deep breath, exhaled, and cupped her chin. "In all that time, you have somehow thought your love was not important in the grand plan of what you saw as *my* life, *my* truth."

He had to stop then, and it took him a moment to continue. His voice was thick with emotion. "You could not have been more wrong, Shandiin. You have always been what made my life whole. Even if your magic had worked on me, I'd still have known part of me was missing. I would just have been...lost, without understanding why."

She grimaced. "I've hated myself for what I did to you. But I thought I'd done the right thing. I thought I had left you whole. I was so sure, when you walked away that night..."

"I let you go. I played a part because you needed me to, and because you were right. I had important work to do, and I had to let you go to do it. Almost everything you said was right – except when you called me a paragon. That's not me, Shandiin. It's you. It's always been you."

She blinked, and her lips parted in surprise as she stared at him.

After a moment came her slow, wicked smile. "What the hell, Romeo. I bet you say that to all the girls."

She was back. He took a relieved breath, then spread his fingers through the fiery wealth of her hair and kissed her lips, holding her between his hands as he had always held her in his heart.

The End of Book 3 of Prophecy's Daughter.
To find out what happens to Shandiin, Khedran, and their people,
watch for Book 4: PALADIN

GLOSSARY

Admech, (ad-MEK), the sea of grass, plains on the eastern border of the original Azlatan.

Allasar, sixth High King of Azlatan, father of Khedran.

Amhara, (am-HAR-a), is a Chaine word combining 'love' and 'respect.' It has two meanings. In the first, it describes a relationship between people. Respect is possible without love, but love without respect is not. Love with respect is amhara. In the second meaning, it is a word of requirement relating to everything in existence, and includes a note of gratitude.

Amharen (am-HAR-en), a Chaine word for the special bond created by amhara. The Chaine do not marry; this bond is as close as they get.

Anzihi, (ANZ-zi-high), were the mind-controlled subjects of the god Phaelon in Book 2 of this series (Penumbra.)

Assemblage, a meeting of all Dominion royalty ordered by the High King.

Azlatan, (AHZ-la-tawn), originally the nation of 77 collected Dominions ruled by a single High King, bordered by the western sea and the great eastern cliff separating it from the central grasslands called the Admech. After arrival of the Earthers, the entire continent was named Azlatan.

Aztlan, the name of the starship that brought the original colonists to the planet Hiraeth. The name is taken from the mythical paradise from which the Aztecs came, and is also the name of a secret project on Earth that genetically engineered the family of heroes. (See Heroes of Earth below.)

Ben Canard, Vice-Premier of the Earthstar; his brother is Premier.

Black Guard, the High King's army, the central army of Azlatan. Originally made up of 10 Legions, each commanded by a Legion Master.

Brend, Dominion King of Ordhold. His older brother Jon was convicted of treason when he refused to defend Azlatan in the Prophecy War.

Cabre, (Kaw-bray), called the "King's City," lies at the edge of the sea which is Azlatan's western boundary.

Camion, (CAM-mee-on), previously the bonded servant to the High King. He and all others so bonded by order of the god Phaelon were freed when the goddess Chaos left Hiraeth, taking with her all the gods and their magic. He is now the Mayor of Cabre.

Chaine, (Chain), a powerful redhaired race of warriors who sailed to Azlatan from the west in the reign of the sixth High King and became the allies of Azlatan. They have a titled leader, "The Chaine," but are basically anarchists with their own philosophy and culture. They mine a metal called "Chaine gold" which is sought for its strength. The Chaine people traditionally wear leather filigreed with Chaine gold for protection.

ChanDethe, (Chan-DEATH-ee), was the mystic messenger of the goddesses Liethe and Chaos, and could appear as cat, bird, or horse.

Chaos, the goddess also known as the Sunqueen, was the secret identity of Shandiin (The Chaine) during the thousand years before she left Hiraeth to take the magic of the gods and free the people.

Compatri, (Com-PAW-tree), Compatri are chosen by the High King for personal reasons of trust and respect and are rare. They wear an emerald star on the collar of their uniform.

Congress, gathering of Sundancers, their version of "Council."

Council, a gathering for trial purposes in Azlatan, made up of the High King and selected royalty from the Dominions. Meetings are held in the Council Hall of Penumbra. The High King's rule is autonomous, but he generally abides by the findings of Council.

Daimaine, (Die-MANE), until the gods were taken from Hiraeth, was the goddess of Death and Justice and the power behind the rule of the High Kings, who protected their people from her evil nature. She secretly tormented the High Kings from the time they each turned sixteen. Her human form was Diane.

Damon Alexander was known as the creator of Project Aztlan, which created genetically engineered superior people. He was assassinated along with the majority of his creations; at the time of Earth's destruction only four were left: Zion, Egypt, Sarnath, and Roland. Some took his last name in his honor.

Danon, (DAY-nun), Compatri to the High King and his close friend as well as Shandiin's.

Diane Fairchild, Shandiin's daughter and twin of Leah. She was a scientist who became the goddess Daimaine on Hiraeth.

Dominion. There were 77 dominions in the original realm of Azlatan. The ones named in this book include Tesna, Lajan, Druna, Vanhold, Denori, and Ordhold.

Dominion royalty, any of the Kings or Queens of the 77 kingdoms within Azlatan, all subject to the High King.

Duine (Dinna). Before the Prophecy War Azlatan had been divided into two races, the Rioch and the Duine. Duine were servants to the Rioch.

Earthers, term used on Hiraeth for Earth's survivors aboard the ship Earthstar.

Earthstar, the ship designed by Zion Alexander for the Right Church. It was originally left to orbit the destroyed Earth with the planet's last survivors.

Egypt Alexander, one of the genetically engineered Heroes of Earth, best friend of Shandiin.

Farbet, (FAR-bet), Compatri to High King Allasar and later High King Khedran; also Master of the Tenth Legion, known as the Queen's Guard.

Heroes of Earth. Zion, Egypt, Roland, and Sarnath. They are the four genetically engineered heroes who saved the majority of Earth's survivors. There were others who were similarly engineered, but they were all murdered before the Earth ended. Their individual DNA shows up to some extent in most of the planet Hiraeth's population. The High Kings of Azlatan are descended from Khandor, the only individual who carried only their DNA.

High King(s), the ultimate rulers of Azlatan, created through a combination of science and magic; they all have emerald eyes that mark their special bloodline. They are bred to be incorruptible and have unnaturally high standards. The bloodline of the High Kings has inherent gifts to bolster their purpose, which is to serve their people through their leadership. The gifts include a 'command voice' that transmits to the mind of everyone in sight, accentuating their authority; a presence that causes them to be recognized as the kingdom's ultimate authority without need of insignia; and charisma that also causes a thrall to fall over most anyone who meets them, a thrall of wonder and sometimes love. All of this is in addition to their special beauty and intelligence. Their most secret gift is the gift of empathy, the ability to read the emotions and truth of others. It is rarely used, because it is an invasion of privacy affecting both parties.

Hiraeth, (Hi-RITH), an ancient Welsh word expressing a spiritual longing for home, a home that perhaps is real only in the heart, a home that is everywhere and nowhere. It became the name of the planet colonized by Earth's survivors who arrived in the starship Aztlan.

Iesse, (I-ESS-ay), inner mountain stronghold of the Sundancers, between the Plain of Admech and the Khaibara mountains that flank the continent's eastern sea. The Sundancers call those mountains the "Wall of the World."

Jael, (Jay-EL), younger half-brother of Khedran, full brother of Varady. Jael is psychic.

John Garcia, Captain of the ship *Earthstar.*

Khaibara, (Ky-BAR-a), an ancient fortification at the top of the Everwinter Pass, named after the far eastern mountains where the original colonists landed on Hiraeth (see definition for "Iesse.")

Khalen, (KAY-len), the first High King. He was engineered on Earth and traveled to Hiraeth. He never made it to Azlatan. He sacrificed himself to Daimaine in exchange for relinquishing her power to the High Kings' authority, thus protecting the people from her power.

Khandor, (KON-dor). He and Khalen were engineered on Earth. Khandor was the second of the special bloodline with added capabilities. He became the second High King, and direct ancestor of Khedran. He ruled Azlatan years 1-250.

Khedran, (KEY-drun), seventh High King.

Kimhi, (Kimmy), woman of Xanthe who became that city's leader.

Leah. Shandiin's daughter, became the goddess Liethe when magic overtook Hiraeth.

Legion Master, commander of a Legion of the Black Guard.

Liethe, (Lie-ETH-ee), was the goddess of healing, light and love. She was depicted with a blindfold, carrying a cat. Her mortal form was Leah.

Lilith, redhaired Hero of Earth, was killed just before the Earth ended.

Magdalena, rebel and secret spy on the Earthstar.

Majia, (Maj-HEE-a), giant white snowcat of Ordhold.

Marre, (MAR-ray), Khedran's wife, the High Queen of Azlatan.

Mary Elenna, immigrant teacher of Earth's history at the Cabre Institute of Higher Learning.

Morgana, also known as Morgan le Fay among other variations, this mythical woman represents death, darkness, and deception. Diane took this as her title on the *Earthstar.*

Ordhold, (ORD-hold), the mountainous northern Dominion of Azlatan where the young King Khedran spent exile between the ages of 16 and 18.

Paladin. The noun paladin means a champion of a cause. While the French word paladin means warrior, its meaning has grown to include any chivalrous or heroic person, and the word is surprisingly used with very few variations throughout many languages.

Penumbra, (Pen-oom-bra), the obsidian palace of the High Kings, was given to them by the goddess Daimaine. It has been the ancestral home of the High Kings for a thousand years.

Phaelon, (Fail-on), was the God of Order, who had no human form but was created from the artificial intelligence that had operated the ship *Aztlan.*

Prophecy War. Phaelon promised Hiraeth's humans a thousand years of peace to be followed by war, when Azlatan was invaded and almost destroyed. Shandiin saved the people by leaving and taking the gods and their magic with her, but the war continued without magic.

Queen's Guard, the Legion assigned to the High Queen, is also the Tenth Legion of the Black Guard, which is stationed in Cabre.

Rammorth (Ram-MORTH) Range, mountains north of Cabre, south of Ordhold.

Ravinn, the eighth High King, grandson of Khedran through his daughter Shandi. His father was The Chaine Roinn.

Rhiathe, formerly Princess of the Dominion of Alaura, High Queen to Allasar, mother of Khedran; she died in childbirth. She was born mortal but is the goddess spirit of the planet Hiraeth.

Rioch (Ree-awk). Before the Prophecy War Azlatan had been divided into two races, the Rioch and the Duine. Duine were servants to the Rioch.

Roinn (Rowan.) This name was given to the Chaine heroes who won their contests for wit and battle, and thus became second in command of their people. The name was retired with the heroic death of the seventh and last Roinn, who was the father of the eighth High King, Ravinn.

Roinnda (Ro-in-dah), the continent claimed by the Chaine people, is named for their hero Roinn and Khedran's Compatri Danon, who were both killed by an assassin.

Roland, one of the genetically engineered Heroes of Earth, who remained behind on the ship *Earthstar* when the other three heroes traveled on to the planet Hiraeth. He jokingly uses the last name "Bond" because he's a "spy."

Sarnath, (SAR-nath), one of the Heroes of Earth, but who is mysterious as he is psychic and has visions or memories of another life.

Shajii, (SHA-gee), young Chaine woman who had been mentored to become The Chaine.

Shalmira, (Shal-MEER-ah), warhorses protected by the Sundancers; they have a special bond with their riders.

Shandi, (SHAN-dee), daughter of Khedran and Marre, named for Shandiin.

Shandiin, (Shan-DEEN), found as an infant and raised by the Navajo, apparently immortal. On Hiraeth she became The Chaine (title), leader of the Chaine people, and was secretly the goddess Chaos, the Sunqueen.

Spectacle of Retribution. The regime aboard the starship *Earthstar* instituted capital punishment in the form of an ancient torture when prisoners were "drawn and quartered." They modernized it as a televised autopsy performed on the living.

Star Blade, the magic sword gifted to the Line of the High Kings by Daimaine; it vanished when the gods were taken from Hiraeth.

Stareven, the beginning of the warm season.

Starfall, beginning of the cold season, presaged by a fall of stars (meteor shower.)

Starships. With the destruction of their home planet, the survivors lived on huge ships designed by Zion Alexander. The *Aztlan,* along with other starships, traveled to Hiraeth, taking the people who colonized that planet. The other ships were lost after they landed on Hiraeth and were taken out to sea by a tsunami.

The *Earthstar* became home of all other survivors and most of its inhabitants have never been on a planet.

Sundancers, the nomads of the east, led by Varady.

Tahmond (Tah-mund), word for the priests of the departed gods.

The Bridle, a constellation of stars seen from the realm of Azlatan.

The Chaine, title for the leader of the Chaine people.

Varady, (VERA-dee), leader of the Sundancers. He is half-brother to the High King, but has different gifts, and is known for his compassion.

Xanthe (Zahn-thay), is a city in the far south of the steppes of Admech. It was established by the God of Order for the purpose of invading Azlatan and overthrowing the High King and his race.

Zion, genius leader of the Heroes of Earth, is a polymath scientist who designed the starships that saved the last of Earth's humanity.

MEET THE AUTHOR

Susan L. Alandar has written fantasy since she was a child. She grew up on Robert Heinlein and Ray Bradbury and Madeline L'Engle, discovering epic fantasy (Tolkien, of course) about the time Heinlein broke into adult work with *Glory Road*. But she gave up the fragile hope of a writing career when she became an abandoned mother of two and needed a stable income. In retrospect Susan would say she needed the raw experience of the real world to bring her writing to life. Now, years later, she has returned to her fantasy world of Hiraeth, ready to share The Daughter of Prophecy series with the world.

ACKNOWLEDGEMENTS

When I was left alone at the death of my husband Jim (one of those with honor and compassion), my two daughters encouraged me to return to the stories they had loved in their childhood but that I had finally put aside. So I dug out an old manuscript and started typing the words from paper into a computer. As I did, I found joy return to my spirit. I found enthusiasm, and purpose. Hiraeth and her occupants welcomed me home, and...because I understood more... became more.

So I thank my beloved redhaired girls, Rose and Kimberley, for their faith in me. And I thank the wonderful person I found, Keri-Rae Barnum of New Shelves, who has guided me through the practical part of writing fiction. And, most importantly, I thank all three for supporting my newfound courage to quit writing in secret.

www.ingramcontent.com/pod-product-compliance
Lightning Source LLC
Chambersburg PA
CBHW070206310726
48976CB00001B/231